All My Tomorrows

Sequel to 2009 Golden Crown
Literary Society Award Winning
'Yesterday Once More'

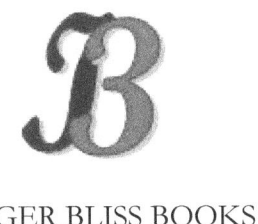

BADGER BLISS BOOKS

All My Tomorrows

DEDICATION

I dedicate this book to my wonderful wife, Barbara "Bliss" Sawyer. She is the most fantastic sounding board and collaborator an author could ever want. She listens to me when I hit a wall and talks me off the ledge when all I want to do is delete the damned manuscript from my computer and be done with it. She sparks my imagination and alas, occasionally my anger, when she suggests something brilliant that of course, requires a total rewrite. But rewrite it I do, because she is most often right. She is my rock...she is my love...she is my heart. I love her dearly and I always will.

I promise to you, my love...all of my tomorrows.

ALSO WRITTEN BY KAREN D. BADGER AND
AVAILABLE FROM BADGER BLISS BOOKS:

ON A WING AND A PRAYER
YESTERDAY ONCE MORE
THE BLUE FEATHER
ALL MY TOMORROWS
1140 RUE ROYALE

The Billie/Cat Commitment Series:
 IN A FAMILY WAY
 UNCHAINED MEMORIES
 HAPPY CAMPERS
 COLLECTIVE IDENTITY
 SWEET ANGEL
 RELATIVE-LY SPEAKING

www.badgerblissbooks.com

All My Tomorrows

Sequel to Yesterday Once More

B

A BADGER BLISS BOOK

By

Karen D. Badger

This is a work of fiction. All characters, locales and events are either products of the author's imagination or are used fictitiously.

ALL MY TOMORROWS

Cover picture and design by Karen D. Badger

A Badger Bliss Book
Published by Badger Bliss Books
Georgia, VT 05468

www.badgerblissbooks.com

ISBN 13: 978-1-945761-03-4
ISBN 10: 1-945761-03-2

Second Edition, August, 2016

Printed in the United States of America and in the United Kingdom

ACKNOWLEDGMENTS

As always, I want to thank my beta readers for the amazing job they did on the first read-through for this book. They include my mom, Ellie Atherton (the best mom a girl could ask for), Donna Brown (friend extraordinaire), Carol Poynor (the cutest Werther's Lady ever) and of course, my wife Bliss. Your help not only prevents me from looking like a total moron, but also helps make my editor's job so much easier. Speaking of editors, many thanks to Natty Burns for all her hard work and effort on my behalf. You guys rock!

PROLOGUE

SHELBURNE, VERMONT, 2105

Kale and Andi sat at the kitchen table waiting for Jordan to wake up. Andi had brewed her third cup of coffee when she commented on Jordan's absence.

"Maybe we should check on her. It's nearly ten o'clock. It's totally unlike her to sleep past seven," Andi said.

"You're right." Kale rose to his feet and headed toward Jordan's room. He stopped in front of her door.

"Jordan? Jordan, you're going to sleep the day away if you don't get your lazy butt out of bed."

Kale listened for a response, and became alarmed when none came. By this time, Andi had joined him in the hallway.

"She isn't answering me," Kale said. He reached for the handle and pushed the door open. Inside, Jordan lay in the same position she had been in when they left her the night before. He frowned and approached the bed.

"Jord?" he said.

She didn't reply. He glanced at Andi helplessly.

Andi touched the side of Jordan's face with her palm. "She's warm…but not hot," Andi said. She leaned in closer. "Jordan. Sweetie, wake up." She gently patted the side of Jordan's face. "Come on, time to get up."

Jordan turned her head to the side to escape Andi's touch.

"Oh, no you don't. You're not getting off that easily," Andi said. "Come on, wake up," she repeated, patting the side of Jordan's face again.

"No," Jordan moaned. "Go away."

"Not a chance. The day is nearly half over. We have a lot of work to do."

Jordan brushed Andi's hand away, but Andi persisted. Finally, Jordan pushed herself into a seated position. "Okay, okay, I'm up. Sheesh! Can't a girl get any sleep around here?"

"We woke you because we were worried. You've been sleeping for over twelve hours," Kale said.

Jordan looked at him. "Are you serious? What time is it?"

"Almost ten," he replied.

Jordan threw herself back onto the bed and covered her eyes with her hands. "Why am I still so tired?" She sat up once more. "All right. I need to get up." She swung her legs over the edge of the bed and placed her feet on the floor, then leaned forward to stand up. She rose halfway and then grasped her thighs. "Oh, my God."

Kale and Andi were immediately by her side. Kale wrapped his arm around her back. "Sit," he said.

"No, wait. Just let me hold on to you for a minute," she replied as little by little, she forced herself to stand erect.

With one hand on Andi's arm and the other on Kale's, Jordan took a tentative step forward and grimaced. Her eyes suddenly flew open.

"What is it?" Andi asked.

"It hurts," she replied. A grin split her face. "It hurts. My legs actually hurt."

Kale stared at her intently. "Are you telling me you feel pain in your legs?" he asked.

"Yes, that's exactly what I'm saying." Jordan watched the frown appear on Kale's face. "That's a good thing, isn't it, Kale?"

"A year from now, it would be a good thing. Two weeks after implant surgery—I'm not so sure. Jordan, it's too soon for the implant to be working. It should take months, if not years for the electrical impulses emitting from the implant to promote enough nerve regeneration for you to feel pain."

Jordan released her friends' arms and walked gingerly across the room to her bathroom. She stopped at the door and looked back. "I, for one, refuse to look a gift horse in the mouth. Give me a few minutes and I'll join you for coffee."

Kale and Andi interpreted the dismissal for what it was and left Jordan's room. On their way back to the kitchen, Kale was deep in thought.

"Are you okay?" Andi asked as she wrapped her arms around Kale's waist.

Kale shook his head. "Something isn't right about this. She severed her spinal cord sixteen years ago. There is no way the implant could restore synapse connection after only two weeks. Hell, even if the injury were brand new, it would take longer than that."

"Maybe it's phantom pain. I've heard amputees say countless times that they still feel pain in the limbs that are no longer there. Maybe that's what she's experiencing."

"I guess that could be it, but still, something doesn't feel right about this."

* * *

Jordan stepped into the shower and allowed the water to cascade over her body for several minutes. She leaned against the wall of the shower and reveled in the feel of the needle-like spray bombarding the skin on her legs with endless tingles of sensation. Tears mingled with water as the alien feelings overwhelmed her, yet she was reluctant to turn off the water for fear the sensation would also cease. A loud knock on the bathroom door shook her from her reverie.

"Jordan? Are you okay?" Andi called through the door.

Jordan turned off the spray and reached for her towel. "I'm fine. I'll be right out." She stepped out of the shower and methodically dried her body from the top down. When she reached her legs, she very slowly massaged them with her towel and was amazed at how soft the terry cloth felt against her skin.

This is freaking awesome!

Jordan stood in front of the vanity and tossed her hair with her fingertips. As she manipulated her wet hair into place, she saw something that disturbed her.

"What the hell?" she said out loud as she leaned in closer to the mirror. "Is that gray hair? That's odd. Mom didn't gray until she was nearly fifty. God, I hate getting older." She scrutinized herself closer.

Lewis, you need to take better care of yourself. I can see the beginnings of wrinkles here. Get a grip, girl, you're only thirty-two. At this rate, you'll look like Grandma Moses by the time you're forty.

A second knock at the door interrupted her scrutiny. "I'll be out in a minute, Andi."

"It's Kale. You've been in there an awfully long time. Are you sure you're okay?"

Jordan looked at the ceiling. "I'm fine. Really, I am. I'm coming out right now, so if you don't want to see me naked, you should get out of my bedroom. Here I come," Jordan warned.

She pushed the door open just in time to see her bedroom door close behind Kale. She chuckled as she entered her bedroom to get dressed. Moments later, she joined her friends in the kitchen for coffee.

"What the hell took you so long?" Kale asked. "Usually, your morning routine takes half the time mine does."

"You want the truth?" she asked. "I couldn't resist the feel of the shower spray on my legs. Guys, it's the most amazing thing to actually feel again. I could have stayed in there all day."

Andi sat back in her chair and looked at Jordan. "Something's different about you. I can't quite put my finger on it, but something is different."

Jordan chuckled. "It's probably my gray hair. Can you believe it? Look," she said as she tilted her head for Andi to see the dense shock of gray beginning at the back of her head. "I don't remember seeing that there yesterday."

Kale suddenly put his coffee cup down and rose to his feet. He approached Jordan and swung her around to face him, chair and all.

Jordan nearly fell out of the chair at the sudden movement. "What the hell are you doing?"

"Don't move," he told her as he carefully examined her face, and then the gray hair she pointed out earlier. "Bend over. I want to see your incision."

The next thing she knew, Kale was pacing angrily back and forth across the kitchen. "Goddamn it. Damn it all to hell. No wonder the implant is working already." He approached Jordan and dropped to one knee. "I hate to break this to you, but the time travel experiments are over. You got that? Finished."

Jordan's eyes opened wide. "Why?" she demanded.

Andi looked just as shocked as Jordan at Kale's declaration. "Kale, I don't understand," Andi said.

Kale approached Jordan once more. "Bend forward again."

Jordan did as she was told and Kale once again lifted her shirt. "Andi, look at the incision on Jordan's back. What do you see?"

Andi looked at Jordan's back, frowned, and then leaned in for a closer look. "It's barely discernable," she exclaimed.

"Exactly. She had spinal surgery just two weeks ago. At the very least, there should still be red, welted scar tissue there." He pointed at the incision site on Jordan's back. "Any doctor or nurse—hell, any mother who's put a bandage on her child's scraped knee would tell you that incision was made maybe twenty years ago, instead of two weeks."

Jordan sat upright and looked at Kale. "What the hell are you talking about?" she demanded.

"Come with me," Kale said as he took her hand and led her to the bathroom. Andi followed them and leaned against the bathroom door. "Here, stand with your back to the mirror. Now look." He gave her the hand mirror.

Jordan angled the mirror so that she could see the area around the incision on her back as Kale lifted her shirt yet again. "Oh my God," she said in nearly a whisper. Jordan put the mirror down and faced Kale. "What does this mean?" she asked.

Kale ran a hand through his hair. "It means that each time we send you through time, your body ages by God only knows how many years. That's why the implant is working so quickly. The time travel is adding years to your body, giving the nerve endings adequate time to grow over the injury site."

5

Jordan sneaked a look at Andi. A knowing gaze passed between them as she recalled an earlier conversation they had about how traveling back in time might have a potential affect on the aging process.

"From Einstein's experiments, we know time is gained when traveling backward and lost when traveling forward. I can only assume that each time we send you back, the actual transfer process accelerates time for you. Once you arrive there, time moves at a normal pace, but during the actual transfer, it moves faster," Kale said.

"Then why wouldn't the aging reverse on the return trip?" Jordan asked.

"I can answer that one," Andi interjected. "There probably *is* some amount of reversal, but theory dictates that time gained by traveling backward is much larger in magnitude than time lost traveling forward, so the amount of reversal would be minuscule compared to the aging."

"Jordan, we can't risk sending you back again. Judging by the change in your physical state just since the last transfer, it's almost as though the aging effect is cumulative. In other words, the rate of aging appears to be increasing with each transfer. At this rate, you'll die from old age in no time."

"I have to go back," Jordan insisted.

"I can't do it, Jordan. I won't risk it. Look at you. You look like you've aged at least fifteen or twenty years over the past three transfers. You had surgery just two weeks ago and yet the implant site has the appearance of a scar that healed years ago. It's obvious to me that you don't even need the implant anymore. I'm sure if Peter opened the injury site right now, all synapse connections would be restored. If we could have accomplished that one thing without causing you personal harm, all of this would be worth it, but I'm not willing to risk your death, or be the cause of your premature death from old age."

Jordan walked directly up to Kale and grabbed the font of his shirt. "Well, I'm willing to risk my death and old age because without Maggie in my life, it won't be worth living anyway."

Kale put his hands on his hips and closed his eyes. "Jordan, I don't want to lose you," he whispered.

Jordan released the front of his shirt and cupped his face. "Sweetheart, you will never lose me—regardless of where I am." She paused for a moment for her message to be absorbed. "Kale, imagine your life without Andi," she said softly. "I need you to do this for me. Please."

Kale closed his eyes as if to shut out the war raging in his mind between his own heart and Jordan's desires. He opened his eyes to find only desperation in Jordan's blue eyes.

"Please," she whispered once more.

* * *

"Okay, Kale. You need to use these time coordinates. They should land me very close to when I need to be there."

Kale took the piece of paper from Jordan and looked at it. "Remember, you promised to come back as soon as you've taken care of things, okay?"

"Yes, I remember," Jordan replied. "I don't break my promises."

"And then, no more time travel, right?" Kale reiterated.

"No more. Got it," Jordan replied nonchalantly.

Kale narrowed his eyes at Jordan. "Why is it that I don't believe you? What is going on in that mind of yours?"

Jordan adopted a surprise look on her face. "Who, me?"

"Jordan," Kale said.

Jordan threw up her hands in frustration. "All right, all right. No more transfers. I got it."

Kale turned his attention back to the control console as he typed in Jordan's time coordinates. "Good. I'm just about ready to go."

Jordan took her cue from Kale and climbed onto the platform. Just then, the door to the lab opened.

"Wait. Don't you dare leave without saying goodbye to me," Andi shouted as she hurried to the time machine. She reached forward and embraced Jordan warmly, then kissed her full on the lips. "Take care of yourself, girlfriend. I love you."

Jordan smiled. "I love you too, Andi. And you too, you pain in the ass," she shouted across the room to Kale.

"Yeah, yeah, whatever," Kale responded teasingly.

Jordan drew her knees into her chest and wrapped her arms around her legs, then lowered her forehead to her knees. "Okay, blast off," she shouted as Kale powered up the rings.

Moments later, she was gone.

"I love you too, Jordan," Kale whispered.

* * *

Jordan landed on the dirt floor of the barn with a thud. She pushed herself into a seated position and looked around to be certain she had not been seen. Suddenly, she heard a voice.

"Hey, Shawny-baby. How's Mommy's good boy this morning?"

It's Maggie.

Jordan crept behind a nearby saddle rack near Shawny's stall to shield herself from Maggie's view. She watched as Maggie saddled her horse.

"How would you like a ride, sweetie? It's a beautiful morning. The air is crisp and the sun is shining off the snow. A nice fast ride will do us both some good, and when we get back, I'll give you an extra helping of oats to eat while I cook breakfast for Jordan. That's a good boy."

Jordan waited impatiently as Maggie saddled her horse.

"Okay, dumpling, let's go for a ride," Maggie said as she mounted her horse and gently prodded the steed forward through the barn. Soon, she was gone.

Jordan emerged from behind the saddle rack and ran as fast as she could to the house. She threw open the kitchen door and ran directly through the house into Maggie's bedroom.

"Jordan! Jordan, get your ass out of bed." She flung the door to the bedroom wide open. It hit the wall behind it with a resounding bang.

"What the hell?" the sleeping Jordan exclaimed as she quickly sat up in bed.

"Go after her. Quickly, or you'll lose her forever. This is your last chance," Jordan screamed from the doorway.

"Who are you, old woman?" Jordan demanded as she

scrambled out of bed and pulled her jeans and boots on as fast as she could.

"Never mind who I am. Just hurry. For God's sake, please hurry. You know what's at stake here. She just rode off. You have very little time." She scurried out of Jordan's way as quickly as she could to avoid the two of them making bodily contact as the younger Jordan ran past her.

* * *

Without stopping, Jordan grabbed her canvas barn jacket from the hook by the kitchen door. Within moments, she ran the distance between the house and barn and flung the barn door open. She ran directly to the pile of tack being held for repair and realized Maggie's saddle was no longer there.

Oh no. Maggie, please don't tell me you are using the defective saddle.

Jordan desperately searched several empty stalls until she came across one containing a magnificent mustang steed. She talked soothingly to the animal as she first threw a blanket and then a saddle over the horse's back.

"Come on, big guy. We've got a job to do."

Minutes later, she led the horse out of the stall and climbed into the saddle. With a quick jab to the horse's ribs, she was on her way at a full gallop across the snowy fields, heading for the western edge of the property bounded by Lake Champlain.

The old woman made her way through the empty farmhouse and stepped onto the porch outside the kitchen door. From her vantage point, she could see Jordan speeding across the plains.

"Godspeed, Jordan. Please reach her in time. This is her last chance. This is *our* last chance."

Then she slowly descended the stairs and walked toward the barn.

* * *

Jordan agonized about how long it was taking to cover the distance between the house and the lake. In her desperation, she was oblivious to the biting cold that chafed her cheeks while she rode. Nearly a half hour later, the frozen lake came into view. The sight encouraged Jordan to dig in her heels and push her steed nearly beyond its limits as their speed increased and she felt airborne.

Maggie, please stay away from the edge. Please. I'm coming, my love, I'm coming. Please let me reach you in time.

Jordan pushed her mount as hard as she could and almost gave up hope until she spotted Maggie on the horizon, galloping freely across the plains, directly toward the edge of the cliffs.

"Maggie!" she screamed. "Maggie, stop."

Jordan's screams were ineffective. The distance between them and the sound of the crashing surf below the cliffs drowned out any chance that Maggie would hear her.

Jordan silently asked her horse for forgiveness as she dug her heels in once more in an attempt to get just a little more speed out of the animal. Her efforts paid off as she began to close the distance between them. Again, she attempted to call out to Maggie, and again, her efforts were for naught. Finally, when she had closed the distance to within thirty feet, she heard a shot ring out. Maggie's horse suddenly reared up very close to the edge of the cliff.

* * *

"Kale, Jordan left us a message. It's time to bring her home," Andi said as she entered the lab.

"Okay. Let's do this," Kale replied, powering the system up.

"Ten seconds to surge," Andi said. "Ten, nine, eight, seven, six, five, four, three two...ready...surge."

* * *

Maggie stood in the saddle in an attempt to steady herself and calm the animal as it continued to rear up.

"Maggie." Jordan shouted once more. She was now only twenty feet from Maggie.

Maggie looked up and saw Jordan just as she lost her footing and began to tumble off the horse.

"No." Jordan screamed, reaching for anything she could cling to. Just as her fingers made contact with the collar of Maggie's jacket, she felt the now-familiar tingling in her body as though every muscle had fallen asleep and was now awakening. She realized immediately what was happening. "Kale. No. Not now. For heaven's sake, not now." she screamed.

* * *

The power surge passed over Kale and Andi as they watched Jordan appear on the platform. Then, the unthinkable happened. Jordan's figure began to fade again as though she were somehow resisting the retrieval.

"Do something!" Andi shouted.

"I...I don't know what to do," Kale said.

They stood by helplessly as Jordan began to fade away. Then, as suddenly as it began, the process reversed itself and Jordan appeared once more on the platform.

"Power down," Andi ordered, running toward Jordan.

Kale powered down the rings as fast as he could. Moments later, he ran toward the machine where Andi had climbed onto the platform and gathered Jordan into her arms. She was rocking the frail, gray-haired Jordan back and forth while cradling her close to her breast.

"Andi?" Kale said softly.

Andi looked at Kale with tear-filled eyes. "She's gone, Kale. She's gone."

CHAPTER 1

SHELBURNE, VERMONT
SEPTEMBER 23, 2018

"Good Morning, John," Maggie said as she entered the barn.

"Mornin', Maggie."

"What's on your agenda today?"

"Well, I'm fixing to repair this pitchfork. The handle is loose. After that, I have some hay bales to stack."

"The wagon with the bales is out in the barn yard. Would you like me to bring them in for you?" Maggie asked.

"No ma'am. I'll take care of it, right after I fix this pitchfork."

"All right then," Maggie said. She shoved her hands deep into the front pockets of her jeans and walked into her horse's stall. "Hey, Shawny. How's my guy this morning?"

John stepped out of the tack room. "Where's that wind coming from? Did you leave the barn door open, Maggie?"

Just then, a flash of light appeared in the area of the barn where the hay bales were stored, drawing John's attention. "What in tarnation—?"

Maggie's exited Shawny's stall a moment later. "John, are you sure you don't want help with the hay?"

Suddenly, her attention was drawn to a cracking sound above her head. A split second later, she found herself tackled to the ground as a large metal winch hit the dirt with a resounding thud, right next to her.

"Get off me." Maggie scrambled to her feet. "What the hell

happened?" she said as she watched her would-be rescuer also stand and brush herself off.

"John," Maggie screamed. "John, I need you in here, right now."

Maggie circled the heavy winch then looked up at the rafters. "Son of a bitch—I could have been killed," she exclaimed.

John ran into the barn from the tack room, just as a petite woman with short blonde hair entered the barn.

"Maggie. What happened?" John asked.

Maggie pointed at the winch. "*That* is what happened. John, I need you to inspect the rafter this thing was hanging from. Something caused it to snap, and I want to know what."

"Yes, ma'am," John said.

The petite woman shot a questioning look at Jordan. "What happened?" she asked, placing a comforting hand on Maggie's back.

Maggie rubbed her forehead. "I don't know. I was walking toward Shawny's stall when all of the sudden this woman—" Maggie gestured at Jordan "This woman appeared out of nowhere and tackled me to the floor. The next thing I knew, the winch was sitting in a crater on the floor, exactly where I'd just been standing."

The smaller woman wrapped her arms around Maggie and hugged her. "Thank God you weren't hurt," she said. "I'll investigate this. I promise we'll get to the bottom of it."

Maggie cupped the side of the woman's face and smiled. "Thank you, Jan."

Maggie turned abruptly and looked at Jordan. Her brows knit together as she considered the woman who had saved her life. She watched Jordan shift her weight from foot to foot, uncomfortable under Maggie's intense scrutiny. Maggie extended her hand.

"And you are?" she asked.

"Jordan. Jordan Lewis," she replied as she shook Maggie's hand.

Maggie smiled, clearly aware of the effect she was having on Jordan as she saw Jordan struggle to look away. "Well,

Jordan, I guess I am indebted to you. I can't thank you enough. If you hadn't come along when you did, that winch would have killed me."

Jordan inhaled deeply. "You're welcome," she replied. "When I heard the rafter crack, I pretty much acted on instinct."

"Thank God for instinct," Maggie declared. "So, the question is who are you and what were you doing in my barn?"

"Ah…ah…I was actually looking for work," Jordan began, "No one answered the door at the house, so I came to the barn."

Maggie smiled again. "Work, huh? Well, why don't you join me for a glass of lemonade while we talk about it?"

Jordan smiled back at her. "I'd like that."

* * *

Maggie filled two glasses and handed one to Jordan, who was seated at the kitchen table. Maggie leaned against the cupboard and assessed Jordan as she drank.

"So, Jordan, where are you from?" Maggie asked.

"I'm actually from the area," Jordan replied.

Maggie sipped her drink. "I see. So, what kind of work are you looking for?"

Jordan sat back in her chair and crossed her legs. "Well, my parents raised horses, so I have experience in the care and training of horses, and I'm pretty good with my hands," she added.

"Hmm," Maggie murmured as she watched a wide array of expressions cross Jordan's face. "Is it safe to say you'll need to bunk here as well? I mean, assuming I hire you, of course."

Just then, the kitchen door swung open and Jan entered. Both women turned their attention to her.

"Did you find anything?" Maggie asked.

Jan shrugged her shoulders. "Not really. I climbed into the rafters and examined the beams. Odd as it sounds, that particular beam snapped for no apparent reason. It was probably a defective beam."

Maggie frowned. "That seems strange. The winch has been hanging from that beam for the past two years, and there's been no sign of failure. What did John have to say about it?"

Jan shifted her weight from foot to foot. "John didn't look at it. I told him I would take care of it."

Maggie frowned. "Well, I'll call the contractor who built the barn and have him repair it for me."

"I can repair it," Jordan interjected.

Maggie raised her eyebrows. "You can?"

Jordan stood. "Like I said, I'm good with my hands."

Maggie grinned. "Okay." She turned to Jan. "Jan, this is Jordan Lewis, our new ranch hand."

Jordan extended her hand to Jan, who pointedly chose not to shake it.

"I've got to get back to the barn. John needs a hand offloading the feed," Jan said. She turned abruptly and left.

"Humph," Maggie exclaimed as she looked at Jordan. "That's not like her. She's normally so friendly. Please accept my apologies."

Jordan smiled. "No problem. I'm sure she's still just shaken up by your close call."

"Maybe," Maggie replied absently.

"So, if you'll point me in the direction of your tools and wood supply, I'll get to work on that rafter," Jordan offered.

Maggie smiled. "You don't waste any time, do you?"

"No, Ma'am," Jordan replied.

* * *

The broken rafter was just beyond the end of the hayloft but close enough that Jordan was able set up an extension ladder on the floor of the loft and lean it against a rafter adjacent to the break. Once the ladder was in place, Jordan carried up a few pieces of two-by-six lumber and placed them across two rafters in order to create a scaffold for herself.

Jordan was nailing the last plank in place when Maggie appeared in the barn below.

"Hey there," she called up to Jordan. "How's it going?"

Jordan looked down "I've just built the work platform. I'm about to inspect the beam now."

"Do you mind if I join you?" Maggie asked.

"Not at all. Come on up." Jordan climbed down the ladder

and waited for Maggie to join her in the loft. "You go ahead of me. I'll hold the ladder," Jordan offered.

"Okay," Maggie said.

Once Maggie was standing securely on the scaffolding, Jordan climbed the ladder and joined her. The platform was relatively narrow, so Jordan had to hold on to Maggie as she shimmied past her in order to get close enough to inspect the break.

"Okay," Jordan said. "Let's see what the problem is here. Hmm…this is odd."

"What is it?" Maggie moved in for a closer look.

"Well, after what Jan said, I expected to see a ragged break. If this was caused by a defect in the beam, the break would most likely be splintered, jagged, and at an angle."

Jordan pointed to the end of the rafter still in place. "Look here. This beam has been cut with a saw. Look at how straight and clean this edge is."

"That *is* odd," Maggie said. "I wonder who did that…and why?"

Jordan's eyes narrowed. "What I'd like to know is why Jan said there was no apparent reason for the break."

Maggie frowned. "You don't suspect Jan, do you?"

Jordan shrugged. "Maggie, I don't even *know* Jan, so I'm in no position to judge her. I just think it's odd that she inspected the break and found nothing strange about it."

"Well, to tell you the truth, Jan is really good with the animals, but she doesn't know which end of a hammer to use to drive a nail. I doubt she would have realized the significance of this clean cut. I will call the original contractor and ask him about it. Would you mind talking to him?"

"No," Jordan replied. "Sounds like a good idea. In the meantime, I'll repair this."

Maggie smiled. "Okay. If you don't mind, I'd appreciate it."

"Consider it done." Jordan smiled sweetly at Maggie.

Maggie's gaze lingered on Jordan for several seconds. Finally, she chuckled. "Forgive me for staring, Jordan, but I've never met such a competent woman, especially not one as attractive as you."

Jordan blushed. "Well thank ya, ma'am," she said in a mock southern drawl. She tucked her thumbs into her belt. "Yer not such a bad looker yerself."

Maggie laughed. "And you have a sense of humor as well. A very nice combination. Okay, good luck with the repair. I've got to get ready for a meeting with the Shelburne selectmen in about an hour. If you need anything, ask John."

Jordan nodded at Maggie. "All right then. I'll just take a few measurements here. Do you need help with the ladder?"

"No, I'll be fine. I should be back in a couple of hours. I'll show you around the farm and get you settled into the bunkhouse when I get back. Is that okay?"

"That's fine. Have a good meeting."

Maggie smiled once more. "Thank you. I'll be back soon."

CHAPTER 2

When Maggie returned to the barn later that day, she found Jordan standing in the hook of the winch as John raised her to the rafters and lowered her again. "Okay, John, this time we'll hook onto a pallet of feed and see how that goes."

Maggie leaned quietly against the doorway of the barn and watched Jordan hook the winch to the straps supporting the feed pallet before climbing on top of the bags.

"Okay, John, take it up."

Jordan held on to the rope just above the winch as John slowly raised her and the pallet to the level of the hayloft. "Looks good from here," she announced. "Take it down."

John slowly lowered the pallet to the floor of the barn. When it was stable, Jordan jumped off and turned to John. "Good as new," she proclaimed. "You should be able to unload the feed safely now."

"Thank you, Jordan. Maggie will be happy to know the rafter is fixed."

"Yes, I am very happy," Maggie said from her position by the door.

"Maggie–you're back," Jordan exclaimed. "How long have you been standing there?"

Maggie walked up and linked her arm with Jordan's. "Long enough to watch your acrobatics. Do you always test out your own work like that?"

Maggie led Jordan out of the barn and across the yard.

"Well, I do have a habit of using myself as a test subject. I figure if I put myself at risk, I'll do a better job."

"I like that level of personal commitment," Maggie said. "I think you and I are going to get along just fine."

"Okay, here is the bunkhouse," Maggie said as they mounted the steps to the cabin. Maggie pushed the door open and stepped aside so Jordan could enter first.

"Wow. This is really nice," Jordan observed. She looked around the well-furnished bunkhouse. It was built in an L shape off one side of the farmhouse and extended behind the main house. "Does anyone else live here?"

"No, you are the only one right now, so you get your pick of beds."

"So, I take it John and Jan don't live on the farm."

Maggie smiled. "John lives about a mile down the road. Jan does live here, just not in the bunkhouse."

Jordan turned red with embarrassment. "Oh, I…ah…well, that's really none of my business."

Maggie touched Jordan's arm. "No, I don't mind. In fact you should probably know that my lifestyle is a bit unconventional. You see, Jan is my…well, let's just say she's my significant other. Is that going to be a problem for you?"

Jordan said, "No. Why should it? What you do in the privacy of your own home is your business. I do have one question for you though."

"And that is?"

"Considering Jan's status in your household, am I to take instructions from her as well as you?"

Maggie grinned. "Absolutely not. Like I said, Jan is good with the animals, but not very proficient in other things. No, if there is something to be done around here, I will be the one to direct it."

"Well that's a relief," Jordan replied.

Maggie cocked her head to the side. "How so?"

"Because judging by her reaction in the barn earlier today, I don't think she likes me very much."

Maggie chuckled. "Don't let her bother you. She tends to be a bit territorial, but she's all bark and no bite. So, take your pick of the bedrooms and make yourself comfortable. Take a look around, settle in, and let me know if you need anything. Okay?"

Jordan shoved her fingertips into her back pockets. "I don't think I need anything right now. Oh, wait. Maybe some paper and a pen? I like to keep a journal, and I don't have anything with me right now to record today's entries."

"Not a problem. I'll go fetch it for you right now. I assume your diary is in your luggage?"

"Er...yes. My diary is in my luggage. Now that I have a job, I'll send for it. With any luck, it will be here in a couple of days."

Maggie crossed her arms and cocked her head to one side. "So I guess you'll need something to sleep in as well?"

Jordan turned red and looked at the floor. "Well, I thought about washing my things out in the sink tonight and just sleeping in the nude."

"You'll do nothing of the kind. Come with me. I have several old T-shirts here that my Dad left behind when they moved to Florida. Come pick out what you'd like to wear. He wasn't a very big man. There may even be some jeans and shirts of his that you can wear until your luggage arrives. As for the personal items, you're a few inches taller than I am, but it looks like we wear pretty much the same size jeans, so I'm sure I have some underclothes you can wear."

"You don't have to do that, Maggie."

"No, I don't, but I want to. So, come with me," Maggie said.

Jordan followed her from the bunkhouse into the kitchen of the farmhouse.

As they stepped into the kitchen, Maggie turned to Jordan and smiled. "Dinner time is normally a community affair around here, and everyone pitches in—however, I must warn you, if you can't cook, you usually end up doing the dishes."

Jordan grinned. "Well, I guess I'll be sporting dishpan hands 'cause I burn water."

Maggie chuckled. "Well, luckily for you, I can cook. In fact, I usually end up doing most of the cooking around here."

Jordan followed Maggie from room to room as she pointed out areas of the house. After the tour of the living areas was complete, Maggie led Jordan down the hall to the bedrooms. "That's my room," she said, pointing out the first door they passed on the left. "The bathroom is right across the hall, and down here at the end is a suite of rooms that my parents used when they lived here."

Maggie pushed the door open to her parent's suite. "Okay, let's see," she began as she opened a dresser drawer and pulled out a few T-shirts. "These should fit you." Maggie pulled open another drawer. "Also, here are some blue jeans that Dad sometimes wore. Like I said, he wasn't a large man. He was maybe three or four inches taller than you are, but he was pretty slim. If the cuffs are too long, just roll them up."

Maggie handed the pile of clothes to Jordan. Then she led Jordan back into the hall to her own bedroom. She pushed the door open and, instantly, the scent of patchouli reached Jordan's nostrils. Jordan inhaled deeply as she stepped into the room. "Hmm," she said unconsciously.

Maggie noticed Jordan's reaction. "It's patchouli. Do you like it?"

Jordan looked into Maggie's eyes. "It's my favorite scent," she replied.

Maggie smiled. "It's my favorite as well."

Maggie's gaze held Jordan's for a tad longer than would be considered conventional. After a moment, she inhaled deeply and regained her sense of awareness.

"Underclothes," Maggie said as the open a dresser drawer and pulled out a few pairs of panties, some socks, and a couple of bras. "I'm a 34C. Will that work for you?"

"Perfect," she replied as she accepted the clothing. "Maggie, I don't know how to thank you enough."

"No thanks necessary. After all, if you hadn't come along when you did, I probably wouldn't be here. That winch hit the floor exactly where I was standing. It surely would have killed me. I should be thanking *you*."

Jordan grinned and shook her head. "You probably would have seen it in time to get out of the way, but like you said, no thanks necessary."

Again, a silence fell as they stared at one another for what seemed like an eternity. Finally, Jordan broke the reverie. "Ah, I guess I should be getting settled in."

Maggie snapped out of her trance. "Of course, of course. Oh, let me get you some paper and a pen before you go."

Maggie retrieved a small journal from the bedside table

and handed it to Jordan.

"Here. This is a spare journal I haven't used yet. I keep diaries myself, you know. I realize how important it is to organize your thoughts at the end of the day."

Jordan grinned as she accepted the book and pen. "Thank you, Maggie. You know, something told me you were the diary type."

"Really?"

"Yes, really," Jordan replied. She added the diary to the growing heap of things tucked under her arm. She looked at Maggie. "So, if you were writing today's entry right now, what would it say?"

Maggie looked up at the ceiling and squinted her eyes. She raised one hand for emphasis as she spoke. "It would say September 23, 2018. This is the day I almost died. Luckily, my beautiful blue-eyed guardian angel came to my rescue."

Jordan cleared her throat. "Well, I guess I should go settle in. Thank you again."

"You are welcome. Can you find your way out?" Maggie asked.

"No problem," Jordan replied. "This place already feels like home."

* * *

Maggie kicked off her boots, stripped off her blue jeans and flannel shirt, and threw everything into a heap by the side of the bed just as Jan entered the room.

"Wow. Now that's what I call a nice welcome," she exclaimed.

Maggie walked to her dresser to retrieve a tank top that she slipped over her head.

Jan frowned. "So I take it you're not interested in making love tonight."

Maggie stood in front of the dresser and tousled her curly hair in front of the mirror. "Jan, it's been a long day, not to mention a little frightening."

Jan pretended to be interested in something on the dresser. "How so?"

"For starters, having a three hundred pound metal winch nearly fall on my head this morning—that's how so. Do you realize I could have been killed? Thank God Jordan was there."

"There's something odd about that one," Jan replied.

Maggie tuned to look at her. "Why do you say that?"

"What do you know about her? Where does she come from? What did she do for a living before she came here? Have you asked her any of those questions yet?"

"I know that her family raised horses. I know that she is from somewhere around this area, but she hasn't specified exactly where yet. I know she seems to know what she's doing on a farm. I know she's good with her hands, and I know that if she hadn't been here today, I wouldn't be standing here talking to you right now. For me, that's all I need to know."

Jan snorted. "I'll bet she's good with her hands."

Maggie stomped up to Jan and stopped within inches of her. "What exactly to you mean by that?" she demanded.

"Don't tell me you haven't noticed how attractive she is," Jan said. "Are you going to pursue her like you did me when I first came to work for you?"

"The way I remember it, that pursuit went both ways," Maggie replied.

"Yeah, well I'm not sure she's going to be a welcome addition to the crew. She has kind of a know-it-all attitude."

"Oh, really? Just how much time have you spent with her to come to that conclusion?"

"I don't need to spend time with her. I think I'm a pretty good judge of character, and she doesn't look like a farmhand to me. She looks more like she should be sitting behind a desk or teaching school or something like that."

Maggie placed her hands on her hips. "Well, I'll have you know that she's very capable of working a farm. She inspected the rafter after you said it was probably a weak point in the wood, and she found where someone or something had mechanically cut through the boards."

"What?" Jan exclaimed. "How the hell did she come to that conclusion? I looked at the boards myself and saw no such thing."

"Well then, either you didn't really look or you didn't know what you were looking at because she showed it to me. It was clearly cut, not broken and not splintered."

Jan paced back and forth across the bedroom, clearly agitated. "I don't like what you're implying, Maggie. You shouldn't be letting this Lewis character put those kinds of thoughts in your head. She'll be nothing but trouble for us. Mark my words."

Maggie intercepted Jan's path as she crossed the room. "Let's get one thing straight, Jan," Maggie said in a stern voice. "When it comes to this farm, there is no *us*. This is *my* farm, and I will run it the way I see fit. Is that clear?"

* * *

Maggie entered the kitchen carrying several envelopes from the mailbox and noticed Jordan was on the phone. She thumbed through them as she waited for Jordan to finish her phone call.

"No sir, I inspected the board myself. In my opinion, it looks as if it was cut mechanically. The break was straight and clean instead of jagged and angled as I would expect it to be if the board had snapped under the weight of the winch."

Jordan paused for a moment. "Okay then," she said. "I'll let Miss Downs know one of your carpenters will be here today around noon to inspect the board. All right. Thank you. Goodbye."

"What did he say?" Maggie asked without looking up.

"He's sending a man over at noon to inspect the beam."

Maggie threw the last envelope into the bill pile and then looked up at Jordan. "Wow. Daddy never looked that good in those jeans."

Jordan blushed. "Stop that. You're embarrassing me."

Maggie crossed her arms in front of her. "Hey, how would you like to accompany me to an auction?"

Jordan shrugged. "Sure. If you want me to, I'm game."

"All right then. Give me a minute to freshen up, and I'll be right with you. Help yourself to some lemonade while you wait. I won't be long."

"Take your time, I'm on the clock," Jordan joked then took the pitcher of lemonade from the refrigerator.

Jan walked in and stopped short when she saw Jordan making herself at home. "Does Maggie know you're helping yourself like that?" she asked curtly.

"As a matter of fact, she does. I'm actually waiting for her to freshen up. We're going to a horse auction," Jordan replied.

Anger sparked in Jan's eyes. "I guess it will be a threesome then," she stated briskly.

Maggie breezed into the kitchen. "Okay, I'm ready."

She stopped short when she saw Jan.

"Oh, Jan, I'm glad you're here. The building contractor is sending a man over in about an hour to inspect the damaged rafter. I think it might be beneficial for you to meet with him. I am taking Jordan with me to the Mustang auction. We'll be back later this afternoon."

Jordan locked eyes with Jan. If looks could have killed, Jordan would be dead.

CHAPTER 3

Maggie caught Jordan covertly looking at her as she sat in the passenger seat of Maggie's pickup truck. "Okay, I give up. What do you find so interesting that you feel compelled to stare at me?" she asked.

Jordan turned red with embarrassment. She covered her face with her hands. "I'm sorry. I just can't help myself," she confessed.

Maggie's interest was piqued. "No, I'm flattered, actually. But why can't you help yourself? Really, I want to know."

Jordan looked surprised. "You mean you don't know?"

Maggie glanced at Jordan quickly then turned her attention back to the road. "Know what?" she asked sincerely.

Jordan shook her head. "Well, I'll be damned. Maggie, you are a beautiful woman. In fact, you are more beautiful in person than in print."

Maggie frowned. "When exactly did you see me in print?"

"Ah. Well, I did a little research on you and your farm before I came to apply for the job. I found a picture of you that was taken at some county fair a few years back."

Maggie appeared to be deep in thought. "Hmm, I see. Do you really think I'm beautiful?"

"I'm surprised you have to ask that question. I would think you'd have suitors lined up for a mile."

Maggie chuckled. "Well, it's pretty much common knowledge around town that Jan and I are a couple, so there haven't really been any offers for quite some time now."

"Did you date much before Jan?"

"A little, but I had a bad experience with a girl named Jess when I was in my twenties, and that pretty much turned me off to relationships for a while. Jan is my first serious relationship in a long time."

"How long have you and Jan been together?"

Maggie thought for a moment before answering. "For about four years."

"Hmm," Jordan said.

Maggie tossed her a sideways glance. "What is that supposed to mean?"

"Well, I guess I just don't see that she's your type."

Maggie was taken aback by Jordan's comment. "And just why do you feel you're qualified to know what my type is? Hell, you've only been here for two days."

"You're right. I apologize, but it just doesn't feel right to me. Don't ask me why. It just doesn't."

"I don't appreciate you talking about Jan that way. *I* decide what my type is, not you. Jan suits me just fine, thank you very much."

Maggie and Jordan rode along in silence for a few moments. Finally, the silence became unbearable. "So, what exactly do you think my type is?" Maggie asked.

Jordan appeared to be deep in thought. "Well, I guess your type would be someone who was your intellectual equal, someone who could give you good advice yet know when not to cross boundaries. That person should complement you physically as well. You are a very beautiful woman. Don't take this the wrong way, but your feminine nature doesn't fit the profile of someone who can run a farm all by herself."

Maggie glared at Jordan. "Okay, let me get this straight. First you tell me my partner is stupid, and she gives bad advice, and then you have the audacity to imply I can't run a horse farm properly because I'm too feminine?"

"No. No. That's not what I meant. Look, I'm digging a hole for myself that I won't be able to climb out of if I keep running my mouth, so let's just forget I said anything."

"Oh, no. You're not getting off that easy, Jordan. Now, explain what you meant."

Jordan placed her hands on her thighs and dropped her head back to look at the ceiling of the truck. She inhaled deeply then turned her head to look at Maggie. "Okay. Let me just say that most of the feminine women I have known in the past are pretty high-maintenance, and quite frankly, they tend to prefer someone more on the butch side to take care of things for them."

Maggie slammed her foot down hard on the brake, bringing the truck to a grinding halt on the dusty country road. Jordan nearly went through the windshield. She was only able to stop herself at the last minute by quickly placing both hands on the dash.

"What the hell?" Jordan exclaimed.

"Get out," Maggie demanded.

"What?"

"I said, get out. You're fired."

Jordan turned in her seat to face Maggie. "Why am I fired?"

Maggie leaned across the seat toward Jordan. "You're fired because anyone who doesn't respect who I am and what I can do is not welcome on my farm. Now get your ass out of my truck."

"When did I say I didn't respect you?" Jordan spat back.

"You called me high-maintenance." Maggie's voice had risen an octave.

"Like hell I did."

"You said that feminine women look for butch women to take care of them," Maggie insisted.

"Wrong," Jordan shouted back. "I said you don't fit the profile of someone who can run a farm alone. Sheesh, woman. Do you always look for a fight where there isn't one?"

Both women fell silent. Jordan reached for the door handle and set one foot on the ground before Maggie took her arm.

"Where are you going?"

"I'm fired, remember? I'm going back to the farm to collect my things."

"No. Don't go. Please get back into the truck."

Jordan looked at her for a few moments, then shifted her weight back into the vehicle and closed the door. She stared straight ahead.

Maggie had both hands on the steering wheel as she looked out over the hood of the truck. "I'm sorry," she said.

Jordan continued to sit silently, staring out the windshield.

Maggie turned in her seat to face Jordan. "I said, I'm sorry. I misunderstood what you said. Forgive me?"

Jordan tilted her head down and to the left so she was looking at Maggie out of the corner of her eye. "Only if you rehire me," she said, trying to hide a grin.

"Done," Maggie replied.

"And give me a raise," Jordan added.

Maggie's anger immediately erupted again. "Why you...."

Jordan grinned and leaned forward to face Maggie. She pointed her index finger at the angry redhead. "Got you," she teased.

"Jesus Christ. You are exasperating."

"Yeah, but I'll grow on you."

"Like hell you will," Maggie replied, trying to fight a smile.

Jordan and Maggie sat staring at each other for several long moments. Try as she might, Maggie was unable to erase the smile from her face. Finally, Jordan broke the standoff.

"I think we're going to be late for the auction."

Maggie's head snapped back. "Shit, you're right. Hold on. It's going to be a wild ride."

* * *

"Hi, Mom. How are you and Dad doing?"

Maggie paced back and forth across the living room as she held her cell phone to her ear. "That's good. Is Daddy's cough getting any better? Great. I'm sure it's just a cold. If it's not gone in another week, promise me you'll take him to the doctor's and have it checked out. Okay? I'll talk to you in a few days then. Give Daddy a big hug for me. Okay, Mom. I love you both. Goodnight."

Jan placed the book she was reading in her lap. "How are Mom and Dad?" she asked as Maggie sat on the couch with one leg curled under her.

"They're doing okay. Dad still has a cough, but Mom says it's getting better."

"That's good. Have they said any more about putting the farm in your name?"

"Not really. I know Dad hired a lawyer to set things in

motion, but it will take a few months before anything is finalized."

"Still, your parents aren't getting any younger," Jan said.

"Jan, I said Daddy is taking care of it. Now, I don't want to discuss this anymore."

Jan raised her hands into the air. "Fine. Whatever you want."

A tense silence fell between the women. Jan broke it. "So, how was the auction?"

Maggie placed both feet on the floor. She leaned forward and rested her forearms on her thighs. "Things went great. We were able to secure about a half-dozen mustangs. It appears our Jordan knows her animals. Those horses came from quality stock."

Jan cocked an eyebrow at Maggie. "*Our* Jordan?"

Maggie sighed deeply. "Jan, why do you always have to nitpick everything I say? Look, I don't want a fight. I'm going to bed."

"Suit yourself," Jan returned as Maggie stomped away.

By the time Maggie reached their bedroom, she was furious. *Why does she always have to have the last word? Sometimes I regret ever becoming involved with that woman.*

* * *

The next morning, Jordan rose early and headed to the north pasture to mend fences. She worked in the hot sun all day, and by the time she returned to the house, she was in desperate need of a shower. She rode her horse into the barn and dismounted, then took the reins and led the animal into its stall. After feeding and watering the horse, Jordan meticulously brushed him until his coat was gleaming. As she turned to leave, she was startled by Maggie who was standing in the entrance to the stall.

Jordan jumped. "Jesus! You scared me. How long have you been standing there?"

Maggie leaned against the post with her arms crossed in front of her. She grinned sheepishly. "Oh, for about five minutes," she replied. "You really do a nice job with the animals, Jordan. You have a knack for it."

Jordan took her hat off and dusted it as she spoke. "Well, like I said before, I had horses while growing up. Mustangs, in fact. They're beautiful animals."

"Yes, they are. You've been in the north pasture all day, right?"

"Yeah, mending fences. And now I need to shower. I'm kind of filthy and smelly."

Maggie's gaze roamed up and down Jordan's tall frame. Jordan was wearing a plaid button-down shirt with the sleeves rolled back to her elbows and the tails tucked into soiled blue jeans. She had on a brown leather vest, a bandanna around her neck, and a well-worn pair of cowboy boots. Tucked in her back pocket were the leather work gloves she'd used to handle the barbed wire fencing. Her shoulder-length brown hair was damp with sweat. She'd tucked the wayward locks behind her ears.

"I see your luggage arrived," Maggie said.

"Yes it did." A few moments passed in silence until Jordan broke it. "I really should shower. I'm a mess."

Maggie grinned. "I happen to think you look fine. I like a woman who isn't afraid to get dirty doing a hard day's work."

Jordan smiled. "Looking fine and smelling fine are two different things." Jordan walked past Maggie into the main part of the barn.

"Jordan?" Maggie called out. Jordan stopped and turned around. "Would you care to join us for dinner? At the risk of sounding full of myself, I'm a pretty good cook."

As if on cue, Jordan's stomach replied for her, loud enough for Maggie to hear. Jordan turned red with embarrassment.

Maggie laughed. "I'll take that as a yes. Dinner is at six o'clock sharp."

* * *

At precisely six, Jordan knocked on the front door of the farmhouse.

"Hey, Jordan, come in. Wow. You clean up real good," Maggie exclaimed. She noted with approval the freshly showered shine in Jordan's hair and the clean, well-tailored slacks and shirt she was wearing.

Jordan stepped across the threshold and handed a bouquet of wildflowers to Maggie. "I saw these out in the north pasture this morning while I was mending fences. I ran out and picked a few. I hope you like them," she said.

Maggie accepted the flowers, inhaling their aroma. "They're beautiful. Thank you." She closed the door behind Jordan. "Jan is pouring wine in the living room. Go on and join her while I put these in water."

Jordan pushed open the door between the kitchen and living room and passed through.

Jan was standing by the fireplace looking pensively at the flames while she sipped a glass of wine. She looked up when Jordan entered the room. She smiled and extended her hand. "Jordan. It's so nice you could join us."

Jordan was taken aback by Jan's polite and friendly manner but offered her hand anyway. Jan's handshake was firm.

"How do you like the job so far?" Jan asked.

"I like it just fine. I appreciate Maggie giving me a chance."

"Good. Maggie and I have great plans for this farm. We have been thinking about opening a riding school for handicapped children. Maggie just loves kids. In fact, we've considered having one of our own or maybe adopting one or two in the near future."

"I'm sure Maggie would make a great mother," Jordan replied.

Maggie entered the room carrying the bouquet of flowers Jordan had given her. "Jan, look at the beautiful flowers Jordan picked." She placed the vase on the fireplace mantel then turned to face them. "So, is anyone hungry?"

"Famished," Jan replied. She directed Jordan into the dining room.

Jordan held Maggie's chair for her then sat in the seat to Maggie's left. The table was nicely set for three and a crisp garden salad waited in the center of each plate. An array of salad dressings was clustered in the center of the table.

Maggie gestured toward them. "Help yourself."

When they'd eaten the salad, Maggie excused herself,

returning a few moments later with platters of fried chicken, mashed potatoes, and corn on the cob. "I hope you like chicken," she said to Jordan as she placed the platter on the table.

"I love chicken. It all looks so delicious," Jordan said as she filled her plate.

As soon as they had served themselves, Jan reached into the back pocket of her jeans and pulled out a folded envelope. "Oh, Maggie, I forgot to tell you that this letter arrived by registered mail today. It's from your father's lawyer."

Maggie's eyes narrowed as she reached for the letter, and her eyebrows arched high on her forehead as she realized the letter had been opened. "You opened it?" she asked.

Jordan's gaze moved from Maggie to Jan.

Jan behaved as if opening Maggie's mail was something she did on a regular basis. "Yeah, I thought it was important enough to read right away. You were gone to town, so I opened it. It's actually good news," she explained.

Maggie lowered her chin to her chest and rubbed her forehead with her right hand. "I really wish you hadn't opened it."

"What's the big deal?" Jan asked. "You would have read it to me anyway. After all, it concerns me as well."

Maggie put both hands down on the table hard. "I fail to see how this letter concerns you," she said firmly.

Jan shrugged. "Well, we have talked about getting married, Maggie. I think the fact that your father has signed the deed of the farm over to you definitely concerns me."

Maggie took the napkin off her lap and put it on the table beside her plate. She rose to her feet. "Jan, could I please see you in the kitchen?"

"Sure," Jan said brightly as she followed Maggie.

"What the hell was that all about?" Maggie asked in a high-pitched voice.

"I don't know what part of it you don't understand, Mags. Your father transferred the deed of the farm to you. It's all yours now."

"And what does that have to do with *you*?" Maggie asked.

"Maggie, you and I have talked about getting married some day. When that happens, we'll want to add my name to the deed. That way, the farm is protected in the event something happens to either one of us."

"Look, Jan. We have company. This is not the time to have this conversation. I am going back into the dining room, and I am going to enjoy dinner with Jordan. You are welcome to join us if you want, but I don't want to hear another word from you about this deed. Is that understood?"

"I actually thought you would be glad to hear the news. Forgive me for living."

"Jan, that doesn't even warrant a response. Now, I'm going to finish my dinner. You can come with me or not. Your choice."

* * *

Maggie reentered the dining room alone.

"Jan sends her apologies. She's decided to have dinner later."

"Oh, that's too bad. Is she feeling okay?" Jordan asked.

Maggie sat down and spread her napkin in her lap. "She's fine. Let's just enjoy our dinner, okay?"

* * *

After dinner, Jordan excused herself and stood to leave.

"Do you have to go so early?" Maggie asked wistfully.

"I promised John I would help him unload the hay crop in the morning. We're meeting at seven, so I really should get settled in for the night."

"But you haven't had dessert yet."

"That's okay. Dinner was so good, I ate too much anyway. Maybe I'll take a rain check on dessert?"

"Deal," Maggie replied. "Let me walk you to the bunkhouse."

"You don't have to do that, Maggie," Jordan objected.

Maggie put her hands on her hips and grinned. "I know I

don't."

Jordan offered her arm to Maggie, who slipped her hand into the crook of Jordan's elbow.

A few minutes later, they stopped in front of the bunkhouse door and Maggie released Jordan's arm.

Jordan shoved her hands into her pockets. "Maggie, I want to thank you for dinner. It was the best fried chicken I've had in a long time. I appreciate the invitation."

Maggie looked into Jordan's eyes and smiled. "You are welcome. I enjoyed having you. However, I must apologize for Jan's behavior." Maggie crossed her arms in front of her and hugged herself close. "Brrr. I can't believe it's getting cool at night already," she complained.

"Are you cold? Sheesh, how inconsiderate can I be? Let me get you a jacket. Wait right here," Jordan said as she slipped into the bunkhouse, emerging seconds later carrying a jean jacket. "Here, put this on."

Jordan helped Maggie into the jacket and then rubbed the redhead's upper arms to warm her up. "Is that better?" she asked.

"Much. Thank you."

Maggie took a step closer and looked into Jordan's face.

"I need to kiss you," Jordan whispered as she lowered her mouth to Maggie's.

Maggie parted her lips and felt Jordan's tongue explore the moist cavern within. A wave of liquid desire coursed through her as the kiss deepened. It was a full minute later that Jordan finally broke the kiss and leaned her forehead against Maggie's so they could both catch their breath.

"Oh, my God," Maggie whispered hoarsely.

Jordan took a step back. "I'm sorry, Maggie. I shouldn't have done that."

"*You* didn't do that...*we* did," Maggie said. "I'm the one who should apologize."

"No, I take full responsibility. You have a partner, and I should know better than to interfere with your relationship. Jan doesn't deserve that," Jordan insisted.

Maggie placed her index finger on Jordan's lips. "You're

right. She doesn't, but I'm sure you can see that things are not perfect with her. In fact, things have been a little shaky for some time. Maybe you were right earlier...she is assuming."

Maggie wrapped her arms around herself and walked a few feet away. "I don't know, Jordan. I need time to think about Jan. I need to process what I am feeling for you. I'm sorry if I am sending confusing signals. Please forgive me."

Jordan inhaled deeply and nodded.

Maggie smiled and stood on tiptoe to place a gentle, chaste kiss on Jordan's lips. "You need to sleep. I'll see you tomorrow. Good night," she said.

CHAPTER 4

Early the next morning, Jordan directed pallets of hay bales into the loft as John lifted them with the hoist and pulley. She had a perfect view of Maggie as she sauntered into the barn wearing Jordan's jacket.

Maggie greeted John brightly. "Good Morning."

John tipped his hat with one hand while maintaining a firm grip on the pulley rope with the other. "'Mornin', Maggie."

"Nice jacket," Jordan called down from the loft.

Maggie looked up quickly. Her face lit up happily as she grabbed the sides of the jacket, spreading them out while turning around in a circle as though modeling a coat. "Thank you. Do you like it?"

"It's great. You have good taste," Jordan responded.

Maggie smiled. She drove her hands deep into her pockets and shrugged her shoulders. "Are you almost finished? I was hoping you'd be free to ride with me to the north end of the property. I'm meeting my carpenter up there to go over plans for a new barn."

Jordan looked down at John. "How many more do we have, John?"

"Lookin' like two more. Why don't you go ahead with Maggie, and I'll finish up here."

"No, a promise is a promise. We're going to finish this before I leave," Jordan responded. She looked again at Maggie. "Give me about twenty minutes, and I'll be with you. Okay?"

"Sounds good. I'll go straighten up the tack room while I wait." Maggie grinned.

Jordan stepped into the hook of the winch and rode it down to barn level to help John secure the next pallet.

John watched Maggie nearly skip away before he looked at Jordan with raised eyebrows.

"What's that look for?" Jordan asked curiously.

"I'm surprised she didn't blow a cork," John replied.

"What do you mean?"

"Well, Maggie sometimes isn't very patient when she wants something."

Jordan put her hands on her hips. "Really? Has she ever lost patience with you?"

"Nope, not me, but Jan's been on the receivin' end a few times. Let me tell ya, what they say about redheads and tempers is true in her case."

"I know what you mean. She seems to lose her temper quite easily. I can't imagine it would have taken much for her to blow up at Jan."

John ran the winch straps under the pallet and looped them over the hook then eyed her conspiratorially over the pallet of feed. "Well, to tell ya the truth, if it was me, I'd have been mad too."

Jordan grabbed the hook and stepped onto the edge of the pallet. "Take her up, John."

John winched Jordan and the load of feed to the level of the loft where she stepped onto the platform and pulled the pallet over far enough to settle lightly on the deck as John slowly released the tension on the rope.

"Okay, John. That's enough." Jordan unhooked the straps from the pallet and once more slipped her foot into the hook. When John had her lowered to the floor, she handed the straps back to him. She waited for him to thread the straps through the final pallet. "So, exactly what did she do to make Maggie so angry?"

"Well, Maggie was away for a couple of days about a month ago, showin' some of the mustangs at a horse show in the next town. One of Maggie's favorite mares took sick while she was gone. Jan was supposed to be keepin' an eye on the place but instead of taking care of chores, she pretty much lorded over the farm like she owned it. Anyway, when Maggie came home and saw the shape her mare was in, all hell broke loose."

"Wow. Maggie must have really been upset."

"I was in the barn here, cleaning stalls when she returned. I could hear her yellin' at Jan from here, not that I blame her none. Jan really should'a been taking care of things while she was gone instead of playing queen of the castle."

Jordan pulled the straps through the bottom of the pallet and looped them over the hook. "That must have put a strain on their relationship."

"Climb on. She's going up," John instructed as he pulled the slack out of the winch rope.

Jordan stood on top of the pallet while John winched it into the loft. Once the pallet was safely settled in the loft, she unthreaded the straps from the pallet and hung them back on the hook. "Winch it up, John."

John pulled the winch rope until the metal hook made contact with the pulley high above them in the rafters then he tied the rope off on the railing of the staircase leading to the loft. By the time he had taken care of the winch, Jordan had descended the stairs of the loft and met him at the bottom.

"So why does Maggie keep her around?" she asked.

John looked at Jordan. "Well, I reckon she loves her," he replied.

Jordan's brow furrowed into a deep frown.

John put his hands on his hips and shook his head back and forth. "I thought as much," he said, almost sadly.

"What?" Jordan prompted.

"You're in love with her," he stated rather than asked. "I've seen how you light up when she walks into the barn."

Jordan looked everywhere but at John. "Ah, I don't even know her yet."

"Don't matter how long you've known her," John replied. A few moments of silence fell between them before John spoke again. "You know Jan won't be happy about this."

Jordan's attention was suddenly drawn away from her conversation with John. She turned to see Maggie standing nearby with her arms crossed impatiently in front of her. She immediately wondered how long Maggie had been standing there.

"So, how long are you going to keep me waiting?" she asked.

Jordan grinned. "Patience woman," she exclaimed teasingly. "Some of us have work to do around here."

Maggie swatted Jordan's behind with the leather gloves she was holding. "Mind who you're talking to, Missy. You're liable to get yourself fired again."

"Yeah, yeah, yeah," Jordan replied dryly. "Whatever."

John's eyebrows rose on his forehead as he watched the playful interaction.

Jordan looked at him and winked. "So, John, did you say you needed some help with the feed bags next?"

"Oh, no you don't," Maggie quickly interjected as she locked her arm with Jordan's. "You're coming with me to the north pasture, remember?"

Jordan slapped her palm on her thigh. "Oh, yeah. I almost forgot. You know, Maggie, I think I'll be needing that raise now, considering how valuable I am around here."

"I'll give you a raise you little shit, right at the end of my foot if you don't shape up," Maggie laughed.

Jordan looked at John and shook her head. "Women," she exclaimed, which earned her a quick kick in the pants by Maggie.

* * *

Jordan rode beside Maggie on the way out to the north pasture. "This is a beautiful farm," Jordan said. "I've always thought so."

Maggie looked at Jordan and frowned. "Have you seen the farm before?"

"Huh?" Jordan asked. "What do you mean?"

"You just said you've always thought the farm was beautiful. That sounds like you've seen it before."

"I meant, I always thought Vermont was a beautiful state. It goes without saying the farmland is the best part of it."

"I couldn't agree more," Maggie replied.

Jordan chastised herself for being so careless with her words.

They rode on in silence for the next minute or two before Maggie posed another question.

"Have you lived in Vermont long?"

"Yes I have, all my life in fact. I've traveled a lot, but my heart is right here. This is where I want to spend the rest of my life."

"So, what did you do before you came to me looking for work?"

"I was affiliated with the University of Vermont. I worked in the lab there."

Maggie looked at the field ahead of her as she spoke. "Doing what?"

"Well, I did some work with injured animals."

"It sounds interesting. You'll have to tell me about it some time. But right now, I'm going to kick your butt in a race to that outbuilding over there."

Maggie dug her heels into the side of her horse and galloped across the field.

"Hey, No fair," Jordan called. She kicked her own horse into gear. Jordan pushed her horse as fast as she dared and slowly closed the distance between them, but was unable to catch up before Maggie reined her horse to a stop at the hitching post in front of the barn. She was out of breath by the time she caught up.

Maggie grinned broadly. "Not bad for a femme, huh?"

Jordan pulled her horse along side Maggie's and leaned forward until her face was within inches of the redhead's. "A sneaky femme, maybe. That was no fair."

"I never claimed to be fair," Maggie replied. She climbed out of the saddle and tied her horse to the hitch. Maggie glanced at the stunned look on Jordan's face. "Are you coming?"

Jordan dismounted and tied her horse next to Maggie's.

Maggie waited for Jordan to join her before entering the barn. "We've set up an office of sorts in this barn for the contractors. They are also storing the raw materials in here."

Jordan looked around at the rough lumber that was organized by board width and length. There were piles of boards stacked neatly in each of the horse stalls as well as in the loft. "I take it you don't use this barn for livestock?" she asked.

"Not right now. It's kind of small for what I am planning,"

Maggie replied.

Jordan crossed her arms. "And what exactly are you planning?"

"A breeding center for Mustangs. The new barn will be large enough to board several studs and mares and will include a special birthing wing."

"I see. Where will the new barn be erected?"

"Right next to this one, actually. I'll reuse this space as a supply shed. As you can see it's not really big enough for anything else," Maggie explained.

"I see," Jordan remarked as she walked around. When she reached the opposite side of the room, she turned and faced Maggie. "So, Maggie, I have a question for you. The Vermont state horse is the Morgan. Why the passion for Mustangs?"

Maggie's smile brought a twinkle to her green eyes. "Why Mustangs? I like their spirit. They remind me of me, actually…fiery disposition and hard to tame."

Jordan cocked an eyebrow and walked toward Maggie. "You're hard to tame, huh? Well, I've broken a few spirited fillies in my time."

Maggie took two steps forward and stopped directly in front of Jordan. She put her hands on her denim-clad hips and looked up into Jordan's face. "Oh, you have, have you?"

"Yes, I have."

"Maggie. Are you in there?" said a decidedly male voice from outside the barn.

"Shit. It's Dave," Maggie exclaimed.

"Dave?" Jordan asked.

"Dave is the contractor I told you I was meeting here, remember? Why else did you think I asked you to come out here with me?" Maggie looked toward the barn door. "I'm in here, Dave."

Just then, the door to the barn swung open and admitted a large, lumberjack-looking, barrel-chested man. "There you are," he said. "Sorry I'm late."

"I'm not," Jordan said under her breath, just loud enough for Maggie to hear.

Maggie, who had been standing in front of Jordan, gently

kicked her shin.

"Ow!" Jordan's complaint drew the man's attention.

Maggie immediately stepped in. "Dave, this is Jordan Lewis. She started working for me a few days ago. She's the one who checked out the rafter that broke in the main barn."

Jordan extended her hand to meet Dave's. "Nice to meet you," she said as her hand disappeared into the much larger one presented to her.

"Likewise," Dave said as he released Jordan's hand. He then turned to Maggie. "So, I have the new plans if you'd like to go over them."

"Yes. Please." Maggie replied as Dave unfolded the blueprints on a nearby desk.

For the next hour, the three of them poured over the plans, and made minor changes to the location of a few walls and windows.

"Okay, I'd say that just about wraps it up," Dave said.

"Good. When do we break ground?" Maggie asked.

"I can have a crew here on Monday. Is that soon enough?"

Maggie clapped her hands together. "Wonderful." She glanced at her watch. "Wow. It's already noon. Where does the time go? You're welcome to come back to the house for lunch if you'd like, Dave."

"Thanks for the offer, Maggie, but I have another appointment at one."

Dave extended his hand to Jordan once again. "Jordan, it was nice meeting you. Oh, and by the way, I agree with your assessment on the rafter. That board was cut mechanically. Natural weak points in wood don't break that cleanly. I'm not sure if that cut was made before or after the rafter was up, but it was definitely created manually."

Jordan nodded. "That's exactly what I thought. Thanks for verifying it."

"No problem. I've got to run. I'll be here with the crew first thing Monday morning."

"Thank you, Dave," Maggie said. "Have a great weekend."

Jordan and Maggie watched Dave leave. As soon as the barn door closed behind him, Jordan looked at Maggie pensively. "So exactly why did you ask me out here?"

"Maggie? Maggie, where are you?"

Maggie threw her hands into the air at the sound of Jan's voice. "Is this freaking Grand Central Station or something?" she complained angrily. "In here, Jan," she called.

Jan pulled the barn door open and stepped inside. When she saw Jordan, she crossed her arms in front of her. "Humph. When I saw two horses tethered outside, I kind of figured she was with you."

"Jordan and I just went over the blueprints for the new barn with Dave. She actually made several good suggestions. So what brings you here, Jan?"

"I was in the house pouring a glass of lemonade when the phone rang. I let the answering machine pick it up and couldn't help but overhear the message being left. Your father's lawyer called. He left a message for you to call him back. It has something to do with the deed to the farm," Jan explained.

Maggie frowned. "Hmm, I wonder what that's all about?"

"I don't know, but I thought you might want to call him back right way. Maybe Dad needs some information from us or something."

"Maybe," Maggie responded.

An uncomfortable silence fell over the trio as Maggie waited for Jan to leave. When it became obvious that no one was moving, she addressed Jan directly. "Is there anything else you need, Jan?"

Jan shifted from foot to foot. "Well, I was wondering if you're coming home for lunch."

"I have a few more items to go over with Jordan. We'll be along soon. Why don't you get a head start?" Maggie suggested.

Jan approached the table with the blueprints spread out on it. "Actually, I'd like to see the changes you've made in the layout. After all, the design contains my input as well."

"I'm going to head back to the house," Jordan said. "John could use some help with the feed delivery."

Maggie tried to stop Jordan from leaving. "Why don't we ride back together and get some lunch?"

"No, I think I'm going to skip lunch today. I'll see you back at the house."

With regret, Maggie watched Jordan leave while Jan remained bent over the blueprints with a self-satisfied smirk on her face.

* * *

"Mr. Pritchard, I don't see why my father needs to name a second beneficiary on the deed to the farm. Yes, I know none of us will live forever, but I still don't see why he...look, just send me the paperwork, okay? I want to see exactly how it's worded. All right. Thank you."

Maggie hung up the phone. A deep frown creased her forehead.

"What did he want?" Jan asked anxiously.

"He said Daddy added a second beneficiary to the deed. Apparently, someone put it into his head that he needed a backup in the event I died before he did. Where on earth did he get that harebrained idea?"

Jan shrugged. "Beats the hell out of me, but I guess it makes sense."

"Well, it makes no sense to me. If he deeds the farm to me, it is up to me to name a beneficiary I'd want to leave it to, not him. I'll just review the paperwork and if I don't like what it says, I'll get Daddy to change it." Maggie yawned loudly. "Damn. I'm beat. I'm going to bed."

Jan looked at her watch. "It's a little early for me to turn in. I think I'll read for a while. I'll be in soon."

"Suit yourself." Maggie replied.

As soon as Maggie stepped into her darkened bedroom, her attention was drawn to the light shining from the bunkhouse. She walked to the window and stood beside it. From her vantage point, she could see Jordan writing something at the desk.

What kind of spell have you cast over me, Jordan Lewis? Why do you enchant me so?

* * *

Maggie paced back and forth across the bedroom trying to decide out how to break the news to Jan. In her heart, she knew their relationship had been on a downhill spiral for some time, but she had not been able to summon the courage to end it. She was still pacing when Jan finally came to bed.

"You're still up. I expected to find you asleep," Jan said.

Maggie wrapped her hands around her middle. "Jan, we need to talk."

Jan's face grew ashen. She sat on the edge of the bed. "I've been expecting this. You're attracted to her, aren't you?"

Maggie raised her hands out to the sides. "Jan, this is not about Jordan, it's about our relationship no longer working. It's about you being presumptuous. It's about you taking me for granted. It's about you taking liberties you shouldn't be taking."

Jan rose to her feet and planted her hands on her hips. "What the hell does that mean?"

Maggie ran her hand over her forehead. "Jan, I feel like you are trying to control me. It seems that you are making plans and decisions that *I* clearly should be making, or at the very least, we should be making together."

"You're talking in riddles, Maggie. What decisions you are talking about?"

"Let me give you a few examples, Jan. You told Jordan we were getting married and planned to have a baby…and you are being oddly persistent about the deed to the farm. What are you up to, Jan? Something doesn't feel right about that."

Jan paced back and forth, clearly agitated. "This isn't about us getting married, Maggie, and this isn't about the deed to the farm. This is about Jordan and you know it. You're attracted to her, aren't you?"

Here's your chance, Maggie. Be honest with her. Don't blow it.

Maggie sighed and threw her hands up. "I don't know what to say, Jan. Yes, I'm attracted to her. I can't help it."

Jan sat on the edge of the bed. "Goddamn it. I knew it."

Maggie walked a few feet away and then turned around. "I tried to resist what I was feeling, Jan, but I couldn't. There is something about her that draws me in. I feel like we have known each other forever."

"Have you slept with her?"

"How can you even ask me that question? No, I haven't slept with her."

Jan stood once more and crossed her arms. "So what does this mean for me?" she asked. "I love this farm. I have put my heart and soul into training the horses for the past few years. In some ways, I feel like this place is my own. Please don't ask me to leave all of this, behind."

Maggie rubbed her hands across her face in a gesture of frustration. "Jan, I appreciate everything you've done for me and I have nothing but good things to say about what you've done for the farm, but I don't know if it's fair to ask you to stay, especially considering...."

"Especially considering how you feel about Jordan?" Jan finished Maggie's sentence.

Maggie dropped her chin to her chest. "Like I said, Jan, this isn't about Jordan. I'm sorry. I never wanted to hurt you."

"Do you want me to leave, Maggie?"

"I'm not asking you to leave if you don't want to. You are right. You have worked hard to make this farm a success."

Jan stood and walked to the closet to retrieve a suitcase that she carried to the bed. "Okay. I will respect your wishes, Maggie. Like I said, I don't want to walk away from everything I have worked for over the past four years, so if it's all right with you, I'll just move into the bunkhouse with Jordan for now."

Maggie's eyes grew wide. "Do you really think that's a good idea, Jan?"

Jan paused on one of her several trips back and forth between the chest of drawers and suitcase. "Well, if this is not about Jordan, then that shouldn't be a problem, should it? And besides, if I want to stay, I don't see that I have any other choice."

"Okay," Maggie said softly before leaving the room.

* * *

Jordan felt a chill in the air as she made her way across the barnyard. Considering it was late November, she knew it was only a matter of time before early snow fell. She pushed the door open and stepped into the warmth and immediately turned her back to the room to take her jacket off and hang it on a hook beside the door. When she turned around, she met Jan face to face. Her eyes widened with surprise.

"Hey, roomie," Jan said.

Jordan frowned. "Roomie?" she asked.

"That's right. Thanks to you, Maggie has no use for me in her bed anymore."

Jordan walked to the refrigerator and took out a beer. "I don't know what you're talking about," she replied, taking a swig from the bottle.

Jan rose to her feet. "Well, no matter. Just know I have my eye on you. Don't make the mistake of getting in my way, understand? I don't take kindly to anyone who gets in my way."

Jordan walked directly up to Jan and leaned down toward the shorter woman. "Look, I don't know what's up with you and Maggie, but don't make the mistake of threatening me. Understand? I don't take kindly to anyone who threatens *me*." Jordan walked away and went to her room.

CHAPTER 5

Jordan reached forward, turned off the water and drew back the shower curtain. As she squeezed the water out of her hair, she heard a loud incessant pounding on the front door of the bunkhouse. *Who the hell could that be?* She grabbed her towel, wrapped it around herself, and cautiously made her way to the door. "Who is it?" she called out.

"Maggie. I've brought a few things that Jan forgot at the house. May I come in?"

Jordan opened the door and stood there, one hand holding the towel together above her breasts.

Maggie's eyes opened wide. "Oh. I see I caught you at a bad time. I'll come back later," she said, turning to go.

"No. No, it's all right. Come in." Jordan stepped aside and allowed Maggie to enter the bunkhouse.

Maggie held a bag of clothing in front of her. "Jan left these at the house last night. Is she here?"

"No, she's already gone to the barn. That was a nice little surprise you sent my way last night."

"Oh," Maggie exclaimed. "I'm sorry about that, but she offered to stay in the bunkhouse, and I wasn't going to pass on the opportunity to break things off with her without a fight."

"Maggie, you really put me in an awkward situation. What were you thinking?"

Maggie reached out to touch Jordan's arm. "I'm sorry, Jordan. I had to do it. It wasn't fair to continue the charade. Things haven't been good between us for a while now."

"So, why here? Why didn't she just leave?"

Maggie shoved her hands into her pockets. "She didn't want to go...and to tell you the truth, she's good at what she does and I really didn't want to lose her."

Jordan shivered.

"Jordan, you're cold. As much as I like seeing you in just a towel, you really should dry yourself off and get dressed."

Jordan smiled. "You're right. Make yourself comfortable. I'll be right back." She turned around and began to walk toward the bedroom.

"God, Jordan. What happened?" Maggie exclaimed.

Jordan stopped short. She looked at Maggie questioningly. "What do you mean?"

Maggie took several steps toward Jordan then stopped in front of her. "Turn around," she said.

Jordan did as asked and turned her back to Maggie. The towel hung loose and low on Jordan's back. Jordan stood as still as possible as she felt Maggie's breath very close to her still-wet skin.

"What happened to you?" Maggie whispered as she traced the length of Jordan's scar from the middle of her back to where it disappeared behind the towel just above her bottom.

Jordan shivered, more from Maggie's touch than from the cool air on her back.

"Horse riding accident. I was sixteen at the time," Jordan replied.

Maggie traced the scar once more, but this time, ventured beyond the towel barrier. Jordan stood very still.

Suddenly, Maggie's hand became very still as her fingers encountered a foreign object. "Jordan, what is this?" Maggie asked as she pulled the towel down lower on Jordan's back. "It vibrates," she exclaimed. "What is it, some kind of sex toy?"

Jordan chuckled as she reached back and held Maggie's hand against the implant bulging through her skin.

"The vibration you are feeling is due to an alternating electrical charge coming from an energy storage unit…kind of like a power pack. The small box-like structure bulging from the skin is a spinal implant."

Maggie quickly retracted her hand. "A spinal implant? You mean like bionic parts?"

"Kind of," Jordan replied. "You see, the horse riding accident I mentioned a moment ago? I was paralyzed from the waist down. The implant restores mobility."

Maggie walked a few feet away from Jordan then turned around. She placed one hand on her hip while she rubbed her forehead with the other. "You're paralyzed?"

"I was until the implant. I guess you could technically say I still am."

"Do you have any feeling below your waist?" Maggie asked.

"Well, so far, no. No sensation on the skin at least. I will admit however, when you kissed me, I felt some very distinct fluttering deep within my abdomen."

"I...I never knew something like this was possible. You're paralyzed, yet you can walk. I didn't know science had advanced that far already."

"Maggie, there are things you don't know about me that I promise I will explain when the time is right. Please just trust me for now, okay?"

Maggie frowned. "Trust you? Hell, I don't even *know* you. Jordan, this is a major deal. How long did you think you would be able to hide this from me?"

"I wasn't trying to hide it, Maggie. It's just not exactly dinner conversation, you know?"

Maggie crossed her arms in front of her and paced back and forth. She looked apprehensively at Jordan.

Jordan took several steps toward Maggie, but stopped abruptly when Maggie put her hand up. "Jordan don't, please. I need time to digest this."

Jordan stepped back. "I'm sorry. Would you like me to pack my things and leave?"

Maggie walked toward the door then turned to look at Jordan. "Do I want you to leave? No. Not unless you want to."

Jordan looked down at the floor. "I don't want to," she said softly.

When she looked up, Maggie was gone.

* * *

For the next several weeks, Jordan fell into a routine of chores as well as repairs to fences, outbuildings, and grounds. During that time, Maggie made herself conspicuously absent and communicated with Jordan through notes left on the bunkhouse door or through messages hand carried to her by a very smug Jan.

Jordan had free access to Maggie's home, but rarely encountered her. When their paths did cross, Maggie always had an excuse about select board meetings to attend or chores to be done and excused herself with little more than a cursory goodbye.

Jordan spent most evenings standing by the window waiting for the light to come on in Maggie's bedroom so she could catch a glimpse of the redhead. Her heart was heavy with regret. Maggie's revulsion with her condition was something she hadn't anticipated.

Three weeks after Maggie discovered the implant, she asked that Jordan help with the barn raising. Jordan looked forward to it, as she knew Maggie was deeply involved in the project and would no doubt be a frequent visitor on the jobsite. By the time she joined the crew, the footing had already been poured and the wall frames erected. Jordan arrived on the jobsite with her tool belt in hand and immediately climbed the staging to assist with the rafter assembly.

From her vantage point in the rafters, Jordan could see Maggie moving around the site, reading blueprints with Dave and assisting in various ways. Unbeknownst to her, Maggie stole every opportunity possible to glance upward when she was certain Jordan wasn't looking. Jordan was working side-by-side with one of the carpenters when one such opportunity arose.

"Wow, that redhead down there is really hot," the carpenter commented to Jordan.

Jordan glanced down at Maggie who was talking to Dave several yards below them. "Forget it Don. Somehow, I don't think she'd be interested in you," Jordan chuckled.

Don looked offended. "And, why not? I'm a good-looking guy. What is she, a dyke or something?"

Jordan raised her eyebrows at the man. "You *do* realize she's the boss, right?"

Don snorted. "I don't care who she is. I answer only to Dave."

"Whatever," Jordan replied as she drove a spike into the rafter Don was holding level. "Okay, your turn."

Don retrieved a spike from his tool belt and began to hammer it into the wood. When he realized Maggie was looking up at them again, he took his attention off what he was doing for a brief moment to smile at her and promptly lost his footing.

"Whoa!" he yelled as he struggled to maintain his position on the beam.

Jordan tried to reach the man, but in his attempt to catch himself, he released his end of the rafter. It pivoted toward Jordan as it was being held aloft only by the spike she had driven into it moments earlier. Jordan had all she could do to maintain her own balance on the beam as she avoided the swinging rafter, and watched helplessly as Don fell to the floor of the barn.

Maggie screamed as he narrowly missed landing on her.

"Don't touch him," Jordan said loudly as she scrambled across the beam toward the ladder. "Please, don't move him."

Jordan climbed down the ladder as fast as she could. "Call an ambulance, quickly." She fell to her knees beside the fallen man and touched the side of his face gently. Maggie, Dave and several of the crewmembers circled them helplessly.

"Don? Don, can you hear me?" she asked.

Don blinked his eyes and tried to nod his head.

"Don't move your head, Don, okay? Help is on the way. Can you breathe? Blink twice for yes, once for no."

Don blinked twice.

"Good." Jordan looked up at Dave and Maggie. "I need something soft to stabilize his neck, towels, pillows, rolled up blankets, anything. Please hurry."

"I have some blankets and towels in the truck." Dave turned and ran out of the barn.

Maggie squatted down next to Jordan. "What can I do to help?" she asked anxiously.

Dave returned carrying a blanket and several towels. He handed them to Jordan. "I'm afraid they're not very clean," he said.

"I don't think he'll care at this point." Jordan reached up for the blankets and gave one to Maggie. "Cover him up while I stabilize his neck. It will help to prevent shock."

Maggie and Dave worked together to drape a blanket over Don while Jordan rolled two of the towels and placed them on either side of Don's neck then held them there to prevent him from moving his head back and forth. She then lowered her ear to his mouth to monitor how laboriously he was breathing. Satisfied that his airway was unobstructed, she smiled at the man.

"Help is on the way, Don. Hang in there, buddy. Are you feeling pain anywhere?"

Don blinked his eyes twice.

"Is the pain in your neck?"

Two blinks.

"How about your arms and legs?"

One blink.

"Can you move your fingers and toes? Do it gently, and don't lift your hand or foot."

Jordan watched as Don wiggled his fingers and moved his foot. "That's good, Don. Just lay as still as possible. I think I hear the ambulance coming."

"I'll flag them down," Maggie said as she rose to her feet and ran out of the barn.

Moments later, two EMTs rushed into the room carrying medical kits. Maggie followed close behind. One EMT took over Jordan's position by Don's head while the other assessed his bodily injuries.

"What happened?" asked one of the EMTs.

"He fell from the rafter," Dave replied.

The EMT looked upward. "Wow. That's at least fifteen feet."

The EMT who was kneeling beside Don's head looked up. "What's his name?"

"His name is Don. Don Feldman," Dave answered.

"Who secured his neck?" he asked.

"I did," Jordan replied. "I also assessed his respiration, which appears to be even. There doesn't appear to be any radiating pain. Most of the pain is centered in his neck. He is also able to move extremities such as fingers and toes. With any luck, the injury will be isolated to muscle pain and not affect the vertebra beyond C2."

Maggie's eyes grew wide as she listened to Jordan speak with the emergency personnel.

The EMT attending at Don's head glanced up at Jordan. "You seem to know a lot about spinal injuries. I take it you're either a doctor, or you've had such an injury yourself?"

Jordan shrugged. "Something like that," she replied as she met Maggie's gaze.

"Okay. Jim, we'll need the backboard, neck brace, tape and gurney," the EMT instructed his partner. He then looked down at Don. "We'll have you out of here in a jiff, Don. You're in good hands."

Over the next ten minutes the EMTs worked to carefully secure Don to the backboard before loading him into the ambulance.

"I'd better follow them to the hospital," Dave said.

"Yes, of course," Maggie replied quickly. "Do whatever is necessary. I'll cross my fingers that his injuries are not too extensive."

Jordan, Maggie, and the remaining carpenters watched as the ambulance drove away. While Maggie dismissed the rest of the crew for the day, Jordan walked away and collected her tools, then headed toward the old farm truck she had driven to the construction site. As she climbed into the driver's seat, Maggie ran toward her.

"Jordan," she called out.

Jordan remained in the truck and waited for Maggie to reach her. She sat quietly looking out the windshield.

Maggie stopped by the driver's door. "Hey," she said.

Jordan nodded but continued to look straight ahead.

Maggie shoved her fingertips into the back pockets of her jeans and kicked the dirt around gently with her toe. "Look, Jordan, I know you're angry with me, and I don't blame you, but that was quite a bombshell you dropped on me a few weeks ago."

Jordan looked at her. "I hoped it wouldn't matter."

Maggie shrugged. "I don't know if it matters or not. It…it just took me by surprise."

"Well, for that, I apologize," Jordan replied stoically.

"Jordan, don't be that way," Maggie exclaimed.

Jordan's head turned sharply in Maggie's direction. "How the hell do you want me to be?" she asked angrily.

"Honest, for one," Maggie replied.

Jordan could feel the anger rising in her chest as she gripped the steering wheel tightly.

"I have been completely honest with you, Maggie."

"Not completely. You said yourself there were things you couldn't explain right now."

Jordan continued to stare straight ahead.

Maggie sighed deeply. "Look, Jordan, I don't want to argue with you."

Jordan shook her head. "You just don't understand."

Maggie put both hands on the window frame and leaned forward. "Then why don't you explain it to me?" she suggested firmly.

Jordan reached across the bench seat and threw the passenger door open. "Get in."

* * *

Jordan and Maggie drove to the western fringe of the property to where the land abruptly fell off to the lake. An uncomfortable silence settled over them as they both stared out at Lake Champlain.

Maggie turned in her seat to face Jordan. "Tell me about your accident."

Jordan dropped her hands from the steering wheel and allowed them to fall into her lap. She stared at them for several minutes before she looked at Maggie.

"Like I said, I was sixteen at the time. I was riding my horse, Sally, who by the way was a mustang. Anyway, I was riding Sally across the field and she stumbled and threw me. I landed pretty hard, and at an angle that broke my back at the L1 vertebrae, just below the small of my back. I was in a hover…ah, I mean, a wheelchair until I was thirty."

"Oh, my God. How old are you now?" Maggie asked.

"I'm thirty-two."

Maggie did a quick calculation in her head. "So, you were in a wheelchair for fourteen years? How awful for you."

"Awful doesn't even begin to describe it, Maggie. I grew up on this…er, I mean, I grew up on a farm very much like this one, and I felt so incredibly useless stuck in that chair. I spent a significant amount of time after school in the barn with my father. I helped as much as I could with the horses, and we enjoyed small carpentry projects together, but I didn't venture far from the property. I was an only child and my parents were somewhat older than those of other kids, so it was a pretty lonely childhood."

"Where are your parents now?" Maggie asked.

"They died in a car accident when I was twenty-six."

Maggie was crestfallen as she imagined the emotional and physical pain and suffering Jordan must have endured in her life. "I'm sorry," she whispered softly.

"Thanks," Jordan replied without looking up.

"So how did you come to have the implant?"

Jordan lifted her head and pressed it against the headrest. "I volunteered for a spinal implant development project being conducted at the University of Vermont Spinal Institute. They almost didn't accept me because my injury was so old, but I persisted and eventually, they gave in. This is actually the second implant. The first one lasted for two years then failed several months ago. So far, this new one is working well."

Maggie tilted her head to the side. "So, how does the implant work? I mean, you walk like there is nothing wrong with you."

"The implant sends alternating electrical pulses to both sides of the injury site and in theory it encourages the nerve endings to begin growing toward one another. Hopefully, some day soon, they will bridge the injury site and grow together. In the meantime, I have restored mobility, and with any luck, at some point, the nerve endings in my skin will wake up and smell the coffee too," Jordan explained.

"I had no idea that medical science has progressed so far.

It's like a miracle," Maggie exclaimed.

Several more moments of silence passed as Maggie digested the information Jordan had given her. Finally, she touched Jordan's hand. "Jordan, close your eyes," she said softly.

Jordan turned her head to face Maggie and drew her brow into a frown. "Why?"

"Humor me, please," Maggie replied.

Jordan dutifully closed her eyes and waited for Maggie's move.

"Can you feel this?" Maggie asked as she rubbed Jordan's knee with her hand.

"No." Jordan's eyelashes fluttered.

"No, no, no, don't open your eyes. Do you feel this?" Maggie ran her hand along Jordan's thigh.

Jordan concentrated hard but failed to feel any direct stimuli. "No," she said impatiently.

Maggie allowed her hand to roam across Jordan's abdomen and into the crevice between her legs. "How about this?"

Jordan dropped her chin to her chest without opening her eyes. "No. I don't feel anything."

"Surely, you can feel this," Maggie said as she slipped her hand into Jordan's shirt.

Jordan stiffened, but kept her eyes closed.

"Yes, you can feel that. How about this?" Maggie reached far enough inside Jordan's shirt to feel her left breast and capture her nipple between her fingers.

"Ah," Jordan exclaimed as a sudden bolt of desire shot directly to her core. Her eyes flew open and she pressed her own hand into her abdomen. She looked at Maggie. "Do that again."

Maggie applied pressure to the hardened nipple. Once more, Jordan nearly doubled over.

"Damn," Jordan quivered as ripples of pleasure ran through her. She looked at Maggie. Her eyes were wild with wonder and desire. "I can feel that deep within my core. It feels incredible."

Maggie smiled. "This is your first time, isn't it?" she asked softly.

Unable to speak, Jordan just nodded. To Jordan's dismay, Maggie retracted her hand from inside her shirt.

"Well, your first time will not be in the front seat of a beat up old truck. Drive us home."

CHAPTER 6

Jordan left a large cloud of dust in her wake as she accelerated the old pickup truck across the plains and nearly brought it to a screeching halt in front of the farmhouse. She jumped out of the driver's side and quickly ran around the front of the truck to open Maggie's door for her. Maggie took her hand as she stepped out of the truck. Together they ascended the porch steps and came to a halt at the top.

Jan was standing inside the house, just behind the screen door. "Well, well, well. Isn't this interesting," she sneered.

Jordan took a step toward the door, but was stopped by Maggie who glanced at her and silently communicated that she would handle the situation.

"Don't start, Jan. Has the hospital called yet?" she asked.

Jan narrowed her eyes. "Hospital? Why would the hospital call?"

"One of the carpenters fell out of the rafters directly to the floor of the new barn. We had to call an ambulance to come after him. Jordan stabilized his neck until they got here. I hope he's going to be okay," Maggie explained.

Jan put her hands on her hips. "No, they haven't called yet."

Maggie reached for the screen door handle and pulled it open. Jan stepped aside to allow them to enter. Maggie nervously paced back and forth across the room as she spoke.

"Jan, I need you to go to the hospital to follow up on this for me. This is very important. I'm afraid the carpenter might hold the farm liable, and I need to be sure he's going to be okay. The last thing we need is for a lawsuit, never mind losing the farm in the process."

"We'll lose the farm over my dead body," Jan exclaimed angrily. "Who was it?"

Maggie tried to remember the man's name. "Don something."

"Feldman," Jordan supplied. "Don Feldman."

Jan was clearly surprised. "Don Feldman? I know him. Quite the ladies' man, or at least he thinks he is. Which hospital did they take him to?"

"Well, it was the Shelburne Rescue Squad. I would assume they'd take him to the UVM Medical Center," Maggie replied.

"Okay, I'll go check it out. I'll be back in a few hours," Jan said.

"Take the truck. The keys are still in it," Jordan called after her.

Maggie and Jordan watched as Jan ran down the porch steps and jumped into the truck. Seconds later, all that remained was dust. Maggie closed the house door and leaned her back against it. She reached a hand out to Jordan. Jordan walked toward Maggie and, without touching her, leaned forward and placed a tender kiss on the redhead's lips. She then took one step back and extended her hand, into which Maggie willingly slipped hers. Jordan gently pulled her away from the door and led her toward the bedroom.

Jordan pushed the bedroom door open and allowed Maggie to pass through before her. She closed the door behind them and pulled Maggie into her arms. They stood there for what seemed an eternity, with Maggie's face pressed close to Jordan's chest. Jordan could feel Maggie tremble in her arms. "You're trembling. Are you okay?" she asked.

"I'm fine. I just want you so badly, I'm having a problem containing my desire," Maggie explained.

Jordan released her hold and took Maggie's face between her hands. "You are so beautiful," she whispered as her mouth descended once more.

She gently teased Maggie's lips, caressing them with her tongue, asking for permission to enter. Maggie was hardly able to breathe as she parted her lips and readily accepted Jordan's tongue into her mouth.

"I want you," Jordan rasped, barely able to contain her desire.

Maggie's ardor grew as she pulled Jordan's hair to force her closer. "Make love to me," she insisted breathlessly before plunging her tongue into Jordan's mouth, tasting and caressing in a duel for dominance before breaking for air.

Jordan's hands wandered freely over Maggie's body. She placed her hands on Maggie's bottom and squeezed. Maggie sighed aloud. A low growl emitted from Jordan as she pulled Maggie's shirttails out of her jeans and ran her hands under the shirt and over the creamy white skin of her back. Maggie arched her back in an effort to press herself into Jordan's touch.

Within moments, Jordan released the clasps of Maggie's bra. As the bra released, an almost orgasmic wave of relief filtered through Maggie's body. Jordan then unbuttoned Maggie's shirt, and pushed it off her shoulders only far enough to trap her arms in the process. Her lips explored Maggie's neck as she continued to push the shirt down off her arms. The shirt drifted to the floor, followed closely by Maggie's bra.

Not to be outdone, Maggie deftly made short work of the buttons on Jordan's shirt as her garment joined the growing pile on the floor. Maggie admired the toned muscles of Jordan's arms as she ran her hands over her deltoids, across her collar bones, and down over her breasts. Within seconds, Maggie pulled Jordan's sports bra off over her head and threw it on the floor. Skin to skin they embraced. Nipples hardened against one another.

An involuntary spasm wracked Jordan's body.

"Are you okay?" Maggie asked.

"I am feeling things I've never felt before, Maggie. It's a bit overwhelming."

"Do you trust me, Jordan?" Maggie asked.

"With my life."

"Then relax and enjoy this. I promise not to hurt you."

"I believe you, Maggie."

Jordan pulled led Maggie to the side of the bed. She lowered her mouth once more to Maggie's neck and nuzzled her ear as her hands teased and squeezed her nipples to full erectness.

"Jordan," Maggie moaned as she grasped Jordan's hand and encouraged more.

Jordan's hand left Maggie's breast to unbuckle her belt and

jeans. She eased the zipper down to gain valuable operating room as she slipped her hand inside. Jordan nearly doubled over with lustful hunger as she found the evidence of Maggie's passion while alien pangs of passion flooded her own core.

"Maggie. You are so wet. My God, what you do to me."

"Please, baby, I need more," Maggie begged as she reached between them to unzip Jordan's jeans and push them off her hips.

Jordan kicked her jeans off then lowered herself to one knee as she pulled down Maggie's jeans and panties and helped her to step out of them. She then dropped to both knees and pressed her face into Maggie's abdomen and firmly gripped the bulbous curves of Maggie's bottom.

"Maggie, I need you," Jordan whispered.

Maggie grasped the sides of Jordan's arms and encouraged her to stand. She pushed Jordan's panties to the floor. Eagerly, they embraced and lowered their entwined bodies to the bed, where they lay in each other's arms like braided rope, kissing, exploring and breathing common air.

"I am so in love with you," Jordan confessed.

Maggie rolled on top of Jordan and placed one finger on her lips. "Shh, don't say that. You barely know me."

Jordan smiled. "I have known you for a hundred years, and I will love you for a hundred more," she replied as she reached down between them and slid two fingers inside of the woman above her.

Maggie dropped her chin to her chest, her red hair falling into Jordan's face. She moaned loudly as she pressed herself down onto Jordan's hand.

"Jordan, baby, that feels so good."

Jordan gained the upper hand and rolled Maggie onto her back. She continued to plunge into her lover as she grasped a handful of Maggie's hair at the back of her head and devoured Maggie's mouth. Maggie's moans became louder and Jordan could feel the vibration of her voice echo between their mouths.

Jordan suddenly retracted her fingers. Maggie moaned in protest. "Jordan, no, please, I need you."

"Shh, relax my love," Jordan whispered as she placed

gentle kisses along the length of Maggie's collarbone.

Maggie placed her hands on Jordan's head and pushed her downward.

Jordan chuckled. "All in good time, my love. All in good time."

Jordan continued to place butterfly kisses across Maggie's breasts until she reached her nipples, which she absorbed into her mouth, one by one and captured between her teeth. With the sensitive nub gently held captive, Jordan flicked each one with the tip of her tongue until Maggie shuddered with delight. Jordan allowed her hands to run freely over Maggie's abdomen as her mouth slowly made its way southward. Maggie's hips rose to meet Jordan's mouth, demanding satisfaction.

Then, just as Jordan captured Maggie's sweet spot between her teeth, she drove two fingers once again deep into Maggie's core. Maggie's chest arched off the bed and she was unable to contain the scream of desire erupting from her throat.

Maggie's body began to stiffen as her muscles tightened around Jordan's fingers. "Harder, baby, please," she begged as Jordan increased her rhythm.

Jordan held her close as Maggie's body arched off the bed and she cried out her release.

"Let it go, Maggie. Let it go. I want all of you, forever," Jordan whispered gently as Maggie's orgasm subsided.

Jordan gathered Maggie into her arms and held her close as her breathing returned to normal and the pleasurable tension left her body.

Several moments later, Maggie rolled Jordan onto her back. "Your turn," she said. "I want this first time to be special for you."

"Just being here with you makes it special, Maggie," Jordan replied.

Maggie dropped a delicious kiss on Jordan's lips then licked her way along Jordan's jaw line to her ear. Maggie's tongue penetrated the cavity. Jordan moaned as she felt a wave of desire invade her abdomen. The intensity of the invasion was unsettling and ecstatic. She had never felt so out of control in her life. She began to tremble.

Maggie raised her head and looked at Jordan questioningly. "Are you all right?"

Jordan forced a smile to her lips, but was unable to chase away the tears at the corners of her eyes. "I'm okay. A little nervous, maybe, and a lot scared, but I'm okay."

"Do you want me to stop?"

Jordan tucked a lock of wild red hair behind Maggie's ear. "No, love. Don't stop. I want you to make love to me. Please?"

Maggie smiled and placed another deep kiss on Jordan's lips. "Anything you want, lover. Anything you want."

Jordan tilted her head back as Maggie kissed her throat. With her tongue, Maggie traced her flesh to the indentation where Jordan's collarbones met above her breastbone. The erotic feel of Maggie's tongue circling the indentation drove her crazy as she grasped the sheets on both sides of her body and arched herself closer to Maggie.

Maggie took her cue from Jordan and moved downward, biting Jordan's skin along the way. Each gentle strike brought a spasm to Jordan's abdomen. Maggie stopped at Jordan's breasts and gently ran circles around each erect nipple before sucking them one at a time into her mouth and capturing the hardness between her teeth. She flicked the sensitive nub with her tongue repeatedly.

Jordan's hands flew up to Maggie's head. Maggie looked up. "Harder, please," Jordan urged. Veins protruded from Jordan's neck and her face and chest were flushed crimson as she strained against the ripples of desire spreading through her.

Never before had Jordan felt such intensity of emotion. Any other experiences paled in comparison to what Maggie was doing to her. "Maggie, I need you. Please release me," she begged.

Maggie once more moved downward, not stopping until she could smell the aroma of Jordan's readiness. "Hmm, lover, you are indeed ready for me, aren't you?" she cooed as she slipped her tongue between the folds of Jordan's womanhood.

To Jordan's dismay, she had absolutely no feeling from Maggie's caresses.

Maggie continued her efforts for the next few minutes until

she realized there was no change in Jordan's demeanor. She raised her eyes and looked at Jordan over the expanse of her abdomen and saw the apology in her lover's eyes as she mouthed the words, *I'm sorry.* Maggie raised her head and cocked it to one side.

"I'm sorry, love. I don't feel anything. I'm so sorry." Jordan began to cry.

Maggie was confused. *Didn't she say she felt the burn of desire in her abdomen?*

Not wanting to admit defeat, without warning Maggie plunged two fingers deep inside of Jordan. Curling her fingers upward, she thrust in and out of Jordan, massaging her most sensitive spot with each thrust.

Jordan's head slammed back into the pillow. "Ah!" she screamed out. "Don't stop. Please, don't stop."

Tears rolled down both women's faces as Jordan's thrusts matched Maggie's. Jordan grasped the bed sheets on both sides to anchor herself as her hips rose higher and higher off the bed. Waves of desire pummeled her body as Jordan's orgasm raced through her, setting every nerve ending on fire.

For what felt like an eternity, ripples of aftershocks ran through Jordan's body as Maggie held her close. Finally, the spasms subsided, and Maggie gently slid her hand out of her lover then wrapped her arms around Jordan, who was crying uncontrollably. "It's okay, baby. You are safe. Let it go, lover. Relax."

Jordan was nearly incapable of speech as sobs tore through her chest. "I love you, Maggie," Jordan said as she burrowed her face into Maggie's neck.

"Hmm," Maggie replied as she continued to hold the fragile woman.

Before long, Jordan relaxed and drifted off to sleep in Maggie's arms. Maggie turned her head and placed a delicate kiss on Jordan's forehead.

"I love you too, Jordan," she whispered.

* * *

Maggie glanced at the digital clock and saw three-o-four

flash on the LCD. *What time did Jan leave for the hospital? It must have been just after noon.* She turned her head slightly and placed a gentle kiss on the back of Jordan's head, then wrapped her arms around her as she spooned herself behind Jordan. "Wake up, lover," she whispered softly into Jordan's ear.

Jordan moaned and rolled over to face Maggie then took the redhead into her arms and held her close.

"I don't want to wake up. I want to stay like this forever," she replied without opening her eyes.

"I, too, would like nothing more, but Jan will be back soon. Our attraction is difficult enough for her to accept without her seeing us this way."

Jordan rolled onto her back and laid her arm over her eyes. "Ah, Jan. I forgot about her." Jordan sat up and threw her legs over the side of the bed. "Okay. I guess we'd better get dressed."

Jordan stood beside the bed and stretched her arms high above her head. Unable to resist temptation, Maggie rolled to Jordan's side of the bed where she climbed to her knees and wrapped herself around a naked Jordan from behind. Jordan's arms immediately came down to reach behind her and pull Maggie close.

"God, you feel good, Maggie," Jordan said huskily as the flames of desire once again began to flicker within her.

Maggie allowed her hands to roam freely around Jordan's abdomen as she pulled herself closer to her. One hand slipped lower to cover Jordan's mound, where she stroked gently.

Jordan looked down and saw where Maggie's hand rested, and although she could not feel her hand from a tactile standpoint, the psychological effect was overwhelming as a spasm tore through Jordan, nearly doubling her over. "If you keep that up, we'll never get out of here before Jan returns," she warned.

Maggie kissed Jordan's back. "I know, but you make me feel so alive. All I want to do is make love to you."

Maggie placed a trail of kisses along the scar running down Jordan's back. Finally, she sat back on her heels and ran her hand over the area where the implant protruded from Jordan's skin. "Does it hurt?" she asked.

Jordan couldn't feel what Maggie was doing but knew instinctively what she meant. "No, I don't feel it at all. In the beginning, the constant vibration kind of drove me crazy, but I hardly notice it now. It's a small price to pay for mobility."

Maggie patted the mattress beside her as she settled herself into a seated position on the edge of the bed. "Sweetie, sit. Talk to me for a bit."

Jordan sat beside Maggie, then reached up and tucked an errant lock behind Maggie's ear. "Yes my love?" she asked.

Maggie looked directly into Jordan's eyes. "When my mouth was on you, you didn't feel anything, but when I entered you it was amazing how you reacted."

Jordan smiled. "I know. I was so afraid that I would feel nothing at all, but when you were inside of me, I…well, it felt so intensely overwhelming I thought I might explode. When the orgasm hit me, I nearly lost consciousness it was so intense. I have never felt anything so wonderfully satisfying in all my life. I don't know how to thank you enough for helping me experience that, especially for the first time."

Maggie kissed Jordan tenderly then ran her index finger along the side of Jordan's face. "No thanks necessary, sweetheart. You are an incredible lover. You've made me feel more alive in the past two hours than I have ever felt. Thank you for coming into my life."

Both women's attention was suddenly drawn toward the open window as the sound of a vehicle approaching broke them out of their desire-induced haze.

"Shit," Maggie exclaimed. "That's probably Jan."

Maggie quickly jumped up and grabbed her robe from behind the adjoining bathroom door. "I'll intercept her in the kitchen while you get dressed," she said.

Maggie donned her robe and ran through the living room to the kitchen as Jan walked in the door. Jan was immediately suspicious of Maggie's attire.

Jan raised her eyebrows. "A little afternoon delight?" she asked accusingly.

"What I was doing is none of your concern," Maggie replied.

Jan narrowed her eyes. She walked to the bar and poured herself a drink.

"Jan, what did you find out at the hospital?"

Jan rested her backside against the bar and crossed her ankles. She casually sipped her drink.

"The doctors say Don is a lucky man. It appears he landed directly on his back and just fractured a few vertebrae, but the X-rays don't show any permanent damage. He'll be laid up for a while, but they predict a full recovery."

"That's great news," Jordan said from the hallway leading to the bedrooms.

Jan sneered as Jordan came into view. "Got my answer," she said as she downed the rest of her drink and placed the glass on the bar with a resounding thud. "I've got work to do. I'll catch up with you two later,"

She turned and walked out of the house.

CHAPTER 7

Early the next morning Jordan stepped into the common room of the bunkhouse just as Jan entered from outside. After setting up the coffeepot to brew, Jordan turned around and leaned against the counter and crossed her booted feet at the ankles. Her hands rested on the countertop on each side of her reclining torso.

"Are you always up and about this early?" Jordan asked.

Jan diverted her eyes from the mail she was reading to glance at Jordan. "Only when I have business to attend to," she replied abruptly. She returned to reading her letter.

Jordan allowed the next few moments to pass in silence as the coffee brewed. It wasn't long before a beep at the end of the brewing process signaled that her much needed morning energy was ready for consumption. Jordan turned and retrieved two mugs from the cupboard and filled them both with the dark amber liquid. She held one out to Jan.

Jan looked up from her letter once more and cocked an eyebrow at Jordan in surprise.

Jordan continued to hold the cup out to her. "Look, Jan. These past few weeks have been awkward at best. It seems we're going to be roommates for a while, so we might as well make an effort to at least be civil to one another."

Jan relented and accepted the cup from Jordan. "Thanks," she said tersely.

An awkward silence fell between the women as they each sipped their coffee. Finally, Jan cleared her throat. "I, ah, I have some correspondence to take care of. Thanks again for the coffee."

Jordan nodded and watched as Jan retreated to her bedroom and firmly closed the door behind her.

* * *

Maggie was waiting for Jordan in the barn when she arrived a short time later.

"Hey, you," Maggie greeted her with a smile. "Sleep well last night?"

Jordan grabbed her saddle and threw it across the back of a regal Mustang mare she had affectionately named Sally in honor of her own childhood horse. "I slept okay."

"Where are you going?" Maggie asked as she watched Jordan secure the saddle in place.

"Out to the new barn raising. I was thinking last night that it won't be long before snow falls. We don't have much time to finish the shell before that happens. I thought I'd get a head start before Dave and the rest of the crew show up."

"Well then, I'm going with you," Maggie replied as she saddled her own horse. "Surely there's something I can do to help."

Jordan traced her gloved finger along the side of Maggie's face. "Sweetheart, I will have no problem finding something for you to do."

Maggie smiled and raised her eyebrows seductively. "I think you'll find me to be an efficient helper."

Jordan placed her foot in the stirrup and gracefully swung herself into the saddle. "Come on, then."

The two steadily made their way to the site of the new barn where they released their horses to graze in the corral then entered the old barn to retrieve Jordan's tools.

Maggie looked on as Jordan draped her tool belt over her waist and adjusted it into place. "You look very butch in that tool belt," she said suggestively.

Jordan grinned devilishly and retrieved a screwdriver from her belt. "Let me know if you need something screwed. I'd be happy to oblige."

Maggie reached forward and grabbed the front of Jordan's shirt and pulled her close. "I definitely have something you can screw," she said as their mouths met.

Maggie explored Jordan's mouth for several moments before she pulled back and smiled. "Well, lover, as much as I'd like to sample your handyman wares right now, we are bound to get caught if we take this much further. I will, however, hire your services later tonight."

Jordan chuckled and kissed Maggie passionately once more. "Tonight? Mmm, a midnight rendezvous?"

"Well, once I have you in my bed, there's no way I'm letting you leave. You can call it a sleepover, imprisonment, confinement, a hostage situation. Call it anything you want, but you're not leaving."

"Sounds like fun, but aren't you worried about Jan missing me when I don't come home tonight?" Jordan asked.

Maggie cupped the side of Jordan's cheek with her palm. "I broke things off with Jan nearly a month ago. She has to get used to it some time."

Jordan took Maggie's hand from her face and held it to her lips then placed a delicate kiss in the palm. "I like the way you think," she whispered hoarsely.

In the distance Jordan and Maggie could hear sounds of vehicles approaching. The hum of the motors grew louder as they neared. Finally, the sound of male voices competing with each other signaled that the work crew had arrived.

Jordan leaned in to kiss Maggie deeply once more before stepping back to allow Maggie to exit the barn before her.

* * *

During the next several weeks, Jordan worked side by side with the carpenters to complete the outer structure of the barn while Maggie split her time between supervising the finishing touches on the inside and with Jan's help, maintaining the day to day workings of the farm. Jan was uncharacteristically stoic during those weeks, no doubt attributed to the fact that Jordan spent most nights with Maggie and leaving her on her own in the bunkhouse.

The relationship between Maggie and Jan became distant, with communication focusing on the day-to-day workings of the farm. The relationship between Jan and Jordan was strained, but polite—a fact that both surprised and unnerved Jordan, considering the veiled threats Jan had delivered to her the day she moved into the bunkhouse.

Just before Christmas, the barn was finished. To celebrate the occasion, Jordan erected a small Christmas tree inside the main foyer of the barn. The entire construction crew and their families were invited to a holiday celebration, which began with a wine and cheese social in the grand room of the new barn followed by a home-cooked dinner at the farmhouse.

The farmhouse was gaily decorated with lights and garland. A large Christmas tree stood proudly in the corner of the living room beside the fireplace. The tree was festively adorned with lights and ornaments, new and old, including several that Maggie had made as a child.

Dinner was a huge success, followed by a gift hunt for the crew's children in the main barn. Part way through the evening, Jan claimed she had a headache and returned to the bunkhouse.

It was well into the evening before the last guests departed. Jordan and Maggie walked them to their cars then returned eagerly to the house to take advantage of the blazing fireplace. They threw an array of blankets and pillows on the floor near the flames, creating a romantic nest.

"Make yourself comfortable while I pour the wine," Jordan suggested.

"Okay, love. I'll tend the fire," Maggie replied.

When Jordan entered the living room carrying two glasses of wine, she found Maggie sitting in front of the flames, surrounded by pillows. She approached Maggie and handed her one of the glasses.

Maggie smiled up into Jordan's face. "Thank you, lover. Come sit with me," Maggie added as she patted the floor next to her.

Jordan sat on the floor next to Maggie and sipped her wine. She couldn't help but stare at the woman beside her.

"What are you thinking, Jordan?"

Jordan reached forward with her free hand and traced the edge of Maggie's cheek. "I am thinking that I am the luckiest woman in the world. I am thinking that you are so beautiful you take my breath away. I am thinking that I want to spend the rest of my life showing you just how much I love you."

Maggie smiled and looked down into her wine glass, deep in thought.

"My turn to ask. What is on your mind?" Jordan asked.

"I guess I'm waiting to wake up and discover this is all a dream. I have never known anyone like you, Jordan. There is something so mysterious about you, yet I feel like I've known you forever. I feel safe with you, yet I hardly know anything about you. Who are you, Jordan Lewis?"

Jordan kissed Maggie tenderly. "I am the woman who loves you with all her heart. I am asking you to trust me, Maggie. I promise I will tell you everything you want to know in time. Just know that I will never hurt you."

Maggie yawned loudly.

"You are tired, my love. It's been a very long and hectic day. Here, let me take your wine," Jordan said as she took Maggie's glass and placed it on the hearth. "Come here, lie with me. Close your eyes and enjoy the warmth of the fire."

Maggie rested her head on Jordan's shoulder and draped her arm across Jordan's midsection as they lay together on the pillows. Jordan kissed Maggie's forehead. "Close your eyes, my love. Relax. I will keep you safe." Moments later they were fast asleep caressed by each other and by the slow flickering glow of the fire.

* * *

The next morning, Jordan woke up alone among the pillows strewn in front of the fireplace. She sat up and looked around groggily. When she realized where she was and how she came to be there, she smiled broadly.

"Are you going to sleep all day?" Maggie teased as she walked into the living room fully dressed. Maggie scooted away as Jordan playfully reached out for her legs. "Oh, no you don't," Maggie exclaimed.

"No fair," Jordan responded as she lay back down among the pillows. A glance at the clock told her it was only seven. She watched Maggie button the cuffs of her shirt. "Where are you going so early this morning?" she asked.

"I'm going to take a ride out to the north pasture. Wanna

come?"

Jordan placed her hands behind her head. "Actually, I thought I'd fix the broken spindles on the porch then start breakfast while you're gone. I'm not much of a cook, but I can do breakfast."

Maggie smiled. "You won't get an argument from me, but make it brunch if you would. I will probably be gone for a few hours." She squatted down beside Jordan and kissed her temptingly. "I'll be back in a while, lover."

Jordan watched Maggie leave, then climbed to her feet and tried to iron out the wrinkles in her clothing with her hands before heading into the kitchen to set up the coffee pot. While the coffee brewed, she showered and dressed in clean clothes then went out to the porch to assess which spindles needed to be replaced.

"Jordan, do you know where my saddle is?"

Jordan turned to see Maggie stroll toward her from across the barnyard. She stopped working on the repairs to the front porch to give Maggie her full attention. As always, Jordan felt a rush of desire pass through her whenever Maggie was around. "You're still here? I thought you headed to the north pasture a while ago."

"I can't find my saddle. I've been looking for it for the past half hour."

"Your saddle isn't in the barn?"

"No. I put it on the stand yesterday when Shawny and I returned from our ride but it's not there today. I was wondering if maybe you moved it."

"No, I didn't. In fact, I haven't been in the barn yet this morning. The saddler was here yesterday, wasn't he? Maybe he thought it needed repair and took it back to his shop."

Maggie stopped in front of Jordan and placed her hands on her denim-clad hips. Her curly red hair splayed in several directions from beneath her cowboy hat. "Hmm. That's possible, I suppose. I need to check on the horses in the north pasture and you know Shawny doesn't do well with saddles he's not used to."

Jordan looked into her emerald green eyes and smiled.

"Why don't you take my horse? I'm sure Sally would love the exercise."

Maggie smiled and touched the side of Jordan's face. "You are so sweet, my love. I just might do that." She stood on tiptoe to place a kiss on Jordan's lips.

Jordan's arms immediately circled Maggie's waist and her hands found their way into the waistband of Maggie jeans as the kiss deepened. Jordan's hands delved deep, firmly grasping Maggie's buttocks and pulling her close to her own heated core.

"Hmm," Jordan moaned. "I want you again, my love."

Maggie drew her lips away from Jordan's to catch her breath. "God, if you keep that up, I'll never get out to the north pasture."

"Well, you could always send Jan out to check on them while we make better use of our time," Jordan suggested slyly.

"I would, but she doesn't seem to be around right now. She's been behaving pretty erratically. One moment she's stuck to me like glue and the next, she's nowhere to be found."

Jordan picked up her hammer and dropped it into the sling attached to her tool belt. "Well, if you ask me, I think she's trying to win you back."

Maggie blushed then gently punched Jordan's shoulder. "Get out of Dodge. She is not."

Jordan advanced one step in Maggie's direction and took the redhead's face between her hands as their eyes locked. "Trust me love, she wants something. Why else would she stay?"

Maggie wrapped her arms around Jordan's waist and pulled her close. "Well, lover, you have nothing to worry about. She can try all she wants. It's you I love and nothing she can do will change that."

"Well, the feeling is mutual. Now go on. Take Sally to the north pasture. I'll call the saddler for you while you're gone. Okay?"

Maggie turned to head back to the barn. "Okay. I'll see you in a few hours."

Jordan's eyes were glued to Maggie's swaying hips as she made her way back to the barn. After a few minutes, Maggie re-emerged riding Jordan's horse waving her hat in Jordan's direction as she galloped toward the north pasture.

When Maggie was finally out of sight, Jordan entered the house and called the saddler who said he didn't have the saddle.

Jordan hung up the phone then went into the kitchen for a glass of water before continuing the repairs on the front porch. As she was filling her glass, she looked out the window above the kitchen sink and caught a glimpse of a figure covertly exiting the barn on foot. Suspicious, Jordan decided to investigate.

So as to not call any unusual attention to herself, Jordan sauntered toward the barn as she had done countless times before. Once inside, she allowed her eyes to become accustomed to the darker environment before looking around. She searched the horse stalls, but found nothing unusual. She even spent a short amount of time petting Maggie's horse, Shawny. Strangely, upon exiting Shawny's stall, she immediately noticed that Maggie's saddle was hanging on the rail, right where Maggie said she always put it.

Maggie, was this saddle really not here earlier today, or are you losing your marbles, girlfriend?

The saddle was hanging over the rail with the right side facing the rider. Jordan quickly inspected the saddle, then turned to walk away, but stopped short when something caught her eye. She turned back to the saddle and grasped it with both hands. In one quick movement, she lifted the saddle, spun it around and placed it back on the rail so that the left side of the saddle was facing outward.

Jordan lifted the stirrup and threw it over the top of the saddle, then reached down to grasp the belly strap.

"What the hell? How did this get here?" Jordan reached under the saddle and quickly released the buckle holding the belly strap. With the strap in hand, she proceeded to cross the barnyard toward the bunk house. She stopped before the bunkhouse door and banged loudly. "Open this goddamned door."

The door flew open and Jordan came face to face with Jan. Jordan thrust the belly strap toward her. "Care to explain this?"

CHAPTER 8

Jan looked at the belly strap Jordan held in her hand. "It's a belly strap. Surely you know that," Jan said sarcastically.

Jordan turned the strap over in her hand. "No, I mean this."

On the underside of the strap was a metal burr, embedded deep into the leather.

Jan took the strap from Jordan and looked at it closely. "It looks like a burr to me."

Jordan placed her hands on her hips. "That's exactly what it is. Care to tell me how it got there?"

"How the hell am I supposed to know that?" Jan replied angrily.

Jordan grabbed the strap from Jan and folded it in half. "This strap came off Maggie's saddle, which, by the way, went missing this morning and then miraculously reappeared just after I saw you sneak out of the barn. If she had ridden Shawny with this burr in the belly strap, he would have thrown her. She could have been seriously hurt, or worse."

Jan crossed her arms and cocked her head to one side. "So? Why are you telling *me* this?"

Jordan leaned in close. "Because if anything happens to Maggie, I will hold you personally responsible," she answered vehemently.

"Now, why would I want to harm Maggie?" Jan asked defensively.

"That's the part I haven't figured out yet. I would have half expected me to be your target, not her," Jordan replied.

Jan stepped in defiantly close. "Then I guess maybe you're the one who should watch her back."

"What's going on here?"

Jordan turned quickly to see Maggie standing on the bunkhouse porch behind her. After acknowledging her presence, she turned back to Jan and stared directly into her face while addressing Maggie's question. "Nothing. Everything's fine. Jan and I were just making sure we're on the same page."

Jordan looked down at the strap in her hand then shoved it inside her jacket before she turned to face Maggie once more. "Are you ready for brunch?"

Maggie smiled broadly. "You bet I am. I'm famished." She looked over Jordan's shoulder. "Would you like to join us, Jan?" she asked.

"No, thanks," Jan replied. "I've had breakfast already."

Maggie linked her arm into the crook of Jordan's elbow. "All right then, let's eat."

* * *

"Hmm, this is wonderful, Jordan. Where did you learn to cook so well?" Maggie asked as she chewed a forkful of French toast.

Jordan chuckled. "Actually, I'm a lousy cook. This just happens to be one of the few things I can make without poisoning myself. My friend Kale taught me how to make it."

"Kale? That's an unusual name. Male, right?"

"Definitely male," Jordan replied. "He's my best friend in the world, and my surrogate little brother. He's such a sweet guy. He's kind and considerate. We actually shared a house together for a couple of years. For the longest time he was convinced he was in love with me, that is, until Andi came along."

"Andi? Pretty androgynous name. Male or female?"

"Andi is all girl. A very beautiful one at that, and smart too. She's a physicist. Andi, Kale and I all worked together at the lab." Jordan smiled wistfully as she thought about her friends.

Maggie touched Jordan's hand. "You haven't seen them in a while, I take it?"

Jordan pushed her food around on the plate as she shook her head. "I didn't realize until now how much I would miss them."

"Well, maybe we can invite them to visit, do you think?"

Jordan looked at Maggie and smiled. "Maybe," she replied.

Maggie took a bite of sausage. "Oh, when I came back from the north pasture, I noticed you found my saddle. Where was it?"

"Actually, Mags, I didn't find it. It was right where you always put it."

"No way! I swear to you, Jordan, it was not there when I went to saddle Shawny this morning."

"Well, for what's it worth, I believe you," Jordan replied.

"So who would have taken it? And who brought it back?" Maggie asked.

"I'm guessing it was Jan," Jordan said. "John is on vacation until after the holidays and she's the only other one around beside you and me."

"What would she want with my saddle?"

"That's just what I was trying to find out when you interrupted us a while ago."

"Jordan, what I interrupted was some type of confrontation. I'm not blind, you know. I could have sworn Jan was dealing okay with the breakup. Wanna tell me what you were discussing?"

Jordan sat back in her chair. "Nothing, really. I was just making sure she and I understood one another."

Maggie narrowed her eyes at Jordan. "Why don't I believe you?"

Jordan stood and collected their dishes, then placed an inviting kiss on Maggie's lips. "Trust me, sweetheart. I'm just looking out for things, especially for you."

"I don't need looking out for, Jordan. I'm a big girl and I can take care of myself."

Jordan carried the coffee pot back to the table and refilled their cups. "I'm sure you can, sweetie, but it never hurts to have help." Jordan returned the coffee pot to the hot plate. "Tell me about your ride this morning. How are the horses?"

"Oh, I stopped at the new barn to check on the foals. They are doing really well...."

Jordan sat down and enjoyed her coffee as Maggie talked excitedly about the foals, the farm and life in general. For Maggie's benefit, she maintained the smile on her face, but inside, she was seething.

Jan, I won't let you screw this up. That is a promise, she thought fervently.

* * *

Maggie sat at the kitchen table studying several official-looking documents. As she read, she jotted notes on a pad of paper nearby. Her attention was suddenly drawn to the sound of stamping feet on the porch just outside the kitchen door.

Jordan pushed the kitchen door open and stepped inside. "Damn, it's colder than a witch's tit out there," she cussed as she bent over to remove her boots.

Maggie chuckled. "And just how cold is a witch's tit, my love?" she asked coyly.

"Cold enough to produce milkshakes." Jordan grinned. "Sometimes I think your parents have the right idea. Florida in January sounds like a wonderful thing."

Jordan hung her coat on one of the hooks by the door then rubbed her hands together as she approached Maggie. She stood behind her and looked over her shoulder.

"What are you reading?" she asked.

Maggie glanced up at Jordan. "I'm just reviewing the Planning Commission guidelines before I draft the proposal for the riding school," she explained, returning her attention to the documents.

"I can imagine there will be a lot of rules and regulations we'll have to follow and safety upgrades to make the farm safe and suitable for the kids," Jordan predicted.

"I'm afraid you're right. The problem I'm having, though, is trying to put limits on the definition of handicapped, one that doesn't exclude too many of the more disabled children. I really don't want to limit any child with a disability from taking lessons, but I guess it will be unavoidable if we can't make it totally safe for them."

Jordan leaned over Maggie as she read and nuzzled her cold nose into Maggie's neck.

"Yeeow!" Maggie screamed as she squirmed away. "Your nose is cold."

Jordan laughed evilly as she shoved her cold hands into the neckline of Maggie's shirt.

Maggie jumped up from the table. "Jordan Lewis," she shouted. "Stop that."

Jordan adopted an apologetic look on her face as she opened her arms for Maggie. "I'm sorry love. Come here and I'll make it up to you."

Maggie cautiously stepped into the circle of Jordan's arms and allowed herself to be embraced lovingly. After a few moments, she relaxed and returned the hug.

Without warning, Jordan pulled Maggie's shirt up and planted her cold hands on the middle of the redhead's back.

"Ah," Maggie protested as she wiggled out of Jordan's embrace. "Why you little shit," she yelled.

Jordan grinned. "Uh, oh. Time for a hasty retreat."

She turned and made a quick exit into the living room with Maggie hot on her tail. Once in the living room, she threw herself on the couch and put her arms up to protect herself as Maggie grabbed a throw pillow and pummeled her with it. In between hits, Jordan managed to work a pillow out from behind her to enter into the battle. Before long they were both on their feet and engaged in a full-fledged pillow fight. Many minutes later, laughing so hard their sides hurt, the two women dropped side-by-side onto the couch.

Jordan moved to the end of the couch and half-reclined. She beckoned to Maggie. "Come here, you."

Maggie eagerly dove into Jordan's arms. They lay there entwined with Maggie's cheek resting on Jordan's chest.

"Hmm, this feels good," Maggie cooed. "I love listening to your heart beat."

Jordan kissed the top of Maggie's head. "It beats only for you, love."

"How is it that you so easily walked into my life and stole my heart?" Maggie asked.

"Actually, I didn't walk into your life, I transported into it. You see, I'm really a scientist from the future and I traveled here via a time machine to intentionally invade your life," Jordan replied.

Maggie raised her head and looked directly into Jordan's eyes. She smiled widely. "You are such a kook sometimes," she exclaimed. She leaned in and kissed Jordan on the nose, then laid her head back onto Jordan's chest. "Don't ever change, sweetheart. I love you just the way you are."

* * *

Maggie and Jordan chose to spend a cold winter evening reading in bed. Maggie lowered the book she was reading into her lap and looked at Jordan sitting in bed beside her. "Jordan?"

Jordan looked away from her book. "Yeah?"

"Will you marry me?"

Jordan's head snapped back. She was clearly surprised by Maggie's unexpected question and was left speechless.

"Don't look so shocked."

"Ah…ah…ah…I'm sorry. Your question just took me by surprise," Jordan replied.

"I don't know why it should. I mean you've been here for five months now, right? I don't know about you, but I pretty much felt the attraction the minute I set eyes on you."

Jordan nodded. "I think I was in love with you before I met you," she said.

Maggie placed her hand on Jordan's arm and playfully pushed her away. "Get out of here," she exclaimed. "How could you possibly love me before you met me?"

"Let's just say an angel visited me in my sleep. She had wild curly red hair, and looked an awful lot like you. She told me everything about you. I couldn't help but fall in love the moment I saw you."

Maggie smiled. Try as she might, she could not take her eyes from Jordan. "Jordan, I love you so much. I have never felt this way about anyone before. I can't begin to tell you what your smile does to me. There are so many emotions that run through me when you look at me. It seems that you can see deep into my soul."

Jordan reached forward to cup Maggie's face between her hands. She placed a delicate kiss on her lips. "I am so glad you love me, Mags. I have wanted this for so long. You have no idea what I've been through to get here."

Maggie smiled and blinked rapidly to clear her vision that had become cloudy with unshed tears of joy. "I do love you, Jord. I love you beyond anything in my life's experience. I want so badly to be the object of your desire, your partner in heart and in soul. I dream of a life together in body, in spirit, and in name."

Jordan took Maggie's hand and raised it to her lips then kissed her open palm. She felt Maggie quiver as she looked into her eyes. "I want to share your life, my love. I want to laugh with you and cry with you. I want to help you achieve everything you ever wanted in life. I want to be by your side through all the good things, and the bad things too. I want to spend every day of the rest of my life looking into your beautiful green eyes, even when we're old and gray and rocking beside each other in our chairs on the front porch, even when we have just one tooth between us and you have to change my diapers. If that isn't love, I don't know what is."

Maggie wiped an errant tear from the corner of her eye as she laughed at the verbal picture Jordan had painted with her words. "You are such a goofball sometimes. So, as one member of the mutual admiration society to another, does that mean you'll marry me?"

Jordan grinned. "Yes, my love. I'll marry you."

Maggie squealed with delight as she threw her book on the bedside table and stood on the bed. She danced around joyously as Jordan laughed.

"Now who's the goofball?" Jordan exclaimed.

Maggie threw herself at Jordan and straddled her lap. She took Jordan's face between her hands and kissed her soundly. "I love you so much, Jordan. Thank you for loving me, too."

"That is so easy to do, Maggie. I was gone the first time you visited me in my dreams."

Maggie looked confused. "You are a complicated woman, Jordan. You talk in riddles sometimes. I realize there are things about you I don't know, but my heart is telling me to trust you anyway."

Jordan nodded. "Thank you, my love."

Maggie grinned. "I'll call the justice of the peace tomorrow and…."

"Whoa," Jordan exclaimed. "Slow down a bit, sweetheart. Why don't we plan this out? I want it to be special, not just the two of us standing in front of a total stranger saying I do."

"Jordan, I don't want to put it off forever."

"Neither do I, love," Jordan replied. "Let's wait until the weather breaks, say, maybe April or May?"

Maggie nodded. "Okay. I'll compromise. My birthday is April sixteenth. That's about a month from now. I'm still going to call the justice of the peace tomorrow though. It's not too early to begin planning."

Jordan smiled. "What am I getting myself into here?" she teased. "I hear redheads are notorious for determination and hot tempers."

Maggie whispered into Jordan's ear. "I'll show you hot, but it won't be my temper."

"Oh, God," Jordan exclaimed as she scooted down in the bed taking Maggie with her.

CHAPTER 9

Jordan walked across the yard and stepped into the barn. She stopped short when she heard voices.

"Did you hear the news?"

Jordan recognized John's voice as she waited for the reply to his question.

"News? No. I'm pretty much out of the loop these days."

Jan. Jordan's interest was piqued as she covertly listened to the conversation.

"Well, Maggie was in here about an hour ago to take Shawny for his morning ride, and she told me she and Jordan are getting married."

"What?" Jan shouted angrily. "Say that again?"

"I said Maggie and Jordan are getting married. Apparently she proposed last night and Jordan said yes. Maggie was all smiles this morning. I haven't seen her that happy in a long time."

"Jesus Christ," Jan exclaimed. "Did she say when?"

"She said something about having it on her birthday," John replied.

"April sixteenth," Jan whispered nearly under her breath.

John looked at the date on his watch. "Well, it looks like we're going to have a party in about a month."

"Damn," Jan cursed.

John frowned. "Look, Jan. I know you and Maggie used to be together, but maybe you should just accept that she's in love with Jordan now and just let it go."

Jan took several steps toward John and stopped within a foot of him. "Look, old man, I don't have to accept anything. I knew that Lewis woman would be bad news the moment I laid eyes on her. I won't just sit back and let her take everything away from me."

Jan's attempt to intimidate John did not sit well with him. "Well, I reckon I wouldn't be making an enemy of Jordan seeing as she'll be your boss soon."

"We'll see about that," Jan spat as she turned to leave.

Jordan quickly stepped out of the barn and pretended to enter for the first time, just as Jan was leaving. "Good morning, Jan," she said cheerily.

"Fuck you!" Jan stamped past Jordan and headed to the bunkhouse.

Jordan watched her go as she continued to enter the barn. Stopping face to face with John, she asked, "What's up with her?"

"Well, she ain't very happy with the fact that you and Maggie are getting married."

"I see," Jordan replied.

"Well, I think it's grand," John said as he extended his hand to Jordan. "Congratulations."

"Thank you John." Jordan looked around. "So, what can I do to help you today?"

"You don't need to help me with anything, Miss Jordan," John replied.

Jordan put her hand on John's shoulder. "John, I'd appreciate it if you cut the Miss Jordan shit, okay? I'm still just Jordan, and I still want to pull my weight around here. So, what do you say you and I clean the stalls together?"

John smiled. "You got it, Jordan."

* * *

Jordan spent the entire day in the barn with John, cleaning stalls, stacking hay bales in the loft, and doing general repairs. As the sun began to set, she called it a day and sent John home. As she crossed the yard toward the house, she noticed a truck approaching the barn from the north pasture.

The truck was soon close enough to read the name on the door. J. T. Robinson, Artesian Well Drilling.

The well in the north pasture. Maggie, do you realize what you have just done?

Jordan immediately went in search of Maggie. "Maggie!

Maggie, where are you?" she called when she entered the kitchen.

"In here," Maggie replied from the living room.

Jordan found her in the far corner of the living room sitting at the desk organizing paperwork. Maggie turned to face her as she approached and smiled broadly.

"Hey baby," she said.

Jordan forced herself to remain calm. She realized that there was no way Maggie could have realized the ramifications of placing the well in the north pasture. "Hi love. Hey, I just saw an artesian well-drilling truck come out of the north pasture."

"They're finished already? That was fast," Maggie replied.

"I didn't realize you were having a well drilled."

Maggie shrugged. "I almost didn't remember about it myself," she said. "It's actually been scheduled since last fall. It was supposed to be finished at about the same time the new barn was, but Jack Robinson fell behind due to some health issues. By the time he was able to get back to work, it was winter, so it had to wait until now."

Jordan nodded. "I see. So, where in the north pasture did you have it dug?"

Maggie continued to sort her paperwork as she talked to Jordan. "Well, that's the unfortunate part. It's pretty far from the barn. Jack couldn't find a spring to tap into any closer. I'm afraid we'll have to lay pipeline between the new well and the barn for it to be useful."

"So, it's out in the middle of the field?" Jordan asked.

"Unfortunately, yes." Maggie stopped what she was doing and turned to face Jordan. "Why the sudden interest in the well?" she asked.

"Maggie, did the contractor produce evidence that the land is dry around the vicinity of the barn?"

"No. I just assumed he was right. Jordan, what are you implying?" she asked.

"I'm working on a hunch here, Maggie. Could I ask you to humor me by getting another opinion?"

"I guess so," Maggie replied hesitantly, "but I just paid

three thousand dollars to have that well dug."

"Maggie, if my hunch holds true, it will cost a lot less money to have the well re-dug than it will to hire Robinson to lay pipeline."

Maggie threw up her hands. "Okay. You're the boss on this one."

"Thank you, love," Jordan replied as she kissed the top of Maggie's head. In doing so, she glanced at the paperwork laid out across Maggie's desk. "What are you doing?" she asked.

"Ugh. Tax time. Every year I have to sort out receipts and bills in preparation for having the taxes done. I hate it."

"How about next year, I set up a spread sheet on the computer so you can keep track of debits and credits as they occur? Then, at the end of the year, all you have to do is print out reports in any flavor you want. Sound good?" Jordan asked as she glanced again at the paperwork.

As she looked away, something caught her eye. It was a letter from Pritchard and Yeats law firm, the firm that handled Maggie's father's estate.

"That sounds wonderful. But I'm afraid I'm not very computer literate," Maggie replied.

Jordan continued to stare at the paperwork—at one document in particular.

Where have I seen that logo before?

Jordan replied, "It's easy, love. I wouldn't mind holding your hand through it until you're comfortable doing it yourself."

Maggie grinned. "I'm game. Any reason to hold hands with you is good."

Jordan committed the name above the logo to memory in the event it came to her later. "Okay, sweetie. I'm going to leave you alone so you can finish what you're doing. How about I start dinner?"

Maggie was immediately on her feet. "Baby, no offense, but I think I'll make dinner."

Jordan tried to look offended, but was secretly glad. The last time she'd tried to make dinner, they ended up ordering take-out. "I really don't mind, Mags."

"The paperwork can wait. I'll make dinner," Maggie

insisted.

"Well then, let me help, okay?" Jordan suggested.

"Only if you promise not to burn the water this time," Maggie teased.

Jordan chuckled. "Deal."

* * *

Jan had made herself scarce since she discovered Jordan and Maggie were to be married. She spent a great deal of time training and exercising the horses and avoided the immediate area of the farmhouse during daylight hours. Jordan did, however, notice that Jan spent a significant amount of time in the barn after John left for the day and after Jordan and Maggie retired to the house.

After finding the burr on Maggie's saddle, Jordan rose early each morning and went to the barn to search for evidence of what Jan was up to, but each time, she failed to find anything. Finally, she sought out Jan in the bunkhouse to confront her.

Jordan knocked loudly on the bunkhouse door and waited for Jan to answer. After several moments of silence, she knocked again. Still, no answer. Finally, she reached down and turned the knob. The door opened easily.

The bunkhouse was dark. Jordan stepped inside and turned the switch on beside the door. Light immediately flooded the common area. Everything was neat and orderly. Jordan walked across the common room and pushed open the door to Jan's bedroom. She stepped inside and turned on the lamp that was on top of a nearby dresser. Again, Jordan found nothing out of place in the room. Jordan began searching drawers for anything that appeared suspicious. A thorough search of each dresser drawer yielded nothing. She sighed deeply and was about to leave the room when she noticed the bedside table had a built-in drawer. She quickly crossed the room and pulled the drawer open.

Jordan stared at the contents of the drawer for several moments before reaching in to extract an envelope. She held the envelope up and realized it was addressed to Maggie, but most discerning was the return address and the familiar logo below it–Pritchard and Yeats, Attorneys at Law. Jordan's hands shook as she opened the flap and removed the letter inside. The letter was dated October 29, 2018.

Damn. That was more than four months ago.

Jordan closed her eyes and tried to remember back four months and suddenly realized why the logo looked so familiar to her. *This must have been the letter Jan was reading the morning after she moved into the bunkhouse. That's where I've seen the logo before.*

She quickly read the letter and became angrier and angrier with each line of text.

"Maggie needs to see this," she decided as she folded the letter and placed it back in the envelope.

Jordan closed the drawer of the nightstand and turned the lights out behind her. She left the bunkhouse then charged directly toward the house. Maggie was in the kitchen preparing dinner.

"Hey, baby," Maggie said as she wrapped her arms around Jordan's middle. "Good news, lover. The new well contractor just called and said they hit pay dirt, or pay water as the case may be. They found a water source exactly where you told them to drill, just off the corner of the new barn. How did you get so smart?"

"That *is* good news," Jordan replied. "I hate to minimize it, but I have some news of my own that is more important, but unfortunately, not as good."

Maggie frowned. "What is it, love?"

Jordan handed the letter to Maggie.

"What's this?" she asked as she opened it.

"Read it," Jordan encouraged.

Maggie extracted the letter from the envelope and read it out loud.

October 29, 2018

Miss Downs, please find below, a description of the information you requested relative to a recent change made to the deed of the horse farm in Shelburne, VT, based on the wishes of your father, Gary Downs.

Based on the addendum, ownership of the farm is hereby transferred to Miss Margaret Michele Downs, with secondary ownership transferred to Miss Janneal Sanford in the event Margaret Down's predeceases her. Since Gary Downs is the author of the above-mentioned addendum, any changes to the intent and contents must be requested only by him, until he is deceased, at which time, changes may be made by Miss Margaret Downs and approved by Miss Janneal Safford.

Please feel free to call our office if you have any questions about this document.

Sincerely,

Jeffrey Pritchard

"Oh, my God," Maggie exclaimed when she finished reading the document. "This is the document I asked them to send to me months ago. I totally forgot about it. Jordan, where did you find this?" she asked.

"In the nightstand drawer next to Jan's bed," Jordan replied.

"Jan? How did she get it?"

"She must have intercepted the mail, Maggie. That's the only thing I can think of. She obviously has a vested interest in making sure the deed stays exactly as it is."

Maggie folded the paper and angrily shoved it back into the envelope. "Well, she has another thing coming to her. I'll call Daddy right now and insist he has this changed immediately. How dare she?"

"Do you have any idea where she is right now, Maggie? I have a thing or two I want to discuss with her as well," Jordan exclaimed.

Maggie reached for the phone to call her father as she responded to Jordan's question.

"Unfortunately, you'll have to wait a couple of days. She's visiting friends out of town. She should be back on Friday. At least that's what she told me."

"Damn," Jordan responded.

* * *

After dinner that evening, Jordan made excuses about a project she was working on in the barn and left Maggie to work through the tax papers. Jordan secreted herself in the hayloft and waited. She had a hunch that Jan was not really out of town. Near nine o'clock, just as Jordan fought to stay awake, the door of the barn slowly opened. Jordan had positioned herself such that she had a clear view of the main area of the barn and sat as still as possible so as to not call attention to herself in the loft.

Jordan watched as Jan crept slowly into the barn and walked directly to Maggie's saddle. Jordan's view of the saddle was blocked by Jan's body, so she was forced to wait patiently until Jan covertly exited the barn before she could investigate what she had done. She wanted so badly to rush Jan, tackle her to the ground, then pummel her senseless with her fists.

When the barn door closed behind Jan, Jordan descended from the loft and approached Maggie's saddle. She inspected it carefully. Jan had cut the right stirrup strap nearly clean through. It was hanging by barely a quarter of an inch of leather.

"Damn you, Jan," Jordan cursed. She was violently shaking and had to consciously stop herself from going after the woman. Instead, she paced back and forth across the barn to calm down and think.

Finally, Jordan made a decision. She took Maggie's saddle and put it into the repair pile for the saddler to collect. She would call him in the morning and ask him to collect it right away and return it by the end of the day on Thursday. She decided not to tell Maggie what had happened. Satisfied that she had an effective plan, Jordan left the barn and returned to the house.

CHAPTER 10

On Thursday morning, Jordan dropped Maggie off at the new barn then drove the old truck across the north pasture. Arrangements had been made with John to pick Maggie up later in the day. As Jordan drove across the field, the sound of shovels rattling in the back kept time with each bump she encountered. Her mind was occupied with the events of the previous night when she had witnessed Jan sabotaging Maggie's saddle. She was thankful Maggie didn't argue with her about riding to the new barn instead of taking Shawny out on his usual morning run. She was hoping the saddler would keep his word and collect the saddle that morning and return it by the end of the day as he promised he would.

Finally, she spotted a mound of dirt in the distance and steered the truck in that direction. After a few minutes, she pulled the truck along side the dirt mound, turned off the ignition, and climbed out. Jordan walked over to the mound and peered over it to see the hole that had been dug in the earth by the well drillers. It was approximately three feet in diameter and was so deep that she could not see the bottom.

"Well, it's not going to fill itself, I guess."

Jordan walked back to the truck to retrieve a shovel from the bed. Within moments, she was hard at work shoveling dirt from the mound into the hole. For the first hour she was unable to hear the dirt hit the bottom. Finally, faint indications began to emerge as each shovel full of dirt slipped into the hole and landed in a soft thud as the soil reached the bottom. Several hours later, the bottom of the hole became visible.

Jordan stopped and drove the head of the shovel deep into the shrinking mound of dirt, then pulled a bandanna from her back pocket to wipe the sweat from her brow. She looked overhead and guessed from the position of the sun that it was near two in the afternoon. She had been shoveling for five hours. Two hours later, she scooped up the last shovel of dirt and held it above the filled-in hole.

"This one is for you, Sally."

Jordan tipped the head of the shovel and allowed the dirt to slowly slip to the earth. She then stood on top of the small mound covering the hole and packed the soil firmly with her boots.

Covered with sweat and dirt, Jordan carried the shovel back to the truck and tossed it warily into the bed. She then climbed into the cab and drove away.

* * *

Twenty minutes later, Jordan parked the truck in front of the barn and climbed out of the driver's seat. She brushed the dust from her jeans and stamped her feet to loosen any dirt she might have carried into the truck on her boots. She then went inside to check out the saddler's handiwork on Maggie's saddle. To her dismay, the saddle was still in the repair pile.

"Damn it!" she shouted.

She then headed toward the house and climbed the two steps leading to the porch. Jordan removed her cowboy hat as she pushed the kitchen door open and stepped inside. The tempting aroma of freshly baked cookies was stronger than her willpower as she reached for a cookie. Next to their cooling rack on the countertop, Jordan spotted a note from Maggie.

Jord, the saddler called and apologized for not making it out today. He had a family emergency. He said he'd be here by noon tomorrow.

Jordan read the note and cursed again under her breath. "Damn. I'll just need to get up with Maggie tomorrow and convince her to take Sally out again since her saddle won't be usable on Shawny."

"Jordan is that you?"

Jordan turned to look at the door leading to the living room as she heard her name called out. "In here…in the kitchen."

"Hey, you'll ruin your dinner," Maggie scolded as she caught Jordan taking a large bite of the luscious morsel.

"No chance of that happening, I'm famished."

Maggie approached Jordan and tried to wrap her arms around her waist. Jordan took a step back. "Whoa. I'm dirty and sweaty from working in the field."

Maggie crossed her arms. "Well then, get in the shower. Dinner will be ready soon."

Jordan saluted her while clicking her heels. "Yes ma'am." She kissed Maggie on the cheek. "I'll be back shortly."

In her bedroom, Jordan stripped off her dirty clothes and threw them into the hamper. She then reached behind the shower curtain and turned on the water. She stood in front of the vanity and removed her watch as the temperature of the water normalized. Once in the shower, Jordan relished the pulsating warm liquid. She basked in the feel of the needle-like spray as it massaged muscles worn sore by what seemed like endless shoveling. Remembering she needed to cleanse off the sweat and grime, she lathered and rinsed to revitalization.

Jordan remained under the spray for a long time with her eyes closed and her hands braced on the sides of the shower as the water rinsed the soap from her hair. Suddenly she felt a presence behind her. She willed her eyes to remain closed as she felt hands slide across her hips and abdomen while a soft, supple body molded itself against her from behind. One hand slipped downward, coming to rest in the curly patch below her navel while the other hand pressed firmly on her abdomen.

Jordan allowed her forehead to contact the shower wall as Maggie's fingers slipped between her folds. She moaned loudly.

Oh my God, I can feel it. I can actually feel it. Was it because I filled the well? Just enjoy it, Lewis. Shut up and enjoy it.

* * *

"Jordan! Jordan, get your ass out of bed."

"What the hell?" Jordan exclaimed as she quickly sat up in bed and saw an old woman standing in her bedroom doorway.

"Go after her, now. Quickly, or you'll lose her forever. This is your last chance."

"Who are you, old woman?" Jordan demanded as she scrambled out of bed and pulled her jeans and boots on as fast as she could.

"Never mind who I am. Just hurry. For God's sake, please hurry. You know what's at stake here. She just rode off. You have very little time." The old woman scurried out of the way as quickly as she could to avoid making bodily contact with Jordan as she ran past her.

Without stopping, Jordan grabbed her canvas barn jacket from the hook by the kitchen door and ran the distance between the house and barn. She flung the door open and went directly to the pile of tack being held for repair and realized Maggie's saddle was no longer there.

Oh no! Maggie, please don't tell me you are using the defective saddle.

Jordan desperately searched several empty stalls until she came across one containing a magnificent mustang steed. She talked soothingly to the animal as she first threw a blanket and then a saddle over the horse's back.

"Come on, big guy. We've got a job to do."

Minutes later, she led the horse out of the stall and climbed into the saddle. With a quick jab to the horse's ribs, she was on her way in a full gallop across the snowy fields, heading for the western edge of the property bounded by Lake Champlain.

Jordan anguished over how long it was taking to cover the distance between the house and the lake. In her desperation, she was oblivious to the biting cold that chafed her cheeks while she rode. Nearly a half hour later, the frozen lake came into view. The sight encouraged Jordan to dig in her heels and push her steed nearly beyond his limits as their speed increased and she felt airborne.

Maggie, please stay away from the edge. Please. I'm coming, my love, I'm coming. Please let me reach you in time.

Jordan pushed her mount as hard as she could and almost gave up hope until she spotted Maggie on the horizon, galloping freely across the plains, directly toward the edge of the cliffs.

"Maggie," she screamed. "Maggie, stop."

Jordan's screams were ineffective. The distance between

them and the sound of the crashing surf below the cliffs drowned out any chance that Maggie would hear her.

Jordan silently asked her horse for forgiveness as she dug her heels in once more in an attempt to get just a little more speed out of the animal. Her efforts paid off as she began to close the distance between them. Again, she attempted to call out to Maggie, and again, her efforts were for naught. Finally, when she had closed the distance to within thirty feet, she heard a shot ring out. Maggie's horse suddenly reared up very close to the edge of the cliff.

Maggie stood in the saddle in an obvious attempt to steady herself and calm the animal as it continued to rear up.

"Maggie," Jordan shouted once more. She was now only twenty feet from Maggie.

Maggie looked up and saw Jordan just as she lost her footing and began to tumble off the horse.

"No," Jordan screamed. She leaned as far as she dared out of her saddle, reaching for anything she could cling to. Just as her fingers made contact with the collar of Maggie's jacket, she felt the now-familiar tingling in her body as though every muscle had fallen asleep and was now awakening. She realized immediately what was happening. "Kale. No. Not now. For heaven's sake, not now," she screamed.

Jordan held on to the collar of Maggie's jacket with all her might as she fought the transfer. "Kale, please...not now," she shouted as the grasp she had on the saddle-horn barely kept her from falling off the horse and over the cliff with Maggie.

Don't drop her, Jordan, she said to herself. *If you let go, she will die and you will be sucked back to the future without her. Kale can only retrieve what he has sent. As long as you hold on to her, he won't be able to retrieve you.*

"I've got you. I've got you," Jordan said. Maggie's feet skid across the ground as Jordan half-carried, half-dragged her away from the cliff.

Jordan dropped Maggie to the ground only when the last residual of the transfer process faded away. She scampered off her horse and ran to Maggie, dropping to her knees on the ground beside her.

"Maggie. Maggie, you're safe," Jordan cried as she gathered Maggie into her arms and held her close. "Thank God, I got here before it was too late. I couldn't live through that one more time."

Maggie clung to Jordan like there was no tomorrow. She was crying uncontrollably.

"It's okay, Mags. I've got you," Jordan whispered while failing miserably to hold back her own tears. Jordan could feel Maggie trembling in her arms and drew her in closer. "Let it go, sweetheart. You're safe now."

For the next several minutes, Jordan held Maggie in her arms and rocked back and forth, cooing assurances that she was safe and that everything would be okay. Soon, the trembling subsided and Maggie began to relax.

"Are you okay?" Jordan asked as she tucked a lock of red hair behind Maggie's ear.

Maggie nodded. "I could have died. Thank God you reached me in time."

Unable to keep the tearful timbre from her voice, Jordan choked back a tear and said, "Yes. I couldn't live with myself if I screwed that up again."

Maggie frowned. "What do you mean?"

Jordan took Maggie into her arms again and hugged her tight. "I haven't been totally honest with you, Maggie. I have so much to tell you, but it's so far off the wall, I don't know where to start. Just know that you're safe for now and I'll do my best never to let anything happen to you again."

"What happened here today, Jordan?"

"You were destined to die, Maggie. You were supposed to fall over the cliff to your death. Thank God I reached you in time."

"How is it you know that? You're scaring me."

"Let's just say I had a little help from a couple of friends. Like I said, I have a lot to tell you, but right now, we need to get back to the farm. I have an issue to deal with that can't wait."

"Issue? What issue?"

"I'm not ready to disclose that yet. I need to verify a few things first."

Maggie frowned. "Jordan, you're talking in riddles. I demand to know what's going on here—now!"

Jordan took Maggie's hands and held them close to her heart. "I promise I'll tell you everything as soon as I've had a chance to confirm my suspicions, but right now, I need to get you home. You're still trembling from shock." Jordan climbed to her feet and extended her hand to Maggie. "Come on, let's head back."

Maggie accepted Jordan's hand up. "Shawny?" Maggie said while looking around for her horse.

"Shawny is fine. He's gone back to the barn. I'm sure John will take care of him. We'll have to ride double on my horse."

Jordan helped Maggie into the saddle then swung herself up behind her. She reached around Maggie and grasped the saddle horn in front of her while grabbing the reins with the other hand. Maggie wrapped her arms around Jordan's and held on tightly. Before heading back to the farm, Jordan directed her mount to the spot where Maggie's horse reared, and noticed a brightly colored bag near the edge of the cliff. "Did this draw you to the edge of the cliff, Maggie?" Jordan asked softly.

Maggie nodded. "It was so out of place here on the snow-covered ground. I wanted to see what it was, but then I heard the gun shot and Shawny reared. It must have scared him."

"That's just what I thought. Come on, let's go home."

* * *

Jordan saw Jan walking toward the barn as she and Maggie approached the barnyard. "Hold on Maggie," Jordan said as she kicked her heels into her horse's side and prompted the animal into a gallop. Jordan could see the surprise on Jan's face as the sound of the horse's hooves speeding toward her drew her attention. Jan beat a hasty retreat across the yard and into the barn.

"Jordan, what are you doing?" Maggie complained as she held on tighter.

"Taking care of business," Jordan replied as she reined the horse into a quick stop in front of the barn door. "Stay right here," she said as she threw her leg over the side of the horse and dismounted, then ran into the barn.

"Jan, you're a dead woman," Jordan screamed as she ran into the barn and tackled Jan inside one of the stalls. Jan managed to break free and grabbed a whip from a hook inside the stall.

"Stay back, Lewis, or I swear I'll use this," Jan said.

"Like fuck I will," Jordan said as she lunged at Jan.

Jan swung the whip around and struck Jordan on the arm. Seemingly unfazed, Jordan grabbed the end of the whip and pulled Jan toward her. She hauled back and landed a punch squarely on Jan's jaw, sending her tumbling into the soiled straw inside the stall. She grabbed Jan by the neck and pulled her to her feet then slammed her against the side of the stall, her face a mere hair's breadth away from Jan's.

"You failed this time, asshole," she said.

"I…I don't know what you mean," Jan said, barely able to breathe. "I've been right here at the farm all day."

"You know damned well what I mean," Jordan hissed.

Jan struggled against Jordan's superior strength. "You're choking me. I can't breathe."

"Jordan, let go of her," Maggie said, suddenly appearing behind them.

Jordan glanced over her shoulder. "She tried to kill you, Maggie."

"You don't know that, Jordan."

Jordan kept her hate-filled eyes trained on Jan. "I do know that." She looked at Jan. "And you do too, don't you, you piece of shit. Only you didn't count on me being there to save her, did you? Well guess what, asshole, thanks to Kale and Andi, I made it this time. I've be on to you for quite a while now, only I wasn't able to get the timing right until today."

"Jordan, I said, let her go," Maggie insisted again. "You have no proof Jan had anything to do with this."

"Like hell I don't. I have years of proof, Maggie. I have the letter from the lawyer, I have repeated trips trying to save you from falling over the cliff, each time failing and having to live through your death over and over again…and I have your diaries."

Maggie took a step back. "You have my diaries? Jordan, my diaries were buried between the walls of the bedroom years ago."

"Let go of me," Jan rasped once more.

Jordan tightened her grip on Jan's neck and growled into her face. "You are one lucky piece of shit. I'd kill you right now if it wasn't for Maggie. I swear you won't get away with this." Jordan released Jan and watched her sink to the ground as she gasped for breath. Jordan turned to Maggie and reached out to touch her.

"No. Don't touch me," Maggie took another step back. "Who are you Jordan? I don't even know you," she said as she turned her back and walked out of the barn.

During Jordan's confrontation with Maggie, Jan picked herself up from the ground and brushed the hay from her jeans. She picked her hat up and planted it squarely on her head. "Looks like both of us are out," she said.

Jordan turned toward Jan and pointed in her face. "I know what happened to Maggie today was no accident. I know that you cut the strap on her stirrup. I saw you do it. I am aware that you placed that bag on the edge of the cliff, knowing she would go to investigate it, and I am aware that you are the one who fired the shotgun and made Shawny rear just as she was close enough to the cliff to fall over. I lived it over and over, each time just seconds too late to save her from falling–except for today that is. Kale and Andi managed to send me here just in time to save her. Do you have any idea what it was like to lose someone you love more than life itself?" Jordan's body shook with rage.

"You are fucking crazy, Lewis," Jan spat out.

"Call me what you'd like, but I can prove all of it beyond the shadow of a doubt. The only thing I need to do is convince Maggie, and once Maggie is convinced, we'll go to the police."

"You do know this farm is in my name," Jan said.

"What I know is that you coerced Maggie's father into adding your name to the deed then kept the lawyer's letter from her when it came in the mail so she wouldn't find out what you did. Oh, and by the way, I have the letter in my possession to prove it."

Jan frowned. "You had the audacity to go through my personal things?"

Jordan pushed her hard in the middle of her chest, nearly sending her to the ground again. "And you had the balls to try to kill Maggie so the property would default to you. I'm telling you, Safford, you are going down for attempted murder. That's a promise."

Jordan turned on her heel and walked half way to the door before stopping to address Jan once more. "I don't own this place, so as much as I'd like to, I can't fire your ass, but know this—I will be watching you like a hawk and if you give me any reason to believe Maggie is in danger again, I will kill you with my bare hands. You got that?"

CHAPTER 11

"Maggie, Maggie, please open the door," Jordan said as she stood in the hall outside their bedroom. "I can explain everything."

"Go away, Jordan."

"Like hell, I will. You owe it to me to listen to what I have to say. I've been through hell to get to this point and I'll be damned if I'm just going to walk away from you now."

The door swung open suddenly. "*You've* been through hell? What about me? I was the one who almost died out there today."

"Will you just listen to me, please?"

Maggie crossed her arms over her chest. "Okay, you have five minutes."

"Maggie, I know this is going to sound insane, but over the past several months, I have lived through today several times. I've traveled my way to you over and over again, yet you died before I could reach you. Do you have any idea how that has ripped me apart inside? Losing you was the most agonizing thing I have ever lived through. Losing you again and again was nearly unbearable. I was so afraid I would be too late again."

Maggie stared at her like she had a third eye in the middle of her forehead. "You're right, it's insane. How the hell does someone die multiple times? And who are you to blame poor Jan for all of this? Hell, she wasn't even out there with us this morning."

"Poor Jan? Seriously? Maggie, she's been plotting your demise for months now. She talked your father into putting her name on the deed to the farm. I'm telling you, she staged that accident this morning so you would fall over the cliff and die, conveniently leaving the farm to her."

"That's bullshit, Jordan. What is wrong with you? I specifically told Daddy I didn't need her name on the deed. I called and asked him to take her name off. You were there when I made the call."

"Yes, but unless you told her, Jan doesn't realize you did that. She still thinks the farm is in both your names."

"Jordan, I'm done talking about this." Maggie walked past Jordan, through the living room and into the kitchen. Jordan followed close behind. Maggie grabbed her jacket from the hook by the back door.

"Where are you going?" Jordan asked.

"I'm going to talk to Jan myself," Maggie replied.

"Then I'm going with you. I don't trust her."

Maggie turned around and pushed Jordan backward. "Listen to yourself. Do you know how crazy you sound?"

"I love you, Maggie. Call me crazy if you'd like, but I will do everything in my power to keep you safe. I can't lose you again. I just can't."

"There you go, talking in riddles again."

"Then let me explain."

"You'll get your chance, but first, I want to talk to Jan…alone."

* * *

Jordan went directly to the barn to see if Jan was still in the stall, while Maggie made her way across the yard to be bunk house. Jordan found the stall empty and began searching the rest of the barn when John entered.

"John, have you seen Jan?"

"Sure did. She left about twenty minutes ago. She said she's had enough of the bullshit around here, pardon my French, and she was fixing to head out."

"She left? Like in permanently gone?" Jordan asked, relief flooding her chest.

"It appeared so. She left with a duffle bag slung across her shoulder. I assume she had her clothes in it."

"Well, I'll be."

"Good riddance, I say. I didn't much like her anyway. Like

I've said before, when Maggie would leave for a few days, she'd strut around like she owned the place, bossing everyone around and pretty much making life miserable. Good riddance, I say."

"Did she say where she was going?" Jordan asked.

"No. She just said she needed to leave before the shit hit the fan. I can't say it enough. Good riddance."

"I can't say that I disagree with you, John."

Jordan entered a stall containing a large black mustang and began saddling the animal.

"Going somewhere, Jordan?" John asked.

"I'm going to take a ride out to the lake for a bit. If Maggie asks, you can tell her that's where I've gone and that I'll be back soon. But first, I need a new bit for my horse," Jordan said as she went to the tack room.

Once inside the tack room, Jordan opened the panel in the floor beneath the workbench and retrieved the bottle that was inside the cubby. She removed the cork and slipped a piece of paper inside the bottle, re-corked it, then put it back in the cubby.

Dear Kale and Andi. Just a quick note to let you know I made it on time. I was able to save Maggie. Thank you for all of your help. I love you guys.

Jordan left the tack room and retrieved her horse then rode it out of the barn and headed at a full gallop toward the lake.

* * *

Maggie knocked on the bunkhouse door and waited for a reply. After a few minutes of silence, she knocked again. "Jan? Jan, its Maggie. Are you in there?"

When no reply came, Maggie opened the door and walked into the common area. It was neat and tidy.

"Jan?" she said once more as she crossed the room and opened the bedroom door. Again, she was met with an empty room.

"That's odd. It looks like no one is living in here," Maggie said under her breath. She began rummaging around in the dresser and found all of the drawers empty, as was the closet. The adjoining bathroom was also void of all sign of habitation.

"What's going on here?" she said as she went back into the bedroom. It was then that she noticed the note on the pillow. Maggie crossed the room and picked it up.

Dear Maggie,

I don't know what Jordan has told you, but it's all lies. Regardless of what she says, I love you and I would never do anything to hurt you. It's not my fault that your father put my name on the deed. I didn't ask him to do it. He insisted.

Anyway, I wanted to warn you about Jordan. She seems unstable to me. She told me some nonsense about you dying over and over again. I think she's in cahoots with someone named Kale. She also mentioned the name, Andy. I don't know who these guys are, but it makes me suspicious about why she appeared at the farm all of the sudden a five or six months ago. She said something about Kale and Andy sending her here. It sounds like she has an ulterior motive to me. I mean, what do you really know about her? If you fear anyone, it should be her, not me.

I am also writing this letter to say goodbye. I am obviously in the way here. Despite Jordan's odd behavior, I can see how you feel about her and I don't want to stand in the way of your happiness, if that's even possible with Jordan. For some reason, she has it in her head that I want to kill you. I can't imagine why she would think that. Be careful around her, Maggie.

I will miss you and I will miss the farm, especially the horses. Think of me fondly.

I will always love you.

Jan.

"I can't believe she's gone," Maggie said as she folded the letter and slipped it into her back pocket

* * *

Jordan rode her horse to the edge of the cliff where Maggie had nearly fallen to her death earlier that morning. She dismounted and allowed her mount to graze while she found the worn path at the edge of the cliff that led to the rocks below.

Jordan made her way down the trail and walked cautiously among the large boulders and rocks that littered the edge of the lake, scanning the ground in front of her as she walked. It wasn't long before she found what she was looking for.

"There it is," she said as she bent over and picked up a spent shotgun cartridge. She looked at the end of the shell. "Ten gauge. That would have made a pretty loud noise."

She held the shell to her nose and noticed the smell of gunpowder was relatively strong, indicating it had been fired recently and the lingering odor had not yet had a chance to dissipate. Jordan slipped the shell into her pocket and looked around wondering where Jan would have stood as she watched Maggie fall to her death.

She must have ridden back to the farm like a bat out of hell as soon as she fired the shot. Maggie and I sat here on the ground for what seemed like an eternity, holding each other like there was no tomorrow. She had plenty of time to make it back before us, and to make it seem like she had been there all along.

Jordan turned to head back up the trail and suddenly became lightheaded. She had to sit on the closest boulder to prevent herself from passing out. She grabbed her head with both hands as a searing pain shot through her temples. A vision passed through her mind.

Jordan reached Maggie at the bottom of the cliff and knelt by her side. She took special care not to move her to avoid further injury to her neck or back. Instead, she gently brushed the curly locks from the woman's brow and placed her hands on both sides of Maggie's face. She leaned forward so that she was but a hair's breadth away.

"Maggie, Maggie, I'm here. Hold on my love. Please don't leave me. The stable hand will find your horse. Help will be here soon. Please hold on."

Maggie's green eyes fluttered open.

Jordan gasped and fought back the sobs as renewed hope filled her heart. She reached down, took Maggie's hand in her own, and brought the bloodied fingers to her lips to kiss them tenderly. Jordan's eyes never left Maggie's.

Maggie smiled as she fought to keep her eyes open. "Jordan," she rasped as the warmth of her breath created puffs in the cold March air.

Jordan leaned down so she could more clearly hear what Maggie was saying. "I am here, my love."

Maggie took a ragged breath and her brow furrowed in pain, but her eyes remained locked with those of the woman above her. "Jordan, I love you. I always have...through all time."

Jordan's throat was nearly closed with emotion as she held back a sob. "I love you too, Maggie. I always will. Please don't leave me. I need you, my love. Please don't leave me."

Tears cascaded from Jordan's eyes and fell onto Maggie's cheeks as she lowered her face to tenderly kiss her lips. As she raised her head, she watched the life ebb from Maggie's beautiful green eyes. Still holding Maggie's hand, Jordan sat back onto her knees. Her head fell back as a long painful wail escaped her.

"Oh, my God," Jordan said as the vision faded. "Was I here the last time Maggie died? It was so real."

Jordan stood and tested her balance. Satisfied that her lightheadedness had passed, she climbed the trail to the top of the cliff, mounted her horse and headed back to the farm.

CHAPTER 12

Back at the farm, Jordan took care of her horse then slipped into the tack room to see if Kale had gotten her message. It was still there. Kale and Andi had obviously not seen it.

She climbed out from under the work bench and paced back and forth, holding the bottle and trying to figure out why her message was still there. She thought back to what happened earlier that morning. An old woman had barged into her bedroom, demanding she get out of bed and go after Maggie before it was too late. The old woman looked familiar.

She stopped in her tracks.

Oh my God. Was that old woman me? she wondered. *Andi warned me about possible aging effects with time travel.*

Jordan resumed pacing as she sorted out her thoughts. *I saw a vision of Maggie dying in my arms this morning. Was I supposed to fail again on this trip back? Could it be the vision I had was the older Jordan's memory of my failing on this trip? Did the older Jordan came back yet a fourth time to make sure I got out of the house early enough to save her this time?*

Jordan looked at the bottle in her hand once more.

When I had Maggie by the collar and felt Kale trying to retrieve me, was it really me he was retrieving, or was it the old woman? Kale probably doesn't realize the younger version of me is still here. If not, he may never have a reason to check the communication cubby again and I will never be able to go back.

* * *

Maggie was waiting in the house for Jordan when she returned from her ride to the lake.

"Jordan, we need to talk," Maggie said when Jordan entered the kitchen.

"Yes, we do," Jordan replied.

"Jan is gone."

"I know. John told me. He saw her leave within an hour of us getting back this morning."

"You shouldn't have been so mean to her, Jordan."

Jordan raised her eyebrows. "She tried to kill you, Maggie, and if I hadn't made it on time, she would have succeeded. I for one am glad her sorry ass is gone. At least now I don't have to worry about her hurting you again."

Several moments of silence passed between them, until Maggie spoke again.

"Jordan, I want you to be honest with me."

"I'm always honest with you, Maggie."

"I want to know who Kale and Andi *really* are."

"I've told you about them already. Kale and Andi are my family," she said.

"Do they live around here?"

"They live closer than you think. At least Kale does."

"Is Kale your brother?"

"He's about as close to a brother as a person can be without actually being related. I love him very much, and Andi too."

"I want to know who they really are, Jordan, and what role they *really* play in your life."

Jordan crossed her arms over her chest. "Why the twenty questions, Maggie?"

"It's occurred to me that I don't know anything about you. All I know is that you came into my life and turned my world upside down. You seem to know your way around this farm like you've been here before, yet I have lived here all my life and I only met you for the first time when you showed up here looking for a job six months ago.

"You are evasive about where you come from, you have this electronic device installed in your back that you claim has the power to cure paralysis and based on your handling of the farmhand who fell from the rafters while building the new barn this past fall, you have some type of medical background. And now, you're spewing all this craziness about me dying several times and your failed attempts to save me...at least until this morning, that is," Maggie explained, the timbre of her voice raising with each sentence. "That's why the twenty questions, Jordan. Now I deserve an explanation."

* * *

Jordan knelt in front of the fireplace and cleaned out the ashes before building a teepee with kindling wood and setting fire to a pile of crumpled newspaper stuffed in the center of them. She watched the fire grow in strength as the kindling caught and the fire spread, all the while, contemplating what she was going to say to Maggie.

Damn, this is hard. Where should I begin? She's going to think I'm insane. I guess I would too if I were in her shoes.

Jordan's attention was drawn to the kitchen door as it opened and Maggie entered the living room carrying two tall glasses of iced tea. She handed one to Jordan, then sat on the couch.

"Thank you," Jordan said as she sipped her tea then put the glass down on the hearth. She added two larger pieces of firewood to the kindling before collecting her glass again and standing in front of the fire. She faced Maggie.

"Where should I start?" she asked. "Is there anything in particular you want to know first?"

"Why don't you start with telling me about yourself. Who are you, Jordan? Where do you come from? Did you target me specifically, or was I just the lucky winner in your quest to find work?" Maggie asked, a tinge of bitterness in her voice.

Jordan stared for a long time at the ice cubes floating around inside her iced tea, trying to come up with the best way to answer Maggie. Finally, she cleared her throat. "Who am I? I am Jordan Marie Lewis, Doctor Jordan Marie Lewis...."

"I knew it," Maggie whispered out loud.

Jordan continued. "Like I said, I am Jordan Marie Lewis and I grew up at 1029 Pheasant Hill Road, Shelburne, Vermont."

Maggie leaned forward sharply. "That's not possible, Jordan. This farm is located at 1029 Pheasant Hill Road,

Shelburne, Vermont. If you had grown up here, I most certainly would have run into you once or twice over the past thirty years, don't you think?" she asked sarcastically.

Jordan waited patiently for Maggie to finish before she continued. "I was born on September twentieth in the year 2073."

Maggie jumped to her feet. "No fucking way! Jordan, 2073 is fifty-four years from now."

"I know."

Maggie began to pace. "Jan was right. You *are* unstable."

Jordan stopped Maggie by grabbing her arm. "Jan said that?"

"Yes. She left this letter in her room for me to find." Maggie fished Jan's letter out of her pocket and handed it to Jordan. She waited patiently while watching the expression on Jordan's face change from anger to resignation as she read the letter.

Jordan handed the letter back to Maggie. "I suppose you believe her?" she asked.

"At this point Jan sounds far saner than you do. How the hell could you be here right now if you won't even be born for another fifty-four years? It's not possible, Jordan. It's just not possible."

"If you give me a chance to explain without interrupting me, I'll tell you how it's possible."

Maggie sat down again and nodded. "Fair enough. Please continue."

"Like I said, I was born on September twentieth in the year 2073, at the University of Vermont Medical Center in Burlington. My parents bought this farm two years before I was born."

"Your parents bought my farm in 2071?" Maggie said, disbelief weighing heavily in her voice.

"I searched the Shelburne, Vermont town records and discovered the farm was owned by Gary and Sharon Downs from 1985 until 2019. I assume they were your parents. Then a woman named Janneal Safford owned it from 2019 until 2031. It was purchased next by Leland and Marion McKenzie who owned it until 2048 when the deed was transferred to Carl and Rachel McKenzie, most probably their son. Carl and Rachel sold the farm to my parents in 2071. I was born two years later. When my parents died, the deed passed to me."

"The land records actually say Jan owned my property? I don't believe it," Maggie said.

Jordan picked up the newspaper that was sitting on the coffee table in front of Maggie and tossed it into her lap. Look at the date, Maggie. What year is it?"

"2019."

"Yes, 2019. The land records indicated Jan obtained ownership of this farm in 2019. Tell me, Maggie, if I hadn't made it to you in time this morning, what would have happened?"

Maggie looked up from the paper, bewildered. "I…I would have died."

"Yes, you would have died and ownership of the farm would have gone to Jan, just like the letter from the lawyer said it would. Remember the letter I found in Jan's nightstand indicating your father added her name to the deed?"

Maggie picked up the letter. "I admit the fact you found this is Jan's room is suspicious, but I called Daddy and took care of this problem."

"Yes you did, but only because I made you aware of the letter. If I had never appeared on the scene and brought that letter to your attention, you would have never known and Jan would have inherited the farm when you fell to your death this morning."

Maggie fell silent while Jordan collected her thoughts. "So where was I? Oh, yes, when my parents were killed in an auto accident two years ago, which was in 2103 by the way, ownership of the farm passed to me. Kale moved in with me shortly thereafter and in fact, he still lives here today."

Maggie stood and began to pace once more. "Jordan, you are freaking me out here."

Jordan watched Maggie process the information she had given her.

Maggie stopped in front of her. "Okay, let's assume what

you say is true. How is it you are here, standing in front of me when you haven't even been born yet?"

"I have Kale and Andi to thank for that, but before I get into any detail about *how* I got here, let me give you a little background about *why* I'm here," Jordan offered.

"Okay. I'll bite. Why are you here, Jordan?"

"I'm here because you summoned me."

CHAPTER 13

"I summoned you?" Maggie asked skeptically.

"Yes. You haunted my dreams for several years in fact," Jordan replied. "Only, I didn't realize it was you until I found your diaries."

Maggie rubbed both temples with her fingertips. "This is sounding more and more insane by the minute."

Jordan reached out to rub Maggie's back. "Are you okay?"

Maggie flinched under Jordan's touch and moved a few feet away. "I'm fine. A little overwhelmed maybe, but fine. I just don't know what to believe."

Jordan inhaled deeply and tried not to show Maggie how much her reaction hurt. "I'm getting ahead of myself again. Let me start with my childhood on the farm."

Maggie sat down once more and picked her iced tea up from the table beside the couch.

"Not too long after I got here the third time—" Jordan said before Maggie interrupted her yet again.

"Third time? I don't remember you showing up here multiple times."

"I carried memories of the failed attempts, but for you, every time was the first time. The first time, my implant failed and I was completely immobile when I landed, so I went back immediately. The second time, we were way off and I appeared just moments before Shawny came back from the pasture without you. You were already dead. The third time put me here several months before your death."

"I really wish you'd stop saying that. A person can only die once. According to you, I've died, what...three or four times, yet I'm sitting here talking to you right now. Give me a break, Jordan."

Jordan lowered her chin to her chest and sighed. "Maybe

we should just drop it for now," Jordan suggested.

Maggie put her drink on the coffee table in front of her. "I'm sorry if I sound skeptical, but you have to admit this story of yours is a bit off the wall."

"I asked you to give me a chance to explain. I'm being totally honest with you about everything, Maggie. Yes, I know it all seems too incredible to be true, but it is. I've lived it."

Maggie sat back on the couch. "Okay. Please go on. I'll try to keep an open mind."

"Thank you. Like I was saying, not long after I got here, you noticed the scar on my back and I've kind of explained how it happened already, but let me put things into context for you. When I was growing up on the farm…this farm, we had several horses, mustangs in fact, just like you have. I pretty much grew up on the backs of horses. There wasn't a horse I couldn't ride. Even the feisty ones were no real challenge. When I was fifteen, one of our mares gave birth to a beautiful foal that I named Sally after an old song my parents loved called 'Mustang Sally.' I loved that horse and quickly became her human."

"One day, when I was sixteen, Sally and I went for a ride into the north pasture. I totally lost track of time and before I knew it, dusk was falling, so I climbed onto Sally's back and kicked her into high gear. She ran so fast, I felt like we were flying. It was an amazing feeling…that is, until she stepped into an old rotted well. We both went down. She threw me over her head and I landed at an odd angle. My back was broken at the L1 vertebrae, just below the small of my back. My spinal cord was completely severed. Unfortunately, Sally didn't make it. I think that hurt more than my own injuries. I was in a hover-chair until I was thirty."

Maggie frowned. "The well in the north pasture? Jordan, is that why you insisted on having it re-drilled closer to the barn? Is that the well you fell into?"

"Yes. Filling that well back in was the most cathartic thing I have done since I've been here. I suppose I created quite a few paradoxes by doing that. It is quite possibly one of the reasons I have restored feelings in my legs today. Anyway, I'm off on a tangent again. Where was I? Oh yes, I was sixteen when the accident happened. I was in the hospital for several months, but when I got home, I started having this recurrent dream where I re-lived the accident over and over again. The dreams stopped when I left for college, but the moment I moved home after my parent's death, they started up again. They didn't come every night, but they occurred on a pretty regular basis. There were several times Kale would wake me because I disturbed him by screaming or calling out in my sleep."

"Was Kale your boyfriend?" Maggie asked.

Jordan chuckled. "Hell no, not that he didn't try to convert me to men once or twice. As I've already said, Kale is like a brother to me. I met him when we were both assigned to the spinal implant project. He needed a place to live and I had an extra bedroom. He's been with me every since."

"So, you're a doctor? I kind of thought you knew something about medicine, judging how you stabilized that construction worker who fell from the rafter."

"I'm not actually a certified medical doctor although I did attend medical school as part of my degree field. I'm a research scientist with a PhD in the field of kinesiology and spinal cord injuries. Anyway, once again, I digress. As I said, Kale and I were both assigned to a research project at the University of Vermont Spinal Institute on the development of a spinal implant designed to restore mobility to victims of severed spinal cords. Being a victim myself, I volunteered to be the test subject. They almost didn't accept me because by then, my injury was fourteen years old, but in the end, they gave in."

"I'll never forget the day I saw the scar on your back, Jordan. Do you remember? You had just gotten out of the shower and answered the door of the bunkhouse wearing just a towel that drooped in the back. When you opened the door, my body reacted to you viscerally, but when you turned around, it kind of freaked me out to see such a large pronounced scar, and even more so when you explained that you were really a paraplegic. I should have pressed you harder for more details then. Maybe we wouldn't be here having this discussion now if I had," Maggie said.

"What I remember about that day, Maggie, is holding my

breath when you ran your finger down the length of the scar on my back. My heart was bursting at the seams with desire for you, but then you became extremely alarmed and upset when you hand encountered the battery pack under my skin. In my entire life, I never felt more like a freak than I did that day."

"I'm sorry for reacting that way, Jordan. It was just so unexpected."

"I know. Anyway, the implant I have right now is actually the second one we developed. The first one lasted for two years until one morning, Kale woke me for breakfast and my legs refused to support me when I tried to get out of bed. They had to remove the original implant and I ended up back in a hover-chair until the new one completed testing."

"So what has all of this got to do with me *summoning* you here? Whatever the hell *that* means," Maggie asked.

"Well, I had some down time while recovering from the removal of the first implant and I was feeling pretty depressed and angry about being stuck in a hover-chair again. I have to admit I wasn't very nice to Kale during that time."

"Wait…you've mentioned the word hover-chair a few times. Don't you mean wheelchair?" Maggie asked.

"Yes and no. A hover-chair serves the same function as a wheelchair, but it floats on air rather than having wheels."

"No freaking way! It actually floats?"

"Yes, but essentially, it's the same thing as being in a wheelchair would be today."

"Jesus. This sounds like something out of a science fiction novel," Maggie said.

"In a way, it *is* like science fiction. Technology makes some pretty incredible leaps and bounds over the next few decades. But again, I digress…after the fourth or fifth time I blew up at Kale, he pretty much reamed me a new asshole and told me to stop feeling sorry for myself and suggested I do something to take my mind off my own self pity so, I decided to redecorate the house, starting with my own bedroom, which by the way, happens to be the same room you're in. That's how I found your diaries between the walls."

"No way. I don't believe you," Maggie said.

"I'm not lying to you, Maggie. I read your diaries over the next few weeks. I found myself falling in love with the young woman who wrote such impassioned words. Reading your diaries led me to do research on your life. That's when I discovered through the Burlington Free Press archives, that you died in a horse riding accident in 2019. Don't you see...we were both thrown from our horses, only I survived and you didn't. I convinced myself that the common thread of our accidents was the connection that led to my recurrent dream. I am convinced you were trying to reach me through that dream.

"The Burlington Free Press made a big deal about how you were an expert horsewoman. It made no sense to me how an accomplished horsewoman would simply fall from her horse to her death, unless there was something dark and sinister behind it."

"Isn't that a little far-fetched, Jordan? I admit it's a little freaky that we both had horse accidents–supposedly on the same farm, but it's not uncommon for accidents to happen on farms."

"What I haven't told you yet, Maggie is that the dreams became real. Until I found your diaries, the dreams were simply a replay of my accident with Sally. After I found the diaries, the nature of the dreams changed. There were several dreams that felt more real than dreamlike. For starters, you were in them. There were dreams in which you were a teenager and dreams with you as a young woman. There were even a few that were interactive.

"Do you remember writing in your diary about a girl named Jess who challenged your virtue right here in this very room and in this very spot by the fireplace? I think you were maybe twenty-two at the time and she was ridiculing you about still being a virgin?"

Maggie bolted to her feet. "You *did* read my diaries. I have never told anyone about that event...ever. I wrote it in my diary, but never told another living soul about it."

"Do you remember her trying to force herself on you when she suddenly got a cramp in her leg?"

Maggie stood there, her eyes wide with fear as she shook

her head yes.

"That was me, Maggie. I was there. I was in an actual wheelchair, but for some reason, I couldn't get it to move forward, so I climbed out of the chair and crawled over to you and Jess and dug my nail into her calf as hard as I could to get her to let go of you.

"Then there was another entry, I think when you were still in high school. You came home rip-roaring mad that someone named Amy Gokey called you a lesbo. You marched into your bedroom and threw yourself on the bed, right beside me and ranted that just because you weren't impressed with the grabby-feeling boys, and just because you liked to wear jeans and no makeup, that it didn't make you a lesbian. Do you remember that entry?"

Maggie hugged herself and looked around the room with a panicked look on her face. "That was the day I realized I was attracted to women. Jordan you're scaring me. How did you get my diaries?"

"I told you, I found them when I remodeled by bedroom, eighty four years from now. Maggie, I felt…and I still feel you were trying to reach me through those dreams. I don't know if it was the connection we have through our accidents, or maybe it's this house, but it was real and I became obsessed with you. Before long, I realized it wasn't obsession at all. I was falling in love with you. Imagine how I felt, falling in love with someone who died nearly one hundred years earlier.

"Kale was convinced I had gone off the deep end. He was concerned that if the Spinal Institute discovered what was going on in my head, that they would decide I was too unstable to be the recipient of the second implant."

"Jordan, this is just too far-fetched and incredible to believe. I mean, it's 2019 and you're standing here in front of me, yet you claim you were born in 2073. How is that even possible?"

"Kale made it possible. Kale and Andi. I will forever be in their debt. It's because of them that I am here today. It took four tries to get it right, but I finally made it in time to save you from falling over that cliff this morning."

"And exactly what did they do to deserve such praise, Jordan?"

"They sent me to you. They sent me back in time."

"Oh, for crying out loud. How stupid do you think I am? Time travel? Seriously?" Maggie exclaimed.

"I am being totally serious, Maggie. Why would I lie about something like that?"

"I don't know. Maybe you *do* have an ulterior motive, just like Jan implied."

"And what could that motive possibly be, huh? The farm? It'll be mine in another eighty-four years anyway. Maggie, I gave up everything to be here with you, including my best friends and a job that had the potential of helping millions of people. It was a huge risk that the implant could have been totally and permanently non-functional here, just like it was the first time I transferred, or it may have failed in some way *after* I arrived. That would have left me totally helpless and without a way to support myself. Hell, in this time in history, I don't even exist yet. I risked everything to get here in time to save you, Maggie."

Maggie stood in front of Jordan, her hands defiantly perched on her hips. "Prove to me that I was supposed to die today, Jordan. Prove it to me. Then maybe, just maybe, there's a chance that I'll believe you."

Jordan hung her head low and shook it side to side. "I can't prove it to you. The land records, your death certificate, the newspaper articles are all a part of the future. I didn't think to bring them with me. Hell, I'm not even sure they'd survive the transfer. All I have is knowledge, and the love I feel for you in my heart. I'm sorry that's not enough for you."

Jordan stood by the fireplace with her hands shoved into her pockets as Maggie sat silently on the couch. Finally, Jordan spoke. "Maybe I should go," she said.

"Maybe you should."

Jordan nodded, and with a heavy heart, left the room.

CHAPTER 14

Maggie sat on the couch and listened to the sounds of Jordan rummaging around in their bedroom, presumably collecting her things. The emotions going through her heart were a mixture of fear, remorse and regret. Part of her wanted to go to Jordan and beg her to stay. The other part of her was terrified that Jordan had just spun this terrific, convoluted and unimaginable lie about who she was and where she comes from. Jordan's tale was just too incredible to believe, yet there were parts of the story that Maggie couldn't deny.

What she said about my diaries was true. How could she have known about my encounter with Jess if she hadn't read about it? She must have stolen my diaries then repaired the wall. It's behind the dresser after all. I would never even know unless I moved the furniture.

Maggie made a quick decision. As soon as Jordan left, she would check for herself.

Moments later, Jordan came back into the room, carrying her duffle bag. "I guess this is goodbye," she said to Maggie.

Maggie avoided Jordan's eyes, lest she cave and change her mind. "Wait here for a minute," she said as she left the room, returning a few minutes later with a handful of cash.

Jordan backed up a few steps. "I don't want your money, Maggie."

Maggie handed the money forward. "It's not my money, it's yours. It's this week's wages. You've earned it. You're going to need it until you can get back on your feet."

Jordan took the money and shoved it into her front jeans pocket. "Thank you," she said softly. She picked up her duffle and slung it over her shoulder. "I should be going then."

Maggie just nodded, not trusting herself to say anything as she fought back remorseful tears. She stood rooted to the spot while Jordan walked past her and toward the front door. As soon as she heard the door close behind Jordan, she sank to the floor onto her knees and cried heart-wrenching tears. Several minutes later, the crying stopped as she knelt there on the floor, listening to the deafening silence around her.

* * *

Jordan allowed tears to cascade down her face as she walked the mile from Maggie's farmhouse to the main road. She had no idea where she would go, or what she would do, but she had to come up with a plan to win Maggie back. Her life was simply not worth living without her. Maggie was the whole reason she had left her future life behind and risked everything to traverse time to be with her.

By the time she reached the end of the drive, Jordan had her tears under control. She turned left onto the main road and began walking toward the town of Shelburne where she hoped to find lodging for the night.

A few hundred feet down the road, a pickup truck pulled off the road in front of her. As Jordan approached the side of the truck, the driver leaned out the window. "Do you need a ride?" the driver asked.

Jordan was wary about accepting rides from strangers, but this person appeared safe and unassuming. The driver was a woman, about her own age, wearing blue jeans, a flannel button up shirt and a cowboy hat. She had long dark hair, pulled into the pony tail at the nape of her neck.

"Don't worry, I don't bite. I promise you're safe with me," the woman said. "Get in."

Jordan walked around the truck, opened the door and climbed into the front seat beside the woman. She extended her hand. "Jordan Lewis," she said.

"Glad to meet you, Jordan Lewis. My name is Gina Delarm. Where ya headed?"

Jordan looked down at her duffle bag she placed on the floor between her feet, then back at Gina. "That's a good question."

Gina put the truck in gear and pulled back onto the road. She drove the two miles into town then pulled into the parking lot of the general store. She shut off the engine and turned to face Jordan. "Wanna talk about it?" she said.

"I don't even know you," Jordan said.

"Sure you do. I'm Gina. Remember?" Gina grinned.

For some reason, Jordan felt comfortable with this woman. "Truth is, I have no place to go. I've been working for Maggie Downs for the past several months and we had a falling out and she asked me to leave."

"Well, Maggie's temper is going to get her into trouble one of these days. What did you do to piss her off?"

"You know Maggie?"

"I know her very well. My wife and I are good friends with her, although it's been a while since we've seen her. Her blood has always run a little hot. It's gotta be the red hair." Gina waited for Jordan to answer her question, but was greeted with silence. "So I'll ask again, what did you do to piss her off?"

Jordan's lip began to tremble. "Maggie almost died today."

"Are you shitting me? Really? How?"

"She took Shawny out for a run this morning and was attracted to a brightly colored bag that was on the ground near the edge of the cliff by the lake. Just as she got very near the edge, a shotgun went off and the horse was spooked into rearing up. She would have fallen over the cliff if I hadn't reached her in time and grabbed her at the last second."

Gina frowned. "Did you go on this ride with her?"

"No, she went on her own, but I managed to catch up to her in time to keep her from going over the cliff."

"How did you know she was in danger?"

Jordan sighed deeply and rested her head against the back of the seat. She wiped the tears from her eyes then turned her head sideways to look at Gina. "That is a very difficult question to answer. In fact, attempting to do just that is why she asked me to leave."

"You're in love with her, aren't you?" Gina asked.

Unable to find her voice through choked-back tears, Jordan just nodded her head.

Gina started the truck up again and backed out of her parking space.

"Where are we going?" Jordan asked.

"I'm taking you home with me. Something doesn't feel right about this and I intend to get to the bottom of it."

"I'm not so sure that's a good idea. If you'll just direct me to the nearest motel, I'll get out of your hair and be on my way."

"No, I don't think so. My gut tells me there's more here than meets the eye, and I always listen to my gut, and beside, you said yourself you had no place to go."

* * *

After about a ten-minute ride out of town, Gina turned the truck into a gravel driveway and pulled to a stop in front of a saltbox styled contemporary home.

"Sam? Sam, I'm home," Gina called as she exited the truck. "She's probably in the greenhouse," Gina said when Sam didn't answer. "Follow me."

Jordan grabbed her duffle bag. "I'm not so sure about this, Gina. Sam may not appreciate an unexpected guest."

"Don't you worry about Sam. If I told her about meeting you and then came home without you, she'd have my hide. Come on. You've got to see Sam's garden. It's amazing."

Gina took Jordan's arm and led her around the house to the back.

As they emerged into the back yard, Jordan was unprepared for the massive greenhouse that lay before her. She followed Gina from chilly March temperatures into the balmy greenhouse where there was every kind of vegetable imaginable laid out in neat, weed-free rows.

"Amazing is an understatement," Jordan said to Gina as she took in the expanse of the garden.

"Who do we have here?" Sam asked as she walked out from behind a dense group of cornstalks, revealing herself to Jordan. She had a basket of freshly picked vegetables hanging from one arm.

"Sam, this is Jordan. Jordan, my wife, Sam," Gina said.

Sam extended her hand. "Nice to meet you, Jordan."

Jordan was tongue-tied. Sam was one of the most stunning women Jordan had ever seen. She was about Jordan's height, slim, and with dark mocha skin and wildly curly black hair. Her dark brown eyes sparkled with merriment as her dimples deepened with her wide smile.

"My God, you're beautiful," Jordan said before blushing a bright crimson red. "Ah, I mean, nice to meet you too, Sam."

Sam threw her head back and laughed.

"Sam, Jordan has just come from Maggie's farm and she needs a place to stay for the night," Gina said.

Sam looked surprised. "Maggie's?" She looked at Jordan. "What did you do to piss her off?"

Jordan looked at Gina, who tried to hide her smile behind her hand. "I get the impression Maggie has somewhat of a reputation," Jordan said.

Sam put her hand on the small of Jordan's back and led her out of the greenhouse. "Don't get me wrong, we love Maggie like a sister, but she can be a bit of a hothead. Come, we can talk more in the house. You're just in time for dinner. I'm going to throw together a stir-fry with these wonderful vegetables."

* * *

"Great dinner, Sam," Jordan said as she finished the last bite on her plate.

"There's plenty more," Sam said.

Jordan held up her hand. "Thank you, but I'm stuffed."

"How about a beer?" Gina offered.

"Sure, that sounds great," Jordan replied.

"Can I get you a glass of wine, love?" Gina asked Sam.

Sam kissed Gina. "Why don't you and Jordan retire to the living room while I clean up the dishes, then I'll pour myself some wine and join you."

"Would you like some help with the dishes?" Jordan asked. "Maggie did all the cooking, so I was relegated to cleanup. I've gotten pretty good at it if you'd like help."

Sam watched Jordan's face as she spoke. "You're in love with her, aren't you?" she asked.

Jordan fell silent.

"No need to answer," Sam said. "I can see it on your face. Go. Enjoy your beer. I'll be with you in a few minutes."

Jordan accepted the beer from Gina and followed her into the living room.

"Have a seat," Gina said. Gina waited for Jordan to settle in on the couch before continuing. "So, how did you meet Maggie?"

"I went to the farm looking for work. No one answered the door at the house, so I went to the barn looking for someone in charge. I didn't find anyone there either, at least not right away, so I started exploring the barn. Soon, Maggie came in looking to saddle her horse and just as I approached her to introduce myself, I heard a loud crack over head and realized a heavy metal winch had broken the rafter. Quite by instinct, I tackled Maggie to the ground and the winch hit the floor of the barn right where she was standing."

"No shit? Wow, Maggie was lucky you were there," Gina said.

"I think I was the lucky one. I don't know if it was out of gratitude or not, but she hired me on as a farm hand that very afternoon. I've been working for her ever since."

"How long ago was that?"

"Six months."

"Well that explains why we haven't seen much of her of late," Sam said from the kitchen doorway. She sauntered across the living room, wine glass in hand, and snuggled in beside Gina on the couch. "Is Jan still around?" Sam asked.

Jordan frowned. "No, she isn't. In fact, she left today."

"That's one woman I won't miss," Gina said. "I didn't like how she tried to control Maggie. How did you manage to get rid of her?"

"She's the other reason we've haven't seen much of Maggie lately. That woman gets under my skin," Sam added.

"I think she was behind Maggie's accident this morning. I cornered her in the barn when we got back and let her know I was on to her. She left about an hour later," Jordan explained.

"You think she intentionally tried to kill Maggie? Why would she want to do that?" Gina asked.

"Wait a minute. Someone tried to kill Maggie this morning?" Sam said.

"Jordan seems to think so. Apparently, she was lured to the edge of the cliff by the lake and her horse was intentionally spooked so it would throw her from the saddle over the cliff. I guess Jan is the prime suspect," Gina explained.

"Is Maggie all right? Should we go pay her a visit?" Sam asked.

"Maggie is fine. I got to her in time to keep her from falling…just barely, I might add," Jordan said.

"So what makes you think Jan is behind it?" Gina asked again.

"Jan convinced Maggie's father to put her on the deed to the farm such that if Maggie died first, the farm would go to her. I think Jan set her up to fall off the cliff this morning. I also think Jan is the one that cut the rafter holding that winch several months ago," Jordan said.

Gina whistled. "Holy shit. It sounds like Maggie is lucky to have you around. So, why did she ask you to leave?"

"She learned that my appearance at her farm six months ago was not by chance. I had been trying to reach her for quite some time. I knew I had to get here in time to prevent her death. Understandably, that scared the shit out of her, and she asked me to leave."

Gina leaned forward. "You aren't some kind of stalker, are you, Jordan?" she asked in a firm voice.

"I came here to save her, not hurt her. I love her, Gina. I would die for her."

CHAPTER 15

Maggie pulled the dresser away from the wall and picked up the sledge hammer. After a few firm swings at the wall, she had a hole big enough to put her hands into and pulled several larger pieces of sheetrock away. She continued to enlarge the hole until she managed to remove the entire bottom of the four-by-eight sheet at least two feet up from the floor, exposing all four studs the sheetrock was nailed to. She knelt on the floor amid the dusty mess and inspected the area between the studs. There, still wrapped in cloth, were all six of her diaries, two between the first and second studs, two more between the second and third studs and the final two between the third and fourth studs. Notwithstanding the sheetrock debris, they were just as Maggie left them months earlier when she decided on a whim to turn them into a time capsule of sort. All six diaries were untouched.

Oh my God. She was telling the truth, Maggie thought. *They're all still here. She didn't steal them. Could she really be from the future?*

Maggie thought back to when she first met Jordan. She'd been in the barn one morning, getting ready to take Shawny out for a ride when all of the sudden, Jordan lunged at her from out of nowhere, tacking her to the dirt just before that metal winch fell from the rafters.

Maggie now found herself wondering if Jordan's presence in the barn was the coincidence Jordan tried to pass it off as. *Could she have been there intentionally? Could she have traveled through time and arrived just before the winch fell? Could she have known I was in danger? This sounds so insane.*

Over the next several weeks, she had spent more and more time with Jordan, and before long, she felt herself anticipate the sunrise each morning because it would mean seeing Jordan's smiling face at the breakfast table.

Then she saw the scar that ran from the middle of Jordan's back down to her buttocks and learned that she was a paraplegic.

If she is really from the future, it makes sense that the implant would seem beyond what is currently possible with today's medical technology.

"What was it that she said to me that day? *Maggie, there are things you don't know about me that I promise I will explain when the time is right,*" Maggie said out loud. "Is this time-travel business what she was trying to tell me about in her own covert way?"

As she knelt in front of the torn out wall, Maggie remembered the first time she made love to Jordan. Having been paralyzed since she was sixteen, Jordan had spent the previous fourteen years with no sensation in the lower half of her body, but with the help of the spinal implant she was slowly beginning to feel surges of desire deep within her core when Maggie would touch her in certain ways.

Maggie's eyes flew open as she recalled what Jordan had said in the middle of love making…

"I am so in love with you," Jordan confessed.

"Shh, don't say that. You barely know me," Maggie replied.

Jordan smiled. "I have known you for a hundred years, and I will love you for a hundred more."

"I have known you for a hundred years and I will love you for a hundred more," Maggie repeated out loud. "What did she mean by that? Was she talking about what she learned from my diaries? How can that be? How could Jordan have read my diaries if they are still buried here in the wall just as I left them? Could she be telling the truth?"

Maggie thought back over the past several months for other clues. She recalled brief comments made after making love in front of the fire one night.

"How is it that you so easily walked into my life and stole

my heart?" Maggie asked.

"Actually, I didn't walk into your life… I transported into it. You see, I'm really a scientist from the future and I traveled here via a time machine to intentionally invade your life," Jordan replied.

Maggie raised her head and looked directly into Jordan's eyes. She smiled widely. "You are such a kook sometimes."

Maggie sat back on her heels and covered her face with her hands. "It's been there all along. The clues, the hints. I've just been too blind to see it. I do love you, Jordan. I should have trusted you. What have I done, Jordan? What have I done?"

CHAPTER 16

Jordan repacked her duffle bag and slung it over her shoulder. She picked up her shoes and quietly padded through the house toward the front door where she sat down on a bench to put her shoes on. Just as she rose to her feet and reached for the door handle, she heard a noise behind her.

"Going somewhere?"

Jordan looked back to see Sam standing at the top of the stairs.

"I thought I'd head out early. I've got to figure out what to do next if I'm going to move forward with my life," Jordan said.

Sam reached her hand out toward Jordan. "I forbid you to leave before breakfast. Now put your bag down and come help me."

Sam led Jordan into the kitchen and pulled two mugs from the cupboard. "The coffee pods are next to the machine. Creamer is in the fridge. I drink mine black," she said.

Jordan inserted the first pod into the coffee maker and waited patiently as it brewed. "How long have you and Gina known Maggie?" Jordan asked as she handed the first cup to Sam.

Sam answered her as she gathered ingredients for omelets. "Gina has known her since grade school. They grew up together. I've only known her for about ten years. That's when I met Gina."

"Where did you two meet?"

"We met in college. We both attended Vermont Tech. Gina is a veterinarian and studied animal husbandry there. I studied agriculture."

"Hence your gardening skills," Jordan observed.

"Yes."

"Is Gina the vet for the area?"

"Are you asking if she takes care of Maggie's horses?"

Jordan blushed. "I'm that transparent, huh? Yeah, I guess that's just what I'm asking."

Sam leaned her hip against the cabinet and tilted her head to one side. "I get the feeling there's more to you than meets the eye, Jordan Lewis. I mean, the reason you sought Maggie out is a bit odd, and maybe even alarming, but I don't sense any danger in you."

"Otherwise Sam wouldn't be comfortable allowing you to stay in our home," Gina said from the doorway. "I've learned to trust Sam's instincts."

Sam smiled when she saw her wife. "Good morning, love. Coffee?" she asked.

Gina walked over to Sam and kissed her tenderly. "Yes, please."

"I've got it covered," Jordan said as she pulled another mug down from the cupboard and slipped a new pod into the machine.

"I caught Jordan trying to sneak out before breakfast," Sam said.

Gina raised her eyebrows at Jordan. "Big mistake, my friend. Sam doesn't let anyone leave here on an empty stomach. So, what are your plans from here?"

Jordan leaned her backside against the cabinet and crossed her legs at her ankles. "Truthfully, I don't know. I have a little money from my job on the farm, so I should be okay for a few weeks if I can find a relatively inexpensive place to live. I know what I'd *like* to do, but it will take considerable money to get it off the ground."

"What kind of skills do you have besides being a farm hand? Maybe we can put you in touch with potential employers," Gina offered.

Jordan debated with herself whether to be truthful with her new friends. She thought for a moment before answering. "I am a research scientist with a PhD in kinesiology and spinal cord injuries."

Gina nearly choked on her coffee. "Are you shitting me? A research scientist? Really?"

"Yes, really."

"Why would someone with your background want to be a farm hand, Jordan?" Sam asked as she slid the first omelet onto a plate.

"I needed to be close to Maggie. Besides, I grew up on a horse farm so I really do know my way around horses."

"Well, the University of Vermont has a program that's associated with the Medical Center. Maybe they could use another research scientist," Gina suggested.

"There's also Dartmouth-Hitchcock Hospital in Lebanon, New Hampshire. That's about a ninety-minute drive from here," Sam added. She slid the second omelet onto a plate and handed one each to Gina and Jordan. "Here, eat them while they're hot. Mine will be done in just a minute."

A few minutes later, all three women sat round the small table in the breakfast nook, enjoying their breakfast.

"So, Jordan, what is it you want to do that requires so much money?" Gina asked.

"I have knowledge and experience that no one else has in this day and age relative to treatments for spinal cord injuries. I'd like to open my own privately funded foundation to further those studies. I believe I can realize significant gains in restoring mobility for victims of spinal cord injuries in a relatively short amount of time."

"You're very sure of yourself, Jordan. Why such a high level of confidence?" Sam asked.

Jordan stood and turned her back to her friends. "Because of this," she said, pulling up her shirt to expose the scar on her back.

Sam stood and approached Jordan. "My God, Jordan, what happened to you?" she asked, running her index finger down the scar.

Jordan sighed. "Maggie had the same exact reaction," she said, a tell-tale catch in her throat. Jordan reached back and moved Sam's hand lower down her spine and pressed it into a spot just to the right of center between her two back pockets of her jeans. "Feel this," she said.

Sam's eyes opened wide. "It's vibrating. Gina, feel this,"

she said."

Gina reached forward and also felt the vibration. "What the hell is it?" she asked.

Jordan turned around and tucked her shirt back in. "It's a spinal implant, design to restore mobility."

"Whoa, wait a minute here. Are you trying to tell us you have a spinal cord injury?" Gina asked incredulously.

"Yes. My spinal cord is completely severed at the L1 vertebrae. As a vet, Gina, you surely understand what that means."

"You're damned right I do. It means paralysis…complete and permanent. How the hell are you standing here if you're a paraplegic?"

"The implant sends alternating electrical pulses to both sides of the injury site and allows a synthetic bridge to be established, thus restoring mobility. In theory, these impulses encourage the nerve endings to begin growing toward one another. Hopefully, someday soon, they will physically bridge the injury site and grow together. In the meantime, I have restored mobility, and with any luck, at some point, the nerve endings in my skin will wake up too," Jordan explained.

"Holy shit. I didn't realize spinal cord research has progressed so much," Gina exclaimed.

"It hasn't," Jordan replied. "But with my help, I'm hoping it will."

Gina carried her plate to the sink, rinsed it and put it in the dishwasher. "This changes everything, Jordan."

"What do you mean?" Jordan asked.

"I mean, I'm going to put you in touch with some philanthropist friends of mine. Once they hear what you have to say, I'm betting they'll be willing to throw some money behind your plan."

"Gina, that's a great idea," Sam said. "Jordan, go put your bag back in the guest room. You're not going anywhere."

"I appreciate your hospitality, ladies, but I don't want to overstay my welcome," Jordan said.

Gina put her hand on Jordan's shoulder. "Bullshit. Do as Sam says. You can pay us back when you're rich and famous.

Now go take care of your bag and while you're doing that, I'll call my friends."

* * *

At two o'clock that afternoon, Jordan and Gina sat in the waiting room of one Phyllis Neese, Attorney. Jordan's leg bounced up and down nervously.

"Relax. Phyllis is a nice person. Don't be so nervous," Gina said.

"I feel like I should be more prepared. In the past when I've applied for grants, I spent hours and hours preparing presentations and organizing research results to justify funding. This feels way too casual. Hell, I'm wearing jeans, for Christ's sake. I feel so unprofessional."

"Phyllis won't be concerned about the way you look. She'll be more concerned about your brain and your potential results than the fact that you're wearing jeans."

"Sometimes, talking to the money guys is more difficult than you think. They are usually focused on the bottom line rather than the benefits of your research."

"I think you'll find Phyllis to be a horse of a different color," Gina said. "She specializes in medical disability cases, so she'll at least understand the lingo. And besides, it's not like the money is coming directly out of her pocket. She represents investors. All you need to do is convince her that this is an investment worth making."

"That might be harder than you think," Jordan mused.

"How can you lose? You are proof that it works." Gina pointed out.

Just then, the door to the waiting room opened and a middle-aged woman entered. "Ms. Neese will see you now," she said.

"Take a deep breath, Jordan. It'll be fine," Gina said as she rose to her feet and offered her hand to Jordan.

Gina walked into Phyllis Neese's office in front of Jordan. The lawyer rose to her feet and met her half way across the room. "Gina," she said, hugging her. "It's so nice to see you again. How's Sam?"

"Sam is great. She sends her love."

"How did her garden do this winter? Nancy is looking forward to the rhubarb."

"Nancy's strawberry-rhubarb crisp is the best. Is she planning to enter it into the Champlain Valley Fair this year?"

"You bet she is."

"Well, I'll be sure to tell Sam to set some aside for her as soon as it's ripe enough to harvest."

Jordan observed the interaction between Gina and Ms. Neese and immediately liked the woman.

"Phyllis, I'd like to introduce you to Dr. Jordan Lewis. Jordan, this is Phyllis Neese," Gina said.

Jordan extended her hand to Ms. Neese and shook it warmly. "So nice to meet you, Ms. Neese," she said.

"Phyllis. Call me Phyllis. So, Gina tells me you have a proposal that requires funding."

"Yes. It's more of a research project at this point, but I have evidence and experience that will significantly shorten the development time. I'm afraid I don't have a formal presentation for you today."

"The presentation to the investors will come later, after you convince me your project is worth funding. Now tell me, Dr. Lewis what is it you need funding for?"

Jordan walked from one end of the room to the other, feeling Phyllis's eyes on her as she walked. She returned to the center of the room and stood in front of her. "I have a cure for paralysis resulting from a complete severance of the spinal cord," she said.

Phyllis jumped to her feet. "No freaking way. How is that possible?"

"I hesitate to divulge the details at this point, Phyllis. Just know I've spent the last several years working on a method to restore mobility for millions of SCI victims who currently have little to no hope of walking again without the assistance of some huge, clumsy exoskeleton."

"How do I know you're telling me the truth? You realize you are asking for millions of research dollars, but yet are not giving me anything to base it on."

"What I am asking for is a chance to present my case to the scientists you currently have working on SCI mobilization projects," Jordan explained. "If they see the merit in my proposal, then yes, I will be asking for millions of research dollars and the right to lead a team of scientists in the development of a cure for complete spinal cord injuries."

"Do you have X-rays or MRI's from test subjects to verify your injury?" Phyllis asked.

"They have been done, but unfortunately, I do not have access to them."

"Well, then they will need to be done again before we go to the investors."

"I'm afraid that will not be possible."

Phyllis looked long and hard at Jordan. "You're not making my job easy, here, Jordan."

"I apologize for that, but I am confident I can sell my case to a group of scientists who will truly understand the potential in what I have to say."

Phyllis scribbled several notes on the notepad in front of her. "By the way, Dr. Lewis, what is your background?"

"I have a PhD in kinesiology and spinal cord regeneration techniques."

"I assume you have the credentials to back up your education?"

Jordan fell silent for a few moments. "No, Ma'am, I don't have access to those documents either. What I have for proof is the knowledge and experience that I am willing to share with other research scientists. I am also willing to go before your most knowledgeable experts on spinal cord injuries for either a written or oral exam."

"But you have no records of either the medical procedures or your credentials?"

"No, Ma'am, I do not."

"That might be a problem. Let me talk to my investors. If they are willing to listen to your case, I will set up a meeting with them."

"And their SCI scientists," Jordan added.

"Yes, and their SCI scientists."

CHAPTER 17

Maggie spent the rest of the day cleaning up the mess she had made in her bedroom by tearing out the sheetrock in front of the diaries. She would have to hire a contractor to repair the wall, but at least she had peace of mind that Jordan was not lying to her. It was nearly dark when she finished. Electing to forgo dinner, she poured herself a tall glass of wine and started a fire in the living room fireplace. She threw several large pillows on the floor in front of the hearth and sat on them, contemplating the flames. The house was empty and dark...and very lonely. John had gone home for the night, and she was alone.

She replayed her last conversation with Jordan, over and over again, while trying to make sense of what Jordan was telling her.

Is it really possible she traveled through time? What did she say...her parents died two years ago in 2103, so that means she was living in the year 2105 before she came here. That's eighty-four years from now. Will time travel even be possible in eighty-four years?

Maggie sat with her knees up and arms wrapped around her shins. She rested her forehead on her knees and began to cry.

How will I live without you, Jordan? I have never loved another human being the way I love you. Why does life have to be so complicated?

She propped her chin on her knees and stared at the fire once more.

I wish I would have let you explain how you knew I was in danger. You said I died over and over again. What do you mean by that, Jordan? It's so hard for me to even imagine it. I am so angry at myself for not giving you the chance to explain.

Maggie drained her wine glass and refilled it with the bottle she had placed on the hearth in front of her.

Where are you, Jordan? Where did you go? What you said earlier is right, you don't exist in 2019. You have no social security number, no credit cards, no cell phone, no history at all. Hell, you don't even have a car or a valid driver's license. Sweetheart, how will you survive? I'm so sorry for not listening to you. I'm so worried about you. Jordan, please come home.

Maggie refilled her glass a third time, emptying the remainder of the wine into her glass. She wrapped her arms around her shins once more and allowed the tears to roll down her face.

What good is having this farm if I have no one I love to share it with? Maybe you should have let me die, Jordan. You have risked everything in your life to save mine, and what did I do to repay you? I threw you out. I didn't believe you. I didn't trust you. I am so sorry.

Maggie drank the rest of the wine in her glass then put it on the hearth and laid her head on the pillows. Within moments, she was asleep.

* * *

Maggie awoke the next morning with a nagging headache. She rolled over and looked at the ceiling and wondered why she wasn't in her bed. It was then she realized she had fallen asleep on the pillows in front of the fireplace.

"Oh my God," she said, pushing herself into a seated position. "I can't believe I drank that whole bottle of wine last night. No wonder I've got a headache."

Maggie climbed to her feet and tossed the pillows back onto the couch, each time fighting the pounding in her head as she bent down to pick up the next pillow.

"Remind me never to drink wine again," she said to no one in particular.

She shuffled into her bedroom and looked at herself in the mirror. "Maggie, you look like death warmed over," she said out loud as she took in appearance. There were dark circles under her eyes and her curly red hair was even more unruly than usual. She began stripping her clothing off then threw them into the laundry basket located beside the dresser…directly in front of where she had torn the sheetrock from the wall.

Maggie sat heavily on the bed and looked at the hole in the wall. "Jordan," she whispered as her handiwork reminded her of what had transpired the day before.

"Jordan, where are you? Where did you sleep last night?"

Maggie fought back tears as she stripped off the rest of her clothing and headed to the bathroom to shower.

"Good Morning, John," Maggie said as she entered the barn to saddle Shawny for their morning ride.

"'Morning to ya, Miss Maggie," John replied. "I take it Jordan is sleeping in?" he asked. "She promised to give me a hand stacking the hay bales today."

Maggie threw the saddle over Shawny's back then stopped to look at John. "Jordan is gone, John."

John lowered his chin to his chest. "That's a pity, Ma'am. She was good people. Seein' as you and she were supposed to get married soon, I thought…."

"Well, she's gone. She left last night." Maggie resumed saddling her horse.

"I know I shouldn't be so bold, but Jordan was my friend. Do you mind me askin' why?"

"We had an argument over something she was keeping from me…something she should have shared with me when she first arrived."

"You mean the time travel thing?" John asked.

Maggie pulled the belly strap tight then stopped short. She walked over to John and stood directly in front of him. "What did you say?"

"I asked if it was about the time travel thing."

"You *knew* about that? She told you, but kept it from *me*?" Maggie said, her anger escalating once more.

"No, Ma'am, she didn't tell me about it."

"Then how the hell did you know?"

"I was in the tack room fixing one of the pitch forks, when all of the sudden, a wind kicked up inside the barn, so I peeked my head outside the tack room into the barn proper to see if you had left the main door open. A flash of light lit up the room in the center of the barn where the hay bales were stored. It only lasted a second or two, but when it was over, there was Jordan, sitting in the middle of the floor, all wrapped up in a ball. She just appeared outta nowhere."

"You *saw* her appear?" Maggie said excitedly.

"I did."

"And that didn't scare you?"

"Yes, Ma'am, it did. I thought she might be an alien or something, but she looked harmless enough. That was moments before she tackled you to the ground and saved you from the winch that fell from the rafters. You talked to her yourself. Did she appear to be dangerous to you?"

Maggie paced back and forth in front of John. "She appeared from thin air just before the winch fell?"

"Yes, Ma'am, and now I'm glad she did, otherwise, you might not be here talking to me about it right now."

"And you never questioned her about it later?"

"No, Ma'am. Like I said, Jordan is good people. Once I got to know her, I could tell she was harmless. It don't matter none to me where she comes from, only that she's good people."

Maggie stood there with her hands on her hips and smiled broadly. "We should all learn to think that way, John. If I was half as open-minded as you are, she would be here today to help you stack those hay bales."

"Do you know where she went?" John asked.

"No, I don't." Maggie rubbed her forehead. "I've been such a fool, John. She tried to explain it to me, but I wouldn't listen. It just seemed too incredible to believe, and now here you are, telling me exactly the same thing." Maggie wiped the tears from her eyes.

John put his hand on Maggie's shoulder. "I know she loves you, Maggie. She's told me so herself. Let me put out a few feelers around town to see if anyone has seen her."

"I'd appreciate that, John."

"Go on now. Take Shawny out for his ride. I've got hay bales to stack."

CHAPTER 18

Gina glanced at Jordan across the front seat of the truck. "I'm surprised you didn't show her the implant or even tell her about your own injury."

"We're dealing with a sensitive research project here, with the potential for very high-stakes political visibility. Neither Phyllis, nor the research scientists need to see the implant. They only need to be impressed enough with my knowledge of how to restore mobility and feeling to a person with a complete SCI," Jordan explained. "One thing I learned from my mentors is that you only divulge what is necessary to get the job done. Exposing anything more will only get in the way of progress, and may even put you at risk."

"What kind of risk?" Gina asked.

"Imagine for a moment that word got out about the implant. What do you think it might be worth on the black market?"

Gina glanced quickly at Jordan then back at the road. "To sell it on the black market, they'd have to take it out of you, wouldn't they?"

"Exactly, and since I wouldn't willingly allow that, what do you think my life would be worth compared to what could be made by cloning and selling this device?"

"Holy shit. I never thought of it that way."

"Hence, the need to keep that piece of information under wraps. What I will be trying to do here is to sell my knowledge and experience *without* putting my life on the line."

"So, how is it that you have no identification and no way to prove who you are or what you've accomplished in your life? I mean, you were obviously born, grew up, and went to school. Hell, you're a scientist. There must be some records of your degree somewhere, not to mention medical records from the implant."

Jordan stared straight ahead, unsure how much she should share with Gina. "There are plenty of records. They're just not accessible to me."

"What the hell does that mean?"

"Look, Gina, you are asking questions I can't answer right now."

"You're not from around here, are you?" Gina asked.

"I grew up on a farm very near here, Gina. I just can't go into any detail right now."

"Are you a fugitive or something?"

"No."

"Damn it, Jordan. You're not giving me much to go on here. Sam and I are willing to help you, but trust can only go so far."

"Gina, the more people who know the details, the more paradoxes it creates, and that's not exactly a good thing."

"You're asking an awful lot of us, Jordan. I mean, the only thing we've got to go on right now is your connection to Maggie, and even that's not good at the moment."

Jordan nodded. "You're right. You and Sam have been nothing but kind and helpful to me, and I'm sorry that I can't divulge more to you right now. I'm thinking that I need to find a place to stay in Burlington, preferably within walking distance of the lawyer's office. Like I said, I have enough money to live on for several weeks. With any luck, we'll get the funding for the non-profit set up soon and I'll be back on my feet. I'm anxious to get a team together and get the ball rolling on the implant development. There are a lot of people out there who can benefit from the progress I've already realized."

"And what about Maggie?" Gina asked.

"What about her?"

"I thought you loved her."

"I love her with every fiber of my being, Gina. I would stop at nothing to get her back, but she needs to be a willing participant in that effort, and right now, she's not. And even if she was, I can't spend the rest of my life being her paid farm hand. I need to do something with my life to prove myself worthy of her. I need to prove that I wasn't lying about who I am and where I come from."

"So you have nothing...no social security number, no driver's license, no credit cards, no cell phone. How the hell did you survive without those things where you come from, Jordan?"

"I had all those things where I come from. I just don't have them here."

"Man. You are making no sense at all."

"I know this all seems very cryptic to you. I guess you can see now why Maggie freaked out and asked me to leave."

"You got that right," Gina said as she took her eyes off the road for a quick glance at Jordan.

"Look, Gina, I know you don't know me, and heaven knows, you have no reason to trust me, but I promise you I only came here to save Maggie. I didn't anticipate her rejection...pure and simple, but it happened and now I have no way to go back to where I came from, so I need to make the best of a bad situation. I need to make something of myself and pay my own way."

"Why can't you go back to where you came from?"

"The path home is no longer available to me. The door has been closed."

* * *

Jordan and Sam stood on the front deck while Gina waited for her in the truck.

"Jordan, are you sure we can't talk you into staying a little longer, at least until your funding has been granted?" Sam asked.

Jordan took Sam's hand in her own. "I really appreciate everything you and Gina have done for me, Sam, but I think it would be best if I go. I've overstayed my welcome already."

"You've been here for less than a week, Jordan," Sam pointed out.

"Well, I feel like I've taken advantage of you and Gina for long enough. Thanks to your help, I have a nicely furnished studio apartment right across the street from the hospital, and I'm within walking distance of the lawyer's office as well. With any luck, I'll be able to arrange for legal identification soon and will be able to purchase a car and a cell phone."

"When is your appointment with the spinal institute?"

"Phyllis set it up for two weeks from now. That should give me enough time to pull together a convincing presentation. I have to admit I'm a little nervous about that meeting."

"Would you like Gina or me to go with you?"

"No, that won't be necessary. I've disrupted your lives enough already."

"It's really no problem."

Jordan squeezed Sam's hand. "No, really. I'll be fine."

Sam opened her arms and took Jordan into her warm embrace. "Take care of yourself, Jordan. You have our cell phone numbers if you need anything. Don't hesitate to call, okay?"

Jordan stepped back out of Sam's arms. "Okay," she said.

"We're still on for dinner on Friday, right? Gina will pick you up after she closes the office. Bring a change of clothes so you can spend a night or two."

Jordan grinned. "You are such a mother hen, Sam."

"I can't help it. It's in my nature to take care of people."

Jordan descended the three steps between the deck and the driveway then looked back at Sam. "Well, don't ever change. You're perfect just the way you are. I'll see you on Friday."

* * *

"Flirting with my wife, are you?" Gina said, a twinkle in her eye.

Jordan reached for her seatbelt and pulled it across her chest. "Damn right I am. You're a lucky woman, Gina. You have a treasure there. I hope you know that."

"I most certainly do, my friend. So, did she try to talk you into staying longer?"

"Oh, yeah."

"The offer is still open, you know."

"I know, Gina, and I love you both for being there for me, but I really do need to be on my own. I've taken advantage of you two for long enough."

"We don't feel that way. There's something about you, Jordan. Something about you that made us trust you right away. It's like we've known you forever, even though it's been less than a week."

"I feel the same about you and Sam. You two have been a godsend to me since Maggie threw me out. I don't know what I would have done without you."

"I'll respect your need for secrecy for now, but I expect you to come clean with us when you can. You know you can trust us."

Jordan nodded. "I know, and yes, as soon as I feel secure and have established myself, you'll be the first ones I tell."

"Fair enough."

Gina and Jordan drove on in silence for several minutes.

"Gina, how often did you see Maggie before I came along?"

"Every couple of weeks...at least we used to see her that often until Jan became intolerable. Why do you ask?"

"I'm kind of concerned about her. Unless she's hired a replacement for me, she's pretty much alone on that farm at night. John is there during the day, but he goes home around five."

"I'll give her a call tonight and check in on her. Do you want her to know you've been staying with us?"

"I wouldn't bother. I'm not sure she'll care anyway." Jordan bit her bottom lip and looked out the side window to keep herself from crying. She covertly wiped the moisture out of the corner of her eye, a movement not unnoticed by Gina.

"Are you all right, Jordan?" Gina asked.

"I miss her," Jordan whispered as her bottom lip trembled.

"Maybe you should call her."

"I don't think she wants to hear from me." Jordan inhaled deeply in an attempt to regain control of her emotions. "Damn. I can't believe how much it hurts."

"You love her, Jordan. I totally get that it hurts."

"Yeah, well, love sucks."

"Sometimes it does, my friend. Sometimes it does. Here we are," Gina said as she pulled into the driveway of Jordan's apartment complex. "Are you going to be okay?" Gina asked.

"How can I not be with friends like you and Sam? I mean, you find me a place to live, you fill my cupboards with food and you put yourselves on call to me twenty-four seven. I'll never be able to repay you."

Gina reached across the cab of the truck and hugged Jordan tightly. "No repayment necessary, Jord. We're glad to help."

"Thanks, Gina, and thank Sam for me again too, okay?"

"Will do. Call if you need anything."

"I will," Jordan said as she climbed out of the truck and waved as Gina drove away.

* * *

Gina tapped the Bluetooth icon on the dashboard monitor and selected speed dial. She had a white-knuckle grip on the steering wheel as she waited for the call to be picked up. "Damn," she said as the call went to voicemail.

"Maggie, this is Gina. We need to talk. Call me."

CHAPTER 19

"Maggie? Maggie, are you in there?" John called out from the front porch. After waiting several minutes for a response, he turned to walk back toward the barn.

"John?" Maggie said from behind him. "Is everything okay?"

John turned around and noticed Maggie standing behind the screen door. She pushed it open as he approached and he instinctively gasped at her appearance. She appeared to have just woken up, despite the fact that it was ten in the morning. She had dark circles under her eyes, her clothes were wrinkled as though she had slept in them, and her hair was unkempt.

"Maggie, are you okay? You haven't taken Shawny out for his ride for the past two days and I was getting kind of worried about you. Do you need me to call a doctor?"

Maggie looked around disoriented. "What time is it?" she asked.

"It's near ten o'clock." John walked closer and could smell alcohol on her. "When's the last time you had something to eat?"

"I'm okay. Don't worry about me."

Just then, John heard Maggie's cell phone ring from inside the house. Maggie seemed to be oblivious to the sound.

"Maggie, this is Gina. We need to talk. Call me."

"Is there something you need, John?" Maggie asked.

"No Ma'am. Just checking to see if you're okay."

"Okay then. I'm going back to bed."

"Yes, Ma'am."

John went directly back to the barn and looked up the phone number for Delarm Veterinary Clinic. He pulled out his cell phone and dialed the number.

"Delarm Veterinary Clinic, Melinda speaking," the

receptionist said.

"Hi, Melinda. This is John from the Downs farm. I'm looking for Dr. Delarm. Is she in?"

"She's actually out of the office today. Would you care to leave a message?"

"Yes, please have her call me. Oh, and please tell her it's urgent."

"I'll page her right now."

"Thank you," John said, offering his cell phone number.

John hung up the phone and paced back and forth across the barn waiting for Gina to call him back. He didn't have long to wait.

"John, this is Gina. Please tell me Maggie is okay."

"How did you know?"

"Is she okay, John?"

"She hasn't been out of the house for the past two days. Its ten o'clock and I just woke her up by bangin' on her door. Oh, and she smells like alcohol."

"Has she been like this for very long?"

"Just since Jordan left three days ago."

"Damn. I'm on my way, John."

"Thank you, Miss Gina. She's been in a bad way since Jordan left. Damned, stubborn woman. She was a fool to let that one go."

"I hear you, John. I'll be there soon."

* * *

Gina brought her truck to a screeching halt in front of Maggie's farm house, a cloud of dust billowing in her wake. She threw open the door and ran into the house uninvited.

"Maggie! Maggie, where the fuck are you?" she shouted as she made her way through the kitchen and living room. Not finding Maggie in either room, she went directly to her bedroom where she found Maggie asleep on the bed. She immediately noticed the large hole in the wall behind the dresser as well as an array of wine bottles on the floor beside the bed. "What the fuck happened in here?"

Before waking Maggie, she went to the adjoining bathroom

and turned the cold water on in the shower. She then went back to the bedroom and shook Maggie awake.

"Noooo," Maggie whined as Gina shook her.

"Let's go. Out of bed, Maggie," Gina said. "Come on."

She pulled Maggie to her feet and dragged her into the bathroom then pushed her into the walk-in shower.

Maggie screamed in protest. "God damn it. Let go of me, Gina. It's cold!"

"You're damned right, it's cold. What the fuck were you thinking, Maggie?"

"Let go of me," Maggie screamed again.

For the next ten minutes, Gina continued to hold her under the cold spray, soaking both Maggie and herself in the process. Finally, she pulled her out of the shower and sat her on the toilet seat. Maggie sat there shivering uncontrollably as Gina grabbed two towels from the linen closet and wrapped one around each of them.

"Don't move," she said to Maggie as she went into the living room and started a fire in the fireplace. She returned five minutes later and found Maggie still sitting on the toilet with the towel wrapped tightly around her. She was shivering so loudly, her teeth chattered.

"Okay, come on. Let's get you out of those wet clothes," Gina said and she led Maggie back into the bedroom and sat her on the bed. Piece by piece, Gina stripped the clothes from Maggie's body until she was totally naked. She then towel-dried her unruly red hair and helped her into a thick terry cloth bathrobe and wool socks.

"All right, in the living room with you," Gina said. She wrapped her arm around Maggie's waist and led her to the wing-backed chair she had positioned directly in front of the fire. "Sit while I find myself something dry to put on," she said. Before going to change her clothes, she added a large piece of wood to the kindling. "There, that should warm things up a bit."

Maggie sat in the chair with a blank look on her face, still shivering from the cold shower.

Gina returned a few minutes later wearing a pair of men's

jeans and a button-down flannel shirt she found in the spare bedroom closet. She assumed they belonged to Maggie's father. She squatted down in front of Maggie. "Okay. You wanna tell me what this is all about?"

For the first time since she got there, Maggie looked directly at her. "You wouldn't understand," she said.

"Try me."

Maggie closed her eyes and allowed tears to squeeze between her lashes.

"Talk to me, Mags."

Maggie kept her eyes closed and shook her head.

"This is about Jordan, isn't it?" Gina finally asked.

Maggie's eyes flew open. "How do you know about Jordan?"

"Four days ago I was driving down Bostwick Road toward the village and I came across a woman walking with a duffle bag slug over her shoulder. It was late enough in the day that I knew she wouldn't get to town on foot until dark, so I stopped and picked her up. She was a little reluctant to get into the truck at first, but I assured her I wasn't an axe murderer or anything, so finally, she relented. It was obvious to me from the moment she got into the truck that she was an emotional wreck. I pressed her to talk about it and she finally admitted that she had been working for you and that after an argument, you and she parted ways."

"I'll bet she had plenty to say about how badly I treated her," Maggie said.

"Quite the contrary. When she mentioned your name, I told her that Sam and I were good friends with you. She loosened up a bit after that and told me about your brush with death that morning on the ridge by the lake and about how she saved you in the nick of time. She also made it clear that she thought Jan was behind it. Is that true, Maggie?"

Maggie nodded. "I would have died if she hadn't caught me in time."

"Anyway, it was apparent to me that she's in love with you and that your falling-out pretty much tore her apart."

"Did she tell you why we fought?"

"She mentioned something about you freaking out when she tried to explain to you how she knew you were in danger that morning."

"You don't know the half of it, Gina."

"No, you're probably right, so why don't you enlighten me."

"She's read my diaries, Gina. She was able to quote things from them that not another living soul knows besides me. Gina, my diaries have been hidden between the walls of my bedroom for quite some time now. I tore part of the wall down a few days ago just to verify they were still there...and they are."

"So that explains the hole in the wall behind your dresser."

"Gina, she claims she's from the future. She claims she owns my farm eighty-something years from now and she found my diaries while remodeling."

"Holy shit!"

"There's more. She broke her back in a horse riding accident when she was sixteen, but she has some sort of bionic device in her back that allows her to walk. She's a freaking scientist, for Christ's sake. At least that's what she claims."

"Do you believe her?"

"I don't know what to believe. Apparently, she fell in love with me through my diaries and when she researched the Burlington Free Press archives, she discovered I died four days ago under questionable circumstances. According to her, she's traveled here through time at least four different times, and until this last time, she arrived too late to save me from falling over the cliff."

"How the hell does one travel through time?"

"She has these two friends, Kale and Andi who are quantum physicists or something like that, who helped her."

"My God, Maggie. No wonder you're a mess over this."

"I don't have another explanation for her knowing what's in my diaries, Gina. They're still in the wall where I placed them. They haven't been moved so she would have had to read them before showing up here for the first time. Oh, I almost forgot to tell you, John saw her transport here."

"What?"

"Yes. He confessed to me, that six months ago, he was in

the tack room when all of the sudden a gust of wind blew up inside the barn even though the doors were closed. When he went to investigate, this blinding blast of light occurred and when it was all over, Jordan was sitting there in the middle of floor. She just appeared out of nowhere. Gina, six months ago is when Jordan arrived at the farm, supposedly looking for work"

Gina stood up from her crouch and walked back and forth in front of the fire. "Well that explains a lot of things," she said.

"What do you mean?" Maggie asked.

Gina stopped pacing and looked at Maggie. "I told you I picked her up from the road four days ago. What I haven't told you yet, is that she's been staying with Sam and me—until today, that is."

Maggie became animated. "You know where she is?"

"Yes, I do."

"Take me to her, Gina. I need to see her."

"I'm not taking you anywhere in the shape you're in, except home with me. Now let's get you dressed then pack a bag and head out."

* * *

"Hey Sam," Gina said as she paced back and forth across her kitchen with her phone held to her ear.

"Hi, love. This is a pleasant surprise. What's up?" Sam said.

"Things are about to get very interesting. I got a call from Maggie's farmhand on my way back from dropping Jordan off this morning. Actually, he called the clinic, but instead of scheduling an appointment like he normally would, he asked Melinda to page me with an urgent call-back."

"Well that doesn't sound good. Is Maggie okay?"

"Great minds think alike, it seems. That was my first thought as well. It turns out that since Jordan left four days ago, she's been holed up in her house, barely eating and drinking a substantial amount of wine, judging by the number of empty bottles on her bedroom floor when I got there."

"I assume you brought her home with you?"

"I did, although she was pretty angry with me over the cold shower I forced her into when I first got there."

"Where is she now?"

"Soaking in the hot tub. She's a mess, Sam."

"Look, it's almost closing time here. I'll be home soon then I'll fix us all a nice hot dinner. Maybe we can get her to talk to us."

"Oh, she's talked plenty already, and what she told me about Jordan will knock your socks off. If she's telling the truth, it sure does answer a few questions I have about her."

"You'll have to enlighten me when I get home."

"I will. I hope the rest of your day goes smoothly, love. I'll see you in a few hours."

"Okay. I love you, Gina."

"Love you too."

Gina hung up her phone and slipped it into her back pocket then retrieved two soft drinks from the refrigerator and carried them out to the hot tub on the back deck. She sat down on a wicker chair next to the tub and handed a drink to Maggie. "How are you feeling?" she asked.

"Much warmer, now. Thank you for the drink," Maggie replied. "I assume you called Sam?"

"Yes, I did. She'll be home in the next few hours. She's as concerned about you as I am, Maggie."

"Well apparently, you've been more concerned about Jordan than about me," Maggie replied, a tinge of bitterness in her voice.

"Not fair, Maggie. Jordan had nowhere to go. When I first picked her up, I didn't even know she was associated with you. Did you expect us to just turn her out?"

Maggie had the decency to look ashamed. "No, I guess not. It just doesn't feel right that she's being portrayed as the victim here. I mean, how would you feel if Sam dropped in on you out of nowhere and claimed she was from the future?"

"Sam could drop in on me from Mars for all I care, and I would still love her. For me, love transcends all things. The question you need to ask yourself is whether you love Jordan enough to accept her into your life regardless of where...or *when* she came from."

"She scares me, Gina."

"Scares you, how? She hasn't been abusive, has she?"

"No, not at all. In fact, she's so tender and loving…more so than anyone I've ever met. It's just that this whole mess is so abstract. I don't know what to believe. I can't help it, Gina. I'm the type of person who needs to touch and feel things to believe them. She's asking me to suspend all disbelief here, and I don't know if I can do that."

"Yet you're miserable without her. Think about that, Maggie."

Maggie nodded and watched the bubbles swirl around her for the next several moments before she looked up at Gina again. "You said you know where she is?"

Gina nodded. "I do."

"Is she okay?"

"Funny you should ask that. When I dropped her off this morning, she asked me to check on you to make sure *you* were okay."

"She did?"

"Yes. She wears her love for you on her sleeve, Maggie. A blind man could see it. On the first day we met her, Sam asked if she loved you and she was so choked up, she couldn't even answer. Sam simply said, *No need to answer, I can see it in your face.*"

"Where is she, Gina?"

"I'm not going to share that information with you if you have no intention of using it, so ask me again if it gets to that point."

Maggie yawned loudly.

Gina pushed the button on the hot tub and shut off the jets. "Out with you," she said. "You obviously need a nap. Sam will be home in a couple of hours. That should give you adequate time to get some rest."

Gina held the towel for Maggie as she allowed herself to be swaddled in terry cloth comfort, then accepted Gina's hand to help her out of the tub.

As Maggie walked through the house toward the guest

room, Gina remembered that they had yet to change the sheets from Jordan that morning. "Maggie, wait. I need to change the sheets before you crawl in. We didn't have time to do it after Jordan climbed out of them this morning."

Maggie turned around sharply. "No, please don't. I need to feel her near me, even if it's only her essence."

"Okay. Head on in then. I'll wake you when Sam gets home."

* * *

Gina met Sam at the door when she got home. The minute she walked into the entryway, Gina grabbed her and pressed her against the wall. She kissed her long and hard then pulled her close for several moments. When she released Sam, she touched her forehead to hers and whispered, "Promise you'll always love me."

Sam dropped her bag to the floor and took Gina's face between her hands. "Sweetheart, you're trembling. Of course I'll always love you. Baby, talk to me."

"I've never seen such raw pain on someone's face as I've seen on both Maggie and Jordan's. Sam, they are dying apart. I don't ever want that to happen to us."

"Not a chance. You're stuck with me, and don't you forget it. Okay?"

Gina nodded and kissed her again. "Thank you."

"You're welcome. Now why don't you come help me get dinner started." Sam stopped part way to the kitchen. "By the way, where's Miss Thang?"

"Miss Thang is right here," Maggie said as she came out of the bathroom and straight into Sam's arms.

"Come here, darlin'," Sam said as she held her close. "How are you doing?"

"I've had better days," Maggie replied. "Can I help you with dinner?"

"If you'd like, then you can tell me what's been going on in the crazy red head of yours."

"Crazy is a good way to put it. It sure feels that way of late."

Gina followed them into the kitchen. "Does this mean I get out of cooking?" she asked hopefully.

"Not a chance. Now drag that cute white ass of yours over here and peel the potatoes," Sam joked as Gina pouted. "And use the potato peeler. I'd like there to be some potato left to actually cook when you're done."

"Nag, nag, nag," Gina mumbled.

"What was that you said?" Sam asked.

Gina perked up. "I said, sure, honey. No problem. I love peeling potatoes."

"That's what I thought you said." Sam winked at Maggie, who chuckled at her friends' antics.

* * *

Sam paced back and forth across the living room. "So let me get this straight. She's from the future?"

"That's what she claims," Maggie said.

Sam stopped in front of Maggie. "Do you believe her?"

"I don't know. I…I don't know what to believe. She's been able to quote things directly from my diaries that I've never told another living soul, yet I tore the wall apart in my bedroom a few days ago to see if they were still there…and they are, so she would have had to read them before I even met her."

"Wait a minute. You diaries were between the walls of your bedroom?" Sam asked.

"Yes. I put them there a while back on a whim, you know, as a time capsule of sorts. I thought it would be fun for someone to find them…" Maggie trailed off.

"In the future," Gina finished for her.

"In the future," Maggie repeated.

Sam sat down beside Maggie and took her hand. "And you say John saw her appear?"

"He claims he did."

"And he didn't freak out about it?"

"John said, and I quote: *Jordan is good people. Once I got to know her, I could tell she was harmless. It don't matter none to me where she comes from, only that she's good people.*"

"Gotta love John," Gina said.

"Well if she's really from the future that would explain the implant in her back. I'm sure spinal cord regeneration techniques will improve significantly over the next eighty or so years," Sam observed.

"Well, if she has her way, it won't take another eighty years," Gina said.

"What do mean, if she has her way?" Maggie asked.

"She has a meeting scheduled with the Vermont Spinal Institute in a couple of weeks to convince them to fund her research on the spinal implant," Gina explained. "I only hope it doesn't backfire and get her arrested."

"Arrested? Why would they do that?" Sam asked.

"Because she has no identity," Maggie explained. "Think about it. She won't even be born for another fifty-four years. You're right, Gina, there is a chance they'll think she's an illegal and have her arrested."

"What are we going to do? We can't let her go to jail, or get deported," Sam said.

"Get deported to where, the year 2105?" Gina said. "No, we need some other way to make her legal."

Maggie stood and walked across the room to stand in front of the picture window, her back to her friends. She stood there, looking out into the darkness in silence for a long time until Sam approached her and put an arm around her shoulder. "Maggie, are you all right?"

Maggie turned and looked at her friend. Tears were falling freely from her eyes. "I know what to do." She looked at Gina. "I need to see her, Gina. Where is she?"

CHAPTER 20

"What do you mean, you know what to do?" Gina asked.

"I'm going to marry her," Maggie replied.

"Whoa, wait a minute," Sam interrupted. "Are you sure you want to do that, Maggie?"

"I may be freaked out about all this future stuff, but one thing I am absolutely sure of, is that I love her. I have loved her almost from the first time I set eyes on her."

Maggie paused to collect her thoughts. "You don't know this, but I actually asked her to marry me several weeks ago. We were going to do it around my birthday, which is only two weeks away, but then the near-death experience and time travel thing changed everything."

"Ya think?" Gina said sarcastically.

"Gina," Sam admonished gently.

"So, how do you think marrying her will make her legal?" Gina asked.

"Well, foreigners who marry US citizens are generally not deported, so I figured—"

"But she still doesn't have any ID. You need to show ID to get a marriage license," Gina pointed out.

Maggie turned back toward the window for several moments. Suddenly, she swung around. "Gina, maybe you can...."

"No fucking way. Don't even go there, Maggie," Gina said. She sat back on the couch and crossed her arms defiantly.

"But—" Maggie started.

"I was a stupid kid then. I have too much to lose now. It's too risky," Gina insisted.

Sam looked back and forth between Maggie and Gina. "What's going on here?"

"When we were in high school, Gina had this little business

going on where she would make fake ID's for people," Maggie said.

"Seriously, Gina?" Sam asked.

"Key word here is high school. Like I said, I was a stupid kid then. We're talking now about a grown-up world and grown-up situation with authorities who could do some pretty severe damage to me if we're caught," Gina explained.

"But Gina, the only person we would have to fool is the town clerk. Once we have a marriage license the rest should be relatively easy. I mean, if the spine institute accepts her, she'll be issued an employee ID and medical insurance cards. That, along with our marriage certificate and a few pieces of mail addressed to her, is enough to establish residency. Once we have residency established, we can see about getting her a social security number."

"You are being way too optimistic, Maggie. I'm pretty sure the spine institute will want her social security number before they hire her, otherwise, *their* asses would be on the line with the federal government," Gina reasoned.

"Not if they want what she has to offer badly enough," Maggie said.

"Are you suggesting they might look the other way and break some rules just to get access to the spinal implant?" Sam asked.

"That's exactly when I'm suggesting. Hell, they might even help get her the documentation she needs to become a legal citizen."

Sam looked at Gina. "I guess it all comes down to just how much risk we're all willing to take...you with the fake ID, Maggie with an illegal marriage license, and Jordan with the possibility the spine institute may not play nice."

"And you?" Gina asked.

"Well, I guess, I'd be a willing accessory to all of it. In the eyes of the law, I may be just as responsible as the rest of you." Sam held her hands out to the side to emphasize her point.

"Okay. Stop right there," Maggie said. "This is becoming way too complicated. I obviously didn't think this through before I opened my mouth. Maybe it's not such a good idea.

You two have no skin in this, and it's unfair of me to ask you to put your necks on the line. I'm sorry."

A silence fell over the three friends. Gina remained on the couch, her arms crossed, Maggie leaned her backside against the window sill and Sam stood there looking at both of them.

"Well then, I guess we should defer this decision to Jordan. I mean, she's the one who is most at risk here," Sam said.

* * *

"Hi Jordan," Gina said into the phone. "How are you settling in?"

"Hey, Gina. There wasn't much to do but put my clothes and groceries away, which was accomplished in about a half hour after you dropped me off this morning. Other than that, I'm pretty much bored out of my mind. I'm used to having an endless list of chores to do on the farm. Did you get a chance to check in on Maggie when you got home?" Jordan asked.

"I did. In fact, she's here with us right now." Gina listened to the silence coming from the other end of the line. "Jordan? Are you there?"

"She's there with you? Is she okay?" Jordan asked.

"Yes on both counts. In fact, she'd like to talk to you, if you feel up to it." Again, Gina listened to silence. "Jordan?"

"I'm here. I…I wasn't prepared for that. I assumed she'd never want to see me again. Is she angry?"

Gina glanced at Maggie who sat beside her on the couch eagerly waiting for the phone. "Is she angry? No, she's not angry. You've actually been the topic of conversation for the past hour or so. Maggie has something important to ask you, and we have plans to make before your meeting with the spine institute."

"What kind of plans?"

"Well, we believe there's pretty significant risk involved with you exposing yourself to the institute, and we need to come up with some sort of plan to mitigate that. The last thing any of us need is for you to be arrested or detained in some way because you can't prove you exist."

"Believe me Gina, *that* thought has crossed my mind

several times since I made the appointment. What do you have in mind?" Jordan asked.

"I think we'd best leave that discussion for when we're face to face, but right now, Maggie wants to talk to you. Is that okay?"

"Damn. Suddenly, I can't breathe," Jordan said.

Gina stood up and stepped onto the back deck, casting a nervous glance over her shoulder at Maggie as she went. "Jordan, are you okay?"

"Yeah, I'm fine, just really nervous about talking to Maggie."

"I totally understand how you feel, but I think talking to her will be good for both of you."

"Has she said anything to you about what happened between us?"

"She's told us more than you probably would have wanted her to, if that's what you're asking."

"So, are you as freaked out about it as she is?"

"I won't lie and say I don't have concerns, but like I told Maggie, I would love Sam, even if she teleported here from Mars. I happen to believe love transcends all things, and if you and Maggie love each other as much as I think you do, I am confident things will work out."

"She said she loves me?"

"She said the time travel thing is a little hard to deal with, but the one thing she is sure of is her love for you. Don't give up on it, Jordan. You guys need one another right now."

Gina glanced into the house through the sliding glass door and saw Sam holding Maggie in her arms. Maggie was crying.

"Gina, I'd rather talk to Maggie face to face. I can call a taxi and be there within an hour if it's not too late," Jordan suggested.

Gina looked at her watch. "It's only seven o'clock. I will come to get you. A taxi from Burlington to Shelburne will cost a fortune. I'll be there in about a half hour. Pack a bag for a couple of nights, okay? Tomorrow is Friday. Sam and I have to work, but that will give you all day for the two of you to work things out."

"I'll be waiting…and Gina, I don't know how I'll ever be able to repay you."

"Your friendship is payment enough. I'll be there soon. Bye."

Gina slipped her phone into her shirt pocket and went back into the house. Maggie and Sam's attention was immediately drawn to her.

"She doesn't want to talk to me, does she?" Maggie said in a tearful voice.

Gina grabbed her truck keys from the key holder on the kitchen wall. "I'll be back in about an hour. I'm going after Jordan."

* * *

Maggie sat on the couch in the living room, nervously fussing with her hair while Sam stood in the window keeping watch. Finally, headlights appeared at the end of the driveway. "They're here, Maggie," she said.

"Do I look okay?" Maggie asked.

Sam walked over to her friend and took her hands. "You are an amazingly beautiful woman, Maggie, but I'm guessing you could look like death warmed over right now and it wouldn't matter to Jordan."

Their attention was drawn to the sound of the front door opening.

Maggie squeezed Sam's hands.

"Sam, we're home," Gina's voice called out.

"In the living room, love," Sam replied.

"Throw your bag on the floor for now, and give me your jacket. I'll hang it up for you," Gina said.

Jordan walked ahead of Gina into the living room and stopped short when she saw Maggie sitting on the couch. She was unable to speak and unable to move as their gazes locked.

Gina walked around Jordan and motioned to Sam to join her. Sam obliged as they walked hand in hand down the hall to their bedroom, leaving Jordan and Maggie alone in the living room.

It was several long moments before Jordan found her voice.

"Maggie," she whispered. She extended her hand forward while consciously fighting to keep her tears in check.

Maggie didn't need a second invitation as she rose from the couch and ran into Jordan's arms, sobbing uncontrollably. "I'm sorry, Jordan. I'm so sorry," she said.

Jordan clung to her for dear life, nearly crushing her in her embrace. "I love you, Maggie. I love you so much."

"You are the best thing in my life, Jordan. I'm sorry I asked you to leave. I was such a fool," Maggie said.

Jordan eased her death grip on Maggie and leaned back to look into her face. She cupped the side of Maggie face with her hand. "No, you're not a fool. The truth does sound crazy. I don't blame you for being afraid. I know this won't be easy to deal with, but know that I love you with everything that I am."

Jordan wiped the tears from Maggie's face. "Please don't cry. It's breaking my heart."

"I'm sorry. I can't help it. There is just so much emotion spilling from my heart right now, I can't contain it."

Jordan lowered her face to Maggie's and tentatively brushed her lips against hers. "Let me love you," she whispered.

Maggie wrapped her hand around the back of Jordan's head and pulled her mouth closer for a deep, probing kiss. "Love me, Jordan. Please."

Jordan scooped Maggie into her arms and carried her to the guest room, kicking the door closed behind them. She placed her on the bed and lay completely on top of her. "I've missed you so much, Maggie. I've missed holding you in my arms at night. I've missed the smell of your hair and the softness of your skin. I've missed the taste of your essence."

Maggie tilted her chin upward to give Jordan access to her neck. "Oh, my God, Jordan. Do you know what you're doing to me right now?"

Jordan slipped her hand into the front of Maggie's jeans and encountered a flood of moisture that caused a spasm to wrack her own body. "Maggie, I need you," Jordan said in a shaky voice."

Maggie reached down and unbuttoned her own jeans then

pulled down the zipper and pushed Jordan's hand deeper into the front of her panties as she lifted her hips. "Ahhh, Jordan, I need more."

Jordan sat back on her knees and pulled Maggie's jeans and panties off and tossed them on the floor. She pulled Maggie's button-up flannel shirt over her head without unbuttoning it and threw that on the floor as well, before making short work of Maggie's bra.

Before she could do anything else, Maggie sat up and began removing Jordan's clothing. "Off with this," she said as she pulled Jordan's shirt over her head followed by her sports bra. As soon as Jordan's breasts were freed from her bra, Maggie suckled her hardened buds, causing Jordan to spasm involuntarily.

"Maggie, as much as I'm enjoying this, I'm going to come right now if you don't stop," Jordan said.

Maggie grinned and turned her attention to the button and zipper on Jordan's jeans, and soon added them to the pile of clothing on the floor.

Jordan shifted her weight to one side and ran her fingers through Maggie's damp curls before plunging deep inside. Maggie's head pressed into the pillow as she moaned loudly, spurning Jordan on to increase the frequency and depth of her thrusts until Maggie's hips arched high off the bed.

"Jordan," Maggie cried as her body convulsed again and again.

Jordan turned her palm upward and curled her fingers to slowly massage the sponge-like tissue at the front of Maggie's vagina. Maggie involuntarily convulsed a few more times, until finally, Jordan removed her hand and gathered her into her arms.

After a few moments, Maggie kissed Jordan tenderly. "My turn to love you," she said.

"This won't take long. I almost climaxed just looking at you in the living room tonight," Jordan joked.

Maggie pushed her onto her back and kissed her way from Jordan's ear to her breasts where she inhaled each nipple, catching the swollen bud between her teeth and flicking it with the end of her tongue.

Jordan caught Maggie's head between her hands and encouraged her to continue. "I'm almost there, Maggie. God, what you do to me."

While suckling at Jordan's breasts, Maggie slipped her fingers inside Jordan's heated core. Almost immediately, Jordan climaxed, lifting both herself and Maggie off the bed with her spasms. The convulsions became so intense at one point that Jordan physically removed Maggie's hand and gathered her into her arms, holding her close as her body continued to endure the orgasmic waves running through it. After a time, the tremors faded, leaving her feeling fulfilled and complete. She kissed Maggie on the head.

"I love you, Maggie. I always will…across all space and time."

"The offer is still open, you know," Maggie said.

"Offer?"

"My proposal. Will you marry me, Jordan?"

CHAPTER 21

Jordan awoke the next morning with a heavy weight on her stomach. She looked down and saw a tangle of red hair sprawled across her chest. Maggie lay partially on top of her; her head on her stomach and her right arm thrown over her thighs. Her left arm was tucked securely under her own torso while their legs were braided. A rush of love, as well as a renewal of desire, invaded her being as she recalled their lovemaking from the night before.

"I love you, Maggie," Jordan whispered, "Yes, I will marry you," she added, having been delinquent with her response the night before.

Jordan gently rolled her body to the right and watched as Maggie slowly slid off and lay on her back beside her. She carefully inched her way to the edge of bed so as to not disturb Maggie, then stood and stretched. Before leaving the room, she pulled the sheet over Maggie then slipped her flannel button-up shirt on in the event Gina and Sam were still home when she went to use the bathroom. The tails of the shirt conveniently extended to mid-thigh. She opened the bedroom door and stepped into the hall, closing it behind her. The first thing she encountered was the aroma of fresh brewed coffee.

"Oh my God, I'm in heaven," she said out loud.

Gina poked her head out of the kitchen and looked down the hall. "What was that?" she asked.

"Coffee. The aroma is orgasmic," Jordan said; her hand on the bathroom door knob.

"Well, judging from the sounds coming from the guest room last night, you would certainly know," Gina teased.

Jordan covered her face with her hands. "Sheesh, Gina. Did you have to say that?"

Gina chuckled. "Go to the bathroom. I'll make you a cup of

coffee while you're in there."

Jordan accepted the cup Gina handed to her when she entered the kitchen. "Thank you," she said.

Gina grinned. "So, I take it you and Maggie made up last night."

"You could say that." Jordan looked around. "Where's Sam?"

"She's already gone to the market. She has a produce delivery coming in this morning and she needed to be there when it arrived."

"What time is it?"

"Seven-twenty," Gina said. "I need to get out of here in the next ten minutes myself."

"So you mentioned something on the phone yesterday about a plan to deal with my identity problem," Jordan said.

"Yeah. Sam, Maggie and I wracked our brains trying to come up with some ideas about how to make you legal. Our biggest concern is that you'll go to this meeting you have with the spinal institute and they'll assume you're an illegal alien and have you arrested."

"I know. I've been worried about that possibility myself. Did you come up with anything?"

"We had lots of ideas, but nothing legal. I hate to say it, but we just might have to resort to something illegal to get it done. It all comes down to how much risk we're willing to take."

"Well, no one is taking any risk except me," Jordan said adamantly. "I won't be having you or Sam…or Maggie for that matter, on the wrong side of the law just to protect my ass."

Gina refilled her travel mug and snapped the lid on. "Well, we can talk about it more this afternoon when Sam and I get home."

She picked up her keys and headed toward the front door. "Help yourself to anything you'd like to eat," she called over her shoulder on the way out.

"Have a great day, Gina," Jordan said.

Jordan rummaged through the cabinets looking for the

spices and finally found the jar of cinnamon. She had already gathered a loaf of bread, four eggs, the container of milk and maple syrup from the refrigerator as well as frozen sausages from the freezer. She cooked two servings of French toast with sausage and brewed another coffee for herself and one for Maggie. After rinsing her cooking utensils and putting them into the dishwasher, she arranged their breakfast on a cookie sheet and carried it to the bedroom. When she opened the door, she found Maggie awake. She was lying on her back and looking at the ceiling.

"Good morning," Jordan said as she approached the bed. "Scoot up," she said.

Maggie complied and pushed herself into a seated position with her back against the headboard. "Wow, this looks wonderful," she said.

"I hope you're hungry."

Jordan placed the entire cookie sheet on Maggie's lap. "Hold on to this for a sec while I climb in," she said then settled herself on the bed beside Maggie.

Maggie smiled. "Thank you for breakfast, love."

Jordan kissed her. "You're welcome. Eat up while it's hot."

"How did you sleep last night?" Maggie asked around a bite of French toast.

"Better than I have in the past several days. Having you beside me makes all the difference. I missed you, Maggie."

Maggie looked down at her plate, a remorseful look on her face. "I missed you too. I'm sorry, I put you through that."

"Sweetheart, look at me. You did nothing wrong. I don't blame you for being afraid. It's not every day someone tells you they're from the future. I'm just happy you've allowed me back into your life."

"What's it like in the future, Jordan?"

"The farm isn't much different. The bunkhouse is gone, and the wall between your bedroom and the adjoining guest room is gone. Oh, and Kale and I remodeled the kitchen, but other than normal paint and repairs on the house, the rest is pretty much the same."

"The barn is still standing too?"

"Yes. In fact, a few months before we started transporting me here, the spinal institute came in and retrofit one end of the barn with an on-site lab so we could finish the implant testing while I was recuperating from the implant surgery."

"What is the world like?"

"Technology has advanced at a remarkable pace. This implant is a good example of that. This wouldn't be possible today without the developments in hardware and software that we've realized over the last fifty years. The political atmosphere played a big part in that."

"What do you mean?"

"Today, in 2019, so many medical advances have been stymied because of the religious beliefs of our lawmakers. Stem cell research has received very limited funding, so the development of cures for some catastrophic illnesses and injuries has been slow and in some cases, non-existent. During the next few years, there will be a shift in the political climate in this country and the scientists who have been waiting in the wings will emerge and progress will happen pretty quickly. It is my hope that I can start that escalation sooner."

"Can you do that single-handedly?"

"Single-handedly? No, but I have something that doesn't exist in 2019. I have the implant and the knowledge of how it was developed and how it works. If I can convince someone to fund a research and development project for me, we can advanced the science of SCI regeneration nearly a hundred years sooner than it would normally happen."

"SCI?"

"I'm sorry. It stands for Spinal Cord Injury."

Maggie fell silent for a moment. "I am seeing a side of you I didn't know existed, Jordan. I mean, I knew you were smart, and I knew you had some medical knowledge, but I never dreamed you were a medical research scientist."

"It's that advanced research knowledge that allowed me to be here today, Maggie. Kale developed the time machine, but both Andi and I helped Kale to fine-tune the quantum physics behind it in order for it to actually work."

Maggie finished her breakfast and put her plate on the

cookie sheet near the foot of the bed. She grabbed her coffee cup she had placed on the nightstand earlier and took a sip. "Tell me about the time travel, Jordan. What was it like?"

"Well, the machine Kale built had a series of concentric rings that when rotating in opposite directions, actually created a synthetic black hole in the center of it."

"Ah, aren't black holes kind of dangerous?" Maggie asked. "Doesn't it like, suck things into it?"

"Generally yes, but we discovered that in order to contain the black hole, we needed to add an outer set of rings, rotating in the opposite direction. Anyway, it took forever to finally progress far enough for Kale to let me try a transfer. Prior to that, we sent inanimate objects, and a monkey through time."

"So you just put this object into the machine and poof, it was gone? Were you able to get it back?"

"Yes, but it took dozens of adjustments to the software before we were able to control *when* to retrieve an object so it came back in relatively the same condition it was when we sent it."

"What do you mean?"

"Well, for example, the first thing Kale sent through time was an old boot, but when he retrieved it, it came back brand new. You see, he retrieved it years too early. Can you imagine what might have happened if he sent *me* through time and when he retrieved me, I came back as an infant?" Jordan chuckled.

Maggie frowned. "You mean he had to wait years to retrieve it? I'm confused."

"No, he actually retrieved it minutes after he sent it, but the significant digits in the software program were off by a couple of nanoseconds, which accumulated over the exact time period we were trying to transcend. Those cumulative seconds all added together, resulted in many years relative to the age of the boot."

"This is too complicated for me to absorb."

"Just know that with a few tweaks to the software, we were able to retrieve the boot relatively unchanged compared to the condition it was in when we sent it. We verified that with a newspaper as well."

"You said you sent a monkey through time?" Maggie asked.

"Yes we did. We actually retrofit the monkey with a vest that had a small camera mounted to it, so we were able to record the transfer process. We retrieved the monkey after only about ten minutes, but the two-hour disk on the camera was full."

"What was on the disk?"

"Some of the most amazing images I have ever seen. When the transfer first began, the recording showed streaks of light, bright colors racing toward them. The speed and direction of the light streaks gave the impression that they were moving down a thin tube at high speed...a tube filled with a million twinkling Christmas lights. To our amazement, the camera continued to work throughout the entire transfer process, including after the monkey landed. There were pictures of the barn...and even a quick shot of you."

"Whoa. Stop right there. You transported the monkey into my barn?" Maggie asked.

"Yes. You see, we transported the monkey *from* the barn in the year 2105, so it landed in the same spot it was transferred from."

"Oh, my God. You are really freaking me out now, Jordan."

"I'm sorry, Maggie. You asked me to tell you what it was like. I'm telling you the truth."

"So, does that means, when you transported, you also landed in the barn?"

"Yes. In fact, that's how I was there in time to save you from the winch that fell from the ceiling."

"Well, that explains how you appeared out of nowhere. Oh, but the way, did you know that John actually witnessed that particular transfer?"

"He did? He never mentioned it to me."

"Well apparently, you made an immediate impression on him during the winch incident and he quickly concluded that you were *good people*, as he put it and saw no reason to be alarmed that you appeared out of thin air."

"Thank God for John."

"So, what was it like?"

"The transfer? Well, it started out with me sitting on the platform in the middle of the rings—"

"Wait a minute. You intentionally put yourself in the middle of a black hole? Are you insane?" Maggie exclaimed.

"Keep in mind, we had already sent the monkey and he came back just fine. Anyway, when the rings neared critical velocity, I began to float then I felt this huge force on my body that pressed so hard against me that is was nearly impossible to breathe. I was completely paralyzed. I couldn't even move my fingers. What came next was this incredible tingling through my entire body, kind of like when the feeling returns after you sit on the toilet too long and your legs fall asleep."

Maggie sat beside Jordan, totally captivated by her words.

Jordan continued. "Everything was dark at first. No light. No sound. It was a total void. It felt like I was suspended and motionless. It was really quite terrifying the first time, and just when I was convinced I would die of fear alone, the space around me exploded into a multi-colored light show with the colors moving in and around each other like a giant kaleidoscope.

"I felt myself being drawn toward the hole in the center of this light show. Interestingly enough, the fear I was feeling simply evaporated. The colors were amazing. I found myself experiencing the colors in ways I didn't know were possible. I could not only *see* them, but I could *feel, smell* and *taste* them as well. Red was warm. Yellow was soft and silky. Green was tart, and blue felt like a gentle breeze. Lavender smelled like the air after a rainstorm. It was very stimulating.

"As I approached the end of this tunnel, everything became calm and peaceful. My heart and mind were filled with a sense of tranquility. At one point, it was so peaceful, I actually wondered if I had died during the transfer, but then suddenly, everything changed and I landed with a thud on the floor of the barn. It took me a minute or two to regain my bearings, but there I was, sitting in your barn behind the hay bales."

"Were you dressed?" Maggie asked.

"What kind of question is that?" Jordan replied.

"Well, in the Terminator movies, the time travelers arrived naked."

"Terminator movies?"

Maggie grinned. "Oh, yeah. I forgot. That would have been way before your time. Hell, the first one was made even before I was born, but they're classic time-travel movies. We'll have to watch one when we get back to the house. We can download them on-demand from the television. By the way, Linda Hamilton is really hot in those movies, but I digress. So, when you landed, that's when you saw the winch falling toward me and you jumped up to save the day?"

"I wish it was that simple," Jordan said. "The first time I landed, my implant wasn't working and I was totally immobile. I had to drag myself to the tack room to leave a message for Kale to retrieve me."

"You actually had a way to communicate with Kale and Andi?"

"Yes. There's a loose board on the floor beneath the bench in the tack room. I actually found it when I was a kid. We agreed that if I put something made of stone in the cubby that it meant I needed to be retrieved, and if I put something metal in there, it meant I arrived okay. So, unable to walk, I dragged myself to the tack room and found a whetstone, which I put in the cubby."

Jordan began to laugh.

"What's so funny?"

"Kale and Andi are pretty much city folk. They had no idea what a whetstone was and had to look it up in a catalog before they realized I was in trouble."

"So, why did the implant fail?"

"Interestingly enough, it was working again when I returned to the future. When I got back, we went to see a physics professor at the university and he told us the electro-magnetic fields I experienced through the transfer process cancelled out the electrical impulses transmitted by the implant. Further transfers were put on hold at that point until we could design a faraday shield to protect the implant."

"Further transfers? How many times did you do it?"

"Three, no, make that four times, but the final trip was made by an older version of me, just about a week ago when I finally got there in time to catch you before you fell over the cliff."

"Okay, slow, down, you're confusing me. You traveled here four times?" Maggie asked.

"Yes. I've already explained the first trip, when the implant failed. The second trip was made and I arrived just moments before you saddled Shawny for that fateful ride…only I didn't realize it at the time. After you left, I spent some time looking around the barn and exploring the barn yard while I waited for you to come back, but when Shawny suddenly galloped into the corral without you I realized I was too late. I was devastated.

"I made some adjustments to the transfer algorithm before the third trip back in order to get me here six months sooner. The *me* you see before you now, arrived during that transfer."

"Wait a minute. You're confusing me here. Did you just say the *you* I see before me arrived during the third transfer?"

"Yes."

"But you said there were four transfers. I don't remember you leaving and coming back again," Maggie said.

"Let me finish and I think it will become clearer. So where was I? Oh, yeah, the obituary said you died from a fall in March of 2019, and I actually arrived near the end of September, 2018. I arrived just before the winch fell from the rafters and nearly hit you."

"Was I supposed to die that day?" Maggie asked.

"No. You actually penned a diary entry for that day indicating you saw the winch falling and managed to mostly get out of the way of it. It apparently nicked you on the shoulder and back and fractured a couple of ribs, but you survived."

"I survived, only to die six months later, it seems," Maggie said.

"Yes. As I was saying, I arrived in September of 2018 and saved you from being hit by the winch, which according to your diaries, I didn't really have to do, but at least it saved you from having to deal with the rib fractures. As you know, you hired me on as a farm hand and as over the next six months we fell in love."

Maggie squeezed Jordan's hand. "Yes, we did," she said.

Jordan smiled and kissed the back of Maggie's hand. "Anyway, according to your obituary, you died on the morning of March 29, 2019. As luck would have it, I apparently overslept and was just minutes too late to keep you from falling over the cliff."

"But...but you weren't too late," Maggie said. "You actually *did* save me."

"Maggie, after we returned to the farm that morning, I rode back out to the edge of the cliff to look around. While I was there, I had a vision of myself racing across the plains trying to get to you on time, only to meet Shawny coming toward me with no rider, and knowing I was too late. You died in my arms. My God, Maggie, it tore my heart out. I wanted to lie down and die beside you."

"But, Jordan, that never happened. You reached me in time."

"On the morning you were supposed to die, I heard a loud bang as someone threw open our bedroom door and it hit the wall. I sat up in bed and saw this old woman standing in the doorway. I will never forget what she said to me. She said, *Jordan, get your ass out of bed. Go after her, now. Quickly, or you'll lose her forever.* I remember asking her who she was and she said, *never mind who I am, just hurry. For God's sake, please hurry. She just rode off. You have very little time.*

"I realize now the older woman was me. Don't you see...I overslept and failed to save you on the third trip and yes—you died in my arms. I must have convinced Kale to send me back one more time to make sure the younger me woke up soon enough to save you. You know what happened next, Maggie. I reached you with just seconds to spare and stopped you from falling over the cliff. The memory I have of you dying in my arms must have been the older Jordan's memory—not mine."

"So there were two of you here at the same time?" Maggie asked.

"It appears so, which explains why the old woman backed out of the way to let me pass. You see, matter can't occupy the same physical space more than once at the same time. Physics also dictates that you cannot occupy the present and the past at the same time nor the present and the future at the same time. If she had touched me, there's no telling what might have happened."

"Jesus, Jordan. This is giving me the creeps."

"I can understand why you feel that way, Maggie, but believe me, everything I'm telling you is the truth. Oh, and something else I haven't told you yet. When I was holding your collar to keep you from going over the cliff, I felt this tingling in my body, just like I felt every time Kale retrieved me from the past.

"I was so worried he would pull me back before I had a chance to save you, but I now realize it was the older Jordan he was retrieving. You see, *I* wasn't in the barn when the tingling began, but I assume *she* was. She would have returned to the barn to be teleported back to the future after waking me up. Also, I was holding you by the collar at the time, and since he couldn't retrieve more matter than he sent, there was no way for him to retrieve this younger version of me as long as I was touching you. I'm sure I felt the tingling because he was retrieving *my* DNA, albeit an older version of it."

Maggie stared at Jordan for several moments in silence.

"What are you thinking?" Jordan said.

"I'm thinking that no one could possibly make this stuff up if it wasn't real. I'm thinking it will be an interesting life living with a time traveler."

CHAPTER 22

"How are you at grilling?" Gina asked Jordan as she lit the grill.

"That depends on whether you like hockey pucks," Jordan replied.

"Then we're screwed, 'cause I specialize in hockey pucks as well. I guess we'll just have to wing it. Grab a couple of beers from the fridge, will ya?"

"Got it," Jordan said.

Jordan stepped into the house and dropped a kiss on Maggie's cheek as she walked by en route to the refrigerator. Maggie and Sam were preparing a salad to complement the burgers she and Gina were about to incinerate.

"Tell Gina not to turn the grill on high this time and to cook them only for five minutes on each side with the grill cover open. I'll be out to check them in ten minutes," Sam said as Jordan made her way back to the kitchen door.

The first thing Jordan noticed when she stepped outside was the white smoke billowing out from under the grill cover. "Ah, Sam said don't turn the grill up on high this time."

"Now she tells me," Gina said as she threw open the lid to expose a neat row of burgers, all ablaze.

Jordan grabbed the metal spatula. "Quick, let's move them to the top rack before they turn to ash."

Between the two of them, they managed to move the burgers and get the inferno under control inside the grill.

"Is the grill on low now?" Jordan asked.

"Yes."

"Okay, I'm going to flip these and move them back to the lower level. Do you have a spray bottle of water handy? When Maggie cooks on the grill, she uses it to keep the meat from drying out. Maybe we can prevent another flare-up as well."

"I'll be right back," Gina said as she went into the house and returned a few minutes later with a spray bottle in hand. "Will this work?"

"I think so."

"The girls wanted to know why I needed a spray bottle. I told them we were hot and needed to cool off," Gina chuckled.

"You know they're going to bust our asses for this anyway, don't you?"

"That's pretty much a given."

"Hmmm, the burgers are nice and juicy, babe," Sam said.

"Thank you," Gina said, sending a sly look Jordan's way.

"So, let's talk about this documentation problem," Maggie suggested.

"I say we wing it," Jordan suggested.

"What do you mean by wing it?" Maggie asked.

"Anyone want another drink?" Gina said as she pushed herself away from the dining room table.

"I'll take another beer," Jordan replied.

"A refill on the wine would be nice," Sam said. "How about you, Maggie?"

Maggie nodded, unable to speak with a mouthful of food.

"What I mean," Jordan continued, "is that if the institute wants what I have to offer badly enough, they'll work with me to obtain, or fabricate, or whatever it takes to get me the documentation I need to live a normal life."

Gina put a beer in front of Jordan. "You seem pretty sure of yourself, Jordan," she said.

"Thanks, Gina. What I have to offer could make someone very rich. I just need to get that message across when I present to the board in a couple of weeks. The return on investment for this research project will be phenomenal."

"I thought you wanted this to be *your* team, with *you* in control of the research," Maggie said.

"I do. I am the only one with the knowledge to make this happen near term. When I present my case, I hope that becomes clear to the investors. I won't do this if they don't allow me to run the project."

"So you're basically going to do all the work to make some billionaire even richer," Gina said.

"That's unavoidable, Gina. In order to develop the implant, I need someone to establish a multi-million dollar, private foundation for me, and before anyone is willing to do that, they will need to feel comfortable that they'll get their investment back, and then some. Unfortunately, that's how the system works."

"And what do you get out of it, Jordan?" Sam asked.

"I will get a substantial compensation package, as well as intellectual property ownership for the implant design. If it takes off as I think it will the patent will be a significant source of income for many years to come. But what I really get out of the deal is the chance to prevent a sixteen year old from spending fourteen years in a wheelchair like I did. That alone is worth any amount of blood, sweat and tears it will take to get this project off the ground."

"Jordan, what are you going to do if they ask how you obtained your experience?" Sam asked.

"That's a good question," Maggie said. "And what will you tell them when they ask about your own injury?"

"I'm not going to tell them about my injury, nor about the implant, and certainly not about the time travel. It'll be really important that none of you divulge that information either."

"But you are proof that it works. Why *wouldn't* you tell them?" Maggie asked.

"Jordan and I talked about this on the way home from meeting with the lawyer," Gina said. "Basically, that information in the wrong hands could put not only the project in danger, but Jordan's personal safety as well."

"I see," Sam said.

"You see?" Maggie said, her voice raising an octave. "Could someone please enlighten *me*?"

"Maggie, you're right. Jordan is the perfect proof that the implant works, but if the wrong person learns that she carries this miracle device around with her, it wouldn't be long before someone tries to take it from her," Sam said.

"Are you suggesting someone might forcibly remove it

from her?" Maggie asked.

"Well I certainly wouldn't *willingly* allow them to take it," Jordan said. "Look, Mags, this implant could easily be reverse-engineered. Someone with the right skills could figure out how to make it work even without my help, but only if they have access to it."

"I don't like the sound of this, Jordan. Why don't you just come back to work on the farm and forget about all this," Maggie suggested.

"I can't do that Maggie. It would be like me asking you to give up the farm. For the past sixteen years, I have devoted my life to someday making this cure accessible to other victims of SCI. I can't…no, I *won't* walk away from it now. Not when I have the chance to make a difference."

Maggie struggled to hold her emotions in check. "So you're just going to walk right into the institute, wow them with your intelligence and experience, and expect them to throw millions of dollars at you." It was more of a statement than a question.

"That pretty much sums it up," Jordan said. "What I need to do is some intensive research into the current state of development for SCI regeneration. I need to find the holes in their theories and I need to determine what their roadblocks are. Then, I need to point out where and how I can help them get beyond those roadblocks."

"How can you be so sure?" Maggie asked.

"I am sure because that's how we started with our own development. My fellow research scientists and I piggy-backed on the failures of our predecessors. These scientists are our predecessors, Maggie. They've already laid the foundation. I just need to provide the building blocks to construct the solution on top of what they've already done."

"And your identity problem, Jordan, how do you plan to deal with that?" Gina asked.

"My proposal will lay out the conditions under which I will participate in this research. Helping me to establish a no questions asked identity will be at the top of the list."

"And if they choose to report you to the government

instead of doing your wishes? What then?" Gina asked.

"That won't happen," Jordan said.

"How can you be so sure?" Maggie asked.

"Because I've done my homework. After you dropped me off at the apartment yesterday morning, Gina, I walked down to the Fletcher Free Library on College Street and did some research on the people who run the institute as well as those who fund it. The primary benefactor is a foundation called JEM Spinal Injury Research Association, administered by a man named Charles Malone. It turns out that Mr. Malone has a teenage daughter who has been confined to a wheelchair for three years now with a completely severed spinal cord. Records indicate he began supporting the institute right after his daughter's accident. If the institute chooses to set up the private foundation to support the development of this implant, I am confident I can have her on her feet within a year. *That* is how I can be so sure."

* * *

Jordan volunteered to load the dishwasher while the others searched for an interesting on-demand movie to watch on television.

"Hey, how about *The Terminator*?" Maggie suggested. "It seems apropos, considering Jordan's situation, don't you think? I told her about it a few days ago."

"That's a great idea," Sam said. "Let me see if I can find it on the menu."

Jordan entered the living room a few moments later carrying wine coolers for everyone. She glanced at the television as the opening credits rolled. "The Terminator, huh? This should be interesting." She passed the drinks out and sat down next to Maggie, draping her arm around her shoulder.

Maggie snuggled into her side. "I've missed this over the past few days, love," she said softly.

Jordan kissed her on the temple. "Me too."

Jordan sat forward in her seat about a half hour into the movie. She rested her forearms on her thighs and stared intently at the screen. "Gina, do you have something I can write on?"

"Sure, let me get it for you," Gina said. She retrieved a small notepad and a pen and handed them to Jordan as she returned to her position beside Sam on the couch.

"What are you doing, love?" Maggie asked.

"This movie is triggering a few thoughts about the implant. I might want to use some of it in the presentation to the institute, or at the very least, file it away for future reference."

"You do realize this is only the first of three movies, don't you?" Gina asked.

"Three?"

"Yeah. They made two sequels."

Sam reached for the remote control and paused the movie. "Well if we're going to do a six-hour Terminator marathon, I need to make some popcorn. Who's with me on this one?"

Maggie was on her feet in an instant. "I am a major popcorn ho. You're damned right I'm with you as long as it's doing the backstroke in butter. Come on, I'll help you make it."

CHAPTER 23

Early the next morning, Gina drove Maggie and Jordan back to the farm. Inside the front door, Maggie stopped and offered to take Jordan's duffle bag to the bedroom.

"No, I think I'll take it with me back to the apartment. I'll need the clothes that are in it."

"You're going to the apartment? I...I thought you might want to come home," Maggie said.

"I have a significant amount of research to do at the medical library if I'm going to be ready for this presentation in two weeks. It'll be a lot more convenient being within walking distance of the library for the next several days. It'll save you from having to drive me into town every day."

Maggie fell silent, a fact not lost on Jordan.

"Are you okay?" Jordan asked.

Maggie nodded without meeting Jordan's eyes. "I'm just a little disappointed. I was looking forward to you being home."

"I'm looking forward to being home too, but everything is hinging on me convincing the institute to fund the implant project. I'll be working some very long hours over the next two weeks getting ready for the presentation. I just thought it would be easier on both of us if I did it from Burlington."

Maggie continued to avoid Jordan's gaze.

Jordan reached forth and took Maggie's chin in her hand. "Sweetie, look at me." She studied Maggie's face closely and watched a parade of emotions cross her features. "Baby, talk to me."

"I'm afraid you'll never come home, Jordan," Maggie said tearfully.

Jordan smiled. "Is that what this is all about? Sweetheart, wild horses couldn't keep me from coming home once I have the information I need for the presentation. I don't think I'll be gone for more than a week. You can join me if you'd like."

Maggie walked a few steps away then turned to face Jordan. "I can't. Without you here to help John, I'll need to pitch in."

"You *do* realize that if my proposal is approved, I'll be pretty much working full time on it for the foreseeable future. You might want to consider hiring another farmhand to replace me."

"I suspect if your proposal is approved, a lot of things are going to change around here."

"That's true, but one thing that will *not* change is my commitment to you. Like I said, I can't begin to describe the planning and effort it took for me to get to you. I am not willing to give up everything the future has in store for us, Maggie. You have nothing to fear. We were destined to be together through all space and time and I promise I'll do nothing to jeopardize that."

Maggie shoved her hands into her pockets and lifted her shoulders to her ears. "Do you want to leave tonight, or tomorrow morning?" she asked.

"That depends on how early you want to get up in the morning. The library will probably open by eight and I'd like to get an early start. I'm sorry you'll have to drive me there, but I have this small issue with having no driver's license in 2019."

"I'm okay with taking you in early. I'd like to spend tonight in our own bed, wrapped in your arms," Maggie replied.

"I was hoping you'd say that," Jordan said.

Maggie looked into Jordan's eyes for several long moments. "I love you, Jordan. I wanted to die when you left. I regretted asking you to leave the moment the words left my mouth. I should have begged you to stay, but this stubborn Irish pride of mine got in the way. Forgive me?"

Jordan gathered Maggie into her arms. "Your stubborn Irish pride is one of the things I love most about you. Please don't ever change. I'm just glad we are here together now. Promise me we'll be more open with one another from now on."

"I promise," Maggie said.

"Me too." Jordan kissed Maggie tenderly. "So what do you

say we head into town for dinner? I'd like to try that Japanese steak house on Shelburne Road near the highway."

"You mean Koto's?"

"Yeah, that's the place."

Maggie stepped out of Jordan's embrace and retrieved her purse from the coat hooks behind the door. "Sounds good to me... and while we're out, I want to stop and add a cell phone to my plan for you. If we're going to be spending some time apart, I'd like for us to be able to contact each other no matter where we are."

"Why don't we wait until I'm actually making some money so I can pay for my own cell phone," Jordan suggested.

Maggie frowned. "Now whose pride is getting in the way? Look, Jordan, if we're going to be married, it makes more sense for us to be on the same plan. It's actually cheaper to have a family plan anyway."

Jordan grinned. "Okay, I'll concede that one to you. So, when did you have in mind for us to get married?"

"Well, we originally planned it to be around my birthday, which is in on April sixteenth. I think it's a Tuesday. Today is the seventh, so we should plan it for either next weekend or the weekend after that."

"I hate to burst your bubble, but we need to solve my identity problem before we can get a marriage license. I'm afraid we may have to put the wedding off until after that happens. My presentation is on Monday, April twenty-second, so with any luck we should have that problem fixed not too long after that."

"Oh yeah, I forgot about that. Okay then, I'll keep the date open ended for now."

Jordan's stomach rumbled loud enough for Maggie to hear it.

"The beast is complaining. Time for lunch. Take your bag to the bedroom then we can head out. While you're doing that, I'll pull the truck up to the door."

Jordan picked up her bag and headed in the direction of the bedroom. She pushed the door open and stepped inside, only to stop dead at the vision before her. Moments later, Jordan climbed into the front seat of the pickup truck and looked at Maggie. "Want to explain why half the sheetrock is torn off the bedroom wall?"

* * *

"You can park over there, behind the building," Jordan said the next morning as Maggie pulled into the driveway of the apartment building.

"You weren't kidding when you said it was across the street from the hospital," Maggie remarked.

"The location is the primary reason I want to hold on to it for a while. Like I said, I'll probably be working late on a regular basis and until I can get a driver's license, it will be easier for me to just walk to the apartment than for you to come in from Shelburne to pick me up every day."

Jordan pulled a key ring out of her pocket and worked one of the keys off the ring. She handed it to Maggie. "Here's a spare key to the place in case you want to stay over with me some nights."

Jordan grabbed her duffle bag and climbed out of the truck after Maggie, then walked hand-in-hand with her to the apartment in the back of the building.

"It's really small, but I don't need much room for sleeping," Jordan said as she unlocked and pushed the door open for Maggie to enter first.

"Wow, this is really cute," Maggie said. "It's small, and a little outdated, but cute." Maggie looked around at the flowered wallpaper, craftsman molding around the window and doors, and original pine flooring. On one side of the room was the bed, a desk and a dresser with a TV on top of it. On the other side was a small sink cabinet with a microwave on the counter top, a small cabinet over the sink, and an apartment sized refrigerator beside it. A small bathroom with a claw-foot tub, toilet and sink adjoined the bedroom.

"The landlord is an elderly lady, who actually lives in the front part of the building. I suspect this room was originally part of the main house."

"It's nice that it's on the back side. That should keep the

traffic noise to a minimum," Maggie said.

Jordan wrapped her arm around Maggie's waist and pulled her down onto the bed. "C'mere, you," she said as she snuggled with Maggie. "As much as I like this apartment, I'm so very glad I won't be living in it full time. I was not looking forward to living my life without you. Thank you for letting me come home."

"No thanks necessary, Jordan. You should have never left in the first place. I was a fool to let you go." Maggie traced the side of Jordan's face with her index finger. "I'm going to miss you when you don't come home."

"I promise it won't be for long. I'll be home in a few days, and if they accept my proposal, I may end up working late a few nights a week until we have a routine established. If that happens, I'll stay here, but other than that, I'll be home in the evenings."

"I'll be so glad when all this uncertainty is behind us," Maggie said.

"Like what?"

"Well, like the approval for your research foundation, getting you legal documentation, getting married. I have so many plans for our lives together, Jordan, but it's all hanging in limbo right now."

"What kind of plans?"

"For starters, I've always wanted to open a riding school for handicapped children. Considering your situation, I want to do that more than ever."

"You like children, don't you? You were so kind and patient with the children of the construction workers when we had the celebration at the end of the barn raising."

"I guess it comes from being an only child. Hell, I don't even have nieces and nephews to spoil. I would have much preferred to come from a larger family."

"I was an only child too, so I totally understand what you mean. The closest things I've ever had to siblings are Kale and Andi." Jordan fell silent for several long moments.

"You miss them, don't you?" Maggie asked.

Jordan wiped a tear from the corner of her eye. "Yes, I do.

Unfortunately, I'll never see them again."

Maggie traced the line of Jordan's brow with her index finger. "Maybe we can name our first born after one of them," she suggested.

"You would do that?"

"If it wasn't for them, you wouldn't be here with me today. Of course, I would do that. For you, and for them."

"Well, I guess I just agreed to have a baby with you," Jordan pointed out.

"Or two…"

"Two?"

"Or thr—"

Jordan quickly put her hand over Maggie's mouth. "Two sounds just about right."

Maggie began singing, "Jordan and Maggie sittin' in a tree—"

"K-I-S-S-I-N-G," Jordan added.

"First comes love, second comes marriage," Maggie sang.

"Then comes Maggie pushing a baby carriage." Jordan ended the childhood limerick by kissing Maggie on the end of the nose.

"I love you, Jordan."

"I love you too, Mags."

CHAPTER 24

Two weeks later…

Jordan walked to the front of the conference room, portraying an air of confidence and poise. She had elected to wear a double-breasted, pin-striped business suit, a crisply starched white shirt and medium height heels. She stood behind the lectern and picked up the remote control to the overhead projection system.

"Good morning," she said. "My name is Dr. Jordan Lewis, Professor of Kinesiology and an expert in the field of spinal cord injury and regeneration techniques. I first want to thank you for taking time out of your busy schedules to grant me an audience. What I will be outlining for you today, is a proposal for the development of a cure for spinal cord paralysis."

Jordan looked around the room at the stunned expressions on the faces of the scientists.

"Yes, you heard me correctly. I use the term *cure* in the literal sense. You see, historically, treatments for complete SCI's has involved a regimen of managed care. I will present to you today, a concept that will not manage a complete SCI, but rather, cure it. I further submit that the age of the injury, while important, is not a deciding factor relative to curing a completely severed spinal column."

Jordan watched as nearly every person in the room furiously scribbled notes on the papers in front of them, with the exception of one man who sat directly opposite her at the end of the conference table. He was a good-looking man, dressed in blue jeans, a white shirt and tie, and a tweed jacket with leather patches on the elbows and a shock of unruly hair. Jordan guessed him to be around her same age. He appeared to be watching her intently; an even, non-responsive expression on his face.

Who does he remind me of? Jordan said to herself as she mentally prepared to begin her presentation.

"Without further ado, let's get started." Jordan turned on the projector and displayed her first slide. "Being in the company of such esteemed medical scientists, I don't need to go into any great detail about the function of a healthy spinal cord.

"Spinal cord injury is most often caused by trauma where vertebrae are displaced and the cord running through them is damaged. Motor and sensory control below the point of the lesion is lost or impaired.

"We all know that while spontaneous function recovery is possible with partial lesions of the spinal cord, deficits persist in a complete separation. Even if partial function is restored during the treatment of a complete SCI, there is almost always some level of permanent disability associated with the injury."

Jordan advanced the slide.

"There have been many research projects focused on repairing completely severed spinal cords. All of these projects used non-human test subjects. Nearly all of them resulted in some level of restored function, but none of them was completely successful."

Jordan continued to advance the slides as she addressed several individual research projects.

"One study, done in 2004, found that by repeated stimulation of the spinal cord, one could modify the spinal circuits and create temporarily functional synergistic movements. The net conclusion here is that it might be possible to stimulate these synergistic movements by implanting electrodes into localized and stable regions of the spinal cord. What is key here, is that as soon as that electrode is removed, the injury and subsequent paralysis persist.

"Another study in 2007 promotes the use of autologous bone marrow cell transplant and bone marrow stimulation. It was hypothesized that by grafting bone marrow cells into the SCI, it promoted the production of neuroprotective cytokines that are known to rescue neurons which typically suffer cell death after such an injury. Unfortunately, significant functional recovery after cell transplantation was rarely found to be achievable with human subjects.

"A third study, done in 2010, suggests the application of aggressive medical resuscitation and blood pressure management can lead to partially restored functions and bladder control. Very high percentages of these patients showed significant improvement in neurological functions within a year of treatment. What is important to point out here is that these trials were done specifically on cervical and thoracic injuries, but no evidence exists that this approach works on lumbar injuries. Again, testing was done on non-human subjects.

"The last treatment option I'd like to touch on is not a treatment at all. It does not address the injury, but rather restores mobility. What I am referring to here is the bionic exoskeleton, originally approved by the FDA in 2014. It is quite ingenious, as it effectively connects this bionic suit to the patient's nervous system. The suit picks up signals from the muscles on the arms and legs and assists the patient to move. The downside of this approach is that it does not treat the injury at all. In addition, the bionic suit tends to be quite cumbersome in size and requires a lengthy learning curve to become proficient with it."

Jordan paused to look around the room. "Are there any questions thus far?" she asked.

A hand raised in the corner of the room. "Yes, my name is Dr. Hollinbeck. I am familiar with several of the studies you have highlighted, but you have yet to mention anything about endogenous stem cells."

"Thank you for your question. That's a great lead-in to my next slide." Jordan advanced the slide and once again addressed her audience.

"So far, I have provided several examples of some very good work carried out by the foremost recognized scientists in our field; however, as I have pointed out, with the exception of the exoskeleton, none of the approaches has thus far been proven to work on human subjects, nor have they resulted in a complete reversal of the injury. I am here today to propose an approach that does both.

"The method I have developed employs a two-pronged

treatment. First, both autologous, or transplanted stem cells, and endogenous neural stem cells, which are already resident in the spinal column, are inserted into the injury site. Second, the stem cells work in conjunction with a device that simultaneously activates millions of genes to promote cell growth, similar to cells types that repair skin wounds in humans. This device immediately restores full mobility and ultimately, over time, repairs the synapse connections over the injury site, leading to the restoration of nerve endings and sensory feeling. The device is self-taught and self powered, and the software is designed to become self-aware as the healing process progresses. In short, it develops its own order of intelligence. I will also add that this approach has already been fully tested and is currently operational in a human test subject."

Jordan paused to drink from the bottle of water on the podium as she covertly looked out over her audience. Her eyes were drawn to the man at the end of the table once more. He smiled slightly at her, his gaze never leaving her face.

Jordan advanced to her next slide. "As you know, a project of this magnitude requires significant funding. I anticipate the development cycle to be approximately one year for the prototype and several years beyond that to fully optimize and perfect an FDA-approved version.

"A list of my terms and conditions, the estimated cost of this development, and the number and types of scientists I will need on the team is outlined in the package I will leave with you at the end of this presentation. The return on investment will be substantial, but the real bonus will be to the thousands, if not millions of SCI victims that will benefit from this development. I thank you for your time. I will now take your questions pertaining to the presentation."

* * *

"Can you believe the nerve of that woman?" Dr. Hollinbeck said. "Look at this list of terms and conditions. She provided us with her name and information about her degree field, but other than that there are no details about her education or work history. That makes me suspicious."

"She seemed well informed to me," the man at the end of the table said.

"No offense, Chuck, but you're just the front man for some rich philanthropist. You have very little background in scientific research. I'm not sure you're qualified to offer your opinion here."

"I agree with Chuck," another board member said. "She definitely seemed to know what she was talking about. I am very curious about this device of hers. She says it's already been proven functional in a human test subject."

"Heaven knows we aren't making much progress on our own," said yet another board member.

"Well I, for one am not convinced she's authentic," Hollinbeck said. "We pointedly asked her how her device works, and she refuses to tell us."

"It's not unusual for an inventor to keep the details to themselves until funding is secured and intellectual property rights are established. It's a sound business decision on her part," Chuck said. "I mean, she wasn't demanding payment up front, just a commitment for funding. We reserve the right to cancel the project if she is unable to deliver."

"I don't know. Something doesn't feel right about this. I mean, she leaves this list of demands with us, yet she won't share any information about who she is. Look at these terms and conditions for Christ's sake. She wants to be in charge of the team. I'll be damned if I'll let her come in and take over my lab, never mind give *me* direct orders. She also wants a generous salary and the IP and patent ownership for the device. What's in it for the institute if she gets all the credit and royalties from the design?"

"She might get IP rights and royalties, but the institute gets the revenue generated from the sale of the device. She was right when she said the return on investment would be substantial," Chuck argued.

Hollinbeck was not to be deterred. "I still don't feel good about this. Look at this last demand. She wants assistance establishing credentials and identity, whatever the hell that means. As far as I'm concerned, it's not my job to see that she gets all the glory for developing this device. If she really wants to sell this to someone, she needs to learn how to be a team player."

Chuck narrowed his eyes in Hollinbeck's direction. "What are you concerned about Hollinbeck, her integrity, or taking direction from a woman and giving her credit for her own innovation?"

"I resent what you are implying, Chuck. Look around this room and ask the others if I give credit where credit is due."

Chuck scanned the faces of the others in the room and was met by evasive or guarded gazes.

"Look Chuck," Hollinbeck continued, I admit I was intrigued by her ideas, but without any data to back it up—and without her willingness to share the details up front—this feels like a scam. The last thing we need is to give her a ton of money only to have her skip town on us. I vote no on this one."

"Are you sure about that?" Chuck asked. "What if she's the real deal?"

"If she's the real deal, then why all the secrecy?"

Chuck sat back in his chair. "Suit yourself."

"So, let's put this to a vote. There are thirteen of us in the room. Raise your hand if you approve her proposal." Hollinbeck looked each member of the board in the eye as one by one, they voted.

Of the thirteen scientists present, only six found the courage to raise their hands and defy their lead scientist.

CHAPTER 25

"Take her up, John," Jordan said as she stood on top of the pallet of hay bales, riding it to the loft where she swung the pallet onto the deck. "Give me a minute to unload these and I'll send it back down again," she said.

"I can come up there and give you a hand with that, if you'd like," John offered.

"Not necessary. It'll just take me a minute or two. In fact, I'm nearly finished already." Jordan hopped onto the empty pallet and gave John the signal to lower it back to the barn floor.

"I'm kind of glad you're home, Jordan. Miss Maggie worked herself into an unhealthy state after you left."

"What do you mean?" Jordan asked as she stacked new bales of hay onto the pallet.

"Well, she was neglecting Shawny and not taking very good care of herself. The morning Miss Gina came after her, I knocked on her door at ten in the morning and she was still in bed. That's not like her."

"Well, I'm back and nothing is going to chase me away again."

"That's good to hear. You're good people, Jordan…and you're good for Miss Maggie."

"Thank you, John."

Jordan stacked several bales onto the pallet in silence before addressing John once more.

"I understand you saw my transfer into the barn on the morning the winch fell from the rafter. Why didn't you ask me about it?" Jordan asked.

"It all happened so fast. I saw the flash of light, and then Maggie came out of Shawny's stall, right into the path where the winch fell and you pretty much acted on instinct and pushed her out of the way. I knew right then that you meant us no harm,"

John explained.

"But weren't you even curious about it, John?"

"Sure I was, but I figured if you wanted me to know, you'd tell me yourself. Besides, if I've learned anything in my life, it's that it don't matter none where you come from as long as you're good people."

Jordan wiped the sweat off her brow with the back of her sleeve. "Well, I certainly appreciate your open mindedness, John. I want you to know I love Maggie with all my heart and I would do nothing to hurt her. I came here to save her from Jan—not to hurt her."

"So, Maggie tells me you're a scientist. I kind of thought as much. You seem smarter than the average person. I wish you all the luck in the world on your research project."

"I've got my fingers crossed that it will be funded, John. I should be hearing from the board at the spinal institute in a couple of weeks about whether they've accepted my proposal."

"And if they don't?"

"Then I'll seek funding elsewhere. I'd like to keep the research local, but I'll go national if I have to." Jordan once again climbed on top of the pallet. "Round two…take her up."

Jordan had just finished unloading the second pallet of hay bales when she heard Maggie calling her name from across the barnyard.

"Jordan? Where are you? The mailman just delivered a letter from the institute."

"In the barn, Mags." Jordan rode the second pallet to the ground as Maggie waited below.

"You go on and take care of business. I've got this next load," John said.

"Thanks, John." Jordan draped her arm around Maggie's shoulder and walked out of the barn with her. Once outside, she took the letter from Maggie and stared at it intently.

"This doesn't feel right, Maggie. It's too soon. My presentation was only this past Monday, just four days ago. I'm afraid that's not a good sign."

"Or it could be a good sign," Maggie said hopefully.

"Sweetie, no one makes a decision to spend this kind of money without thinking about it long and hard, and running it through a lengthy return on investment analysis. Trust me, I've been here before."

"Well, open it," Maggie said.

Jordan tore open the flap and retrieved a one-page, typewritten letter. She quickly scanned the letter then lowered her chin to her chest. "It's just as I thought," she said.

"Let me see it," Maggie said, taking it from Jordan and reading it out loud.

Dear Miss Lewis.

Thank you for presenting your ideas to us this past Monday on your approach to the treatment and cure of complete SCI's. We regret to inform you that your application for a research grant has been denied. This rejection is due to your lack of verifying credentials as a certified expert in the field of spinal cord injury treatments. We feel irrefutable and spotless credentials are a requirement to move forward with a project that would require the degree of funding your proposal implied. We sincerely hope this will not discourage you from continuing your research.

Sincerely,

Dr. Robert Hollinbeck, PhD.

Assistant Director of the Vermont Spinal Cord Institute

University of Vermont Medical Center.

Maggie put her hand on Jordan's back. "Sweetie, I'm so sorry."

Jordan fought hard to hold back her tears of disappointment. "I was so sure my presentation would convince them to fund this project. They are being so shortsighted."

"The letter implies they rejected the proposal because of your lack of credentials. I don't think it has anything to do with the project itself."

Jordan nodded. "I guess I can't blame them. After all, what do they know about me? I'm an unknown entity that literally fell from the sky. I'll need to find a way to fabricate my credentials before I try again. I don't want to risk another rejection."

"That might be best," Maggie said. "Why don't you come into the house and have an iced tea with me before going back to the barn. Okay?"

Jordan nodded as she and Maggie walked toward the house. Just then, her cell phone rang.

"Who could that be? The only people I really know around here are you, Gina and Sam, and this is definitely not one of their cell numbers," Jordan said as she looked at the screen. She pushed the answer button and held the phone to her ear. "Hello?"

"Jordan Lewis?" a man's voice said.

"Yes, this is she."

"Ms. Lewis, my name is Charles Malone and I…"

"Charles Malone. Yes, I know who you are." Jordan looked at Maggie and raised her eyebrows.

"Yes, anyway, I have reason to believe you received a letter today from the Vermont Spinal Institute. Is that correct?"

"As a matter of fact, I'm holding it in my hand right now."

"I'd like to talk to you about that letter, and about your proposal, if I may."

"Of course, Mr. Malone. What time would be best for you?"

"I can be there in five minutes."

"Five minutes? I…I'm afraid I've been working in the barn and…."

"Don't worry about the way you look, Miss Lewis. It's your brain I'm interested in, not your hygiene."

"Well, in that case, Mr. Malone. I'll have a glass of iced tea waiting for you when you get here. We're located at—"

"I have your address from the funding application. I'll find you."

"Okay then. We'll see you soon."

Jordan shut her phone off and slipped it into her back pocket. "I've at least got to wash off the barn dust. Could I bother you to pour us all some iced tea?" Jordan asked.

Maggie smiled. "Of course, love."

Jordan ran up the front steps, taking them two at a time while Maggie followed at a slower pace. By the time she heard the sound of tires on gravel, Maggie had three glasses of iced tea poured, as well as a selection of sweet breads laid out on a plate. "I just heard a car pull up out front, Jordan," Maggie called out.

Jordan entered the kitchen just as they both heard a car door close. She was visibly nervous.

"Calm down, love. It'll be okay," Maggie said. "Deep breath."

A knock on the screen door called their attention to their visitor on the front porch. Maggie opened the inside door then pushed open the screen door for Mr. Malone to enter.

Jordan's eyes opened wide. "You! You were at the presentation," she said.

Mr. Malone stepped forward and extended his hand to Jordan. "Yes. Chuck Malone," he said, firmly grasping Jordan's hand.

"It's nice to see you again," Jordan said. She stared at him for a few seconds, before shaking herself out of her reverie. "I'm sorry, but you remind me of someone."

"I get that a lot," Malone said. He turned to look at Maggie. "So who is this lovely lady?"

"Sheesh, where are my manners? Mr. Malone, this is my fiancée, Maggie Downs. Maggie, Charles Malone."

Mr. Malone shook her hand warmly. "Your fiancée, huh?"

"Is that a problem, Mr. Malone?" Jordan asked.

"Chuck. Please call me Chuck, and no, it's not a problem. It's so nice to meet you, Ms. Downs."

"The pleasure is all mine, Chuck, and since we're on a first name basis, please call me Maggie."

"Maggie it is." Chuck looked around. "You have a beautiful home. It's very comfortable."

"Speaking of comfort, please have a seat. I've poured some iced tea for all of us," Maggie said.

Chuck pulled out a chair and made himself comfortable at the handmade wooden table, then helped himself to the sweet breads on the table in front of him. "These are amazing," he said.

"Maggie's the cook. I'm afraid I burn water," Jordan joked.

"You too, huh? My wife wouldn't even let me in the kitchen. Maggie, you'll have to give me the recipe for these before I leave. My daughter, Jessie will love these."

"How old is she?" Jordan asked as she too bit into a sweetbread. "Wow, Mags, Chuck is right. These are incredible."

"Thanks, love," Maggie said. Then, to Chuck, "So how old is Jessie?"

"Jessie is thirteen, going on twenty."

"God love you," Jordan said. "Speaking from personal experience, raising girls is not a lot of fun sometimes."

"You got that right," Chuck exclaimed. "One minute, she's all sugar and spice and the very next moment, she's having a high-speed come apart over nothing."

"If it's any consolation, it gets better," Maggie said.

"Well, it can't happen soon enough."

"So, Chuck, what brings you out here?" Jordan asked.

"First, I want to tell you how impressed I was with your presentation, Jordan, and I'd like to learn more about how your device works."

"I'm sorry, Chuck. Since the institute rejected my proposal, I will need to seek other funding, and quite frankly, I need to protect the IP for those donors willing to invest in its development."

Chuck smiled. "I like your attitude and your conviction, Jordan, and I totally understand your reluctance to release any IP relative this device, but *I* am that donor willing to invest in its development."

Maggie reached across the table and took Jordan's hand.

"You? Chuck, forgive me for being confused, but it's a well documented fact that you are the primary benefactor of the Spinal Institute, and as you know, they rejected my proposal."

"Correction, Jordan. I *was* the primary benefactor of the Spinal Institute. I have withdrawn my support starting immediately."

"But, why?"

"Let's just say their focus and their priorities diverge with my beliefs. It is time to make a change, for me, and for Jessie."

"Jessie?"

"If you've done your homework on me, and I believe you have, you will know that Jessie has been in a wheelchair for the past three years."

"Car accident," Jordan said. "I read about it. I'm sorry about your wife."

"I was devastated. At least I didn't lose both of them. Jessie was severely injured in the crash. Her spinal cord was severed at the L1 vertebra."

Jordan's gaze darted to Maggie as they exchanged a knowing look.

"Jordan, your presentation has given me a reason to hope again...to hope that someday, Jessie will be able to get out of that chair and live a normal life."

Jordan closed her eyes and inhaled deeply. When she opened them, she looked directly at Chuck. "Chuck, with the right team and the right funding, I am confident I can get Jessie out of that chair and on her feet within a year."

Chuck's hand flew up to cover his mouth in an attempt to stifle a sob that successfully escaped. Tears spilled over onto his cheeks. Jordan reached out for his free hand while Maggie stood and wrapped her arms around the sobbing man. For the next several minutes, no one said a word as Chuck slowly regained his composure.

"I'm sorry," he said.

"No need to be sorry," Jordan said. "I feel your pain, Chuck. Trust me on that one."

Maggie released Chuck and circled around the table to stand behind Jordan, placing her hands on Jordan's shoulders.

"Don't ask me why, but I do, Jordan...trust you, that is," Chuck said. "Do you mind if I ask you a question?"

"Not at all."

"How long have you been out of your wheelchair?"

Jordan could feel Maggie's hands squeeze her shoulders. She tilted her head back to look at Maggie, who simply placed a kiss on her forehead.

Jordan returned her gaze to Chuck. "For about three years."

CHAPTER 26

"How did you know?" Jordan asked.

"I didn't know for sure, but you mentioned during your presentation that your device had already been tested in a human subject and I figured that since the medical community wasn't aware of it then the recipient had to be someone attached to your research. I took a chance that it was you."

"I see."

"How were you injured?" Chuck asked.

"I was thrown from my horse. I was sixteen at the time."

"And how long were you in the chair?"

"Fourteen years."

"Fourteen years? Damn. You said you've been out of the chair for three years now?"

"Technically, I was out of my chair for two years, then back in it for a few months while a second device was perfected."

"So, how does it work?"

Jordan paused.

"Why don't I leave you two alone to talk business," Maggie said as she excused herself. I'll be out in the barn if you need me for anything."

"Okay, love," Jordan replied as she watched Maggie leave. She turned her attention back to Chuck. "Chuck, as much as I want to explain the device to you, I really need to understand what your intentions are."

"My intentions, Jordan, are to do whatever is humanly possible to get my daughter out of that wheelchair. I watched you walk back and forth across the conference room when you gave your presentation earlier this week. Now, you're sitting here in front of me, with full range of motion and absolutely no telltale sign that there is anything wrong with you. If you are speaking the truth and you are indeed the test subject you mentioned in your presentation, then I want that device, and I am willing to pay any price to get it."

"Did you read the terms and conditions I included in my proposal?" Jordan asked.

Chuck sat back in his chair. "I did."

"And—?"

"And I am prepared to meet every one. The funding is not a problem. As I'm sure you know, I have access to the kind of money required to bring this device to market...that, and more if necessary. I am willing to double the salary you asked for, and IP ownership of the device is yours. I will even have my lawyers draft the patent application for you."

Jordan maintained eye contact with Chuck while he spoke. "And the identity issue?" she said.

"That one, I need a little help understanding," Chuck said.

"It's actually pretty simple. I have no way of proving who I am. I have no birth certificate, no social security number and no access to my educational and medical records. Because of that, I can't get a driver's license and I can't get a credit card. I can't even marry the woman I love. Don't get me wrong, Chuck, I'm no slouch. I'm not running from the law and I have no reason to hide other than my inability to prove who I am. I need you to help me establish an identity so I can live life normally."

"Are you an illegal, Jordan?"

"No, I am not. I was born right here in Vermont. I grew up on a farm here in Shelburne. I was educated in one of the finest medical universities this country has to offer…and I can't prove any of it."

"Why? Why can't you prove it?"

Jordan took a deep breath. *Can I trust this guy?* she thought. She looked down at her hands in her lap then raised her eyes to look into Chuck's face. "Because the records don't exist yet."

Chuck narrowed his eyes at her. "They don't exist yet?"

"That's right, and that's all I'm going to say on the matter for now."

Chuck got up from his chair and walked back and forth

across the kitchen, one hand on his hip and the other running over the stubble on his chin. Finally, he stopped in front of Jordan and placed both hands on his hips.

"I'm willing to work with you on this, Jordan, but before I commit to doing something that just might be illegal, I need you to prove to me that you're telling the truth about this device. It's a lot of money and a lot of risk on my part to enter into this contract blind."

"Fair enough," Jordan said. She rose to her feet. "I'll be right back. I'd like Maggie here for this."

"Of course," Chuck said.

Jordan returned several minutes later with Maggie in tow. Chuck rose to his feet when they entered the kitchen.

"What's this all about?" Maggie asked.

"Maggie, Chuck has offered to set up a private foundation to bring the device to market. He's agreed to all of the terms, including resolving my identity problem, but he's asked for proof that I am who I say I am. I know of only one way to do that, and I thought it might be prudent to have you here."

"I see," Maggie said.

"Chuck, please sit. I owe you some background information before I divulge the proof you're asking for."

"Why don't I make a pot of coffee? This might take some time," Maggie said.

"Coffee would be wonderful, love. Thank you."

"Chuck?" Maggie asked.

"Yes, please," he said, never taking his eyes from Jordan.

"Okay. I guess the best place to start is with my own accident. As I mentioned earlier, I was sixteen at the time. I had taken my horse for a ride and we stayed out longer than planned. It was nearly dusk before we headed back from the north pasture. As I rode, I kicked my horse into a gallop and soon, we were flying across the field. About halfway back to the house, my horse stepped into an old well that was covered over with rotted plywood and sod. I suddenly became airborne and landed in such a way that my spine was broken and my spinal cord completely severed at the L1 vertebra."

"L1? That's exactly where Jessie's was severed," Chuck said.

"Yes. Anyway, like I said, it was nearly dusk when we headed back and almost dark by the time the accident happened. I lay there on the cold, dew covered ground next to my dying horse for several hours before I lost consciousness. The next thing I knew, I woke up in the hospital unable to move my legs. Unfortunately, my horse didn't make it."

"That must have been so awful for you."

"What was awful was spending the next fourteen years in a wheelchair. Believe me when I say, Chuck, that suddenly becoming the only handicapped kid in my high school was pretty traumatic. High school is hard enough on a normal kid. You can imagine what it was like for a kid with special needs. I mean, I had no feeling or control over anything below my waist. I constantly needed help reaching things, and with no bladder control, I had to wear catheters and carry around this bag of urine all the time. It was a nightmare. It was experiences like that which contributed to my decision to become a scientist in the spinal cord injury field."

Maggie put creamer and sugar on the table then carried two cups of coffee to Chuck and Jordan. Jordan detained her with a hand on her arm. "Thank you, my love," she said.

Maggie spontaneously kissed her. "You're welcome."

Chuck sipped his coffee as he watched the tender scene. "Great coffee, Maggie. Thank you," he said.

Maggie returned to the counter and poured herself a cup then joined them at the table.

"Where did you go to school?" Chuck asked.

"Johns Hopkins University in Baltimore, and before you waste your time, you won't find any records or transcripts on me there. I graduated in the top one-percent of my class with a degree in kinesiology and specialization in spinal cord injury treatments."

"So how did you go from being in a wheelchair to walking around like your injury never occurred?" Chuck asked.

"After I graduated from medical school, I joined an institute dedicated to the study of spinal cord injuries and potential cures. I was assigned to a project that was developing a device to restore mobility. I worked on it for several years and three years ago, volunteered to be the test subject. It was an uphill battle to convince them to accept me as the candidate because by that time, my injury was already fourteen years old. As I'm sure you know, Chuck, with traditional spinal cord injury treatments, the speed at which you treat it is critical to minimize cell death."

"But they accepted you anyway," Chuck stated.

"Yes, but not without a fight, and not without a lot of good people backing me up, including my roommate, Kale."

Jordan suddenly sat back. "That's it!" she said. "That's who you remind me of, Kale. It's gotta be the hair. I used to tease him all the time about looking like a mad scientist."

Chuck ran a hand through his hair. "Damned mop. There's not much I can do except keep it cut short, and as you can see, I'm overdue for a haircut."

Jordan chuckled. "I'm sorry, Chuck. I didn't mean to tease you."

"No problem. So, go on. You said three years ago they accepted you for the first device. Did it work right away?"

"It did, although I needed to learn to walk again. After fourteen years in that chair, my brain lost all knowledge of how to put one foot in front of the other."

"So the device cured you then?"

"Not exactly. It gave me *mobility,* but I still had no feeling below my waist. I might have looked more normal, but I didn't feel normal."

"You've said the word *first* a couple of times relative to the device. That implies there was more than one."

"That's an astute observation, Chuck. Yes. There was a second device, designed not only to restore mobility, but over time, to restore feeling as well."

"And did it restore feeling in you?" Chuck asked.

Jordan reached across the table and took Maggie's hand in her own. She squeezed it and smiled. "Yes. Yes it did. It was a slow process, and I'm still not fully there, but it seems to be working toward the restoration of full sensation."

"Jessie's doctors insist her spinal cord will never be healthy again and that she's destined to be in that chair for the rest of her life."

"At this point in time, and with the knowledge that exists today, that is true."

"But you said…."

"I said, at this point in time."

"So, how does it work? Your spinal cord was completely severed. How is it you can walk and have feeling below the injury site?"

"That is information I cannot share right now. It's not that I don't trust you, Chuck, but I need to know your offer to fund this research and development is legit."

Chuck frowned. "Like I said, Jordan, I need proof. Your words and your apparent knowledge give me hope that someday Jessie will get out of that chair, but where's the proof before I pour millions of dollars into this project?"

Jordan looked to Maggie. "Sweetheart, could you give me a hand with this?"

Maggie got up and walked around the table to stand by Jordan's side.

Chuck remained seated, intently focused on Jordan and Maggie.

"Turn around, love," Maggie said.

Jordan did as she was asked and turned her back to Chuck.

Maggie pulled Jordan's shirt tail out of her jeans. "Okay, go ahead and unbutton and unzip your jeans."

Again, Jordan followed Maggie's instructions, allowing Maggie to push the waistband of Jordan's jeans just below her hips.

Chuck leaned in as Maggie raised Jordan's shirt, exposing her back from hip to shoulder blades.

"For the love of God," Chuck said. "That scar has got to be nearly a foot long."

Jordan reached back and touched the scar just above the small of her back. "The injury is right here. The scar is so long because of the required access to insert the device and all its trappings."

"Trappings?" Chuck asked.

"Yes. I will explain all of that in good time," Jordan said.

"Give me your hand," Maggie said to Chuck.

He extended his hand to Maggie.

"Feel this," she said.

Chuck's eyes grew large. "What the f—! It vibrates. What is it?"

"It's all part of the device. Again, I will...."

"You'll explain it all in good time," Chuck said for her.

Jordan pulled the waist of her jeans back up and tucked her shirt in, then turned around as she fastened her belt. "Is that proof enough for you, Chuck?"

Chuck stared at Jordan's face for several moments. "Who are you Jordan? Where do you come from? Better yet, *when* do you come from? They don't make things like this yet."

"No, they don't. Not for another eighty years anyway," Jordan replied.

"Will Jessie realize the same results as you?" he asked.

"In theory—yes. In practice, we'll have to see how her body responds. Everyone is different, but I have confidence it will work just fine for her. She has an advantage I didn't have. Two, in fact."

"What's that?"

"First, she's sixteen years younger than I was when I got the device. Children often heal faster than adults. And second, her injury is only three years old, whereas, mine was fourteen years old. Like I said in the presentation, with the right scientists and the right funding, I think I can have the prototype developed in about a year, or maybe even sooner."

Chuck looked at Maggie. "Maggie, do you have a piece of paper and a pen?"

"Sure. Let me get it for you."

Maggie returned a moment later and put the implements on the table in front of Chuck. Chuck slid them toward Jordan.

"Please write your full name, your parent's names, where you were born and your date of birth on this piece of paper just the way you would see them on a birth certificate." Chuck pulled his phone out of his pocket. "I also need a picture of you."

"I'm not so sure that's a good idea," Jordan said.

"You can't have a passport without a picture, Jordan."

Jordan looked at him for a long time, a play of emotions crossing her face.

Chuck put his hand on Jordan's shoulder. "Jordan, I'm asking you to trust me. I promise no harm will come to you or Maggie. I'm not going to turn you into the police. I'm not going to report you to immigration. I need you to cure my daughter. Believe me when I say I will do nothing to jeopardize her chances of living a normal life. The sooner you feel secure in this environment, the sooner you can begin working on this device."

CHAPTER 27

Charles Malone stood before a room of scientists in white coats and waited for the hum of voices to quiet down before he began the meeting. Prominent among them was Dr. Robert Hollinbeck, sitting in the front row.

"Good morning. Thank you for joining me on such short notice," he began. "As you know, my foundation has donated several million dollars to the Vermont Spinal Institute to develop treatment options for people with acute spinal injuries. You also know that nearly two weeks ago, we were presented with a new and novel approach to SCI treatment that claimed not only to restore mobility, but to actually cure the injury. Most of you were at the meeting and will recall the presentation."

Chuck looked around the room and noted several of the scientists were avoiding eye contact with him while Hollinbeck in the front row sat with his arms crossed and a smug look on his face.

"The presentation was given by Dr. Jordan Lewis. You would do well to remember that name, as she is about to become the leading expert nationwide in spinal cord injury rehabilitation."

Hollinbeck stood up. "Where is this going, Malone?" he demanded.

"I'm about to get to that, Dr. Hollinbeck," Chuck said. "You see, after this body of scientists rejected Dr. Lewis' proposal, I went to visit her at her home. It turns out that she herself, has a complete SCI at the L1 vertebrae." Chuck paused to watch the startled reaction spread through the room. "That's right. *She* is the human test subject she mentioned in her presentation."

"But that's impossible," came a voice from the audience. "She seemed totally unimpaired."

"That speaks volumes for the quality of her work, wouldn't you agree?" Chuck asked.

"Was she able to substantiate her claim?" Dr. Hollinbeck asked.

"Yes. She went so far as to show me the scar on her back and further produced evidence of the device beneath the surface of her skin." Chuck looked out over the room and saw regret on the faces of the scientists. "That said, I have come here today to inform you that the JEM Spinal Injury Research Association will no longer provide funds for the development efforts of this Spinal Institute. Instead, those funds will be redirected to a private foundation to be run by Dr. Lewis."

Hollinbeck jumped to his fee. "You can't do that," he exclaimed.

"Not only can I do that, Dr. Hollinbeck, but it is already done."

"I will take this to the board of directors of the JEM Foundation, Malone. You won't get away with this."

"Dr. Hollinbeck, I *am* the JEM Foundation. You see, JEM stands for Jessica Elizabeth Malone, and she just happens to be my thirteen-year-old daughter who has been confined to a wheelchair for the past three years with a complete SCI. Dr. Lewis took the time to research my foundation and to learn that little tidbit of information. Did you?"

"*You* are the JEM foundation? How dare you withhold that information from us? Does Robinson know about this?" Hollinbeck said.

"Dr. Hollinbeck, I recall you calling me, and I quote, *the front man for some rich philanthropist*, and not educated enough to voice my opinion on Dr. Lewis' presentation. Well, Dr. Hollinbeck, I *am* the rich philanthropist. You should be careful about who you treat with such disrespect and contempt. Not only do I find your attitude reprehensible, but your lack of progress and results is unacceptable. Effective immediately, the Spinal Institute will no longer receive funding from JEM. I will leave it to you, Dr. Hollinbeck, to explain that to Mr. Robinson. That's all I have to say on the matter, gentlemen. Good day."

* * *

"Jordan, your phone is ringing," Maggie said from the living room.

"Answer it, would you?" Jordan called from the kitchen.

"Hello?"

"Jordan? This is Chuck Malone."

"Hi, Chuck. Actually, this is Maggie. Jordan went to the kitchen to refill our coffee cups. She'll be back in just a second or two."

"Okay. Maggie, while we wait for Jordan, let me say what a pleasure it was meeting you and Jordan last week."

"Thank you, Chuck. We enjoyed meeting you as well. Jordan couldn't stop talking about how much you remind her of her friend Kale."

"That's a good thing, I hope."

"Very good. She loves Kale very much. Oh, here she comes. It was nice talking to you Chuck."

"You too, Maggie."

Maggie accepted her coffee and handed the phone to Jordan. "Thank you, love. It's Chuck Malone," she said.

"Hi, Chuck."

"Jordan. How are you today?"

"I'm fine, and you?"

"I'm actually feeling quite good. I just had a meeting at the spinal institute this morning and informed them I'm pulling their funding in favor of yours."

"Wow. You don't waste any time, do you?"

"It seems I've wasted enough time on them already. Look, Jordan, do you mind if I come over this afternoon?"

"Hold on, let me ask the boss." Jordan looked at Maggie. "Do we have anything planned for today, Mags?" she asked.

Maggie put down the paper she was reading and shook her head no.

"Looks like a go, Chuck. What time should we expect you?"

"I have to make a stop at home first, so let's say in about an hour. Is that okay?"

"Sure."

"Okay, I'll see you soon."

* * *

Jordan and Maggie stood on the front porch and watched Chuck pull his SUV up to the front steps. He got out and circled around to the tailgate. "Hey ladies," he called out as he lifted the hatch.

"What's he doing?" Maggie asked.

"I don't know. Why don't we go find out?" Jordan replied.

Maggie and Jordan approached Chuck. "Do you need a hand with something?" Jordan asked.

"Nope. After three years, I'm an old hand at this," he said as he pulled a medium sized wheelchair out of the back of the SUV and opened it.

Jordan and Maggie stood by as Chuck wheeled the chair to the side of the car and opened the back passenger door.

"Come on, sweetheart," Chuck said as he lifted the young girl out of the car and placed her in the chair, then swung the chair around to face Jordan and Maggie. "Ladies, I'd like to introduce to you, my daughter, Jessie. Jessie, this is Jordan and Maggie."

Maggie was immediately on one knee beside the wheelchair. She took Jessie's hand in her own and shook it. "Hey, Jessie, I'm Maggie."

"Nice to meet you, Maggie," the girl replied somewhat sullenly.

Instead of squatting down, Jordan stood beside the chair and extended her hand. "Jessie, I'm Jordan," Jordan said, forcing the girl to look up at her. Jordan maintained eye contact with her as she shook her hand. "You and I are going to become good friends," she said.

Jordan noticed how uncomfortable Jessie was at making conversation as the girl looked away. She squeezed Jessie's hand to get her attention once more. "Hey, do you like horses?"

Jessie nodded.

"Maggie, would you mind taking Jessie to the barn? I think

Shawny and Sally might enjoy meeting her." Jordan spoke volumes to Maggie with her eyes.

Maggie smiled. "Of course I will. Come on little one. You're in for a treat," Maggie said as she pushed Jessie across the barnyard.

Jordan turned to Chuck. "How long has she been depressed?"

Chuck shoved his hands deep into his pockets as she watched Maggie and Jessie enter the barn. "Almost from the beginning. As you said, being in that chair is the worst part of this for her."

"Does she know about your association with me? Have you talked to her about the implant?"

"No. I thought it might be good for her to get to know you and Maggie first."

"Okay. I just didn't want to blindside her with anything you hadn't prepped her for."

"I appreciate that, Jordan," John said. "Oh, I almost forgot." Chuck opened the front passenger door of his car and retrieved a legal sized manila envelope. "This is for you," he said as he handed it to her.

Jordan looked between Chuck and the envelope before opening it and retrieving the documents inside. Her eyes opened wide. "Chuck, I can't thank you enough. How did you do this?" she asked as she scanned the birth certificate, social security card and passport she pulled out of the envelope.

"Anything is possible if you throw enough money at it," he said.

Jordan's eyes filled with moisture. "I can't tell you what this means to me."

"Well, I can't tell you what your work means to me, and to Jessie."

"Chuck, I would have helped Jessie regardless of whether you could produce these documents or not."

Chuck nodded his head.

"So, I assume you had to go through illegal channels to do this. Is there anything I need to do to assure neither of us gets into trouble over this?" she asked.

"Just stay on the right side of the law and no one will get hurt," Chuck replied. "The way I look at it, you're not really an illegal. You're just here at the wrong time."

"So you know how I got here?"

"I *suspect* how you got here. What was it like?"

"Bright light, brilliant color, a little pain. Kind of like I would imagine being born would be like."

"Are you able to go back?"

"No, but then, I don't want to. I am here for Maggie, and to help people like Jessie."

Just then, their attention was drawn to the barn where Maggie and Jessie emerged. Jessie wore a huge smile on her face as Maggie pushed her back across the yard and stopped in front of Chuck and Jordan.

"Anyone interested in a horse ride?" Maggie asked.

"Can we, Dad? Can we? Please?" Jessie begged.

"I thought we'd ride out to the north pasture and check on the new foals," Maggie said.

Chuck looked at Maggie worriedly. "Is it safe for her to ride?" he asked.

"She'll be fine. In fact, she can ride in the saddle in front of me," Maggie offered.

"Maggie is one of the best horsewomen I've ever seen, Chuck. I don't think you need to worry."

"Please, Dad," Jessie said, batting her eyes at her father.

He pointed at Jessie and looked at Jordan. "See what I have to deal with? How can I resist that face?"

"Is that a yes?" Jessie said hopefully.

"I guess so, but you need to mind Maggie, okay?"

"I will. I promise," Jessie said excitedly.

"Why don't we all go?" Maggie suggested. "Jordan, we can saddle Trixie for Chuck. She's a pretty gentle mount. Do you ride Chuck?"

"I haven't ridden since I was a boy, but I'm willing to give it a try."

"All right then," Jordan said. I'll go saddle the horses."

"I'll give you a hand, Jordan," Chuck offered as they both headed toward the barn.

Maggie turned to Jessie and put her hand out for a high-five.

* * *

For the next three hours, Maggie, Jordan, Chuck and Jessie rode out to the north pasture and spent time with new foals. When they reached the new barn, Jordan fashioned a make-shift chair out of some hay bales and covered it with a horse blanket so Jessie would have a comfortable place to sit. The smile never left Jessie's face as she fed the young colts and brushed their shiny coats.

"They're beautiful," she exclaimed over and over.

"I haven't seen her this excited and animated for three years," Chuck said to Maggie as Jordan led another foal toward Jessie to be brushed and fed. "I can't thank you enough for your kindness and attention to her."

"Someday I hope to establish a riding school for handicapped children, right here on this farm. I've been researching what it will take to get it off the ground. We've got a lot of work ahead of us...permits, improvements to the farm, including new safety features, and I need to design a saddle that can be used safely, regardless of the child's handicap. It will take some time and money, but I'm determined to do it. Its reactions like Jessie's that fuel my drive to do this," Maggie said.

Chuck nodded. "She seems to have taken a liking to you. She's hasn't been close to anyone since her mother died in the same accident that put her in that chair. Again, I can't thank you enough."

"No thanks necessary, Chuck. She's a lovely young lady." Maggie looked at her watch. "We should probably head back. It will be dusk soon."

Jessie insisted on riding once again, in the saddle in front of Maggie. On the way back Maggie let her control the reins, and she soon learned how to manipulate the direction of the horse by pulling on one rein or the other, all the while receiving direction and reassurance from Maggie that she was doing a good job.

When they returned to the barn, Chuck dismounted first and gave his horse to Jordan as he put his arms out for his daughter to slide into. Maggie and Jordan put the horses in their respective stalls and walked Chuck and Jessie to their car. Jordan opened the back passenger door, but before Chuck could place Jessie inside, the young girl reached out and wrapped her arms around Maggie's neck and kissed her on the cheek.

"Thank you, Maggie. Can we do it again some time?"

"Of course, dumpling," Maggie said.

Jessie then reached for Jordan and hugged her as well.

Chuck raised his eyebrows in surprised then placed his daughter inside the car and buckled her in. He closed the door and faced Jordan and Maggie. "I don't have the words to thank you enough. You have made today very special for Jessie."

"She's a special, girl, Chuck," Maggie said. It was our pleasure."

"What she said," Jordan said with a crooked smile while extending her hand to Chuck.

"I'll be in touch over the next few days to set up the paperwork for the foundation, Jordan."

"Thank you, Chuck."

"No need to thank me. You're giving my daughter's life back to her. I'll talk to you soon."

Jordan draped her arm around Maggie's shoulder as they watched Chuck and Jessie drive away.

* * *

"Hollinbeck, you owe me an explanation."

"It's not my fault, Mr. Robinson. Malone pulled our funding because of that bitch Jordan Lewis," Hollinbeck explained.

"What exactly did Ms. Lewis do?"

"She apparently has come up with a cure for complete spinal cord injuries. Don't ask me how she did it. The technology just doesn't exist today. She tricked us."

"She tricked you? How?"

223

"She said she had already tested the device on a human subject, but what she failed to say is that *she* was the test subject."

"How exactly does that qualify as tricking you?"

"Don't you see?" Hollinbeck said. "Never before in the history of SCI's has a complete break been cured. She was walking back and forth across the front of the room like she had never been injured. Never in a million years would anyone believe she had a severed spinal column. She was vague about her credentials and she withheld information we needed to make informed decisions."

"Yet she was able to convince Malone of her authenticity."

"Apparently. By the way, did you know Malone is the founder of the JEM Foundation?"

"Yes, I did know that. It's public knowledge, by the way. If you had done your homework, you would have known it too."

Hollinbeck fell silent and stared at the floor.

"Your negligence has cost the institute a significant amount of money, never mind potential future recognition and funding. I hold you personally responsible for this, Hollinbeck. If you know what's good for you, you'll make this right. I don't care how you do it, but you need to fix this. Your reputation just may depend on it. Have I made myself clear?"

CHAPTER 28

"Hey Gina, this is Jordan. Are you and Sam up for a cookout and bonfire tonight?" Jordan said into her phone.

"Hi stranger," Gina said. "We haven't heard from you in about two weeks. We wondered if maybe you transported back to the future or something."

"Very funny, Gina. Actually, a lot has happened over the past week or so. I'll tell you all about it when you come over."

"Cookout and bonfire, huh? Hold on a sec."

Jordan listened as she heard Gina ask Sam if she was interested in going to Jordan and Maggie's for dinner. Jordan smiled as she realized that was the first time she had ever heard the farm referred to as Jordan and Maggie's.

"Okay, I'm back," Gina said. "Sam wants to know what we can bring."

"Rumor is she makes a killer strawberry rhubarb crisp."

"Done. We'll bring the fixings and make it at your place. When do you want us to come over?"

"Any time you'd like."

"Well, since you've made me curious about what's been happening with you two, we'll be over in about an hour."

"Sounds like a plan. See you soon."

* * *

"Okay, Jordan, now take the wooden spoon and mix the butter, brown sugar and oats together until it starts to clump, then finish blending it with your fingers," Sam said.

"You seriously want me to put my hands in butter?" Jordan asked.

"Yes, it's the best way to make the crisp layer. Trust me. It will be fine."

"If you say so, Sam."

"I do. Now keep mixing while I spoon the rhubarb mixture into this baking dish."

Maggie walked into the kitchen from the side porch carrying the packaging from New York strip steaks. "Steaks are on the grill and Gina is keeping an eye on them," she said.

Sam looked up quickly. "You're letting Gina cook?" she asked.

"She didn't do such a bad job on the burgers we had at your place a couple weeks ago," Maggie reasoned.

"Ah, actually, they caught on fire, but we saved them before they became hockey pucks," Jordan confessed.

Maggie grabbed the spray bottle and garlic salt from the cupboard. "I guess I'd better give her a hand then."

"How does this look, Sam?" Jordan asked as she tipped the bowl of oats toward Sam.

"Not too bad. Now, go ahead and spread it evenly over the top of the rhubarb, then put it into the oven. I've already pre-heat it to three hundred fifty degrees. Oh, and set the timer for thirty-five minutes."

"Got it." Jordan followed her instructions carefully then grabbed four wine coolers from the refrigerator and carried them out to the side deck. She passed Maggie on the way out.

"After you deliver those, do you mind coming back to help me carry out place settings?" Maggie asked.

"Sure. I'll be right back."

Over the next few minutes, Jordan and Maggie worked to prepare the picnic table on the side deck for four, and then carried out salads and corn on the cob, while Sam and Gina finished grilling the steaks. Soon, they were all sitting around the table filling their dishes and eating their meal.

"The steaks are perfect, Sam," Maggie said.

"We're missing something," Jordan said. She looked around the table for clues. "Ah, steak sauce. I'll be right back." While she was inside, the timer on the oven went off. "Sam, the timer went off. How do I know if it's done?"

Sam came into the kitchen. "Let me take a look at it." She opened the oven door and peered inside. "Nice and golden brown. Perfect," she said. Sam retrieved the pot holder and removed the baking dish from the oven, then shut the oven off. "We're going to leave it right here on top of the stove to cool. By the time we've finished our dinner, it should be cool enough to eat."

"So, Jordan, what's the big news you have to tell us?" Gina asked as Jordan settled into her place at the table.

"Well, I gave my presentation a little more than a week ago to the spinal institute, and within four days, I received a rejection letter in the mail."

"Seriously? They rejected your proposal? On what grounds?" Sam asked.

"On the grounds that I didn't provide any evidence of my educational background or experience. The letter indicated that I was too much of an unknown for them to risk investing that kind of money."

"Well that sucks," Gina said.

"I thought so too until my cell phone rang just moments after I received the letter. The call was from Charles Malone."

"Charles Malone…Charles Malone. Where have I heard that name before?" Gina asked.

"Isn't that the name of the benefactor at the spinal institute? I remember you mentioning him the last time you were at our house," Sam said.

"Yes, that's him. Anyway, he came to the farm and we had a long discussion about the implant. He wants to set up a private foundation to fund the development. We also talked about his daughter."

"Thirteen and wheelchair bound," Gina said.

"Yes. Her name is Jessie."

"So you two talked about the implant. So what happened next?" Sam asked.

"Chuck returned a few days later, with his daughter in tow."

"She is a very sweet young lady, and she took immediately to the horses. We even made time for a horseback ride to check on the new foals," Maggie said.

"She took immediately to *you*, Maggie," Jordan said. "It's

227

almost as though she bonded with you instantly."

"Yes, she did," Maggie agreed.

"So he came to the farm just for you to meet his daughter?" Gina asked.

"That, and to bring me something else. Let's say it was an act of good faith to let me know he was serious about funding the foundation."

"So what did he give you?" Gina asked.

"Give me a minute and I'll show you." Jordan rose from the table and went into the house, returning a few moments later with a manila envelope, which she opened and dumped onto the table."

"Holy shit!" Gina said as she picked up the birth certificate, social security card and passport. "These look amazingly authentic. He must have paid some serious money for them."

"My thought exactly," Jordan said.

"He's put his neck on the line to get these, Jordan," Sam said. "I'd say he's pretty serious about the foundation."

"So now that we have Jordan's identity problem taken care of, who'd like to help me plan a wedding?" Maggie asked.

* * *

Maggie and Sam sat on the front porch swing watching Jordan and Gina toss a baseball back and forth in the barnyard.

"You do know your life is about to take a drastic turn," Sam said.

"I suspect it will," Maggie replied. "For starters, once the foundation is established, Jordan won't be around much. She's actually decided to keep the apartment in Burlington until she understands what her work schedule will be like. If she ends up working late into the evenings, it doesn't make sense for her to drive forty minutes home just to get up five or six hours later and drive back in."

"How do you feel about that?"

"Are you asking me if I trust her?"

Sam shrugged. "I guess I am."

"I trust her implicitly. I'm convinced she wants to keep it

for the sheer convenience, and besides, she gave me a key, so I could drop in unannounced at any time. I don't think she would have done that if she had ulterior motives in mind."

Sam nodded. "I thought as much, but I just want to be sure you're not hurt. You were pretty devastated when you and Jordan split up a few weeks ago, and I don't ever want to see you in that state again."

Maggie rested her head on Sam's shoulder. "Thank you for looking out for me, my friend."

Sam kissed the top of her head. "Any time, little sister. Any time."

They rocked back and forth in silence for the next few minutes.

"Have you told your parents about Jordan?" Sam asked.

"Yes, I have. I talk to them weekly. I haven't gone into any detail about her, for example, they don't know she's a research scientist, but they know she's here and that we are in a relationship. They know that I love her."

"Did they voice an opinion about Jan leaving?"

"They haven't said a word about Jan."

"I assume they'll come for the wedding."

"Yes. In fact, I need to call them tonight and chat about when they can come home so we can get the plans moving."

"Are you going to tell them about Jordan's unique situation?"

"I'll tell them about the foundation, but Jordan and I don't think it's a good idea to tell too many people about the time travel thing. Jordan says that her very presence here will have an effect on the future and she wants to minimize that. Hell, just the fact that she saved me from falling off the cliff will have an effect on the future, but we don't know how that will manifest itself at this point."

"She needs to be careful not to do anything that might change who she is here in this time, or she ultimately may not be the Jordan you fell in love with."

Maggie frowned. "What do you mean?"

"Well, for example what if she did something here that might prevent her from becoming handicapped in the future? If she did that, she probably wouldn't have become a scientist. She'd be a different Jordan all together. Didn't she say it was her injury that prompted her to study spinal cord injuries in college?"

Maggie suddenly sat up. "Oh, my God!"

"Maggie, what is it?"

Maggie ran into the house with Sam right behind her.

"Maggie, talk to me," Sam said as Maggie grabbed the truck keys from the kitchen counter top.

"I've got to fix this," Maggie said as she ran past Sam and out the door.

"Maggie, wait," Sam said as she watched Maggie run across the barnyard and climb into her pickup truck.

Jordan and Gina stopped tossing the ball as the scene unfolding before them between Maggie and Sam caught their attention.

"Where is she going?" Jordan asked as they watched Maggie tear across the field.

"I don't know. We were talking about paradoxes when all of the sudden, she grabbed the truck keys and ran out the door," Sam said.

Jordan grabbed Sam's arms. "What paradox, Sam?"

"We were talking about how things might be different if you had never been paralyzed in your future life."

Jordan's brow creased deeply as she thought about the possible scenarios that might change her own future. Finally, it came to her. "The well," she said. She turned to Gina. "Gina, I need to stop her. Let me take your truck."

"You can take my truck, but I'm going with you," Gina said.

"Me too," added Sam.

* * *

Maggie pulled to a skidding stop beside the filled-in well in the north pasture. She jumped out of the truck and grabbed the pointed shovel from the back, then walked to the edge of the hole. To her surprise, the hole wasn't completely filled. *How can this be? Jordan filled it in almost three weeks ago. It must be the soil settled with the rain.* Just then, Maggie heard the sound of another vehicle approaching. She turned to see Gina's truck stop a few feet away from her. The first one out of the truck was Jordan.

"Maggie, what are you doing? Are you out of your mind?" Jordan exclaimed. She took the shovel from Maggie and began shoveling more dirt into the hole.

Maggie grabbed the handle of the shovel and prevented Jordan from continuing. "No Jordan. Stop. You can't do this."

Gina and Sam got out of the truck and stood by, watching the interaction between their friends.

"Let go of the shovel, Maggie," Jordan warned.

"Or, what? What are you going to do, Jordan?" Maggie challenged.

"Maggie, you don't realize what you're doing here," Jordan tried to reason.

Maggie shoved Jordan backward letting go of the shovel in the process. "No, *you* don't realize what you're doing. Jordan, if you fill this hole, you and Sally will never fall into it. You will never be injured. You will never study spinal cord injuries in college. You will never become a research scientist. You will never meet Kale and Andi, and you will never find my diaries. Jordan, if you fill this well, you will cease to exist in this world. If that's what you want, then fine, fill the goddamned well. I'm going back to the house. This is your decision, Jordan."

"Hold up, Maggie. I'll go with you," Sam said. Sam sent a meaningful look in Gina's direction then followed Maggie to the truck.

Jordan threw the shovel to the ground and closed both hands into fists at her sides. A deep growl emitted from her throat and her whole body shook in anger.

"She's right, you know," Gina said. "Obviously, the hole is still deep enough to cause your accident in the future, but if you fill it to the top, who knows what might happen to you—not to mention what it might do to Maggie."

"Do you have any idea how it feels to be stuck in a wheelchair for eighteen hours a day, every day for fourteen years, Gina?" Jordan asked.

"No I don't, but think about it, Jordan. If you and your horse never stepped into that hole, your entire life in the *future* would be different. Everything that drove you to travel through time to get here would evaporate—including your drive to save Maggie from falling to her death. You would have had no knowledge of Maggie. Who knows, you may have grown up to be a carpenter, or a teacher. You may have met someone, fallen in love and lived happily ever after.

"They say you never miss what you never had, but the truth is, you already have Maggie and if you fill that hole, you may be making a conscious decision to throw all of this away, and then to live with the memories of what you've lost. I would die without Sam, and from what I've seen, I think your love for Maggie is at least as strong as my love for Sam. I would do anything to keep Sam in my life. Are you willing to do the same for Maggie?"

Gina placed her hand on Jordan's shoulder.

"The bottom line, my friend, is whether your love for Maggie justifies allowing the future Jordan to become paralyzed in that fall."

CHAPTER 29

Sam was waiting on the porch when Gina dropped Jordan off at the house. Gina hugged Jordan warmly when she got out of the truck and held the door open for Sam to get in. Sam kissed her on the cheek. "She's barricaded herself in the bedroom. I recommend giving both of you some time to think about the implications of your being here, Jordan."

"It's not like I have a choice, Sam. My portal home is closed."

Sam got into the truck and hooked her seatbelt, then leaned out the window and placed her hand on Jordan's arm.

"I'm not sure it is, Jordan. I think you could go home at any time simply by changing the series of events that brought you here. It just might not be the same home you left."

* * *

Jordan paced back and forth in front of the fireplace in the bunkhouse. A swell of emotions raged through her, so intense she had to run to the bathroom to eject the contents of her stomach. She knelt on the bathroom floor with tears streaming down her face. Anger formed in the pit of her stomach as she beat the floor with her fists until her knuckles were bloody.

"Why? Why does this have to be so hard," she cried out loud.

She curled into a fetal position and thought about the events that had brought her here.

You called to me, Maggie. The dreams...the diaries. I swear you called to me.

Jordan pushed herself to her knees then climbed to her feet.

In slow and emotionally painful movements, she made her way back into the common area of the bunk house and sat on the couch in front of the fireplace.

Are Maggie and Gina right? Would I simply disappear if the hole was filled to the point that it posed no danger to my future self? Would I cease to exist here in this time?

Jordan thought back to her teenage self before the accident. She was sixteen and a sophomore in high school and she was just beginning to realize her attraction to girls. She had dreams, as most young women do. Dreams of becoming an Olympic Equestrian. Dreams of going to veterinary school and eventually setting up a clinic right here on the farm. She had it all planned out, right down to building a new barn in the north pasture to board horses…ironically, right where Maggie had built her new barn just months earlier.

Maggie is right. If I hadn't fallen into that hole, I wouldn't have become a scientist. The whole reason I studied spinal cord injury regeneration was because of my own injury. I wouldn't have met Kale and Andi or Peter. Hell, Kale wouldn't have met Andi if I had never been injured. I didn't realize how many lives I would be changing simply by filling that hole.

Jordan thought about how her life had affected Maggie's so far.

Maggie would be dead right now and Jan would own this farm while quite literally getting away with murder if Sally and I hadn't stepped into the hole when I was sixteen. If I reset the life of my future self, then everything I have done here that affects Maggie will be reset as well. Saving Maggie's life is the direct result of me crossing paths with her in the future through her diaries.

Jordan sat forward on the couch and propped her elbows on her knees, then lowered her head into her hands. She closed her eyes as an intense wave of emotion washed over her, an emotion she recognized as overwhelming love and need for Maggie.

Jordan sat up, wiped the tears from her face then stood in front of the fireplace. "I know what I need to do," she said. Wincing as her injured knuckles scraped the hem of her pocket, she retrieved the keys to the truck and left the bunkhouse. Moments later, she backed the truck up the barn and threw several tools and implements into the back end then headed out to the north pasture.

Maggie stood at the living room window and watched Jordan back the truck up to the barn. Her heart sank as she saw Jordan load additional digging tools into the truck and drive away in the direction of the north pasture.

* * *

It was nearly dark when Jordan returned to the house four hours later, tired and covered in dirt. The blood on her knuckles was crusted over and her fingers were stiff and swollen. She pulled the truck up to the front of the house, turned off the ignition and sat there for several minutes while trying to come up with a way to apologize to Maggie for her earlier indecision. Finally, she decided to just take her knocks as they came and hoped Maggie would forgive her.

Jordan climbed out of the truck and went into the house. All was quiet, like no one was home. She saw Maggie's truck in the yard, so she was sure Maggie was still home. She made her way through the kitchen and living room and finally into their bedroom where she found Maggie asleep on the bed. She stood beside the bed for a time, just watching her sleep and allowing the love she felt for this woman to overwhelm her heart and fill her eyes with a fine mist. Finally, she went to the bathroom and stripped off her clothing before stepping into the shower.

Jordan felt a sense of renewal when she turned off the water and stepped out of the shower. She towel-dried her hair and body, then grabbed her robe from a hook on the back of the bathroom door. The burning feeling on the backs of her hands led her to rummage through the medicine cabinet for salve and bandages, which is what she was in the process of doing when the bathroom door opened, admitting Maggie.

"Oh, I'm sorry, I didn't realize you were back," Maggie said and began to leave.

"No. No, please come in. I'm just about finished in here," Jordan said.

Maggie walked completely into the room and saw what Jordan had in her hands. "What did you do to yourself?" she asked.

"I'm afraid my temper got the best of me," Jordan replied as she turned her hands over to show Maggie her knuckles.

"Jordan," Maggie admonished. "Go sit on the bed. I'll be out to bandage them for you as soon as I pee."

Jordan sat on the edge of the bed and waited for Maggie, hope brewing in her chest after their relatively civil first encounter since the confrontation in the pasture earlier that day. Maggie came out of the bathroom and sat on the bed beside her.

"Give me your hand," she said, and proceeded to apply salve and to wrap gauze around Jordan's knuckles. She avoided Jordan's eyes as she worked. "Jordan, I want to apologize for my behavior earlier today."

Jordan stiffened. *She's apologizing to me?* "No, Maggie. You've done nothing to apologize for."

Maggie taped the gauze then moved on to Jordan's other hand. "How did you say you did this?" she asked.

"My temper got the best of me. When Gina dropped me off, Sam recommended I give us both some time to think about things, so I went to the bunkhouse and did just that. The more I thought about it, the sicker I became until I finally lost my lunch and then beat the hell out of the bathroom floor when I realized what I fool I had been."

Maggie looked into Jordan's eyes after she taped the gauze on the second hand. "What do you mean?" she asked.

"Maggie, I just came back from the north pasture where I not only dug the hole a little deeper, but I covered it with a layer of plywood and sod, just like it was when Sally and I went through it so many years ago."

Jordan raised one bandaged hand to cup the side of Maggie's face.

"When I filled that well a few weeks ago, I didn't realize I was potentially throwing away everything I have worked so hard to have. Everything I have done...everything I have risked

236

to get here was for you. When I was in the bunkhouse earlier today, pacing back and forth in front of the fireplace, asked myself if everything I went through as a teenager confined to a wheelchair, and everything I went through with failed relationships as an adult, and everything I endured during the testing and failures of the implant was worth spending the rest of my life with you. Undeniably, the answer to every one of those questions is yes. Yes, I would do it all over again just to be here with you right now and to be facing such a promising and loving future with you."

Jordan watched Maggie's eyes fill with tears.

"Maggie, I love you more than life itself, and if you'll have me, I will spend all my tomorrows making you happy. I'm asking you to forgive me, Maggie, for I have truly been a fool to risk losing the most precious thing in my life."

Maggie closed her eyes and allowed the tears that clung to the edge of her lids, to roll down her face. She opened them again and smiled through her tears. "I guess we should be planning a wedding then."

Jordan lowered her mouth to Maggie's and kissed her tenderly, then rested her forehead against Maggie's. "Thank you, Maggie." She kissed her once more. "Let me love you."

"Not with those bandages on your hands," Maggie replied. "I will however, submit to sleeping in your arms tonight."

Jordan smiled. "I would love to hold you in my arms while you sleep. I love you, Maggie. Thank you for loving me too."

* * *

"Jordan, calm down. It'll be fine," Maggie said as Jordan paced back and forth in front of the gate.

"Calm down? Mags, they're your parents."

"And your point is?"

"What…what if they don't like me? Hell, your father was ready to just give the farm to Jan."

Maggie stood in Jordan's path on her next pass by the gate. "Stop. Please. Jordan, they'll love you. Trust me."

"How do I look?"

"Good enough to eat."

Jordan grinned. "I'll take you up on that later. Shit! Here come a bunch of people off the plane."

Maggie looked intently at the surge of people coming through the gate. "There they are," she said and began to wave. Once they cleared security, Maggie ran toward them and hugged them fiercely. "I missed you guys so much," she said. "How was your flight?"

"We had a long layover in Newark, of all places. Other than that, it was fine," Gary Downs said.

Maggie stood between her parents and slipped her arms into theirs as they walked toward Jordan. "Mom, Dad, this is Jordan Lewis. Jordan, these are my parents, Gary and Sharon Downs."

Jordan extended her hand first to Maggie's father. "Mr. Downs. It's a pleasure to meet you."

"Likewise, Jordan. But since you are going to be part of the family soon, you need to get over the Mr. Downs thing. Call me Gary."

"Thank you, Gary," Jordan said before turning her attention to Maggie's mother.

"Sharon, or Mom, if you'd like," Sharon said before Jordan could speak. "And may I add that you are quite a beautiful woman. You chose well, Margaret."

"Mom, do you have to call me that?" Maggie whined.

Sharon batted Jordan's hand away. "In this family, we hug," she said, opening her arms to Jordan.

"Thanks, Mom," Jordan said, winking at Maggie over her mother's shoulder.

Sharon slipped her hand into Jordan's arm. "Gary, Margaret, why don't you go on ahead to collect the luggage so I can get to know my new daughter-in-law."

"Better to do as you're told, *Margaret* or there'll be hell to pay," Gary teased.

"My name is Maggie!"

Jordan smiled broadly as Gary took Maggie's hand and dragged her toward the luggage carousel.

* * *

"Who gives this woman in matrimony?" the priest asked.

"I do," Gary said as he stepped forward and stood beside Maggie.

"And who gives this woman in matrimony?" the priest repeated.

"That would be me," Gina said. She stood beside Jordan.

"Please join hands."

Jordan and Maggie joined their right hands.

The priest removed a brown cord from around his neck and handed it to Gary, who wrapped it around their joined hands.

"May this brown cord represent Mother Earth. In her name, we rejoice in the bounty that comes from a loving union," the priest said.

He then handed a blue cord to Gina, who tied it around their joined hands.

"Let this blue cord represent the depth and breadth of the commitment between you. As soft as water, yet as deep as the ocean."

Gary next tied a green cord around their hands.

"Let this green cord represent the ongoing renewal of love required for a healthy marriage. May it always grow and blossom like spring flowers."

Gina then tied a yellow cord around their hands.

"Let this yellow cord represent the warmth and energy of the sun. Let warmth and energy always be present in your everyday lives."

The priest spread his arms open. "Jordan and Maggie, you have chosen to write your own vows. You may now share them with each other and with all present. Maggie, you may go first."

Maggie smiled into Jordan's eyes. "Jordan, you literally appeared out of thin air to rescue me. I summoned you from afar, reaching through the time continuum, pulling you toward me. At great risk to yourself, you came. You came in the nick of time; my knight in shiny armor, riding her steed at full gallop across the plains to save me. And save me, you did. For that, and for so many other reasons, I will love you forever, across all space and time. Thank you for consenting to spend all your tomorrows with me."

Jordan cleared her throat to speak. "Maggie, I never really understood how full life could be until you came into mine. I was broken and damaged, yet you looked beyond my limitations and demanded no less of me. Your love healed me. Your love reached through time and summoned my soul. I could do nothing but follow your call. You say I rescued you, but it is I who was rescued by a fierce red-headed warrior named Margaret…er, I mean, Maggie."

Jordan could hear a chuckle break out among the well-wishers.

Maggie punched her in the arm.

"You made me see that we are not alone in this universe, that our every waking moment impacts those around us, past present and future. Maggie, I vow to make you the center of my universe and to love you for all my tomorrows."

"Nicely said," the priest said. "Now, before I make the final proclamation, Jordan and Maggie asked me to extend an invitation to all of you to join them at the farm afterward for an old-fashioned country cookout."

After the announcement, the priest reached forward and removed the cords from their hands. "Now, without further ado, by the power granted to me by the great state of Vermont, I proclaimed Jordan Lewis and Maggie Downs, joined as one in the bond of matrimony. Ladies, you may kiss the bride."

Jordan tilted Maggie's chin up and placed a series of tender kisses on her lips, then took her into her arms and held her close for several seconds. "I will love you through all space and time," Jordan whispered again in her ear.

"Through all space and time," Maggie repeated.

* * *

"Goodbye, Jen and Dave. Thank you so much for coming," Maggie said to the final guests. She leaned against the door. "Wow, what a long day."

"You got that right," Jordan replied.

"We had a really nice turnout."

"You are well-known and respected in the community,

Mags. I'm not really surprised at the number of people who came."

"I'm glad Chuck and Jessie came. I really like them."

Jordan took Maggie into her arms. "Well, like I said, I think Jessie has really bonded with you. It will be good for her to have another mother figure in her life. I'm sure she misses her own mom. I know I do, and I was in my twenties when my parents died," Jordan said.

"You never really stop needing your parents, I guess."

"I would hope not," Sharon said as she came through the kitchen door with Sam and Gina right behind her. "Sam, Gina and I just finished picking up the kitchen while your father cleaned up the grill."

"We can't thank you enough for all your help," Jordan said. "You've all been a godsend. The cookout ended up being a lot more work than I thought it would be."

"Your father loves to grill. He was in his glory out there today. Don't let him fool you," Sharon said.

"I heard that, Sharon," a voice boomed from the deck.

"We love you, Daddy," Maggie said, a grin splitting her face ear to ear.

"Yeah, yeah, yeah," Gary called out.

"We're going to hit the road," Gina said. "I'm sure you lovebirds don't need us hanging around for any longer than we need to," she joked.

"La, la, la, la," Sharon said as she put her fingers in her ears and escaped to the kitchen."

"I love your parents," Sam said.

"And they love you too," Maggie replied. "C'mere you," she said, hugging Sam close, and then Gina. "Seriously, we couldn't have pulled this off without your help. You two are the greatest besties a girl could ever have."

"Make that the greatest besties *we* could ever have," Jordan added as she hugged her friends and saw them to the door. "Come by for lunch tomorrow. We have tons of leftover food that needs to be eaten," she added as they climbed into Gina's truck.

Jordan closed the door and turned around to see Maggie

opening some of the cards left behind by the guests. One in particular caught her eye as their names were written in the scrawl of a young person, including a heart in place of a dot over the small I in Maggie's name. Jordan lifted the flap and pulled out the card. "Congratulations on your wedding," she read before opening the card. "Holy shit," she said.

"What is it?" Maggie asked.

Jordan handed Maggie the check that was inside the card.

Maggie's eyes grew wide. "Oh my God!" she exclaimed.

"Listen to this, *Dear Jordan and Maggie, we would be honored if you would accept this gift to begin the renovations and upgrades necessary to open your riding school for handicapped children. We cannot think of a better wedding gift for two such wonderful people. Always be happy, Chuck and Jessie Malone.*"

"Jordan, we can't accept this. It's too much. It's $100,000. We can't possibly accept this," Maggie said.

Jordan took Maggie into her arms. "Sweetheart, Chuck Malone is a very wealthy man. Yes, this seems like a huge sum, and quite extravagant for a wedding gift, I might add, but compared to his net worth, this is a drop in the bucket. He wouldn't have done this if it wasn't important to him, and to Jessie."

Maggie looked into Jordan's face through misty eyes. "Jordan, didn't you say his foundation is named after Jessie?"

"Yes it is. The foundation is called the JEM Spinal Injury Research Association. JEM stands for Jessica Elizabeth Malone."

"Then we will accept this gift, on one condition, that we name our school after Jessie as well."

"That's a great idea." Jordan wrapped her arms around Maggie and nuzzled her neck. "Now, I recall someone saying to me that I looked good enough to eat. Just how hungry are you?"

Maggie released a throaty laugh. "I'm starved, but with Mom and Dad in the next room, I think we might be on a diet for a few days."

CHAPTER 30

Jordan climbed out of her car and crossed the parking lot to shake hands with Chuck.

"Thanks for coming, Jordan. I think you'll like the new facility."

"Wasn't this site owned at one point by a semiconductor manufacturer?" Jordan asked.

"Yes, it still is. WorldWide Mainframes, as a matter of fact. They consolidated their operations to the Essex Junction side of the river, making several buildings on the Williston side available for lease. I don't think it will take much to retrofit it for our use. There used to be a module test line in the facility so it's already equipped with the proper clean room configuration for our operating suite."

"Okay, let's take a look."

While they toured the facility, Jordan provided recommendations for the layout relative to designing, manufacturing and testing the new implant.

"I think this will work," Jordan said as the finished the tour. "When do we start renovations? I'd like to be on site when that happens."

"Now that you've approved the site, I'll hire an architect and general contractor and get the ball rolling. I'm guessing they'll have blueprints for us to approve in about two weeks."

Jordan nodded. "That should give me enough time to heal."

"Heal? Are you okay?" Chuck asked.

"Walk me back to my car and we'll talk along the way," Jordan said.

"Okay, let's go then."

"All right," Jordan said as they left the building. "First, speaking of semiconductor manufacturers, we will need the most advanced computer chip available on the market today. It will need to have a MIPS of at least 10 GHz."

"MIPS?" Chuck asked.

"It stands for millions of instructions per second. It's a measure of task performance speed. This device needs to be capable of extremely fast execution speeds to avoid a measurable disruption in signal. A disruption in signal could cause the person to move in a jerky manner instead of fluid motion."

"That makes sense," Chuck replied.

"Also, since the unit will be self-taught, we will need a logic chip capable of millions of computations per second and memory enough to recognize, compute and store repeating events. This chip will be the brain of the device and must have the ability to adapt, become self-aware and develop its own order of intelligence. I won't lie when I say I'm a bit worried about this part of the development."

"What do you mean?" Chuck asked.

"What I mean is that we will be trying to duplicate the device implanted in me using an approach and materials that are quite antiquated compared to how the original device was made. I suspect the physical size of the computer chip we'll be able to obtain will be larger and less powerful than the one in the current device. We may have to piggyback two or more chips to get the same result."

"Will that work?"

"In theory, yes, but I expect the overall implant may be larger than mine. It will all depend on the size and power of the chip...or chips as the case may be. We may have to commission the design of the chip to meet our needs and hope technology is advanced enough to build it."

"I will set up a meeting with WorldWide Mainframes and ask them to present their roadmap to us," Chuck said.

"That would be good. I can give them the specs that we'll need, although I suspect they'll think I'm crazy. I know what I need the chip to deliver. If they can't make that directly, then maybe they'll have ideas on how to achieve it with other configurations."

"Okay, so now tell me about this healing you need to do," Chuck said.

"Ah, yes, the healing. You see, Chuck, I don't have any documentation for this implant. I helped develop it, but I did not personally carry out each and every step of the development. To truly duplicate it, we may need to remove it from my spine and reverse engineer it."

"Are you sure about that, Jordan? If we remove the implant from you, won't you be paralyzed again?"

"I don't think so. Do you recall me saying my incision was so long because we not only needed to install the implant, but all of the trappings as well?"

"Yes, I remember that conversation," Chuck said.

"Well, the trappings are actually electrodes. You see, a series of electrodes are surgically implanted on each side of the injury site, along with both autologous and endogenous neural stem cells. Then, a continuous-wave electrical charge is applied to the electrodes. The electrical charge excites the stem cells and encourages them to adapt to their surroundings. They essentially develop into spinal nerve cells and grow toward one another from both sides of the injury until they create a synapse in close enough proximity to allow nerve impulses to pass from one neuron to the other. In short, the nerve growth weaves a bridge over the injury site and basically heals, or mends the break in the spinal cord while reestablishing the lines of communication between the nerve endings. Once that bridge is weaved and feelings are restored, in theory, the implant is no longer needed."

"There's that phrase again...*in theory*," Chuck said.

"Unfortunately, I am the one and only human test subject, so we won't really know if theory holds until we test it."

"Is there a way we can test whether you still need it without taking it out?"

"That's exactly what we're going to do. I'm afraid I will need your help with that as well."

"How can I help you?" Chuck asked.

"We need to find a surgeon we can trust, someone who will not leak the existence of this device to anyone. It is critical this remain a well guarded secret, for my own safety, and for the success of this project."

"You leave that to me," Chuck said. "I assume we want to do this as soon as possible?"

"In order for me to be ready to help with the renovations, yes, we need to do it as soon as possible."

* * *

Jordan finished dressing as she waited for Dr. Hoffman to return. She didn't have long to wait. Dr. Hoffman entered the room and went directly to the viewing screen. She snapped the films into position over the light panels and turned the back light on. She stood there for a long time, studying the films without saying a word to Jordan.

Finally, Jordan came up behind her. "I'm sure your eye is better trained than mine, but it looks to me like the span has been bridged," she said.

Dr. Hoffman turned around and looked Jordan directly in the eyes. "Who are you?" she asked.

Jordan instinctively knew what she was asking. "I'm Jordan Lewis," she replied.

"Don't play games with me, Ms. Lewis. What I see on this x-ray is physically impossible with today's medicine."

"Correction, it's physically impossible with today's *knowledge*."

"Let me ask the question again. Who are you?"

"I am a doctor and a research scientist, specializing in spinal cord injury regeneration techniques. What you see on those films is a complete spinal cord injury I sustained at the age of sixteen. The spider-like tentacles you see radiating over both sides of the injury site are electrodes. The box you see below the injury site is a combination spinal implant and self-charging battery pack. Upon installation, the device immediately restores mobility. Over time as the nerve endings bridge the injury, feeling is restored as well. I was one of the principle designers of the device and now I intend to apply what I have learned to further its development. Does that answer your question, Dr. Hoffman?"

"But science hasn't advanced far enough for this to be possible."

"I'm standing here beside you, Dr. Hoffman. It *is* possible."

"Why are you here Dr. Lewis? You obviously don't need my help."

"That's where you're wrong, Dr. Hoffman. I *do* need your help. As you can see, I have total mobility...and for the most part, tactile feeling has returned as well, but I need to know if it's the device providing that functionality, or if I am truly cured and no longer need the device."

"What exactly is it you want me to do?"

"I want you to temporarily disconnect the device from the electrodes. Depending on what happens, I may need you to either reconnect it, or remove it all together. I am hoping for the latter."

Dr. Hoffman stared at the x-rays again without speaking. After a time, she said, "Your Mr. Malone offered me a handsome price in exchange for helping you and for keeping my silence. I, however, want more."

"Such as?" Jordan asked.

"I want to be on the team."

* * *

"Baby, I'm worried about your surgery tomorrow," Maggie said as she snuggled into Jordan's side.

"We're only going to disconnect the device. It's just under the surface of the skin. I'll be in and out of there in less than a day. Please try not to worry."

"But what if something goes wrong? What if disconnecting it puts you back in a wheelchair?"

"If that happens, we'll simply reconnect it again." Jordan rolled over so she was lying partially on top of Maggie.

"Maggie, please don't cry," she said as she wiped the tears from Maggie's face. "It'll be fine. I promise."

"Do you trust her?"

"Do I trust who?"

"Dr. Hoffman."

"After meeting with her, I did a little research, and yes, she seems well qualified. She has a very good reputation as a neurosurgeon. More than that, though, she seems genuinely interested in the implant and in the project as a whole. I've decided to add her to the implant team. She'll play an integral role when we reach the testing stage."

Maggie traced the side of Jordan's face with her index finger. "I would want to die if anything happened to you," she whispered. "I have so many plans for our future together. Our whole lives are before us, love. Promise me you won't take any unnecessary risks."

Jordan kissed Maggie tenderly. "I promise."

She kissed her again, a little deeper this time. A surge of desire spread through Jordan's abdomen as she deepened the kiss yet again. She felt Maggie's arms circle her waist, pressing her hands into the small of her back and pushing her heated core into her own.

"Love me," Maggie said.

"My pleasure," Jordan replied as she placed a line of kisses across Maggie's jaw and down her neck. A spasm shot through Jordan's abdomen as she fought to control her own desire. "God, Maggie, what you do to me," Jordan rasped into Maggie's neck.

Maggie's head pressed into the pillow and her chest arched upward as Jordan devoured first one breast, and then the other. She grasped two handfuls of Jordan's hair and held her there as Jordan gently nibbled on the swollen nubs. "Jordan," Maggie whispered hoarsely. "Baby, I need you. Please."

Jordan moved slowly down Maggie's body, tasting her skin and placing kisses along the way. Finally, she reached the golden-red triangle of hair at the apex of Maggie's legs. She glanced up the expanse of Maggie's body and nearly climaxed from the look of passion on Maggie's face. She gently parted the curls and blew a stream of warm air across Maggie's heated core.

"Oh, God. Jordan. I need to feel you inside me. Please," Maggie begged.

Jordan ran her tongue in circles around Maggie's passion point before sucking it into her mouth and flicking her tongue across the engorged bud for several minutes. Maggie pressed her heated core toward Jordan's mouth in a silent plea for more.

"Jordan, please. I need you now."

Sensing Maggie was on the edge of climax, Jordan placed two fingers deep inside her, setting up a rhythm that Maggie fell into cadence with, until finally, she felt Maggie's muscles tighten around her fingers.

"Let it go, love. I want all of you," Jordan said.

A guttural scream escaped Maggie's lips as a wave of orgasmic spasms tore through her. Jordan could feel Maggie's body pulsing against her fingers as she strove to bring as much pleasure to Maggie as possible before the orgasm finally subsided and her body became still. Jordan removed her hand then crawled up the length of Maggie to gather her into her arms. "I love you, Maggie Downs. Through all space and time."

"I love you too, Jordan. You are my heart," Maggie said, fighting to keep her eyes open.

"Sleep, my love," Jordan said.

"No, I need to love you," Maggie said.

"I can wait. Now close your eyes and let me hold you while you sleep."

Try as she might, Maggie was unable to keep her eyes open as she fell asleep in Jordan's arms. Jordan, still heated from Maggie's own arousal, lay beside her, wide awake until finally, the desire subsided and she joined her in sleep.

CHAPTER 31

Jordan lay on her stomach on the operating table. Her head rested on her crossed arms, and she was fully awake. Maggie stood in the balcony above them observing the scene below.

Dr. Hoffman exposed the middle of Jordan's back and applied a local anesthetic. "This shouldn't take long to numb the area, Jordan, since we are only concerned about cutting through the skin at this point."

Without looking up, Jordan called out to Maggie. "Are you doing okay up there, Mags?"

"Right now I'm fine, but I won't guarantee I'll still be on my feet after the doc cuts into you," Maggie joked.

"So I shouldn't be alarmed then if we hear a thud?"

"Very funny, love. Very funny," Maggie replied.

"Do you feel this, Jordan?" Dr. Hoffman asked as she poked Jordan's skin with the tip of the scalpel.

"I don't feel a thing."

"Okay then, here goes," the doctor said as she cut a curved flap over the device and peeled back the skin. "How are you doing, Jordan?"

"I'm fine. A layer of faradic mesh was installed between the device and the skin to protect it from electro-magnetic fields, so you'll have to make a second incision to cut through that. Be careful though not to cut too deep or you'll hit the electrode wires."

"Hey, who's doing this operation, you or me?" Dr. Hoffman joked.

"Sorry, Doc,"

"Okay, Jordan, I've exposed the device." Dr. Hoffman looked at the schematics of the device hand drawn by Jordan based on the x-rays, MRI's and CAT scans taken of the implant. "So, based on your drawing, this red wire right here should be the main power feed to the electrodes," Dr. Hoffman said.

"Be sure to cut it far enough back to be able to splice it back together if the paralysis returns," Jordan said.

"Got it. Here goes nothing," Dr. Hoffman snipped the wire then glanced at the various monitors hooked up to Jordan. "Your vitals look good. Everything is normal. How are you feeling, Jordan?"

"No different from before you cut the wire."

"Okay, here's the moment of truth," Dr. Hoffman said. "Tell me if you can feel this." Dr. Hoffman touched Jordan's foot.

"You're touching my foot."

"Can you wiggle your toes?"

Jordan complied.

"How about bending your knee?"

Jordan bent both knees to a ninety-degree angle, lifting the lower half of her legs straight up.

"Okay. Motion and touch seem to be intact. Now let's try temperature." Dr. Hoffman lifted the edge of the sheet and placed a warm, damp cloth on Jordan's leg. "Tell me what you feel, Jordan."

"Wet, soft and warm," Jordan replied.

"And this?" Dr. Hoffman touched the calf of Jordan's leg with an ice cube.

"Ice. That's freaking cold!"

"Very good. How about this?" Dr. Hoffman touched the other calf with the warm cloth.

"It's the warm cloth again."

"Well, all indications are that at least tactile feelings have remained intact. The only thing left to test is mobility under duress. We've already shown that you can move your legs, but I need to determine if the repaired spinal cord will support your weight and allow you to walk without the device. I am going to put the flap of skin back and place and cover it with a clear plastic bandage so we don't encounter significant bleeding while testing this. Okay?"

"Let's do it," Jordan said. "Hey, Mags, are you doing okay?"

"I'm speechless, Jordan. This is amazing," Maggie said.

Dr. Hoffman folded the flap of skin back into place and applied the clear bandage. "Okay, you'll need to carefully roll onto your side and push yourself into a sitting position. That's it," Dr. Hoffman said as she assisted Jordan.

"Nice moon shot," Maggie said from the observation balcony.

"I'll show you a moon shot," Jordan quipped back.

"Promises, promises," Maggie returned.

Dr. Hoffman chuckled. "Are you two always like this?" she asked.

"Pretty much."

"You're a lucky woman. You both are," the doctor said. "I hope one day to find someone I can have that kind of relationship with."

"You're not married?" Jordan asked.

"Divorced, but that's another story in itself. Okay, I need you to swing your legs over the side of the table and slide off." Dr. Hoffman stood in front of Jordan and prepared to catch her should she fall.

Jordan tenuously placed her feet on the floor and while holding on to Dr. Hoffman's arm, she stood erect. "So far, so good," she said.

"Hold onto my hands. Let's see if you can take a couple of steps," the doctor instructed.

Jordan took a few steps then released the doctor's hands and walked back and forth across the room twice. "Everything appears to work...and nothing hurts, so far," she said.

"Wonderful. So, decision time. Do we cut the rest of the wires and remove the device, or give it a few days to see if anything develops?" Dr. Hoffman asked.

"Just to be certain, you did cut the red wire, right?"

"Yes. That's the one you identified as connected to the power pack," Dr. Hoffman said.

"I can verify she cut the red wire, Jordan," Maggie said from above. "I watched her do it."

"Okay, then, if there is no power going to the device and I haven't lost any feeling or functionality, then I guess it's safe to remove it. I will ask, however, that just like the power wire, you cut the leads such that it…or another device like it, could be reinserted if necessary."

"All right then. Hop back onto the table and let's get this done."

A half hour later, Dr. Hoffman retrieved the device from under Jordan's skin and placed it in a stainless steel tray. She then cleaned the wound thoroughly and stitched it closed before applying the bandage. "Are you still doing okay, Jordan?" Dr. Hoffman asked.

"I'm fine. Are we finished?"

"Yes. You should be able to get up now and get dressed." Dr. Hoffman looked up. "Maggie, if you'd like to join us now that would be fine."

"I'll be right down."

Dr. Hoffman picked up the device and turned it over in her gloved hand several times. "I'm amazed that something so small could be so powerful. I mean, before this, the only device I was aware of that could restore mobility is a big, clumsy exoskeleton."

While Maggie helped Jordan to dress, Dr. Hoffman cleaned the blood and tissue off the device and placed it in a plastic bag. "It appears to have survived well in such a moist environment as human tissue. How long ago did you say this was implanted? Both the imaging we did and a visual inspection of the site, indicate nerves and tissues have grown around the electrode wires still installed in your spinal column. I'm afraid we won't be able to remove them without risking damage."

"Actually I didn't say," Jordan replied as she tucked her shirt in. Just know that it's been a while, and as far as the electrode wires are concerned, they have never caused me any issue, so I don't think leaving them in there will be a problem." Jordan held on to Maggie's shoulder for balance as Maggie bent to help Jordan put her boots on. "Thanks, love," she said.

Dr. Hoffman scribbled something on a prescription pad. "Here's a script for pain meds if you need it. So, as with any other wound, the stitches should absorb in a matter of two weeks. No heavy lifting, and be careful bending for the next several days. Topical antibiotic ointments are okay, and change the dressing daily for the next week. After that, as long as it's not seeping, and not irritated by clothing, you can leave it uncovered. I'd also like to see you in two weeks to check how well it's healing,"

"I dare say you'll see me before then," Jordan said. "I will be finished assembling the team in the next few days, then I plan to schedule a briefing to lay the groundwork for the new implant development. Since you are part of the team, you will be invited, even though your involvement will be later in the process."

"I look forward to meeting the team then. Let me know immediately if anything changes, or if any complications arise. Okay?"

Jordan slipped the device and the prescription into her shirt pocket. "All right. Thank you, Dr. Hoffman."

"Oh, and Jordan, since we're going to be working together, you can drop the formalities and call me Julie."

"Will do. I'll see you in about a week then, Julie."

* * *

Jordan looked at the screen on her cell phone to see who was calling. She smiled and pushed the answer button. "Hi Chuck," she said.

"Jordan. How did your surgery go?"

Jordan could hear the anxiety in his voice. "It went great. The device is in a plastic bag on top of my dresser right now ready for the team to reverse engineer."

"And you? How are you doing?"

"Fantastic. The good news, Chuck is that the implant worked exactly the way it was supposed to. Like I said, it's no longer in my back, yet I have the same degree of feeling and movement I had before removing it."

Jordan listed to several moments of muffled silence. "Chuck, are you still there?"

"I'm here," he said in a choked voice.

"Are you okay?"

"I'm fine. Just a little overwhelmed that we now have

actual hope that a cure is possible for Jessie."

"If we can successfully reengineer the device, then hope is absolutely there. Speaking of which, have you had a chance to set up a meeting with WorldWide Mainframes about the computer chip development?"

"Yes. In fact, that's why I'm calling. They are available for a meeting at two on Friday."

"That's in two days. Let me make sure we have nothing going on then." Jordan looked across the kitchen to Maggie who was stirring the spaghetti sauce on the stove. Maggie gave her a thumbs-up. "The boss says Friday at two is fine."

"Great. Do you think Maggie would mind coming along a spending a little time with Jessie while we're at the meeting? Jessie's been asking to see her again."

"Why don't you bring Jessie here and maybe she and Maggie can ride out to the north pasture again while we're at our meeting. Afterward, we can have dinner here, and maybe a bonfire."

"That sounds like a fine plan. We'll see you around one on Friday then."

* * *

"Gentlemen, Ladies, what I need is a computer chip that is more advanced than anything currently available on the market. I am hoping you are far enough in the development cycle for your next generation lithography for me to be able to take advantage of the increased power and speed it will surely provide." Jordan advanced her slide.

"This chip will be used in the development of a spinal implant, designed to restore mobility and over time, tactical sensation in victims of complete SCI's, or Spinal Cord Injuries." Jordan watched as the engineers present in the room exchanged curious looks with one another.

"The chip must have a MIPS of at least 10 GHz, and preferably more. It needs to be capable of extremely fast execution speeds to avoid a measurable disruption in signal. A disruption in signal could cause the person to move in a jerky manner instead of fluid motion. The speed of the chip must be fast enough to minimize delays to the nanosecond range, imperceptible to the human consciousness.

"The chip must have the ability to be self taught and must be able to perform millions of computations per second. It must contain memory enough to recognize, compute and store repeating events over several years time.

"The chip must be fully programmable and must be able to be powered by the human body itself. Used in conjunction with software that I will help to develop, this chip will be the brain of the device and must have the ability to adapt, become self aware and develop its own order of intelligence."

Jordan stopped to take a question.

"Dr. Lewis, you are describing a chip whose capabilities have not yet been developed, although they are certainly in the roadmap. What you are asking us to do could take years of development. Do you have that much time?"

"No sir, I do not. It is my goal to develop this spinal implant device within twelve calendar months."

"An impossible task," came a remark from the far end of the conference room. "The technology isn't ready for such a challenge."

Jordan held up her hand. "What if I was able to provide a prototype chip that is already known to work?"

The engineer closest to her raised his hand.

"Yes, sir?" Jordan said.

"Dr. Lewis, my name is Christopher Gamache and I am the manager of operations for this facility. If we had an existing chip to learn from, it is conceivable that a copycat of sorts could be developed. The question of time line may however, still be an issue...and depending on the level of difficulty and factors such as yield, defect density and reliability, the chip may be cost prohibitive."

"Mr. Gamache, cost is not a factor, within reason," Jordan said, "at least not in the beginning of the development cycle. Over time, one would expect the cost to decrease as the learning and yield increase."

"That is true, but the time line is still a problem. A normal development cycle, given the technology exists today to support such specifications, is at least two years. You are asking us to be ready in less than one."

"That is exactly what I am asking. However, given the technology exists today to support it, and given enough monetary and manpower resource, I believe it is achievable," Jordan insisted.

"So you have this chip in your possession?" Gamache asked.

"I do."

"And do you own the intellectual property for the chip?"

"I do."

"And you would be willing to allow us to reverse engineer the chip for the purpose of mass producing it. Do I understand you correctly?"

"You understand me perfectly well. I will caution you, however, that under no circumstances can this chip be damaged in any way during the reverse engineering process. I understand the semiconductor manufacturing process substantially well enough to know how a functional module is created with several masking levels, but you will not be able to physically dissect or change my chip in any way, or we will lose our only stencil for duplication. Is that clear to everyone?"

"So, what do you anticipate the demand for this chip to be, Dr. Lewis," Gamache asked.

"There are tens of thousands of people out there today, and hundreds of thousands more to come in the future who suffer from partial or complete spinal cord injuries. If these chips can eventually be made at a cost-efficient price, the return on investment will be continuous and astronomical."

A silence fell over the room for several moments. Finally, Gamache stood and shook Jordan's hand. "Dr. Lewis, your proposal has given us a lot to think about. I will convene a task force on Monday to consider your request then I will schedule a follow up meeting to discuss our decision."

"I appreciate your consideration, Mr. Gamache."

CHAPTER 32

Jordan and Chuck pulled up to the farm house just as Maggie and Jessie galloped into the barnyard on Shawny. "Whoa, boy," Maggie said and the steed came to a stop beside the truck.

"Hi Daddy," Jessie said. "Maggie and I have had a wonderful afternoon. Maggie let me help a baby horse be born."

"Dixie foaled? She was a bit early. Is everything okay?" Jordan asked Maggie.

"The foal is small, but she'll make it," Maggie replied.

"Maggie let me name her and said she could be my horse," Jessie said, her excitement evident in the lilt to her voice.

"Really?" Chuck said. "Owning a horse is a big responsibility, Jess."

"You can bring me by a couple times of week to brush her and feed her, can't you, Dad?"

"Well, I guess. If it's no imposition on Maggie and Jordan, that is."

"Not a problem, Chuck," Maggie said. "Jessie is a joy to be around."

"So what did you name this baby horse of yours?" Chuck asked.

"Foal, Dad. It's a foal, not a baby horse," Jessie replied, rolling her eyes.

Jordan had to look away so as to not laugh out loud.

"I stand corrected," Chuck said. "So, what did you name her?"

"I named her Jezebel, after me...get it? Jessie-Bell?"

"Seriously?" Chuck asked.

"Come on, Chuck. It's cute," Jordan said.

"What if it was your daughter, Lewis?" Chuck said, trying very hard to keep the smile off his face.

"Well, I don't have a daughter yet," Jordan said, winking at Maggie.

"Someday," Maggie said contemplatively before changing the subject. "So, how does goulash sound for dinner?"

"Really?" Jessie exclaimed. "I love goulash. My mom used to make it all the time."

"With sausage in it?" Maggie asked.

"Yes… exactly! Can I help?" Jessie asked.

"Sure you can," Maggie said. "Jord, you're on salad duty."

"Got it," Jordan said. "That's one dish I can't possibly burn."

"I'll give you a hand, Jordan. I can slice cucumbers with the best of them," Chuck said.

* * *

"So, Jordan, how did the meeting go with the semiconductor guys?" Maggie asked around a bite of goulash.

"I thought it went well. They didn't commit to anything. A few of them even complained that what I wanted was way beyond what the technology could support today, but after I offered up the chip we currently have as a prototype, they were at least willing to consider it. They owe me an answer next week."

"You aren't actually going to give them the only chip you have, are you?"

"I won't actually be *giving* it to them, just lending it so they can study it and figure out how to reverse engineer it. I made it clear to them that they couldn't damage or alter it in any way."

"What if they can't build you what you need?" Maggie asked.

"Then we'll have to figure out how to take what they *can* build and adapt it. There's a way around everything if you work at it hard enough."

"But will it work the same way as the current chip?" Chuck asked.

"It should be similar. I may have to adapt the algorithm to make up for the differences, but I think it's doable."

"If it's doable simply by making adjustments in the software, then why push them so hard to make a more advanced chip?" Chuck asked.

"Because the chips readily available today will run out of steam must faster than a more advanced one. Keep in mind that the chip inside the device was made eighty years from now. The one unknown in this whole thing is whether or not the software program, which was also written eighty years from now, will work with a less powerful chip. Bottom line...the more powerful chip we can get our hands on, the more likely our chances for long-term success."

"Wow, Jess, you're doing a good job on your goulash. Would you like some more?" Maggie asked.

"Yes, please."

Chuck narrowed his eyes at his daughter. "Who are you and what did you do with Jessie?" he said. "Sweetie, you never ask for seconds."

"Birthing foals can take a lot out of a person. It builds up an appetite, isn't that right, Jess?" Maggie said.

* * *

Jordan helped Maggie clear the dinner dishes and began rinsing them to put in the dishwasher. Maggie came up beside her and took the dish out of her hand. "Let me do that, love while you go entertain, Chuck."

"I'll help you, Maggie," Jessie said as she wheeled her chair up to the open dishwasher door.

"I'll tell you what, I'll rinse and you can load. Sound like a plan?"

"Works for me," Jessie said.

Jordan kissed both Maggie and Jess on the cheek then grabbed two beers from the refrigerator and went to join Chuck in the living room. She handed a beer to Chuck. "They kicked me out of the kitchen," she said.

"Thanks," Chuck said. "Jordan, I can't believe the change

in Jessie. Since she's met you and Maggie, she's full of life, she seems happier, she's eating better. She's a totally different girl. I can't thank you two enough for everything you do for her."

"Jess is a sweet little girl, and a pleasure to have around. You can thank Maggie for the turnaround. She and Jessie have really hit it off. She'll make a good mom some day."

"So, you and Maggie plan to have kids?"

"We've talked about it. Maggie has it all pretty much planned out…a boy and a girl."

"Jordan, this is going to sound a little off the wall, but if there's anything I can do in that respect...."

Jordan frowned. "Anything you can do?" She stared at him like he had antennae growing out of his forehead.

"Yeah, you know, if you need anything to make that happen."

Suddenly, Jordan's head snapped back. "Chuck, are you volunteering to be our sperm donor?" she asked incredulously.

"And what if I am?"

* * *

"What a beautiful Saturday morning," Maggie exclaimed as she stood in the kitchen doorway and looked at the sun filled barnyard. She pushed the screen door open. "Feel like taking a walk with me?"

Jordan looked up from her computer. "Where are you going?"

"Just to the end of the drive. I forgot to check the mailbox yesterday."

Jordan closed her computer and took Maggie's hand. "I can think of nothing better to do then to take a walk with my best girl. Well, I can think of one *other* thing we could do, but I'm not sure my incision is healed enough for that yet."

"You're incorrigible," Maggie said.

Jordan hip-bumped Maggie as they walked down the mile-long driveway, hand in hand. "I had an interesting discussion with Chuck after dinner yesterday," Jordan said.

"Yeah? What about?"

"He volunteered to be our sperm donor."

Maggie stopped dead in her tracks. "He what?"

"He volunteered to be our sperm donor. He's very impressed with the way Jessie has attached herself to you...and with the changes in Jessie since we've come into her life. He seems to think that you'll make a good mom, based on how you are with Jessie. Then he said if there was anything he could do to help us with that, he'd be willing."

"Jordan, are you ready to have kids?" Maggie asked.

"Well, I'm thirty-three and you just turned thirty-one a few weeks ago. I say if we're going to do it, we shouldn't wait too much longer."

"I know we talked briefly about it, but I didn't think we might do it this soon. I mean, you're in the middle of this implant project. Wouldn't having a baby be a distraction?"

"Mags, if everyone waited until the time was perfect to have a baby, there'd be no people on the earth. Any time is a good time. Since I'm older than you, I thought I might go first. Then in a couple of years, it will be your turn. I'm sure Chuck won't mind being the frozen pop for both."

"How long have you been thinking about this?"

"Chuck only mentioned it to me last evening, but I had a heck of a time falling asleep last night because I couldn't get it out of my mind."

Maggie stopped at the end of the driveway and faced Jordan without releasing her hand. "Do you really want to do this?"

Jordan could see the excitement in Maggie's eyes. "I do. I would love nothing more than to start a family with you."

"Okay. Let's do it."

Jordan took Maggie into her arms and kissed her tenderly. "I love you Margaret Michele Downs."

"And I love you too, Jordan Marie Lewis. Now let me get the mail so we can head back and start making plans to turn the guest room into a nursery."

CHAPTER 33

On Monday morning, Jordan met with her team for the first time. She stood at the head of the conference room and introduced herself to each member as they entered. Finally, all six members of the team, as well as herself and Chuck Malone, were present and accounted for.

"Good morning," she said. "As you know, my name is Dr. Jordan Lewis. I have a PhD in Kinesiology from Johns Hopkins University and a specialty degree in spinal cord injury treatment. This kind man to my left is Mr. Charles Malone. Mr. Malone has graciously agreed to fund a private foundation for the development, generation and testing of a new approach to spinal cord regeneration."

Chuck waived to the group.

"Chuck, please call me Chuck. I am looking forward to knowing each of you better and to working with all of you toward this common goal."

"Thank you, Chuck. Now before we begin with any of the details, I would like to go around the room and ask each of you to introduce yourself and to give us a little background on your credentials as well as your specialty field. Julie, if I could ask you to begin, please."

"Thank you Jordan. My name is Dr. Julie Hoffman. I am a neurosurgeon, specializing in spinal cord injuries. I have a private practice in Burlington, as well as admitting rights at the University of Vermont Medical Center."

"Jason," Jordan said.

A thirty-something African American man in a white lab coat worn over well-pressed dress pants, button-down shirt and tie, stood and introduced himself. "My name is Jason LaPine. I am a graduate of Stanford University. My degree field is

Neurology and my specialty field is in synapse development."

The next person at the table stood and introduced himself. He was a middle-aged man with a graying goatee. "Good Morning. My name is Wendell Graham. I have spent the last twenty five years as an Emergency Room doctor and my specialty field is traumatic injuries."

"Welcome, Wendell. Next please," Jordan said.

A young woman stood up. She was Asian-American and had shoulder length black hair and wore rectangular tortoise shell glasses. "Hi. My name is Carrie Alexander. My degree is in Computer Science and my specialty is in Programming."

The next person at the table was a young man wearing a lab coat over jeans, a Nirvana T-shirt and sandals. "Jackson Callahan, at your service. My degree is also in Computer Science and my specialty is in code development."

"Finally, last, but not least," Jordan said to the final member of the team.

"Good Morning. I'm Tom Lawson. My degree is in Material Sciences and I have extensive experience in semiconductor manufacturing and in medical implement development."

"Semiconductor manufacturing and medical implement development," Jordan repeated. "That's an odd combination."

"On the surface, yes," Tom said, "but so many medical implements require a marriage between computer chips, software, and packaging, that it's become a pretty substantial degree field."

Jordan nodded her head. "So let's see, a Kinesiologist, a Neurosurgeon, a Neurology/synapse expert, an ER and trauma doc, two computer programmers, and a materials scientist. That sounds like a pretty well rounded team to me. Welcome to all of you."

Jordan turned on the projector then got up from her seat and walked back and forth across the front of the room. She could feel all eyes follow her as she moved. Finally, she stopped and faced the group.

"I stand before you, a paraplegic. Seventeen years ago, I suffered a complete SCI at the L1 vertebrae as the result of a horse riding accident."

Everyone in the room sat forward in their seats and displayed some sense of surprise…all except Dr. Hoffman.

"How is that possible?" Jason asked. There is no synapse activity in a complete SCI."

"Jason, you are absolutely correct. From the time I was sixteen, until just recently, there was no synapse activity at the injury site, but there is now."

All eyes and ears were on Jordan as she walked across the front of the room once more.

"Dr. Hoffman, could I ask you to explain these fine folks, what you found when you examined my injury recently?"

Dr. Hoffman rose and faced the room. "As late as two weeks ago, I ran x-ray, MRI, CAT scan and ultrasound tests at the site of Dr. Lewis's SCI. All tests confirmed that nerve and tissue re-growth was evident over the injury site, and that synapse connection was present and active."

"Thank you, Dr. Hoffman."

Jordan advanced the slide and displayed the recent x-ray results evaluated by Dr. Hoffman. "This slide shows the calcified bone fissures at the injury site. This next slide displays the MRI and CAT Scans side by side highlighting a tangle of wires surrounded by tissue growth across the injury site." Evident in all of the images was an outline of the implant device.

Wendell Graham raised his hand.

"Yes, Dr. Graham?" Jordan said.

"I'm sure this question is on everyone's mind…the wires and the box seen in all of the images. What are they?"

"They are the reason we are here today," Jordan said. "You see, team, I was indeed a paraplegic, but due to that box and those wires, I was cured."

Jordan reached into her pocket and extracted the implant device. "This is the box you see in the images. Dr. Hoffman can verify for you that it was removed from my body a little more than a week ago. It was removed for two reasons. First, I no longer need it. It did its job and promoted the re-growth of nerves, tissue and synapse connections over the injury site.

Second, and more importantly, it was removed so this team could use it as a template for creating more devices like it."

"How does the device work?" Jackson Callahan asked.

"Good question, Jackson. The wires you saw in the images are actually a series of electrodes that were surgically implanted on each side of the injury site. Next, both autologous and endogenous neural stem cells were injected on each side of the break. As you know, stem cells are very mutable, especially when excited. We achieve maximum mutability by applying a continuous wave electrical charge from the battery pack to the electrodes. This electrical charge encourages the stem cells to adapt to their surroundings. They essentially develop into spinal nerve cells and grow toward one another from both sides of the injury until they create a synapse in close enough proximity to allow nerve impulses to pass from one neuron to the other. As the nerves grow they weave a bridge over the injury site and mend the break in the spinal cord while reestablishing the lines of communication between the nerve endings. Once that bridge is woven and feelings are restored, the implant is no longer needed and can be removed, just as this one was removed from me."

"How long does this process take?" Dr. Graham asked.

"Mobility is established immediately upon insertion of the device. The electrodes act as a synthetic bridge over the injury site. As long as the bone structure is intact, the device will allow the recipient to walk, run, jump and essentially move normally, however, until the nerve growth has had time to bridge the injury site, there is essentially no feeling below the injury. As the nerves grow toward each other and synapses are restored, feeling below the injury will gradually return until one day, the device becomes redundant. That process of re-growth is dependent on how fast the recipient's body allows it to happen. For that reason, it is difficult to put a time frame on it."

"So you basically want us to reverse engineer and remanufacture the design and functionality of this device, Tom Lawson said. "Isn't that piracy?"

Tom's comments caused a wave of discontent to descend over the room.

Jordan gave the team a few minutes to settle down before answering the question. "Ordinarily, Tom, copying an existing device would be considered piracy however, since I own the design and intellectual property for the device, it is not a matter of piracy. Instead, it is our effort to recreate and improve the design and functionality of the device."

"You own the design of this device," Jason said.

"Yes, I do."

"Then why don't you just submit the specs to a manufacturer and have multiple copies built yourself? Why does it need to be redesigned?" Tom asked.

"Because the specs no longer exist."

Jordan held the device in the palm of her hand for all to see. "This is the only one in existence and it will be used as a stencil to create more. Tom, you will be in charge of working with WorldWide Mainframes to design and build computer chips comparable to the one in this device. I will tell you right now the technology used to build this particular device is far superior to anything we have today. Your challenge will be to come as close as possible to the form, fit and function of the chip inside this device, as well as develop a battery pack that charges itself through kinetic energy produced by the human body."

Jordan walked clockwise around the room, stopping to address team members as she went. "Carrie and Jackson, I actively worked with programmers such as yourselves, to write the algorithms that make this device work. Your task will be to write and test seamless code that will minimize clock delays to the nanosecond level such that any inconsistencies in the timing is indiscernible to the human consciousness. In other words, this device has to produce smooth, non-jerky movements in the recipient."

Jordan walked further around the table. "Wendell and Jason, as neurologist and trauma doctors, you will be responsible for redesigning and adapting the device for use in human beings. You both will be responsible for carrying out several clinical trials with non-human subjects. When the time comes to test the device on a human subject, you again will carry the baton."

Jordan turned to Dr. Hoffman. "Finally, we get to you, Dr. Hoffman. As a neurosurgeon, you will be responsible for inserting prototype devices in our human and non-human subjects, as well as monitoring the health of the recipients through the testing process."

Jordan returned to the front of the room and faced the group. "As for myself, since I have experience is nearly every aspect of this process, I will assist wherever necessary…except maybe with the chip design and manufacture. I will supply the specs for the chips, but, Tom, you'll be pretty much on your own relative to driving it to completion.

"I won't lie to you. This is a very big project with colossal challenges; however, if we are successful, many thousands of people will reap the benefits of our work. This team will go down in the history books as responsible for curing complete spinal cord injury paralysis. None of us will work in a vacuum. Although each of you is responsible to driving specific tasks to completion, we are a team and will lend our expertise to each other when needed. If we encounter a situation where skills are needed outside of what the team is capable of, we will seek that skill and contract it out. We have an internal target of entering beta testing within twelve calendar months. The biggest challenge toward that goal will be acquisition of adequate computer chips.

"Mr. Malone here has offered not only to fund our research and development, but to grant each of you a very generous salary. This is your chance to accept this challenge, or to walk away."

Jordan sat back down at the head of the table and waited. She purposely did not make eye contact with any member of the team so as to no intimidate anyone. After ten minutes of silence, she looked around the room once more then stood at the head of the table. "I will interpret your silence as an agreement to accept this challenge. Welcome to the team. We begin at eight tomorrow."

Chuck walked Jordan to the front lobby. "You were very impressive in there, Jordan. You really know your stuff."

"I am passionate about my work, Chuck. People like Jessie deserve no less."

"It appears we have a pretty capable team. I'm willing to bet they're shitting their pants right now over the challenge you threw on the table, all but Dr. Hoffman, that is."

"You could be right, Chuck. This is probably the biggest challenge any of them have ever faced, but I have confidence in the team. By the way, I noticed you had a problem taking your eyes off Dr. Hoffman during the meeting."

Chuck blushed profusely. "Ah…oh, hell, Jordan. You're into women. Don't tell me you didn't notice how attractive she is. Do you know if she's married?"

Jordan grinned. "Yes, I did notice, and no, she isn't married."

Jordan shoved her hands deep into her pockets and realized she was still carrying the implant around with her. She withdrew it and gave it to Chuck. "Could I ask you to put this into the vault when you check on the renovations? I don't like carrying it around with me. I don't want to risk losing or damaging it."

"Good idea," Chuck said as he accepted the device. "I'll do that right away."

"So like I was saying, I don't believe in doing things half-assed. There are too many people depending on us to do the best we can. Imagine implanting a device into Jessie that wasn't as good as it could be. I just couldn't do that in good conscience."

"I agree with you, Jordan. I am trying hard to treat this like a business proposition but my daughter's future is on the line. Being a parent is difficult sometimes."

"Speaking of being a parent, Chuck, I spoke to Maggie about your offer to help us out."

"And?"

"And we would be honored if you would be our donor."

CHAPTER 34

Jordan left the lobby alone while Chuck went to check on the status of the renovations in the lab. As she walked across the parking lot to her car, a man dressed in a black business suit approached her.

"Dr. Lewis. Dr. Lewis, could I have a moment of your time?" the man said.

Jordan stopped and allowed the man to catch up. "How can I help you?" she asked.

The man grabbed her arm and pulled a gun out of the pocket of his suit coat. "You can help me by not causing a scene," he said as he poked the barrel of the gun into her side.

"What's this all about? Who are you?" Jordan asked.

"Just cooperate and no one will get hurt," he said. "I'm going to let go of you, but the gun will remain pointed in your direction. We're going to walk very calmly toward the black car over there."

"I'm not going anywhere with you. Now tell me what's going on," Jordan said.

The man gave her a firm shove. "I said, get moving."

"No. Who sent you?"

He grabbed her arm. "If you don't do as you're told, there will be hell to pay."

"I'll show you hell if you don't take your hands off me."

The man motioned toward the car. A second later, another man exited the passenger side of the car. He grabbed Jordan's other arm and together, the two men dragged her toward their car where they quickly frisked her, taking her wallet and cell phone, then shoved her into the back seat.

"What the fuck?" Jordan said as she tried to climb out of the car, only to have a chloroform-laced cloth held to her mouth and nose. Within seconds, she was unconscious.

* * *

Maggie paced back and forth on the front porch waiting for Jordan to come home. As dusk fell, Maggie became worried and called Chuck.

"Chuck, is Jordan with you?" she asked.

"No. She left the lab before noon after the kick-off meeting with the team. She's not home yet?" Chuck asked.

"I haven't seen or heard from her since she left the house this morning."

"Did she say anything to you about any stops she had to make on the way home?"

"No. In fact, she said she'd be home earlier enough this afternoon to help our farm hand bring in the first cut of hay. She never came home."

"I don't like the sound of this, Maggie," Chuck said. "Maybe you should call the police."

"I really don't want to do that unless it's a last resort, Chuck. There's a lot at stake here for her *and* for you if the police start asking questions about her."

"I hear what you're saying, Maggie, but I'd rather face the music with the police than to see anything bad happen to Jordan."

"I'm going to call Gina and Sam. Maybe she stopped there on the way home for some reason.

"Okay. Keep me posted."

"I will. Thanks, Chuck. Bye."

Maggie selected Gina's speed dial number and waited for her to answer the phone.

"Hey, Mags, what's up?" Gina said.

"Gina, is Jordan with you?"

"No, she isn't. We haven't seen her since the weekend. I take it she's late getting home?"

"Several hours late, in fact, and she isn't answering her phone. Chuck said she left the lab before noon and he hasn't seen her since. I'm worried about her, Gina. It's not like her to be late without calling me."

"Call the police, Maggie."

"I can't, Gina. Not unless I have real reason to fear she's in danger. The last thing we need is the police digging into her past and finding none."

"Sam and I are on our way. We can at least wait with you until she comes home."

"You don't need to do that, Gina."

"Yes I do. It'll be a little tough kicking her ass from here for making you worry."

"Okay, I'll see you in a bit then."

* * *

The man picked up a scalpel and cut a four-inch incision in Jordan's back. He then inserted an expander and opened the incision wider. After suctioning out the excess blood, he reached inside with a gloved hand and felt around.

"Where is it?" he said out loud. "It's gone. Son of a bitch, it's gone!"

* * *

"Oh, my God, my head is killing me," Jordan moaned as she opened her eyes and quickly closed them again. She grabbed the sides of her head to stop the pounding. She pushed herself into a seated position and looked around through barely open eyes. She was on the ground, beside a dumpster that was hidden behind a stockade fence.

"Where am I?" she whispered.

She looked down at herself and realized someone had removed her jacket and her shoes. Curiously, her shirt tails were also un-tucked and the zipper on her slacks was down.

What happened here? she asked herself.

She took a mental inventory of how she was feeling. *I hope to God nothing happened*, she thought as fears of rape and violation crossed her mind.

Jordan rolled to her side and onto her knees, a motion that shot searing pain through her back, causing her to sit back on her heels. She reached behind to rub the source of the pain.

When she pulled her hand back, there was blood on it.

"What the hell?" she said out loud as she lifted her shirt tails and felt under the fabric. Her fingers encountered gauze—wet gauze. "What the hell happened here?" she said.

Despite the pain, she forced herself to stand, thanking the heavens that she still had control of her legs. As she moved, she realized the pain she was feeling was coming from her skin rather than her spine. She looked at the ground where she had been lying and saw her jacket and shoes has been haphazardly thrown beside her. She also saw a large blood stain on the pavement.

I've got to do something about this before an infection sets in, she thought.

Jordan slipped her feet into her shoes and picked up her jacket. She immediately checked the pockets and found that her cell phone and wallet were still there. *Well, I guess that rules out robbery*, she thought.

Jordan pulled her cell phone from her jacket pocket and looked at the screen. "Tuesday, 7:45 am. Tuesday?" There were also seventeen missed calls from Maggie. Jordan immediately dialed Maggie's number.

"Jordan, where the hell are you?" From the tone of Maggie's voice, Jordan could tell she was out of her mind with worry.

"Maggie. I…I'm not sure where I am. I was abducted in the parking lot of the lab after the meeting yesterday and I just woke up beside a dumpster."

"Someone abducted you?" Maggie was crying. "Baby, are you all right?"

"Actually, no. Someone is after the implant, Maggie. I came to this morning with blood all over the back of my shirt. Someone cut me."

"What the hell do you mean, someone cut you?"

"Someone cut my back open, right over the spot where the implant would still be if Julie hadn't removed it. It's obviously been bleeding on and off for a while. The back of my shirt and slacks are covered in blood, and there was blood on the ground as well."

"Where are you, Jordan?"

"I don't know. Hold on and let me look around a bit." Jordan slipped her jacket on and walked out from behind the stockade fence. Luckily there was no one in sight. "It looks like I'm near some sort of medical facility. I see a sign. Let me get a little closer so I can read it." Jordan began walking toward the sign.

"Damn that hurts," she commented as every movement caused a jolt of pain in her back.

"Jordan, hang up and call 911 right now," Maggie said.

"I can't do that, Maggie. What if they ask questions I can't answer? "Okay, I'm close enough to read the sign. It says, Northwest Medical Center."

"Northwest Medical Center? Jordan, that's in St. Albans. Sweetie, is the Medical Center right there?"

"Yes."

"I want you to go to the emergency room, right now."

"I can't Maggie."

"God damn it, Jordan. Will you stop being so fucking stubborn? I don't need you bleeding out by the side of the road."

"I'm not bleeding that badly. Look, call Chuck and ask him to come after me and to bring Julie with him. The lab is about twenty-five miles south of here. With the morning rush hour traffic, he'll be here in about forty minutes."

"I'm on my way as well," Maggie said.

"Maggie, I would rather you bring a change of clothing to the lab. We'll meet you there."

"Okay. I love you, Jordan."

"Love you too, Mags."

Less than five minutes later, Jordan's phone rang. The name on the screen displayed Chuck's name.

"Hello," Jordan said.

"Jesus Christ, Jordan. What the hell happened? Julie and I are on the way," Chuck said.

"I wish I could tell you, Chuck. After I left you in the lobby, a well-dressed man came up to me in the parking lot. He knew my name. The next thing I knew, he and another guy shoved me into the backseat of their car and chloroformed me. My next memory is of waking up this morning on the ground beside a dumpster with blood all over my clothes. I didn't tell Maggie this, but I was partially unclothed."

"God damn it," Chuck swore. "Hold on, Jordan, Julie wants to talk to you."

"Jordan, tell me about the blood," Julie said.

"Hi Julie. The blood is coming from my back. Whoever did this is after the implant."

"How bad is it?"

"Bad enough to leave a good sized spot on the ground where I was lying. The gauze that's on it is pretty saturated. Hurts like hell too."

"Maggie said you were right outside the Northwest Medical Center. Maybe you should go to the emergency room and we'll meet you there."

"I'd rather not do that, Julie. I don't need anyone asking questions about the implant site."

"I have some medical supplies with me, but you might need sutures, in which case, we'll need to go to my clinic."

"You can look at it when you get here. I'm hoping it's not as bad as it looks. Oh, and Julie, like I told Chuck, I was partially unclothed when I woke up. I'll need you to…."

"I'll check it out, Jordan. Let's hope for the best."

"Thanks, Julie."

A half hour later, Chuck's SUV came to a screeching halt in the parking lot next to a bench Jordan was sitting on while she waited. She was bent over with her hands wrapped around her middle. Chuck and Julie immediately jumped out of the car and ran toward Jordan.

"Come on, Jordan," Julie said. "We've got the seats down in the back of the car. I want you to lie on your stomach so I can check you out while Chuck drives us to my clinic."

Jordan walked haltingly to the SUV and painfully climbed into the back. Julie grabbed her medical bag from the front seat and crawled in beside her. She pulled on a pair of rubber gloves.

"Okay, Chuck, we're in. Let's go," she said as she helped Jordan out of her jacket. "Jordan, can you unbuckle and unzip your pants for me so I can gain access to the wound? Thanks. Damn, you weren't kidding when you said there was a lot of blood."

Julie pushed the waistband of Jordan's slacks below the injury site then lifted her shirt above it. "I'm going to take the bandage off, Jordan. This might hurt a bit."

Jordan gritted her teeth as Julie peeled the blood-soaked bandage back. "I'm going to clean this up a bit so I can tell what I'm looking at. This will sting,"

Jordan's whole body tensed while Julie wiped away the blood seeping from the wound.

"Well that answers one question—it was sutured, although I personally would have used twice as many. There are also several bruise marks on both sides of the incision, indicating clamps or maybe an expander was used to open the wound. That's probably where most of the pain is coming from. When we get to the clinic, I want to do another series of x-rays to see if there is any damage beyond the obvious skin lesion caused by whoever did this to you. I will also put you on an antibiotic, as the incision site is pretty inflamed. For now, I'll put a new dressing on it to hold us until we get to the clinic."

"They must have been pissed when they realized the implant was already removed," Jordan said.

"You may be right."

"Julie, could you grab my phone out of my jacket? I need to tell Maggie to meet us at your clinic instead of the lab. She's bringing me a change of clothes."

* * *

Chuck met Maggie at the door of the clinic when she arrived. Maggie immediately went into his arms. "You're shaking," Chuck said.

"How is she?"

"She's fine. Julie looked at the wound. It's a little inflamed, but nothing a good antibiotic won't take care of. She's doing x-rays now to see if any damage was done at the site."

"Why would someone do this to her?" Maggie asked, the frustration clearly in her voice.

"I've been trying to figure out the very same thing. Jordan thinks someone was after the implant. If that's true, it was obviously someone who isn't aware that it's already been removed."

"Well, now that they know, maybe they'll leave her alone."

"I'm not so sure about that. What this tells me is that we need to beef up security at the lab, and for our key personnel. I mean, if for some reason they manage to get their hands on the implant, they will still need Jordan, or maybe another team member to help them operate or program it."

"Chuck, this scares me. I didn't sign on for this. Jordan was supposed to help develop the new implant then life would go on. We would have a couple of babies, start the handicapped riding school at the farm and grow old together. Instead we have kidnapping and industrial espionage."

"I will do everything in my power to protect her from this point on, Maggie. That is my promise to you."

"I know you will, and I know this is something Jordan has to do, but it still scares the shit out of me knowing that there's someone out there with the power, and the opportunity to do something like this to her."

"After today, the opportunity will no longer be there. I promise you, Maggie, we will get to the bottom of this."

Just then, the door to the waiting room opened and Dr. Hoffman entered the room. "Maggie, you can see Jordan now."

Maggie picked the overnight bag up and followed Dr. Hoffman into the clinic. Jordan was sitting on the edge of the examining table wearing a hospital gown. She immediately went to Jordan and wrapped her arms around her. Tears rolled down her cheeks. "When you didn't come home last night, I was so scared. I nearly called the police."

"I'm so sorry you had to go through that, love." Jordan kissed her on the temple.

"What about you? What did they do to you, Jordan?" Maggie leaned to the side and looked at Jordan's back.

"Julie added a few more stitches and put a fresh dressing on it. It hurts like hell, but I'll be okay."

Maggie held Jordan's face between her hands. "They didn't do anything else to you, did they?" The fear on Maggie's face spoke volumes to Jordan.

"No, they didn't. I specifically asked Julie to check for that. These weren't your everyday thugs and rapists. It was the implant they were after."

Maggie closed her eyes and released a deep sigh. "Thank God."

She picked up the bag on the floor by her feet. "I brought you some clean clothes. Let me help your get dressed, then I'm taking you home. The lab can wait until tomorrow."

Jordan grinned. "Yes boss," she joked.

CHAPTER 35

Jordan woke up the next morning very stiff and barely able to move. "Oh, my God, I feel like I've been dragged behind a car this morning."

"Maybe you should stay home from the lab for one more day," Maggie suggested.

"No, I really need to get this project kicked off. Give me a hand sitting up, will you?" She reached her hand forward.

Maggie helped her to sit on the edge of the bed. "Sit here for a few minutes while I get dressed, then I'll help you stand."

"What's on your agenda today?" Jordan asked.

"The saddler is coming over this morning to discuss ideas I have for the handicap saddle design, then at one this afternoon, I have a meeting scheduled with the permit board to go over the required changes we need to make to open the riding school."

"I wish I could be there with you for that meeting, but I really do need to get this project off the ground."

Maggie bent down and kissed Jordan on the lips. "I understand, love. You also need to remember our appointment with the fertility doctor on Friday."

"Friday? What time?"

"Two o'clock. The appointment is in Burlington. Near the hospital, in fact."

"Okay. Text the address to me and I'll meet you there. While we're in town, I'd also like to stop at the apartment before heading home to pick up the food and clothes I have there and to return the key. Chuck outfitted one room at the lab with cots so if anyone on the team needs to work late into the evening we can just crash there."

"Okay. Are you ready to stand?"

Jordan nodded, then raised her arms and placed her hands on Maggie's shoulders.

"Easy does it," Maggie said as Jordan painfully stood.

"Damn, that hurts. It feels like my back is on fire."

"Turn around and let me take a look at it."

Maggie gasped when she saw Jordan's back. "My God, love. You are black and blue from your waist to the middle of your butt cheeks. No wonder it hurts. There's also some seepage through the dressing. I'll need to change that before you get dressed. Where did you put the bag of supplies Julie gave you?"

"On the table in the kitchen."

"Okay. I'll be right back."

Moments later, Maggie had a fresh bandage on Jordan's incision.

"How does it look?" Jordan asked as she looked over her shoulder at Maggie, who was kneeling on the floor behind her.

"Sore, but at least it's no longer hot. Yesterday, I could feel the heat coming right through the bandage."

Maggie gently kissed the area around the wound, causing Jordan to moan.

"Jesus, honey. You can turn me on even while in pain," she said.

"Well there won't be any of that going on for a few days, so save it up until later, okay? Do you need help getting dressed?"

"No, I think I can manage."

"Okay then, I'll get your antibiotic and a couple of pain killers for you, along with a coffee, while you do that."

"Coffee! You're a lifesaver, Mags."

Maggie kissed her on the nose. "I'll be back in a few minutes."

* * *

Chuck was waiting for Jordan in the parking lot of the lab when she arrived that morning. "Good morning, Jordan. How are you feeling today?" he asked.

"Sore as hell, but I'll survive. Is the team here?" Jordan asked as she walked gingerly toward the building with Chuck.

"They are. I hope you don't mind, but Julie and I filled them in on what happened yesterday. They're all pretty upset, but even more determined now to make this work."

Jordan noticed the two security guards standing in the lobby when they entered and nodded her approval to Chuck.

Chuck held the door open to the conference room for her to enter before him. The team was immediately on their feet and clapping. Jordan held her hands up to silence them.

"Good morning," she said. "So, who's ready to kick some ass on this project today?" She was greeted by positive remarks all around the table. "Good. So, I hope you've all had a chance to go over the detailed technical information I provided to you on Monday.

"We have some amazing talent in this room so please use your experience, imagination and ability to think outside the box to kick this development into gear as quickly as possible. You have all been assigned email accounts and we have access to each other's calendars. I ask that you keep your calendar as up to date as possible so we'll all know what times are available for collaborative sessions and meetings. We will begin each morning at eight with a mandatory status meeting right here in this room where we will put on the table, any issues or concerns each of us is currently dealing with. As I said on Monday, we will each have our focus areas to work on, however, as a team there will be opportunities to help each other as well. This meeting will be the focus for those opportunities, however, I strongly encourage you to involve other team members at any time that a situation warrants it.

"Like I said on Monday, I was intimately involved in the development of the first implant, so I have pretty specific knowledge about how that was achieved. I encourage each of you to schedule time on my calendar if you have any questions whatsoever, or need any advice…or if the situation warrants, you have my permission to interrupt anything I'm doing if you need immediate help with something. My door is always open to every member of the team.

"It is not mandatory that the new device be an exact duplicate of the old one but it is mandatory that the function of the device remain the same, or better if possible. Are there any questions?"

Tom raised his hand. "Dr. Lewis, where is the device currently? I have a meeting scheduled for tomorrow with WorldWide Mainframes, but I'd like to get started today on the packaging."

"Good question, Tom. Let me start by encouraging you to call me Jordan. So, as you know, we believe what happened to me yesterday was an attempt to steal the device. Luckily, I had given it to Chuck before I left the building on Monday. This is currently a one-of-a-kind device with the power to cure spinal paralysis, so you can imagine how valuable it might be on the black market.

"I fear my encounter on Monday may be just the first of many attempts. For that reason, the device will be under heavy security at all times, even when it is in the possession of WorldWide Mainframes during the design analysis. Whoever has the physical device in their possession will have to endure the scrutiny of an armed guard by their side while they have it. Please know that this is not a reflection on you, but an attempt to keep the device from falling into the wrong hands during any potential encounter you may have with unsavory elements while it is in your possession. Once we are far enough along in the development of a new device—far enough along that someone may be able to learn something from its form, fit and function— the level of security around the lab will also be substantially increased."

Chuck raised his hand.

"Chuck, did you have something to add?" Jordan asked.

"Yes. I want everyone here to know that your safety is just as important to this foundation as the security of the device, so if any of you needs or wants a bodyguard, please see me immediately. I would be happy to provide one. I also recommend that you not divulge the nature of this project to anyone outside this room."

"Thank you, Chuck. So, Tom, to finally answer your question, the device is in a secure location inside the lab. I will bring it to you right after this meeting. Are there any other questions?" Jordan looked around the room. "Okay, my office door is open, so stop by if you have a question or need help with anything."

Jordan watched her team file out of the room, then sat in the closest chair and released a painful sigh.

"Jordan, are you okay?" Chuck asked.

"I'm fine. The incision is just a little sore."

"Maybe you should go home and lie down."

Jordan looked at Chuck. "Now, what kind of message do you think that will send to the team? No, I'll stick it out here."

"Well then, you need to take it easy. I don't want to endure the wrath of Maggie if I let you overdo it," Chuck joked.

Jordan laughed. "I hear you, Chuck. I'll be fine, and besides, if I need to, I can always ask Julie to take a look at it."

"Did I hear my name?" Dr. Hoffman said as she was passing the conference room. She stopped and poked her head in. "I didn't want to ask this question in front of the team, but how are you feeling this morning?"

"I'm in a little pain, but as long as I don't twist at the waist, it's tolerable. I don't remember it hurting this much after you removed the device."

"That's because whoever did this to you was apparently a gorilla and didn't take measures to minimize tissue damage and bruising. I'll bet the area around the incision is pretty colorful today."

"Maggie said I'm black and blue from my waist to the middle of my butt cheeks."

"I'll bet. Have you given any more thought about who may have done this?"

"I've thought quite a bit about it, but I have no clue. I mean, it was someone who has access to surgical equipment, and knows how to use it. Whoever did this knew I had the implant, but didn't know it was removed, so I'm pretty confident it's no one associated with the team…not that I suspect anyone on the project, but it certainly does eliminate any doubt."

"Well, I recommend you take it easy today. If you're more comfortable sitting than standing, then work on the software with the IT geeks. I'll stop in throughout the day and check on you, and to change the dressing if need be."

"Thanks, Julie. I really appreciate it."

Julie looked to Chuck. "Chuck, don't let her overdo it today. Pull rank on her if you have to."

"Yeah, like *that* will make any difference," Chuck joked.

Jordan watched Dr. Hoffman leave then struggled to her feet. "Okay, I need to get the device to Tom."

"I'll take care of that, along with a security guard," Chuck said. "You just go to your office and relax."

"Thanks." Jordan stopped him just before he left the room. "Oh, Chuck, before I forget, Maggie and I have an appointment with the fertility doc on Friday. It'll probably take a month or two before we actually do the deed."

Chuck smiled. "No problem. Just let me know."

CHAPTER 36

"Are you ready for this?" the doctor asked.

"More than ready," Maggie said.

"Ditto," Jordan said.

"I assume you've been monitoring your ovulation cycles?"

"Daily," Maggie said. We've been keeping a chart in fact."

"Great. Let me get the specimen then we can begin."

Jordan took Maggie's hand as they waited for the doctor to return. "Are you as nervous as I am?" she asked.

"Are you kidding me? I didn't sleep a wink last night," Maggie replied.

"This will mean a significant change in our lifestyle, you know."

"I'm for anything that will calm these crazy lives of ours down. Falling off cliffs, kidnappings, espionage, having a baby will be easy compared to all that." Maggie looked deep into Jordan's eyes. "Are you happy about this, Jordan? I mean, truly happy?"

"I am. I see how you are with Jessie. You're going to be a great Mom, my love."

"And so are you," Maggie said. "I suspect I'll have to be the tough parent. You are such a soft touch the baby will have you wrapped around its little finger with no effort at all."

A knock on the door announcing the doctor's return, drew their attention.

"Okay, Jordan, I'll need you to scoot down on the table and put your feet into the stirrups. Just a bit further. Okay, that's good."

The doctor inserted a speculum into Jordan's vagina then retrieved from the table a large syringe with a very long, thin tube attached to the end of it.

"I am going to insert this tube into the vagina, through the cervix and directly into the uterus, as far as possible so that when the sperm cells are released, they are as close as possible to the fallopian tubes. There, that should do it. Now Maggie, if you'd come here, I'll ask you to engage the plunger on the syringe. That's it. Good. That's about all there is to it," the doc said as he removed both the tube and the speculum.

Maggie grinned at Jordan. "Was it good for you?"

"Fabulous. My eyes are rolling into the back of my head," Jordan replied.

"You're such a goofball," Maggie said before addressing the doctor. "So what do we do next?"

"We wait and see. I recommend talking care of yourself in the meantime, eat well and get plenty of sleep, and let nature take its course. If it didn't work, we'll try again in a few months."

"Or we can try with me," Maggie said.

"Or we can try with you," the doctor agreed.

* * *

Jordan walked into the Monday morning meeting with high hopes. News from WorldWide Mainframes on the previous Friday indicated they would be able to produce a chip similar to the one in the existing device.

"Good morning, everyone," Jordan said to the team. "I trust you all had a good weekend. So, I'd like to begin this meeting with an update from Tom. Tom, I'd like you to share your news with the team if you would."

Tom rose to his feet. "Last Friday afternoon, WorldWide Mainframes contacted me and indicated they had electronically de-layered the chip in the current device. What they discovered astounded them, as they had never seen a chip with so many transistors and microprocessors on it. They were pretty up front about their current market offering not even coming close to what we were looking for; however, they have a new process in development that uses extreme ultraviolet light, also known as EUV light, to carve transistors directly into silicon wafers.

"The new technology uses a very short wavelength to expose the images into silicon—thirteen point five nanometer wavelength to be exact—compared to the current market offering at one-ninety-three nanometer wavelength. For reference, one nanometer is one-billionth of a meter. The shorter wavelength leads to smaller imaging. Smaller imaging means more room for additional transistors. The larger number of transistors leads to a more powerful and faster microprocessor.

"The EUV process currently in development produces chips that are more than one hundred times faster than the most powerful chips on the market today. WorldWide Mainframes is confident they can build a completed module comparable in capability and speed to the one inside the current device in about six months. They made it clear that without the original chip as a model to learn from, development of such a powerful microprocessor would have taken at least another fifteen to twenty months."

"Thank you Tom. Six months is encouraging. We are already two months into the process, so in six months, we need to develop the self-charging battery pack and begin writing the software code that will instruct the device. Also within that time, we will need to design the smallest possible packaging to hold both the chip and the power pack. The current device packaging contains both. There is an option to make the power pack external to the body, but in all probability, it would not be self-charging. That means plugging in and charging while the recipient sleeps. My first implant was precisely in that configuration, and trust me when I say, it was a major inconvenience having to learn new sleeping habits so as to not unplug yourself while sleeping. By far, it is preferable for it to be contained within the body and recharged kinetically through muscle movement.

"If the chip is truly delivered in six months, that will put us at the eight-month mark, meaning we will have four additional months of testing on non-human subjects in order to stay on our twelve-month schedule. Are there any questions?"

Jordan looked around the room. "Okay then. Have a great and productive day."

* * *

Jordan was sitting at her desk working on the algorithm for the self-charging battery pack when Chuck appeared in her doorway. "Good morning," he said.

Jordan looked up and smiled. "Chuck. I'm glad you're here. I want to ask you a few questions about my abduction two months ago."

Chuck sat down in the chair opposite her desk. "Sure. What's on your mind?"

"Well, Julie feels that the person who cut me has medical knowledge. As careless as they were closing the wound, it was not a butcher job."

"So the person who did this to you was probably a doctor."

"I think so."

"Any idea who?"

"I have a hunch, but I want to verify something with you first."

"Okay."

"When I gave my presentation to the spinal institute, I mentioned that the device had been tested on a human subject, but I'm pretty sure I didn't mention who that subject was."

"You're right, you didn't say who. In fact, I was the only one who figured it out. You'll recall our having a conversation about that at your farm."

"I do remember that. So, here's where I'm going with this...the person who cut me knew I was the human test subject, but *didn't* know that the device had been removed from me just a week or so before I was abducted. The fact that they didn't know it was removed tells me it was not someone from our team...and not someone associated with a team member."

"That's a good thing," Chuck said.

"Yes it is, but it still doesn't explain who it might be. Chuck, I need you to think back to the meeting you had with the spinal institute when you withdrew funding. Did you tell them I was the test subject?"

Chuck suddenly paled. "Oh, my God, Jordan. This is my fault. Yes, I told them. Jordan, I am so sorry. I never thought...."

Jordan reached across her desk and took Chuck's hand in

her own. "Chuck, it's not your fault. Don't believe that for a minute."

Chuck was visibly shaken. "Hollinbeck?" he asked.

"I think so."

"I remember him being really pissed when I withdrew funding. He told me I wouldn't get away with it. I knew he was an arrogant, pompous ass, but I would never have thought he'd do something as stupid as abduction, never mind knocking you out and operating on your without your consent."

"You might want to add medical espionage to that list as well. If the implant had not already been removed, he would have taken it, and God knows what kind of damage he may have done to me…or to the implant in the process."

"You realize we have no real proof it was him," Chuck pointed out.

"You're right, we don't, but I have strong enough suspicions to warrant keeping an eye on him."

* * *

Jordan pulled up in front of the farm house and turned off the ignition. She smiled when she saw Gina's truck parked there as well. She got out of her car and walked toward the front porch, only to be met by Sam, who opened her arms wide and hugged Jordan close.

"Congratulations," she said in Jordan's ear. "I'm so happy for you both."

Jordan grinned. "She told you, didn't she?"

Sam linked arms with Jordan. "You know Maggie. She can't keep a secret to save her soul. So, when are you due?"

"Whoa, slow down. We don't even know yet if the insemination took. We won't know for several weeks. To answer your question, its July now, so *if* it worked, it would be due sometime in April of next year."

"April is a good month. Maggie was born in April. So why did you decide to carry it instead of Maggie?"

"I'm two years older than Maggie, so we figured it was now or never for me. Maggie will carry the next one."

"The next one? This one isn't even born yet and you've

already planned the next one?"

"We talked about have two kids. More, if Maggie has her way, but my vote is for two. So what brings you and Gina here on a Monday night?" Jordan asked, changing the subject.

"Actually it's just me. Gina was called out for an emergency on the Bailey farm. My car was blocking her truck, so she took it instead. She called a while ago to say she'd be late, so I kind of invited myself over. It beats the hell out of hanging around the house alone."

Jordan reached for the screen door and held it open for Sam. "Well, I'm glad you're here. You're staying for dinner, I hope?"

"Yes, in fact, I put stuffed shells into the oven about a half hour ago."

"Hey love," Maggie said as she came into the living from the kitchen. She stepped into Jordan's arms and kissed her tenderly. "How are you feeling?"

"I felt the baby kick today," she said.

Maggie crossed her arms and frowned. "Really?" she said sarcastically.

"Truth is, Mags, I don't feel any different than I did a week...or a month ago. Ask me that question again in a few weeks, okay?"

"I'm sorry. I guess I'm just excited about the prospect."

"Well, I am too, but it will take a while before we know anything. Trust me, you'll be the first to know when—or if—something happens. Sweetie, we aren't even sure if this attempt will work. I don't want you to get your hopes up and then be disappointed. If it's meant to be, it will happen. If not, then we have other options. Okay?"

Maggie just nodded.

"Dinner smells great," Jordan says.

"Stuffed shells. You have Sam to thank for that. How about you come help me make salads to go with dinner?"

"Lead the way, boss," Jordan said as she, Maggie and Sam retreated to the kitchen.

CHAPTER 37

Jordan's phone rang as she sat at her desk, reviewing the schematics of the device containment unit with Tom.

"Hello?"

"Dr. Lewis, this is Security in the lobby. There is a Ms. Downs here to see you."

"Yes. May I talk to her, please?"

"Hi, Jordan. I know I'm early, so if you're not ready to go, I'll just sit for a while and read."

"That's fine, Mags. There's a coffeemaker set up out there. Help yourself to it and relax. I'll be there within an hour."

"Okay. I'll see you soon."

Jordan hung up the phone and looked at Tom. "My wife. We have a dinner date tonight and she's just a tad early."

"We can do this tomorrow, if you'd like," Tom said.

"No, that's all right. She has a book with her. She'll be fine. So, tell me, Tom how we're going to contain the size of this unit? I really don't want it to be substantially larger than this one," Jordan said as she picked the original unit up from her desk. "This is actually the second implant. The first one I had required an external battery pack that I had to wear in a pouch around my waist. Although it provided me the mobility I needed, I had to plug into the wall every night to charge it. It was quite cumbersome, and sleeping was not a lot of fun. This particular unit was redesigned small enough to include the battery pack in the same package as the device. Do you think that will be achievable?"

Tom took the device from Jordan and turned it around in his hands. "I'm not sure we can make it this small because I suspect the module we get from WWM will be larger than the original. In fact, I suspect the module will be about the size of this whole device, but we might be able to design a separate battery pack that would plug into the device, yet still be small enough to implant under the skin."

"That would work."

"Let me think about this over the weekend, then I'll get back to you early next week with a design. I think it's nearly time to pull Jason and Wendell into the project. I can design the battery pack, but I'll need their help in determining how to get it to react with human tissue."

Tom looked at his watch. "August twenty-third. Time is really flying. Five months is not a lot of time to prepare for the arrival of the new modules. I've got my work cut out for me."

"The whole team does, but I have confidence in all of us."

Tom stood up and turned to leave.

"Tom, don't spend too much time on this over the weekend. Enjoy your family, okay?"

Tom grinned and nodded, then left her office.

Jordan picked the device up from her desk and looked at the cut wires protruding from both ends. *With any luck, Jessie will be walking a year from now.* She mentally reviewed the timeline. *If several copies of the new module arrive in January, it will take a month or so to perfect a program that will send the continuous wave pulses at exactly the right frequency to both sides of an injury. That brings us to late February before the clinical testing can begin with the lab animals. We're looking at maybe two or three months of testing with several animals. That will put us in the June time frame of next year. We'll probably want to wait until Jessie is out of school for the summer before implanting. If all goes well with physical therapy, she'll be walking to her classrooms in September just like any other high school freshman, instead of wheeling herself.*

Moisture filled Jordan's eyes as she remembered her first steps after fourteen years in her hover chair. It was an amazingly freeing feeling. She could only imagine how Jessie will feel, being given the gift of mobility just as she was beginning such a tenuous stage in her life.

Jordan closed her fist around the device, then wiped the

tears from the corners of her eyes.

"Gotta put this baby under lock and key," she said aloud, the proceeded to the vault before heading to the lobby to meet Maggie for dinner.

Jordan exited through the secured door into the lobby and saw Maggie sitting with Chuck on one of the couches.

"Hey love," she said as she approached.

Maggie rose to her feet and hugged Jordan. "Chuck was just telling me that the two of you need to go with Tom to a materials conference next month."

Jordan looked at Chuck. "That's true. We just learned about the conference today. I was going to tell you about it at dinner tonight."

"Sorry. I guess I let the cat out of the bag," Chuck said.

"No worries," Jordan said. She looked at Maggie. "It's in Monterey, California. Were you interested in going with us?"

"Actually, I just volunteered to watch Jessie while you're gone."

"If you really want to go, Maggie, Jessie can stay with her nanny," Chuck said.

"No, that's all right. I can go another time. I'm kind of looking forward to spending time with her."

"Okay then," Jordan said. "Are you ready for dinner?"

Maggie looked awkwardly at Chuck. He backed up a step. "Don't worry about me. I'm just here to pick up some paperwork for the financial guys. Jessie and I actually have plans of our own for dinner and a movie. You two enjoy yourselves."

* * *

Jordan and Maggie slipped into the high-backed booth at the local Irish Pub and perused the menu.

"Wow, everything looks so good, I don't know what to choose," Maggie said.

A waiter stopped by their table and placed a couple of cardboard coasters in front of them. "My name is Cody and I'll be your waiter tonight. Can I get you ladies something to drink?"

"I'll have a club soda with lemon," Jordan said.

"That sounds, good. I'll have the same," Maggie added.

"Got it. I'll be right back," Cody said.

"So how's the work coming along on the new device?" Maggie asked.

"It's slow right now. There's not much we can actually do until the modules are ready."

"When will that be?"

Just then, the waiter came back with their drinks. "Okay. Have you decided what you're hungry for?" he asked as he poised his pen over his order pad.

Jordan picked up the menu again. "I'll have a Reuben on rye with French fries," she said.

"And for you, Ma'am?" Cody asked Maggie.

"I'll do the corned beef and cabbage. Thank you, Cody," Maggie said as she handed the menus to him.

"All right. I'll put your orders right in."

Jordan took a sip of her cub soda. "Where was I?" she asked.

"You were going to tell me when the modules might be ready," Maggie replied.

"Oh yes. We expect several copies in January. That's when the fun part begins and when we get to see if all our hard work pays off. Until then, we need to work on the software and the packaging, and of course the power source."

"The science behind this blows me away, Jordan. I never would have thought when you came into my life so many months ago that you were such a genius."

"I just seem smarter to you because I come from a time when these things are already known. In this day and age, scientists are barely scratching the surface of what is already part of medical history where I come from. I am really hoping that our work will expedite cures for spinal paralysis in the future."

"How long before you can implant the first one in Jessie?" Maggie asked.

"I'm hoping we'll be ready by next summer."

"Will she be able to walk right away?"

"Yes, if we've done our jobs right. We won't implant it in her until we're pretty sure it works consistently and reliably in several non-human test subjects."

"How long before the feelings return?"

"That, I don't know. For me, the feelings began to return the third time I traveled here, but according to Andi, the travel itself has something to do with speeding that process up. For a normal implant recipient...I don't know. It could take years. When the original implant was inserted in me, Peter said the feelings would come back gradually."

"Peter?"

"Peter Michaels. He was my doctor and the head of the research team that developed it."

"So you're hoping to implant it in Jessie next summer, then?"

"I hope so. She starts high school a year from now, so I'm hoping she can go on her own two feet."

Maggie smiled broadly. "I'm so excited for her, Jordan. She's a lucky girl to have a father who's in the position to fund your research and development."

"Yes. We're both lucky. Chuck has been able to resolve a lot of issues for me as well."

"I'm looking forward to Jessie spending some time with me at the farm while you and Chuck are gone to your convention. When exactly is that, anyway?"

"BACUS is usually scheduled for late September in Monterey, California...in fact, I think it begins the week of September 30th this year."

"BACUS?"

"Yes, it's stands for Bay Area Chrome Users Society. It's an annual conference for photomask technology development, but there are usually several sessions that focus on materials development as well. Those are the meetings we will be most interested in. We need to understand what materials are out there for semi-conductor development that might be useful to use in the packaging of the module and power pack. There will also be several sessions that deal with the new extreme ultraviolet technology that will be used to build the chips. That isn't vital for us to know, but it should be interesting."

"It's all Greek to me," Maggie said. "So, the week of September 30th is a whole month away. I'll check when I get home, but I think the horse auction is on Friday of that week. Jessie should enjoy going to that with me."

"You do realize she will have to go to school. I believe Chuck will arrange for the bus to pick her up and drop her off at the farm every day."

"That shouldn't be a problem, but she'll need to miss just one day of school if I'm going to take her to the auction."

"Ah, here comes our dinner," Jordan said as Cody approached the table carrying two plates heaped with food.

"Enjoy your dinner ladies, and don't hesitate to flag me down if you need anything," Cody said.

Jordan and Maggie spent the rest of their time at the restaurant enjoying their dinners and discussing the changes at the farm that would be necessary to open the riding school for handicapped children. When they were finished, they paid their waiter and left hand in hand.

A man sitting in the booth directly behind the one Jordan and Maggie used, flagged the waiter down. "Check, please, Cody," he said.

"Here you go, Dr. Hollinbeck," Cody said as he placed the check on the table. "Will we see you tomorrow?" Cody asked.

"As always, of course," Hollinbeck said as he left cash on the table and exited the restaurant.

CHAPTER 38

Jordan woke up the next morning with a roaring headache. "Oh, my God," she moaned as she swung her feet over the edge of the bed and sat up. She propped her elbows on her knees and lowered her head into her hands.

Maggie poked her head into the room. "Do you have time for breakfast?" she asked before Jordan's demeanor set off alarm bells in her head. She knelt on the floor in front of her.

"Hey, are you all right?" she asked as she tilted Jordan's head up by placing her fingers under her chin.

Jordan's eyes were small slits. "Headache," she said.

Maggie got to her feet. "Let me get you something for that," she said.

"No, I've got to go to the bathroom anyway. I'll take care of it," Jordan said.

"Are you sure?"

"Yeah." Jordan pushed herself into a standing position and immediately sat back on the bed. "Damn. All of the sudden I'm dizzy and feel like I going to hurl. I wonder if that Reuben I had last night was bad."

She covered her mouth and stood again, this time forcing herself to make haste toward the bathroom where she fell to her knees and emptied the contents of her stomach into the toilet.

Maggie followed and stopped in the doorway. "Maybe you shouldn't go to work today," she suggested.

Jordan sat back on her heels and closed her eyes. "I have to go. There's so much to do that it takes every bit of resource we have to stay on schedule. I'll be all right. Just give me a minute."

Maggie's eyes suddenly grew wide. "Jordan, what if…what if you're pregnant?" Maggie said.

Jordan's gaze sought out Maggie's face, her eyebrows high on her forehead. "You may have a point there."

Maggie covered her mouth with both hands while her eyes misted over. "Maybe we should call the doctor."

"Why don't we give it a couple more days and if I continue to be sick in the morning, I'll take one of those home pregnancy tests. I mean, if I continue to be sick every day, that's a pretty good sign, but if this is a one-time thing and I'm fine after today, then maybe last night's dinner just didn't agree with me."

"Okay. We'll do it your way, but if we get a positive result on the test, you're going to the gynecologist right away. Agreed?"

"Agreed. Now I need to brush my teeth and get rid of the vile taste in my mouth before I shower."

"I'll have a coffee and breakfast waiting for you when you come out," Maggie said.

"Thank you love. I'd kiss you, but you'd be here puking beside me if you come within six feet of my mouth right now."

On Friday morning, Jordan paced back and forth across their bedroom while Maggie held a white stick in front of her. "How much longer?" Jordan asked.

Maggie glanced at her watch. "Two minutes."

"Longest damned two minutes of my life," Jordan mumbled as she continued to pace.

"How are you feeling?" Maggie asked.

"Fine now that I've puked my guts up for the third morning in a row."

"One more minute," Maggie said.

Jordan stopped in front of Maggie and stood by her side, both of them stared at the indicator on the stick as an image began to form.

"It's green," Maggie whispered, almost as if the image could be chased away by the sound of her voice.

"Well, I'll be," Jordan said as a complete, green plus sign appeared on the indicator. She looked at Maggie with tears in her eyes.

"We did it," Maggie said. "We're going to have a baby!"

"It appears we are."

* * *

Chuck met Jordan at her office when she arrived at the lab that morning. "Running late?" he asked.

"Just a tad. Is the team assembled in the conference room?" Jordan said.

"Yes. The last straggler just wandered in so you're not too late."

"That's good." Jordan entered the conference room and took her seat at the front of the table. "Okay, sorry I'm late. Who would like to start?"

For the next hour, the team reported on the status of projects they were working on, either alone or in collaboration with other team members. By the end of the meeting, they had clear directions from both Jordan and the team on how to move forward.

Chuck followed Jordan back to her office. "You look a little tired today, Jordan. Do you feel okay?"

Jordan smiled. "Actually, I feel a lot better after puking my guts up this morning, and every morning for the past three days. It appears your boys are good swimmers, Chuck."

Chuck frowned for a moment before he suddenly realized what she meant. "You're pregnant? The insemination worked?" he asked.

"Yes on both counts," Jordan replied before finding herself enveloped in Chuck's embrace.

"Congratulations, Jordan. I'll bet Maggie is beside herself."

"That, she is. She tried to make me stay home today. She's got it in her head that I need to pamper myself for the next eight months."

"Maybe she's right."

"Like hell she is. I grew up on a farm, remember? We were friends with several other farm families and I distinctly remember the wives working in the fields until the babies were nearly ready to pop. I have no intention of becoming a helpless preggo. We've got too much work to do for me to be lying in bed all day eating bonbons, not to mention I'd balloon to the size of a whale."

"You'd make a cute whale."

Jordan pointed to the door. "Out! I have work to do. Get out of here before I kick your ass, Uncle Chuck." Jordan grinned.

"Uncle Chuck. I like the sound of that."

"Out!" Jordan yelled again.

"I'm going, I'm going." Chuck smiled ear to ear as he beat a hasty retreat.

* * *

Maggie, Jordan, Gina and Sam all sat around the dining room table laden with salad, lasagna and garlic bread.

"Before we eat, I'd like to make a toast," Maggie said. She reached for a bottle of champagne on ice in the middle of the table and poured some for herself, Gina and Sam.

"This is totally unfair," Jordan said.

"Suck it up love. You know you can't drink alcohol for the next several months." Maggie handed her a champagne flute filled with sparking grape juice, then held her own glass up high. "To motherhood," she said.

"To motherhood," all responded as they clinked glasses and sipped their drinks.

"To aunt-hood," Gina said, followed again by the clink of glasses.

"To the end of morning sickness," Jordan called out, causing everyone to laugh.

Maggie held her glass aloft once more. "To my beautiful, wife for agreeing to go first."

Jordan raised her glass. "To *my* beautiful wife who had better not back out when it's her turn."

"To family," Sam said. "To family we choose. To family we're born into. To Maggie and Jordan who are my sisters at heart. Finally, to the little rug rat I can't wait to spoil, then send home afterwards, full of sugar. We love you guys, and we are so very happy for you both."

Gina put her arm around Sam's shoulder as she finished her toast, her voice heavy with emotion. "You okay?" she asked.

Sam nodded. "I'm fine. I guess I didn't realize how awesome it would be to have a child. I guess I'm envious."

"You know…we *could* fix that," Gina said.

"Seriously? Do you really want to?" Sam asked.

"I'm willing to bet my brother, Todd would donate…that is, if you agreed to carry it. It would be a little odd and a lot icky if I was the one to have it. Just think, the little rug rat would have biological ties to both of us."

Sam's eyes filled with tears as she hugged Gina tight. "I love you, sweetie," she said.

"Don't you know by now there is nothing I wouldn't do for you, Sam?"

Sam kissed Gina tenderly then looked at Maggie and Jordan. "It looks like your little one may have cousins after all."

"Cousins…as in plural?" Gina said.

CHAPTER 39

"Jordan, are you going to be okay on the airplane?" Maggie asked as she helped Jordan pack her suitcase.

"Why wouldn't I be?" Jordan replied.

"Well, I would hate for you to get sick."

"I love to fly. I used to go to conferences all the time when I worked with Kale and Peter."

"Yeah, but you've never flown pregnant, have you?"

Jordan took Maggie into her arms. "Sweetie, I'll be fine. You don't need to worry about me traveling. I'm two months along. The morning sickness almost never bothers me anymore. All I need to do is watch what I eat, lay off the caffeinated coffee and stay away from the booze, oh, and take my pre-natal vitamin every day. See? How hard can it be?"

"I want you to let Chuck manhandle the luggage, okay? You shouldn't be doing any heavy lifting."

"Believe it or not, Chuck is a bigger mother hen than you are. He waits on me hand and foot when he's at the lab."

"He's a good friend, Jordan."

"Yes he is, and he'll make a great uncle. It will be good to have a positive male role model in this baby's life, not that I think two women can't raise well-balanced kids, but if it really takes a village to raise a child, I would like that village to be filled with people like Chuck, Gina and Sam."

"Isn't it great that Sam and Gina have decided to get pregnant?" Maggie asked.

"I'm thrilled about that, Mags. Sam is right—with both of us being only children, Gina and Sam's kids will be the closest things they'll know to cousins."

Maggie put the last piece of clothing in the suitcase and zipped it closed. "Done. I'm going to stand it up over here by the dresser so you can grab it on your way out in the morning."

Jordan wrapped her arms around Maggie and kissed her on the head. "Thanks for the help, love. We should probably hit the sheets if I want to get a good night's sleep to travel on tomorrow."

Maggie removed her clothing and crawled in between the sheets and waited for Jordan to join her. Jordan lay on her back and opened her arms for Maggie, who curled up into her side and placed her head on Jordan's shoulder.

"Chuck will drop Jessie off here when he picks me up in the morning. We'll travel tomorrow and attend the conference from Tuesday through Thursday. We already have meetings set up with some of the vendors on Friday, so we'll travel back home on Saturday. We should be home sometime around seven," Jordan explained.

"I'm looking forward to spending the week with Jessie. While she's at school, I'll be working with the saddler on the new saddle design. I'm hoping he'll have the prototype ready for Jessie to try out before Friday," Maggie said.

"You're going to the Champlain Valley auction on Friday, right?"

"Yes. I'm hoping they have a good stock this year."

"Well, you certainly have a good eye for horses. I'm sure you'll do fine."

Jordan yawned.

Maggie lifted her head and kissed Jordan on the cheek. "Time to sleep, sweetie. I love you."

"I love you too, Mags. Good night, my love."

"Sweet dreams." Maggie placed her hand directly on Jordan's abdomen. "Good night my little one," she said before closing her eyes and allowing sleep to claim her.

* * *

Maggie and Jessie waved the next morning as Chuck drove his SUV down the driveway.

"So, what would you like to do today?" Maggie asked.

Jessie looked up at Maggie from her wheelchair. "I'm hoping to do some riding while I'm here, and I don't mind earning my keep by brushing and feeding the foals in the north pasture."

Maggie pushed Jessie's wheelchair across the yard and up the ramp to the porch. "We'll have plenty of time to do that in the afternoons when you get home from school. How about some breakfast, then we'll take a ride out to the north pasture?"

Maggie put a plate full of scrambled eggs, sausage and toast in front of Jessie then sat at the table opposite her.

"Thanks for letting me stay with you, Maggie," Jessie said. "My nanny is really nice, but she's kinda old and not a lot of fun."

Maggie chuckled. "Well, it won't be all fun and games here either. We need to keep the farm operational on a daily basis. There's always a list of chores to do."

"I can help with the chores. There's a lot I can do, even stuck in this chair."

"Actually, I was going to ask you to help me with something while you're here."

"What's that?"

"Well, as you know, I am planning to open a riding school for handicapped children. The generous wedding gift you and your dad gave us will be used for that project."

"So what do you need me to do?"

"I've been working with my saddler on a saddle designed to make riding safe for someone who is handicapped. I was hoping you would help me test it this week."

"Can I?" Jessie asked excitedly. "If it works, does that mean I can ride by myself?"

"That's the goal."

"Cool. When do we get started?"

"As a matter of fact, I've already started." Maggie rose to her feet. "I'll show you the diagrams I've been working on. I'll be right back."

Maggie returned moments later and rolled out the blueprints on the table in front of Jessie. "Okay, so as you can see, the saddle has a high back with arm rests and leg rests in case the handicap requires restraints to hold the rider in the saddle. Many of the features are modular so they can be removed, or not, depending the degree of help the rider needs."

"That's a good idea. I can sit up on my own, but not everyone with a handicap can."

"Exactly. The saddle needs to be versatile enough to adapt to several levels of disability."

"For the record, Maggie, I see my limitations more as an inconvenience rather than a handicap."

Maggie smiled. "I like your attitude, Jess. So, the saddler will be here this afternoon around two o'clock."

"The bus should be dropping me off around three. I hope he'll still be here."

"He will. I've specifically asked him to arrange his visit around your school schedule." Maggie glanced at the clock. "Oops, we need to get going or you'll miss the bus."

* * *

Maggie stood at the end of the driveway at three and waited for the bus driver to unload Jessie via the hydraulic wheelchair lift.

"Is the saddler still here?" Jessie asked as the wheeled her way toward Maggie.

"He sure is. In fact, he brought the prototype saddle with him and wants you to try it out."

"Really?"

"Really."

Jessie buckled herself into the front seat as Maggie loaded her chair into the back of the truck. Five minutes later, they pulled up to the front porch. Jessie was unbuckled and had the door open waiting for Maggie to bring her chair to the side of the truck.

"You're not excited, are you?" Maggie joked.

"I can't help it. I'm looking forward to riding by myself," Jessie replied.

Maggie helped Jessie into her chair and pushed her to the barn where the saddler was waiting for them. "Mike, this is Jessie. Jessie, this is our saddler, Mike Anderson."

Jessie extended her hand. "Hi, Mike."

"Are you ready to try out the new saddle, Jessie?" Mike asked.

"You bet I am."

"Okay. Wait right here."

Mike entered a nearby stall and led a medium sized horse toward Jessie. On the mare's back was the prototype saddle.

"All right, up you go," Mike said as he scooped Jessie out of her wheelchair and gently placed her in the saddle.

"Hold on to the saddle horn while we strap your legs in, Jess," Maggie said. She wrapped two Velcro straps around each leg, one just above the knee and the other above the ankle. "Okay. Your legs are secure. Now, how does it feel?"

"Pretty good."

"Let's fold these arm rests out of the way. I don't think you'll need them as long as your abdominal muscles are strong enough to keep you from tipping side to side. How is your balance?"

"I feel pretty safe. I don't feel like I'm going to fall off or anything."

Maggie looked at Mike. "I'm glad you made the backrest modular. I'm thinking we can take the top tier off. We can always put it back on if she's having problems sitting erect."

"I agree," Mike said.

He addressed Jessie directly, "Jess, I'm going to reduce the height of your backrest because you seem to have really good control over your balance. If at any time, you feel unsafe, or feel like you are going to fall off, let me know immediately and we can add supports back in. We can even strap you to the backrest if you feel you need it."

"I'm okay for now. Maybe we can take a short ride around the paddock to test it out," Jessie suggested.

"That sounds like a good idea," Maggie said. "Mike and I will walk on both sides of you just in case."

After three turns around the paddock, they returned to the barn. "How does it feel, Jessie?" Maggie asked.

"It feels great."

"Mike, what do you say we saddle Shawny and Sally and

the three of us take a ride out to the north pasture? Do you have time to do that?" Maggie asked.

"Sure do. I'd like to be there the first time it's used on a real ride anyway." Mike looked at Jessie. "Give us a minute and we'll be right with you."

Twenty minutes later, all three riders were on their way across the field to the north pasture. Maggie rode along side Jessie.

"Jess, normally, you would use your legs and feet to control the animal. Since you don't have that ability, you'll have to learn to control it primarily with your hands and voice. What I'd like you to do is to place both hands just above the horse's shoulders and press inward while giving the voice command 'giddy up'. That would be similar to squeezing the horse between your knees. Remember, you'll need to hold onto the reins while you do that in the event the horse lunges forward. Okay, give it a try."

Jessie followed Maggie's commands and soon, the horse was moving in a slow canter.

Maggie kept pace with Jessie as they rode to the north pasture and back, while practicing the 'giddy up' and 'whoa' commands. It was nearly dusk by the time they returned to the barn.

Jessie's cheeks were flushed and her hair was in wild array as Mike helped her back into her chair.

"That was amazing," Jessie said. "Can we do it again tomorrow?"

"We'll see. While you're at school tomorrow, I'll need to think about a way to get you on and off the horse. I think that will be a bigger challenge than designing a safe saddle."

"Maggie, I took several mental notes while we were out relative to improving the saddle," Mike said. "Nothing major, mind you, but it needs a few tweaks. I'll take it with me when I leave. It might be Wednesday before I can get it back to you."

"All right, Mike. It will give me some time to think about the loading station." Maggie shook his hand. "I think we are very close to having a saddle that will pass the tough safety standards the state is imposing on us."

"Better safe than sorry," Mike said. He hugged Jessie. "Maybe we can try out the improvements on Wednesday," he suggested.

"That will be awesome," Jess said. "I can't wait. Thanks, Mike."

Maggie turned to Jess after Mike left. "Let's head to the house and wash off this trail dirt, then get started on homework and dinner. Sound like a plan?"

* * *

Maggie stood in the doorway to the guest room and watched Jessie maneuver herself out of her wheelchair and into bed. "You're pretty good at that," she said.

Jessie sat on the side of the bed. "After three years, you kinda get used to it." A sad expression appeared on her face.

Maggie walked into the room and sat beside Jessie with her arm around the girl's shoulder. "Why the sad face?" she asked.

"It gets really old sitting in this chair every day. Heck, I don't even have control over going to the bathroom. Sometimes it's overwhelming to think I'll be stuck like this for the rest of my life."

"I wouldn't say that, sweetie. The medical community might come up with something to get you out of that chair."

"When? When I'm ninety years old?"

Maggie kissed her on the head. "I understand your frustration, but don't lose hope. I mean, just yesterday, you couldn't ride a horse by yourself, and today you can. See what I mean?"

"I guess."

Maggie stood. "Now let's get you tucked in then you can call your dad to say goodnight." She lifted Jessie's legs while she reclined her torso and soon, they had her comfortably lying in the bed with the covers pulled up to her chest. Maggie kissed her on the forehead. "Good night, Jess."

Jessie wrapped her arms around Maggie's neck and hugged her. "Thanks, Maggie."

* * *

"Hey, love, how was the first day of your conference?" Maggie asked into the phone.

"It was great. We've already picked up a few tips to improve the device," Jordan replied. "How's Jessie?"

"We had a very successful test of the new saddle today. Mike was here when Jessie got home from school and we took a two-hour ride into the north pasture. She was able to ride totally unassisted. You should have seen her face, Jordan. The excitement radiated from her," Maggie said in a voice laden with emotion.

"Are you all right, Mags?"

"Yeah. It's just that she's a young girl living a life of privilege and what made her the most happy was gaining a little independence. When she was on that horse, she was free and totally mobile. I am so looking forward to seeing that expression and that level of emotion in other handicapped children."

"You, my dear, have a very tender heart. Please don't ever change. I love you just the way you are."

"Thank you, sweetie. Oh, before I say something I shouldn't, it became obvious to me in a conversation I had with Jess that Chuck hasn't told her about the implant. She was pretty sad tonight about being stuck in a wheelchair for the rest of her life."

"You're right. Chuck has decided not to get her hopes up before it's been proven to work in the lab animals."

"Well, I told her not to lose hope. She's a very special girl, Jordan. She's so good with the horses. I'm looking forward to taking her to the auction on Friday."

"She should enjoy that. I remember the first auction you took me to. You fired me that day, if I remember correctly," Jordan chuckled.

"That's what you get for calling me a high-maintenance diva."

"Your words, not mine, my love. Look, I've got to run. We're having dinner tonight with one of the suppliers."

Maggie glanced at the clock on her bedside table. The time was nine-fifteen. "That's right. I forgot about the three-hour time difference between Vermont and California. Let me say goodnight then before you head to dinner. I love you, Jordan. I hope you have sweet dreams."

"Love you too, Mags. Sleep well."

CHAPTER 40

"Buckle up," Maggie said as she started the truck. "Are you excited about the auction?"

Jessie nodded vigorously. "You bet I am. How many horses are you going to buy?" Jessie asked.

"It depends on how good the stock is. I'm specifically looking for mustangs, but I'll pick up any horse that has the temperament to deal with young children."

"Do you mind if I turn on the radio?" Jessie asked.

"Go for it."

Soon, both of them were seat-dancing and singing out loud to the catchy beats coming from the radio. At one point, Maggie glanced at Jessie across the front seat and smiled.

I think I'm going to like this parenting thing, she thought to herself.

* * *

Maggie raised her number card high above the crowd to place a bid on the current sale then crossed her fingers as the auctioneer accepted her offer. After a short pause, he said, "Going once, going twice, sold to the pretty redhead."

"Yes," Maggie said as she won the bid on the prized mustang. "Okay, that makes four horses. I think that's enough for one day."

"How will you get them home?" Jessie asked. "They can't ride in the back of the truck, can they?"

Maggie laughed. "No sweetie, they can't. I'll send John after them tomorrow with the horse trailer." She squatted down in front of Jessie. "That last mare I bought is for you," she said.

Jessie's eyes grew wide. "Really? Is it really mine?"

"Absolutely. You'll have to come over on a regular basis to brush and feed her, and you can ride her any time, using the new saddle. You will be responsible for naming her and training her. Do you think you can do that?"

"Yes. Yes, I can." Jessie hugged Maggie fiercely. "Thank you, Maggie. Thank you so much."

"You're welcome, dumpling. Now how about we get some lunch then head back and see how John is coming on the loading station he was building for you."

"Okay."

"All right then. I just need to go pay for the horses and we can be on our way. Will you be okay right here for a new minutes? I'll be just a few yards away."

"Yes."

Maggie kissed Jessie on top of the head. "I'll be right back."

Maggie walked to the cashier's table and settled her purchases then returned to spot she had left Jessie. "Jessie? Jessie, where are you?" Maggie said as panic began to set in deep within her gut. "Jessie!"

"Jordan, my God, Jordan, she's gone!"

"Maggie, calm down. What do you mean, she's gone?"

"I…I went to pay for the horses and when I turned around, she was gone. I only left her alone for five minutes. Oh, my God, Jordan, what am I going to do?"

"Did you call the police?"

"Yes, they're here right now."

"Good. Chuck and I will catch the first plane back, no, wait, he just said he'll charter a plane. We'll be home as soon as possible."

"Maggie, this is Chuck. Did anyone see where she might have gone?"

"Chuck, I'm so sorry. You trusted me with her. I'm so sorry."

"Maggie, this isn't your fault. Did anyone see where she might have gone?"

"The police are questioning bystanders now."

"Is there a policeman nearby that I can talk to?"

"Yes. Hold on a minute." Maggie pulled a police officer aside. "Officer, I have Jessie's father on the phone. He'd like to speak with you." She handed the phone to the policeman.

"Sir, this is Detective Williams," the officer said.

"Detective Williams, my name is Charles Malone and the missing girl is my daughter. Can you—"

"Charles Malone? *The* Charles Malone, as in Malone Industries?" the officer asked.

"Yes, exactly."

"Well, that changes things a bit."

"How so?" Chuck asked.

"This may not be a random kidnapping, Mr. Malone. Considering your wealth, she may have been targeted," the police officer explained. "That also means she may still be alive."

"Please explain yourself, Detective Williams," Chuck said.

"You're a wealthy man, Mr. Malone. If the kidnapper is after ransom, it would be in his best interest to keep her safe… at least until the ransom is paid, which I encourage you not to do without involving the police."

"Miss Downs indicated you were interviewing bystanders. Do you have any witnesses?"

"Actually, we do. We have three witnesses who recall seeing a man pushing a young girl in a wheelchair toward the parking lot. The girl appeared to be unconscious."

"Did any of the witnesses do anything about it? I mean, an unconscious girl in a wheelchair should set off some alarm bells, shouldn't it?"

"Mr. Malone, the bystanders had no way of knowing if that was normal for the girl."

"Did they get a description of the man who took her?"

"Yes sir." Detective Williams opened his notebook and read the eyewitness descriptions to Chuck. "Approximately five foot, ten inches, brown hair, average build, wearing blue jeans and a green polo shirt."

"That description could fit countless men," Chuck said.

"Exactly, Mr. Malone. Mr. Malone, may I ask where you

are right now?"

"I'm in California on a business trip, and soon to board a charter jet to get home."

"I recommend you keep your phone line available in the event the kidnapper calls you, and please, do not negotiate with him without involving the police. We will do everything we can to get your daughter back, but you need to cooperate with us. Do you understand?"

"What I understand, Detective Williams, is that I will do whatever is within my power to bring Jessie home safely—at any cost."

* * *

Chuck shut off the phone and handed it back to Jordan. "The police think she's been kidnapped," he said.

"Kidnapped? Why?" Jordan asked.

"Ransom."

"Chuck, if Jessie was targeted, that would mean someone had to know Maggie was taking her to the auction today. Are you sure it wasn't just a random kidnapping?"

Chuck ran a hand through his hair. "We'd better hope to hell it wasn't some murdering rapist who grabbed Jessie randomly. If Jessie was grabbed because of who I am and what I could possibly pay for her safe return, then they'd be more apt not to abuse or kill her."

Chuck looked at his watch. "The charter jet should be ready to go in about a half hour. We need to get to the airport."

* * *

Maggie ran down the porch steps directly into Jordan's arms as she climbed out of Chuck's truck. She was crying hysterically.

"Maggie. Maggie, sweetheart, please calm down," Jordan whispered as she held her close.

"It's all my fault," Maggie said. "I shouldn't have left her alone."

Chuck came up behind Maggie and took her out of Jordan's arms. He turned her around to face him and held her by the shoulders. "Maggie. This was not your fault. If someone wanted to snatch her, they could have done it anywhere. Hell, they could have taken her from the playground at school. We're here to pick you up before going to the police station. Please don't cry. We'll find her. I promise."

"I'm so sorry, Chuck," Maggie said.

"I know. I am, too. Come on, we should go." Just as Chuck reached for the door handle, his cell phone rang. He pulled it out of the holster on his belt and looked at the incoming number. "Who the hell can this be?" he said as he pressed the answer button. "Hello," he said.

"Is this Charles Malone?" a voice said.

"Yes. Who is calling?" Chuck replied.

"I have your daughter."

"You son of a bitch! Where is she?" Chuck demanded, intense anger evident in his voice.

Jordan leaned in close so she could hear the conversation. Chuck pulled the phone away from his ear and pressed the speaker button.

"Never mind where she is."

"Why did you take her?" Chuck asked.

"You have something I want. If you play nice and give it to me, I'll consider giving your daughter back to you."

"If you hurt one hair on her head, I'll—"

"Don't threaten me, Malone. You are in no position to make threats."

"Is Jessie all right?"

"She's fine… for now, that is."

"I want to talk to her."

"Very well."

After a short pause, Jessie's voice came across the speaker. "Daddy?"

"Jessie. Jessie, honey are you all right?" Chuck asked.

"I'm scared."

"I'm sure you are, sweetie. Daddy will do all he can to get you back. Jordan and Maggie will too."

"Is Maggie okay?"

Maggie stepped forward to assure Jessie she was all right, but Jordan stopped her and signaled for her to be quiet.

"Maggie is fine, sweetie," Chuck said. "Try not to be afraid, Jess. We'll do everything we can to get you back as soon as possible."

"That's enough," the man's voice cut in.

"Who are you?" Chuck demanded.

"Never mind who I am. Now if you want to see your daughter again, you'll do as I say."

"What do you want?"

"I want the device."

Chuck looked at Jordan. "What device?" he asked.

"You know damned well what I'm talking about Malone. If you fail to deliver it, your daughter dies."

"Deliver it where?"

"You'll know that soon enough. Oh, and I want it delivered by Lewis."

Jordan frowned.

"Why Lewis?" Chuck asked.

"No more questions. I will contact you tomorrow with a location."

"You'll get nothing if Jessie isn't part of the drop-off."

"I make the rules, Malone, not you. I will contact you tomorrow." The line fell silent.

Chuck immediately checked his incoming calls and saw that the number was blocked. "Fuck!" he cursed.

"Did you recognize his voice?" Jordan asked.

"No. It was probably disguised anyway."

"Maybe we should call the police," Maggie suggested.

"No. Not yet," Chuck said. "I don't want to take any chances that he'll harm Jessie. It's bad enough she'll be spending the night with that monster. I hope to God he doesn't do something stupid." Tears filled Chuck's eyes as he struggled to continue.

"Jessie is a strong girl, Chuck," Jordan said. "You're right, as long as he doesn't do something stupid, she'll be okay."

"You're welcome to stay here tonight in case he calls back

in the middle of the night," Maggie suggested as they entered the house. "Anyone up for a beer?" she asked.

"Soda for me," Jordan replied.

"I'll take a beer. Thanks," Chuck said. He paced back and forth across the living room. "Who do you think it is?" he asked.

"My money is on Hollinbeck," Jordan replied.

"Do you think so?" Chuck said.

"I don't know who else it could be. I mean, he knows about the device and he knows how powerful it is."

"You could say the same about each and every member of our development team," Chuck pointed out.

"True."

Maggie brought them their drinks. "Jordan, I don't like the idea of you being the one to deliver the device to this guy," she said.

"I tend to agree with her," Chuck added.

"What choice do we have? Like it or not, he holds all the cards here."

"Not all of them," Chuck said. "We still have the device. All we need to do is find a way to get Jessie back without giving it up."

CHAPTER 41

Chuck was awakened early the next morning by his cell phone. "Jessie?" he said eagerly as he answered.

"Malone," a man's voice said. "I want Lewis to bring the device to 1248 Flynn Avenue at ten this morning. She is to come alone. If you involve the police I will kill your daughter *and* Lewis. Is that clear?"

Jordan appeared in the doorway of the guestroom. "I heard your cell phone. Is Jessie all right?" she asked.

Chuck covered the receiver. "He's set up a meeting time. He wants you to go alone. You don't have to do this, Jordan."

"Like hell I don't. Tell him I'll be there."

Chuck held the phone to his ear once again. "Before we agree to anything, I need to know that Jessie is okay."

"Hold on," the man said.

"Daddy?"

"Jess, honey. Are you all right?"

"When are you coming to get me?"

"Very soon, love. Very soon. Baby, are you okay? He hasn't hurt you, has he?"

"No. I'm okay, Daddy. Please hurry. I love you, Dad."

"I love you too, sweetie. Be brave."

"That's enough, Malone. I expect to see Lewis here at ten."

"Ten o'clock," Chuck said out loud as he looked at Jordan. A moment later, the line fell silent.

Jordan looked at her watch. "Ten o'clock is only four hours away. We need to get to the lab."

"What are we going to do?" Chuck asked.

"We're going to get him a device."

Jordan turned to go back to her bedroom and ran headlong into Maggie.

"I'm going with you," Maggie said.

"You can come to the lab with us, Maggie, but I'm on my own for the drop-off," Jordan said. "You'll need to wait, out of sight, with Chuck."

"Jordan, I can't let you do that. You're pregnant, for Christ's sake."

Jordan took Maggie by the shoulders. "I know that love. Believe me, I know. I have no intention of putting our child or myself in danger. I'll be careful. I promise. I just need to get in there, give him the device and get Jessie out."

* * *

It was seven thirty before they stepped into the lab.

"Where's Tom?" Jordan called out as she walked through the lab.

"Right here," Tom said as he poked his head out from behind a piece of test equipment.

"Tom, we have a delicate situation on our hands. I know you've been working on prototype packaging for the computer chip. How quickly can you pull something together that might look authentic to a non-computer person?"

"Jordan, what's going on here?" Tom asked, drawing the attention of the rest of the team. Soon all six team members were gathered around waiting for an explanation.

Jordan looked at Chuck who gave his permission for her to speak. "Okay, I'll be honest with you. Chuck has a thirteen year old daughter named Jessie. Jessie has been in a wheelchair for three years after a car accident took away her ability to walk. As you may have guessed, she is our test subject for the human trials on the new device. Yesterday, she was kidnapped and is being held in exchange for the device. We think whoever is behind this is also the one responsible for the hack job on my back a few months ago."

"So, you want me to create a bogus device to give him in exchange for the girl," Tom said.

"That's exactly what we want to do."

"How much time do I have?" Tom asked.

"We meet him in less than three hours in the south end of

Burlington."

Tom glanced at the clock on the wall. "I'll do the best I can."

Jordan grabbed Chuck's phone out of his hand and threw it to Jackson. "Hey, Mr. IT expert, I need you to determine the origin of the blocked call in Chuck's cell phone. Don't hesitate to ask Carrie for help if you need to."

"Right away," Jackson said.

Julie stepped forward. "Is Jessie okay?" she asked.

"I talked to her this morning," Chuck said. "She's scared, but we think she's unharmed. So far, anyway."

Julie placed her hand on Chuck's arm and squeezed. "I'm going with you for the exchange," Julie said. "If anything goes wrong, it will be good to have a doctor on hand."

"I agree with Julie," Maggie said.

"Okay, but you'll have to stay out of sight. I won't have anything interfering with getting Jessie back safely."

"I understand."

* * *

At ten sharp, Jordan walked into the lower level of the warehouse and looked around. It was empty.

"Hollinbeck," she called out. "Show yourself."

A man appeared at the top of the stairs leading to a loft. "How did you know it was me?" Hollinbeck asked.

"I've been suspicious of you for a long time. I'm pretty sure you're the one who butchered my back a few months ago."

"I have to admit I was surprised to find the device had already been removed. All of this could have been avoided if it had still been there."

"You're one sick son of a bitch, you know that? What I want to know is who is working with you. That wasn't your voice on the phone yesterday," Jordan said.

"You're right. It wasn't. Did you bring the device?"

"I did."

"Jordan? Jordan is that you," Jessie's voice came from above.

Jordan walked quickly toward the stairs, but stopped short when Hollinbeck pulled a gun out of his coat pocket. "Stop right where you are," he said.

"I need to see her. I need to know she's all right," Jordan insisted.

"Not until you give me the device."

Jordan pulled the device out of her pocket and handed it to Hollinbeck. He turned it over in his hand, a smug look on his face as he inspected the casing and the wires protruding from each end. Jordan's gaze never left Hollinbeck's face.

After a few moments, Hollinbeck stepped aside and allowed Jordan to ascend the stairs. He followed close behind with the gun trained on Jordan. The moment Jordan saw Jessie, she ran to her and fell to her knees in front of her. Jessie threw her arms around Jordan's neck and hugged her fiercely.

"Are you okay?" Jordan asked as she held her close.

"I'm okay. I just want to go home," she said.

"I'm afraid that won't be possible for either of you," Hollinbeck said as he paced back and forth in front of a ceiling to floor window overlooking the yard below.

Jordan stood and faced him. "What the hell does that mean?"

"It's really very simple. I can't allow the girl to go because she can identify me. I can't let you go because I need your expertise to make this device work."

"You made a deal, Hollinbeck."

"No I didn't. You made a deal with Robinson, not me."

"Robinson?"

"Carl Robinson. He's the CEO of the Spine Institute. You see, he's not as smart as he thinks he is. All he cares about is making a fortune with this device. I, on the other hand, care about the medical industry finally realizing how brilliant I am. When I release this device to the world, not only will I be rich, but I'll be famous. Robinson threatened to destroy me if I didn't get this device for him, but I've turned the tables on him."

"Whatever happened to your Hippocratic oath? Whatever happened to 'first, do no harm'?"

"Think about it, Lewis. Think of all the people I can help

with this device. Sometimes you have to sacrifice a few to save many. Unfortunately, you and the girl over there will become collateral damage. You, I need to keep around long enough to get this device working. The girl, on the other hand can be eliminated immediately."

Hollinbeck leveled the gun at Jessie.

"You son of a bitch," Jordan said as she lunged forward and grabbed his arm, thrusting it high in the air. The firearm discharged into the ceiling. They wrestled with the gun for a few moments until Jordan managed to lift her foot and place it in the center of Hollinbeck's stomach. She pushed as hard as she could in an attempt to wrench the gun away from him, but only succeeded in sending him backward into the window.

"No!" Jordan screamed as Hollinbeck grabbed her shirt in an attempt to save himself as they both crashed through the glass pane and fell to the ground below.

"Jordan!" Jessie screamed as she wheeled her chair over to the broken window.

* * *

"Jordan!" Maggie threw the car door open and ran across the yard when she heard the gunshot. She was halfway across the parking lot when Jordan and Hollinbeck fell to the ground. Jordan landed on top of him then rolled off onto her back.

"Jordan. Oh, my God, Jordan," Maggie cried as she threw herself on to the ground beside her.

"Maggie, don't move her," Julie yelled as she ran across the yard behind her. "Don't move her, please."

Maggie cried uncontrollably as she rocked herself back and forth. "Jordan, sweetie, please don't die," she cried.

Jordan's eyes opened. "Maggie," she rasped.

By this time, Julie was by her side and kneeling on the ground beside her. "Don't move, Jordan. Chuck called for an ambulance."

"Maggie," Jordan said again as she slipped her hand into Maggie's and squeezed.

"Do as Julie says, love. Please don't move."

"Hollinbeck?" Jordan said.

Julie felt for a pulse on the man lying beside Jordan. "He's gone, Jordan."

"Jessie?"

"Jessie is fine, thanks to you," Chuck said as he carried his daughter out of the building and put her on the ground beside Maggie, then went to kneel at Jordan's head. "Hang in there, my friend. The ambulance will be here in no time."

"Maggie, this is all my fault," Jessie cried.

"No. Stop it. This is his fault," Maggie said, pointing to the dead man.

Jordan squeezed Maggie's hand once more. "Maggie."

"I'm here, love,"

"Maggie, I can't feel my legs."

CHAPTER 42

The EMT's secured Jordan to the back board and carefully lifted her onto the stretcher, then loaded her into the ambulance.

Maggie grabbed Julie's arm before she climbed in behind her. "Julie, Jordan is pregnant. I'm worried about the baby."

Julie's eyes widened. "She's pregnant? Sheesh, Maggie, drop another bomb on me, why don't you." Julie looked at the EMT's. "Go ahead and start the drips."

"Is that safe for her and the baby?"

"It's a Ringers Lactate. It's perfectly safe for both Jordan and the baby. How far along is she?"

"About two months, that is, if she didn't lose it in the fall," Maggie said, her voice breaking with emotion.

Julie took Maggie's hand in hers. "I'll check her out as soon as we get her stabilized. "Are you coming with us?"

"Yes," Maggie said as she climbed into the ambulance behind Julie. She sat on the bench next to the stretcher and took Jordan's hand.

"The baby," Jordan said.

"Don't worry about that right now. I love you, Jordan, no matter what. Always remember that. Just focus on recovering from this mess, okay?"

* * *

Maggie paced back and forth across the emergency room while she waited for Julie to give her an update on Jordan's condition. Chuck arrived about an hour into her wait. He took Maggie into her arms and held her close.

"How are you holding up?" he asked.

"I'd be doing a lot better if they'd just tell me how she is,"

Maggie replied.

"Jessie told me what happened between Jordan and Hollinbeck. Apparently, he planned to kill Jessie and to hold Jordan hostage so she could help him make the device functional. After that was accomplished, he was going to kill her as well."

"That son of a bitch. Good thing for him that he's already dead, because if I ever got my hands on him—"

"Anyway, he pointed the gun at Jessie, but Jordan grabbed his arm and forced it upward. The gunshot we heard was him discharging the weapon while they struggled with it. The next thing Jessie remembered is them falling out the window. She saved Jessie. I don't know how I'll ever repay her."

Maggie took Chuck's face between her palms. "She will not expect repayment, Chuck. She loves Jessie."

"And Jessie loves her. She loves both of you, in fact. We're lucky the two of you came into our lives."

Their attention was suddenly diverted to Julie as she entered the waiting room. Maggie immediately went to her.

Julie took Maggie by the shoulders.

"Okay, here's what I know at this point. She did not lose the baby. It appears Hollinbeck's body absorbed most of the impact. Thank God she was only two months along. She did, however, break her back again."

"Oh, my God," Maggie said as she began to cry.

"Her spinal column has not been severed, but it has been damaged. We have the tangle of electrode wires we left in her spine to thank for that. Without the added strength those wire provided, the damage to her spinal cord would have been much worse. In just the hour or so that she's been here, some of the feelings in her legs has returned, but she is unable to move even her toes. She is being fitted for a body cast right now, to immobilize her spine. Once the swelling has subsided, we'll do more tests to determine how permanent the injuries are."

"Can I see her?" Maggie asked.

"Yes. As soon as her cast is set, she'll be moved to a room. I'll ask the nurses to move a cot into her room for you if you want to stay with her for the next few days. She should be able to go home within a week."

"Yes, please. I'd like that," Maggie said.

Julie turned to Chuck. "How is Jessie?" she asked.

"Jessie is physically okay, but she's feeling pretty guilty about all of this."

"Well, if I know Jordan, she'll set the record straight with Jessie as soon as she's well enough for visitors. How are you holding up?" she asked Chuck.

"I'm okay. Just worried about Jordan."

"Well, I'm here to tell you, she's one lucky lady. We all saw her and Hollinbeck hit the ground with her directly on top of him. Her impact injuries were relatively minor compared to what they would have been if his body hadn't absorbed most of it. She has a tough road ahead of her...I won't sugar coat it, but she's been there before and I have confidence that she'll bounce back quickly."

"Spare no cost in treating her, Julie. I will cover whatever it takes."

Julie nodded. "Okay. I should get back to her." Julie turned to go, then looked back at Chuck. "Could I interest you in dinner once we have Jordan settled in a room?"

Chuck smiled. "That would be nice."

"All right. I'll call your cell phone as soon as she's resting comfortably."

She approached Maggie, who was standing by the window staring out over the city. "Are you ready to see her?"

"Yes, please," Maggie said as she followed Julie out of the waiting room.

Maggie sat by Jordan's bedside holding her hand. "You scared the shit out of me, Jordan," she said.

"Julie said the baby is okay," Jordan replied.

"Yes. Apparently, Hollinbeck absorbed most of the impact for both of you. Thank God you fell directly on top of him," Maggie said.

"She also said I've injured my spine again."

Maggie lifted her hand and brought it to her lips. She kissed the knuckles and closed her eyes in an attempt to hold back her tears.

Jordan squeezed her hand. "I'm sorry to put you through this, Mags."

"I'm just glad you're going to be okay."

"I'll most likely be confined to a wheelchair again."

"For a while, anyway," Maggie said. "Jordan, you have technology on your side. The wheelchair will only be temporary."

"Yes, but it will be several months before I'm healed enough to accept a new implant, and besides, Jessie goes first."

"What about re-implanting the old device back into you? Julie said the injury was in the same location as the last one."

"That's a good idea, love, but we can't do that until we're sure the new implant works. The old one may need additional reverse engineering if we run into unexpected issues. We won't be able to do that if it's back inside my body. Once the new device is operational and Jessie is on her feet, I'll feel comfortable doing that."

"I understand. We need to find a gynecologist who has experience with paraplegic pregnancies since you'll be in a wheelchair until after the baby is born."

* * *

Seven months later…

Jordan wheeled her chair through the lab and stopped at the table on which testing was being carried out on two rats with prototypes of the new device implanted over complete SCI's. She smiled as she watched them wobble across the table with halting, jerky movements.

"Why are their movements so irregular?" Jason asked. "It's almost as though something is interrupting the flow of electricity to the implant."

"Well, both rats are having the same issue, so I would guess the problem lies in the device, not in the rats," Wendell said.

"I know what the problem is," Jordan said.

"Please enlighten us," Jason said.

"Before I elaborate, set up a camera and record their movements for the next twenty minutes or so. We'll need a baseline for comparison after the issue is fixed."

"Okay, Jord, spill it. What's causing this?" Jackson said.

"Significant digits," Jordan said.

"Significant digits?" Carrie repeated.

"Yes. The problem is in your algorithm. As you know, the algorithm supplies current alternately to each side of the injury. I'm willing to bet the code that controls the timing for current delivery has a different number of decimal points on one side of the injury compared to the other. The unequal number of significant digits is causing a slight pause between impulses, causing the jerky movements."

Carrie immediately called up the algorithm and searched through each line of code. "Well, I'll be damned. She's right. Look, four significant digits on the electrodes implanted on one side of the injury and five on the other. Let me fix that right now." Carrie typed a few changes into the code and saved the algorithm. "Okay. I'm ready to load it into the device as soon as we have enough baseline video."

Moments later, the new algorithm was loaded and the rats were once again released on one end of the table and enticed to make their way across the length of the field by food staged at the opposite end. Both rats exited the gate and walked toward the food with steady, event gaits.

"Whoa! That's awesome," Jackson said. "How did you know?"

"Like I said, I've seen it before. The same thing happened when we were testing the original device."

"Well, you just saved us a shit-load of time debugging the problem. Now all that's left is the battery pack. The last thing we need to do is figure out how to teach the body to kinetically charge it," Jackson said.

"You leave that to me," Jason said. "I have some ideas that take advantage of synapse activity and the energy produced during that process. I should be ready to test it in about two weeks."

"That's good news, Jason," Jordan said. "I knew I had faith

in this team for a reason. I…ah.   What the hell was that?" Jordan said as she grasped the side of her bulging abdomen.

"Is the baby coming?" Carrie asked.

Jackson and Jason immediately backed up several feet.

"Not on my watch," Jackson said.   "To quote *Gone With The Wind*…I don't know nothing about birthing no babies."

"I'm with him," Jason said.

"Ahhhh," Jordan said again.   "Okay, something is definitely happening here."

"Where's Julie when you need her?" Tom said.

"Oh for crying out loud," Wendell said.   "She's in labor. It's not contagious, you know.   Tom, call Maggie.   Carrie, please call an ambulance. Jordan, take deep, even breaths. This is your first baby, so it will probably take a while."

"Do you have experience in this kind of thing, Wendell?" Jordan asked.

"I spent twenty-five years as an ER doc, what do you think?" Wendell replied.

CHAPTER 43

"Okay, Jess, while I work with Christopher, I'd like you to show Will how to control the horse with his hands and voice," Maggie said. "Please stay in the ring today. We'll take him out to the north pasture after he has built up a little confidence."

"Sure thing, Maggie," Jessie replied as she maneuvered her horse close to Will.

"All right, young man," Maggie said to Christopher, "Let's get you onto this horse."

For the next two hours, Jessie and Maggie worked with their new students, focusing on balance and control. Both boys had spinal injuries. Will had a complete thoracic injury, immobilizing him from the waist down, while Christopher's partial injury was in the cervical region, effectively making him a quadriplegic, but with limited control over his arms and hands.

Maggie stanchion the horse and used the special lift she had designed, to raise Christopher to a level high enough to move him into the saddle. She then strapped his legs, arms and chest into the leather cradle. She placed the reins into his hands. "Okay, big guy, are you ready to ride?" she asked the boy.

A wide grin appeared on Christopher's face. "I'm more than ready," he said enthusiastically.

"All righty then, let's go."

Maggie mounted her own horse, then reached for the tether on the harness of Christopher's horse. She led him around the paddock several times while instructing him on how to use the reins to dictate the direction the horse would go in. Finally, she brought his horse to a halt near the fence, then rode her own horse into the middle of the arena.

"Okay, Chris. You're on your own, bud. Tap the horse's

side like I showed you, then steer him slowly around the periphery of the ring using the reins. When you get back to where you are now, we'll reverse direction and circle the other way. If you can manage this, you'll graduate to the open plain. Are you up for the challenge?"

"Try to stop me," Chris said.

Maggie watched Chris guide his horse around the ring, while spot-checking Jessie and Will in the next ring. She smiled as Jessie encouraged the young boy to push himself out of his comfort zone.

"Come on, Will. You can do it," Jessie said. "You're not going to fall out of the saddle, so don't be afraid to push yourself. Use your voice. That's it. Good job. Now pull back on the reins to stop him. Fantastic!"

Over the next hour, both boys ran their horses through a routine designed to teach them control over the animals' movements, while their mothers watched from the porch. Every so often, Maggie would glance over at them when they clapped and offered encouragement to their sons. At the end of the hour, she led the boys back to the barn, one at a time and helped them dismount and settle back into their chairs. Jessie was the last one to dismount.

"Race you to the house," Will challenged Jessie.

"You're on, squirt," Jessie said as they two of them took off, leaving Maggie to push Christopher behind them.

"What do you think of this guy, Kathy?" Maggie said as she pushed Christopher over to his mother.

"I'm amazed, and very impressed," Kathy said. "Maggie, I can't tell how good this has been for Chris."

"Well, I've enjoyed every minute of it. Give me five, dude," Maggie said to the boy as she put her hand near his. "Will we see you again next week?"

"You bet," Chris said.

Will rolled his chair over to Maggie. "Can we go see the new foals in the north pasture next week?" he asked.

"That's the plan, Stan. I think both you and Chris are ready for a ride across the plains," Maggie said.

Both boys cheered.

"All right then. We'll see you next week."

Maggie draped her arm across Jessie's shoulder as they watched the boys leave. "What do you say we go unsaddle the horses then have ourselves some lemonade?"

* * *

Maggie took two glasses from the cupboard and put them on the table, then reached for the refrigerator door just as her cell phone rang. She pulled it out of her pocket and looked at the number.

"Hmmm. I wonder who this is." She pressed the answer button and raised the phone to her ear. "Hello?"

"Maggie, this is Tom at the lab."

"Tom? Is Jordan all right?"

"Actually, she's in labor."

"What? Oh, my God. Where is she?"

"The ambulance just took her to the hospital."

"Okay. I'm on my way. Thanks for calling, Tom."

Maggie hung up the phone and looked at Jessie. "The lemonade will have to wait. We're having a baby!"

Maggie pushed Jessie down the porch ramp and helped her into the car. She pushed the Bluetooth feature on her dash and called Chuck.

"Charles Malone," he said when he answered the phone.

"Chuck, this is Maggie. I'm on my way to meet Jordan at the hospital. Jessie's with me. You're about to be an uncle."

"Holy shit. I'll be waiting for you in the parking garage."

As soon as Maggie hung up with Chuck, she dialed Gina and Sam.

"Hey Maggie, how are you, darling?" Sam said.

"I'm about to become a mom. The ambulance just took Jordan from the lab. She's in labor."

"Oh my! Gina and I will be there as soon as we can. Congratulations, sweetie. We'll see you soon."

"One more call," Maggie said as she dialed Florida. "Mom…Dad, you're about to become grandparents. I'm on my way to the hospital right now. Jordan is in labor."

"How wonderful, Margaret! Gary, Jordan is in labor," Maggie heard her mother shout to her father.

"Call us as soon as the little one has arrived," Sharon said. "Congratulations, sweetheart."

"I will Mom…I mean, Grandma. Talk to you soon."

* * *

Maggie arrived at the hospital just as Jordan was being wheeled to the operating room.

"Maggie. Thank God you made it," Jordan said as another contraction tore through her abdomen. "Ahhh."

"And you are?" a nurse asked Maggie.

"I'm Maggie Downs, her wife."

"Come with me," the nurse said.

"Where am I going?"

"We need to get you suited up and scrubbed before you can go into the OR."

Maggie squeezed Jordan's hand and kissed her cheek. "I'll see you there, love."

* * *

Maggie stood to the side and talked to the doctor as the scrub nurse prepared Jordan for surgery. "Doctor Cross, isn't the baby a bit early? I mean, her C-section isn't scheduled for another two weeks."

"Two weeks is nothing to worry about, Maggie. I'm more concerned about the contractions. Jordan isn't able to push, so to minimize the stress on the baby, we need to do the C-section right away."

Maggie looked at Jordan, worry evident on her face.

"Don't look so glum. She'll be fine. This will be over in no time. The spinal should take effect in a few minutes, then we'll get started. I will warn you though that C-sections are pretty gruesome to watch."

"I've birthed countless foals. It can't be much different than that."

333

"We're ready, Dr. Cross," the nurse said.

Dr. Cross winked at Maggie. "Let's go have a baby," he said.

Maggie held Jordan's hand throughout the entire surgery, relaying to her each step in the delivery process. Finally, Dr. Cross reached into the incision with the scalpel and cut the uterus.

"Suction," he said as the excess blood and amniotic fluid were removed.

Dr. Cross reached into the opening of Jordan's uterus and guided the baby's head out. The attending nurse immediately began to suction out the infant's mouth.

"It looks like the baby has lots of brown hair," Maggie said.

"Is it a boy or a girl?" Jordan asked.

Just as the words left Jordan's mouth, Dr. Cross pulled the baby the rest of the way out of the opening. "You have a son, ladies," he said, holding the child high enough for Jordan to see.

"We have a son? Maggie, we have a son." Jordan's voice shook with emotion as she looked into Maggie's eyes.

"We have a son," Maggie said. "I love you so much right now, my heart's about to burst."

"Maggie, do you want to cut the cord?" the doctor asked.

"Yes. Yes, I do." She kissed Jordan once more then accepted the scissors from the nurse. When the cord was cut, the little boy was carried to the scale where he was weighed, measured and bathed. Finally, swathed in a warm, soft blanket, the nurse handed him to Maggie who carried him over to Jordan and placed his head close enough for Jordan to kiss him.

"Hey little man," Jordan said tenderly. "I'm your mamma, well, *one* of them at least."

Maggie looked at him for several long moments, then kissed him on the cheek. "Kale Charles Downs-Lewis. Welcome to the world, little dude," she said.

"Kale Charles. I like that. Thank you, Maggie," Jordan said.

"It seems only fitting to name him after the two men who made all this possible. Do you want to hold him?"

"I was wondering when you'd ask," Jordan joked.

Maggie placed Kale in Jordan's arms then draped her arm across the pillow above Jordan's head. "He looks like you," she said.

"I don't know if that's a blessing or a curse," Jordan remarked.

"Oh, it's a blessing, all right. You're a beautiful woman, Jordan, even all sweaty and bloated after giving birth."

Jordan's eyebrows rose high on her forehead. "Sheesh, do I really look that bad?" she asked.

"You are more beautiful than I've ever seen you, my love." Maggie kissed the top of her head.

"Okay, ladies. Just a few more stitches and we'll have you on your way to your room," Dr. Cross said.

"Sweetheart, why don't you go break the news to the crew. I'll see you in the room. Okay?" Jordan suggested.

"Okay." Maggie kissed both members of her new family and left the OR.

* * *

Maggie walked into the room with a big smile on her face. "We have a son," she said. "Kale Charles Downs-Lewis."

Gina and Sam were the first to embrace Maggie as she entered the waiting room, showering her with kisses.

Sam looked down at her own bulging abdomen. "Do you hear that little one? Your cousin has been born."

"Maggie, we are so happy for both of you. How's Jordan?" Gina asked.

"She's great. They're closing the incision now. She should be moved to her room in about an hour. Wait until you see our little man. He's beautiful. He looks just like Jordan."

"My turn," Chuck said as he patiently waited his turn for hugs. "Congratulations, Maggie. A boy, huh? Wow! I finally have a nephew. How cool is that?"

Jessie pulled on her father's coattails. "Me next," she said, urging Chuck to step aside.

Maggie knelt in front of Jessie and accepted a big hug from her. "I can't wait to hold him," Jessie said excitedly. If Daddy is his uncle, does that make him my cousin?"

"I believe it does," Maggie said.

"Cool. I can't wait to babysit."

"Be careful what you wish for. We might just take you up on that."

Julie finally regained her composure and stood to hug Maggie warmly. "I'm so happy for you and Jordan. So, if Chuck gets to be his uncle, that means I get to be his aunt."

Maggie furrowed her brow and looked back and forth between Chuck and Julie. "Are you telling me what I think you're telling me?" she asked.

Julie slipped her left hand into Maggie's. "You think right."

Maggie looked at Julie's ring finger, then at Chuck. "You sly dog. Come here, you." She hugged him fiercely. "Congratulations. You'll make a wonderful couple."

"Whoa, wait a minute here," Jess said. "You two are getting married?"

Chuck and Julie both nodded.

"Well hot damn. I get a new nephew and a new mom all in the same day," she exclaimed.

"Hey, watch your language. Where did you learn that?"

"Oops!" Jessie said as she looked at Maggie.

Chuck glared at her.

"Hey, how about those Red Sox?" Maggie said. "Wait, I think I hear Jordan calling. We'll be in room two-eleven if you want to stop by," she said as she beat a hasty retreat.

Julie walked into the circle of Chuck's arms. "Kale *Charles*? What a wonderful gift, from such a wonderful man."

CHAPTER 44

Two months later…

Jessie sat on the edge of the hospital bed with her feet dangling down. Chuck and Julie stood in front of her. Jordan was nearby in her wheelchair with Maggie and Kale by her side.

"I don't want to do this, Daddy."

"Look, Jessie, the sooner you do this, the sooner your physical therapy sessions will be over. You haven't been very cooperative with them so far."

Jessie crossed her arms and pouted, a scowl on her face.

"Now, put your hands in mine, and slowly slide forward," Chuck said.

The look of fear on Jessie's face was palpable. "I can't, Daddy. I'll fall."

"You won't fall, Jess. I would never let you fall."

Jess looked at Jordan.

"It's okay to be scared, Jess. I was scared too. Trust your father," Jordan urged.

"You can do it, Jess," Maggie added.

Jess closed her eyes and inhaled deeply, then slid forward until her feet touched the floor and she stopped sliding.

"We have touchdown," Julie said. "All right sweetie, Dad and I will each hold an arm. I want you to lean forward and imagine yourself pushing your feet into the floor while you straighten at the waist. Just like that," Julie said as Jessie stood up.

Her eyes were as big as saucers, then rapidly filled with tears as the emotion of the moment overwhelmed her.

"I'm standing. Daddy, I'm standing!"

"Yes you are, baby," he said, unable to hold back his joyful tears as they rolled down his cheeks.

"Mom, look at me. I'm almost as tall as you are," she said to Julie.

"In a few years, you'll be taller than me," Julie replied, tears glistening in her own eyes. She looked at Chuck from behind Jessie's back and mouthed the words *she called me mom*!

"Okay, Jess. I need you to take a few steps for me," Chuck said. "Your physical therapist said you need to push yourself or it will never happen."

"I…I can't. I'm scared."

Maggie handed Kale to Jordan. "Sweetie, take our son for a moment. I want to try something."

Maggie stood in front of Jessie. "How badly do you want to be an instructor at the riding school?" she asked.

"I really, really want that, Maggie. You know I do."

"Well, just like we've told our students, you have to earn the right to move up to the next level."

Maggie backed up three steps. "If you want to be promoted from helper to full blown instructor, then start earning your stripes right now. Three steps. That's all you need to do to get the ball rolling. Just three steps."

Jess grasped Chuck and Julie's hands tightly and locked gazes with Maggie. She moved one foot forward, followed by the other. With each step she took, Maggie backed up one more. Before Jessie knew it, she had walked all the way across the room. Finally, Maggie stopped and allowed her to take one final step, right into her arms.

* * *

Jordan sat in bed, reviewing lab notes taken during Jessie's meeting with the team earlier in the day.

Maggie came into the room and reclined on the bed beside Jordan. She rolled onto her side and propped her upper body on her elbow. "The little one is down for the night, or at least until his next feeding."

"I'm a little nervous that he's in his own room already. He's not quite three months old yet," Jordan said.

"He'll be fine. He's right next door and the baby monitor

lets us know his every move. "Maggie looked at the papers in her hands. "What 'cha reading?" she asked.

"These are the notes we took while examining Jessie at the lab today. We are all astounded at the progress she's made in just the three short weeks since her device was implanted."

"I know what you mean. I spent some time with her today teaching her how to mount and dismount her horse from a standing position, and how to control it with her knees. She's having to re-learn horse riding techniques again, but she's doing remarkably well."

"She's a determined young lady."

"That, she is. She's almost walking normally after only three weeks."

"I agree. Muscle memory is returning pretty fast for her. It will only be a matter of time before her movements are completely normal. The question is, how long it will take for sensory feelings to return."

"So, is she far enough along in her healing to claim victory on the chip design and function?"

"I'd give it another few weeks, just to be sure nothing goes wrong."

"Another few weeks? Define *few*.'"

"I'd like at least a two-month trial before we do anything with the original device."

"So we're looking at another five weeks?"

"Pretty much."

"Are you nervous about getting the device back?" Maggie asked.

"A little. I'm more concerned about it working properly. With all the poking and prodding we've done on it, I really hope we haven't made it non-functional."

"I guess time will tell. If for some reason it doesn't work, you could always use one of the new devices."

"True. I'm just thankful that this latest injury wasn't a complete SCI. I still have most of the feeling below the injury site, I just can't move my legs. It makes waiting another five weeks in this wheelchair a little easier."

Maggie took the papers from Jordan's hands and placed

them on the nightstand. She then ran the tip of her index finger from Jordan's ear to the tip of her chin. "How about we exercise those feelings below the injury site."

"Yours or mine?" Jordan smiled wickedly.

Maggie glanced at the clock on the bedside table. "Let's see, I just put Kale to bed. That means he'll be awake in three to four hours wanting to be fed again. Three or four hours is enough time to walk on the wild side in both our sugar bushes. Don't you think?"

Jordan rolled over so she was partially lying on top of Maggie. "I'm always up for a wild time as long as it's with you, my love."

Maggie cupped Jordan's face between her hands and stared directly into her eyes. Jordan could see the passion smoldering below the surface of Maggie's green pupils. "Love me like there's no tomorrow, Jordan."

* * *

One year later…

Jordan walked back and forth across the front of a room filled with high-ranking military officers.

"Ladies and gentlemen," she said. "What I am about to propose to you will revolutionize the treatment of our veterans, specifically those who return from war with spinal injuries."

Jordan advanced the slide. "What if I was to say to you that I can cure paralysis caused by complete or partial spinal cord injuries? What if I was able to develop advanced, permanent prostheses that work on nerve impulse alone? What if I said my team and I have developed a functional power pack that is powered by the body using simple kinetics, *and* could be used to power cell phones or electronic body armor in the field?"

Jordan looked at the shocked faces of the people in the room. "Think of the possibilities, ladies and gentlemen. What if in the future, we were able to use this device and this knowledge to grow bulletproof skin, or to re-grow limbs lost to land mines?"

"I'd say, hogwash," a voice said from the back of the room.

"Impossible," came another response.

Jordan listened to several more negative outbursts, all the while nodding her head. "I expected those exact sentiments," she said.

A man sitting near the front of the room rose to his feet. "This is nonsense, Dr. Lewis. You're wasting our time."

"With all due respect, General, I disagree with you. Everything I have said is not only possible, but many of these capabilities have already been developed by my team…or are in process of development."

"With all due respect to you, Dr. Lewis…prove it," the general said.

Jordan walked back and forth across the front of the room one more time before stopping at the head of the table. "Ladies and gentlemen, I stand before you, a paraplegic."

EPILOGUE

UNIVERSITY OF VERMONT
MEDICAL CENTER

SHELBURNE, VERMONT, 2112

Kale glanced at the lab technician assisting him then returned his gaze to the rodent trying furiously to escape his grasp. "Okay, Dave, I'll hold the little bugger while you slightly increase the current to the implant. I'll tell you when to stop."

Kale was in the middle of an experiment on a rat in which damaged musculoskeletal nerves were replaced with synthetic fiber optics. Just as Dave completed the first incremental step, Kale's communicator chimed loudly.

"Hello?"

"Kale, Jordan is hurt. Come quickly."

Kale felt like someone had punched him in the stomach. "Andi? Andi, slow down. Tell me what happened. Where are you?"

"We're in the emergency room. She was on the bus. It went off the road and rolled over. Please, come quickly."

"I'm on my way. Hold on, love. I'm on my way."

The University of Vermont was affiliated with the medical center teaching hospital, and the laboratory was located just on the other side of the parking lot opposite the emergency room. Realizing he could cover the distance between the lab and the hospital quicker on foot than by trying to find his vehicle in the vast parking lot, he set off running, making it to the emergency room within five minutes of Andi's call. Andi met him at the door. He grabbed her by the shoulders. "Where is she?" he asked desperately.

Andi was barely able to speak as she pointed to the door of an examination room. "They took her in there."

Kale was frantic as he ran toward the door, only to be stopped by a resident who would not permit him to enter.

"I'm afraid you can't go in there," the resident informed him.

"I'm afraid I don't care," Kale responded as he tried to push his way past the man. "Let me by," he said.

"No can do. You'll need to see the doctor if you want a status."

Just then, Peter Michaels exited the room Kale was attempting to gain access to. "Peter. Peter, how is she?" By this time, Andi had joined Kale and was clinging tightly to his arm.

Peter took Kale by the arm and walked a few feet away from the door. Andi followed closely. "She's stable. As stable as she can be, considering her condition."

Andi stepped forward. She was clearly distraught as she wiped the tears from her cheeks. "Tell me, Peter. How bad is she?"

Peter looked back and forth between Andi and Kale. "Judging by the severity of her injuries, it's apparent she was violently thrown around the bus."

Peter ran his hand through his hair then looked at his friends and coworkers once more. "All indications are that she's broken her back and probably severed her spinal cord completely."

Andi nearly collapsed and Kale supported her with an arm around her waist. "No," she moaned.

Kale felt he needed to be strong for Andi's sake, and tried not to cry. "Can we see her?"

Peter nodded. "Of course. They'll be preparing her for surgery soon to further stabilize her spine, so you'll only have a few moments. We'll let you know as soon as she's been settled into Intensive Care."

Kale nodded. He tightened his arm around Andi and led her into Jordan's room. Peter followed close behind. Andi was shaking uncontrollably. "She looks so small and helpless."

Kale was unable to speak for fear of losing control. As they approached the bed, they separated, with Andi on one side and Kale on the other. Kale leaned over the small form lying in the bed and kissed her on the cheek.

"Jordan, honey. Daddy's here. Mommy's here too, baby." Andi rubbed the back of the girl's hand as Kale spoke. "You're going to be all right, sweetie. Mommy and I will be right here waiting for you to wake up, okay?"

Andi inhaled deeply to control the tears that cascaded down her face. She leaned in close to the injured child. "We love you, sweetheart. You'll be better soon. Just wait and see."

Peter motioned to them that time was up as the technicians entered the room to wheel the child to the operating room.

Andi looked at Peter and nodded, then turned back to her daughter. "Jordie… the doctors are here to take care of you, but we'll be here when you come back, okay? Mommy and Daddy love you, honey."

Andi and Kale kissed their child tenderly then stood together by the window as they watched the technicians move the five-year-old Jordan from the room.

* * *

Andi paced back and forth across the waiting room as Kale sat hunched over with his head in his hands. Every few moments, Andi blew her nose, left runny by nonstop weeping. Kale felt totally helpless as his baby girl lay clinging to life on the operating table and his wife paced worriedly across the floor in front of him. Few words passed between them as they waited for news of their child.

Finally, after what seemed like an eternity, a man wearing a white lab coat entered the room. He looked at the clipboard in his hand before addressing Kale and Andi. "Mr. and Mrs. Simmons?"

They were on their feet immediately. Together, they approached the man who extended his hand to them. "My name is Dr. Lewis. I'll be evaluating your daughter's condition."

Kale looked at the man's nametag as he firmly shook his hand.

Dr. Jordan Lewis. What the hell?

His eyes moved from the nametag to the man's face. He appeared to be around fifty years old, and something about him felt familiar.

"Dr. Lewis," Kale replied as he shook the man's hand and then stepped aside to afford the same courtesy to Andi.

"How is she?" Andi asked.

Dr. Lewis smiled. "She made it through surgery just fine. I won't be sure about the extent of her injuries or her chances for recovery until I've had a chance to examine her holograph."

"When can we see her?" Kale asked.

"She's being moved to the ICU right now. You should be able to see her in a couple of hours."

Andi noticed the doctor's nametag as Dr. Lewis answered Kale's questions. She gasped and gently elbowed Kale in the ribs to call his attention to the badge. Kale briefly glanced at his wife and acknowledged that he was aware of it.

Dr. Lewis scribbled a few comments on his clipboard. "I encourage you to get something to eat while you wait. There's a cafeteria downstairs that serves hot meals. Neither of you will be of any use to your daughter if you don't take care of yourselves. You can stop by the nurse's station at the ICU afterward and they'll be able to direct you to your daughter's room. I'll check on her as soon as she's settled in."

Kale stopped the doctor as he turned to leave. "Dr. Lewis?"

The doctor stopped his retreat and turned back to Kale. "Yes?"

"We couldn't help but notice your nametag." Kale looked at Andi, and then back at the doctor. "We…we knew a Jordan Lewis. In fact, we were very close to her." He cleared his throat before continuing. "We loved her very much. So much that we named our daughter after her."

Dr. Lewis simply nodded, then left the room.

Outside the waiting room, Dr. Lewis stopped and leaned against the wall. After taking a deep breath, he scanned the papers attached to his clipboard.

Simmons, Jordan. Age 5. Parents: Kale and Andrea

Simmons.

Dr. Lewis pressed the back of his head into the wall and closed his eyes.

It's them!

* * *

Kale stood at the window of Jordan's room and looked out over the city. A canopy of stars stood guard over the night and streetlights dotted the scenery below. Andi sat at her daughter's bedside and hummed nursery tunes in time to the various monitors that beeped in harmony with her voice. Both parents waged internal battles between hope and desperation as they waited for their daughter to regain consciousness.

After a time, their vigil was interrupted by Peter's arrival. Andi looked up at him with expectation and hope on her face.

"Peter?"

Peter walked over to the bed and placed his hand on Jordan's forehead. He addressed Kale and Andi without taking his eyes from the little girl. "She's a beautiful child, very much like her namesake."

Kale approached Peter and placed a hand on his shoulder. "What can you tell us?"

Peter turned to address them. "As you might guess, she's in pretty rough shape. We know her spinal cord is severed, but we have yet to determine just how catastrophic her injury is. I assume you've met Dr. Lewis?"

"Yes," Kale replied. "Do you realize his name is Jordan Lewis? How odd is that?"

Peter's eyebrows rose on his forehead. "Yes, I know. What's even stranger is that he's rapidly building a reputation for new spinal cord regeneration techniques—techniques that are supposed to restore complete sensory communication and feeling in a matter of months rather than the years we would have realized from our own research. He's apparently been doing independent research for the better part of his career, largely funded through a private organization named JEM."

"Do you think he can be trusted?" Andi asked.

"I checked out his credentials thoroughly. He has an

excellent reputation and from all reports, his patients are doing exceptionally well. From what I can tell, he's little Jordan's best chance at this point."

"When do you think we'll know if he can help her?" Kale asked.

Peter inhaled deeply. "Well, Dr. Lewis and I examined her while you two were having dinner. Hopefully, we'll know better tomorrow morning after Dr. Lewis has reviewed the test results."

Kale and Andi absorbed Peter's statement. Peter headed toward the door, but stopped and turned around. "The two of you should go home and rest. She'll be sedated throughout the night so I don't expect she'll be aware of your presence at least until morning."

Andi shook her head. "I can't leave her."

Peter looked at Kale. "I'm staying as well," Kale said.

Peter nodded. "All right. At least take turns napping, okay? You two need to take care of yourselves in order to help your daughter through this."

* * *

Dr. Jordan Lewis entered the Intensive Care Unit the next morning to find Andrea Simmons sleeping with her head resting on her daughter's bed. Kale was pacing the floor.

Kale's attention was immediately drawn to the door as it opened. He reached out to shake the doctor's hand. "Dr. Lewis, good morning."

Andi stirred at the sound of voices in the room. "Kale?" she asked groggily.

Kale walked over to the bed and rubbed Andi's back. "Sweetheart, Dr. Lewis is here."

Dr. Lewis walked over to the bed and shook Andi's hand, then he pulled up a chair and sat down. He motioned for Kale to sit as well.

"Please sit. I have some news for you."

He waited for Kale to sit on the arm of Andi's chair and place his arm around her shoulder to both give and receive emotional support.

"I believe I can help your daughter."

Andi began to weep softly.

Dr. Lewis continued. "I've been working for the past thirty years on a revolutionary method for restoring spinal function in a completely severed spinal cord."

He stopped speaking for a moment both to allow Kale and Andi to absorb what he had said, and to prepare himself for what he had to say next.

"We can't thank you enough," Kale said, wiping the tears from his face.

Dr. Lewis reached into his breast pocket and extracted an envelope. "Before you thank me, you need to read this. You see, there is a reason my first name is Jordan. I was named after my grandmother."

Kale's knees buckled and he slowly lowered himself to the edge of the hospital bed. "Oh, my God. Jordan," he whispered.

Dr. Lewis smiled. "Yes, Jordan—your Jordan. She and Grandma Maggie wed in 2020. My father, Kale, was born through artificial insemination, followed by my Aunt Andrea a year later."

Kale and Andi looked at each other. They were speechless as Dr. Lewis continued.

"You see, I know about how you two helped her transcend time so she could be with Maggie." Dr. Lewis stared off into the distance as he fought the mist that was forming in his eyes. "They were the happiest two people I have ever known in my life. Grandma Jordan lived to the ripe old age of ninety. Grandma Maggie died a year later."

He looked back at Kale and Andi as he continued. "Thanks to you, she was not only a happy woman, but she also brought into the past, all the knowledge and talent required to advance stem cell and spinal regeneration research a century before it would otherwise have been done. Granted, we have really just begun clinical testing on the newest device. Your daughter will become part of that. If her accident had happened even fifty years ago, there would have been little hope of a quick recovery. So, as you can see, it's her you should be thanking."

Dr. Lewis smiled as he watched Kale and Andi attempt to

compose themselves.

"I can't believe it." Kale knelt in front of Andi. "Sweetheart, he's Jordan's grandson. She made it. I always felt like she had, and now thanks to her, our baby has a chance to live a normal life."

Kale lowered his head into Andi's lap while he cried. Andi rested her cheek on top of his head and spoke soothingly to him. "Now maybe you can let go of all the guilt you've been carrying around for the past several years. Not only did she make it, but she made it in time to save Maggie, and thanks to you and your whacky time machine, she was able to live the rest of her life with the one she loved more than life itself."

Dr. Lewis stood and looked at the couple before him. "I can clearly see why Jordan loved you two so much. Here, she wrote this for you before she died more than thirty years ago. My wife found it a few years back in some old papers that were in a trunk my grandmothers owned. It was enclosed in a larger envelope addressed to me. With it, was a note asking me to hand-deliver it to you. I didn't expect it to be under these circumstances, but it seems appropriate. Considering what you three meant to each other, it's only fitting that she continues to help you across time."

Dr. Lewis handed the envelope to Andi. "I'll check back with you later today to discuss little Jordan's treatment." He then smiled at the couple and left the room.

* * *

Kale and Andi walked hand in hand across the pasture toward the tall oak tree. To the right of the tree was a small cemetery where Jordan and both her parents were buried. The couple approached Jordan's headstone and sat side by side with their backs leaning against it. Kale pulled out the letter Dr. Lewis had given them and gingerly opened it. It was several hand-written pages long. Andi entwined her fingers with his and laid her head on his shoulder as Kale held it before them and began to read.

My Dearest Kale and Andi,

I don't know how to begin except to say I dearly love you both with all my heart. Because of your love and sacrifice, I have lived a long and prosperous life with the one person who completes me. I will be forever thankful that you came into my life. I know you compromised everything you believed in to help me realize the love of my life. For that, you have my undying gratitude.

Andi, I am so happy you came into Kale's life. You are the main reason I felt comfortable leaving him. He needs you. You are the other half of his soul. Please take care of him.

I cannot possibly rest until I tell you how I came to be so happy. As it turned out, the final trip back was the charm.

On the morning Maggie was supposed to die, I almost slept through my opportunity to save her. An old woman that looked strangely familiar woke me in the nick of time. At the time, I didn't know who she was, but as I write this and see my own visage in the mirror, I can only thank you for obviously indulging me one final time.

Loving Maggie is the most important thing I have ever done in my entire life. I don't know how I could ever have lived without her. She is even more beautiful in person than she was in my dreams. The first time we made love, it was so incredibly life altering. I was changed forever.

Kale, you once told me that someday I'd be happy that you were around. My dear friend, I was always happy that you were around. You are the closest thing I have ever had to a real brother. Did you ever learn to comb your hair?

Kale and Andi both chuckled through their tears as Jordan teased him from beyond the grave. They continued to read the details about how Jordan had saved Maggie from Jan's deadly plans. As the letter wound down, Jordan explained how the farm had been saved for them.

Kale, do you remember the land records for the farm indicating there were several owners between Maggie's parents and mine? Well, I needed to find a way to assure you and Andi ended up with the farm, so I convinced Maggie to hold on to it until 2071, when my parents came along, and we sold it directly to them. Let me tell you, it was very strange meeting them two years before I was born. They both stared at me in the oddest way, like they thought they should know me. I wanted so much to tell them who I was, but that might have just given them both heart attacks, then I would have killed my parents before my own birth. Talk about the ultimate paradox!

Maggie and I were married a year after the final transfer, and thanks to the wonders of science, we had two children, a boy we named Kale and a daughter named Andrea, after two people I love with all my heart. The two of you made all of this possible for me. I will be forever in your debt and will watch over you and your loved ones for the rest of eternity. That is my promise to you.

Kale, you warned me about not creating paradoxes with my presence in the past, but as I see it, impacts of a positive nature would surely be welcome. So, as you probably know, I continued our spinal cord regeneration research. It is my sincere hope that by taking the knowledge back one hundred years, SCI healing will have advanced at a much faster rate. It's the least I could do to repay the two of you and Peter for all you did for me.

If you are reading this letter, then you have met our grandson, Jordan. We are so proud of him. He has known about where I came from since he was a child. In fact, our children, Kale and Andrea, as well as all six of our grandchildren know. Jordan has chosen to enter the field of spinal cord regeneration to follow in my footsteps. He just completed his internship and will return to school in the fall to pursue advanced training in neurology. He is determined to escalate the progress we have seen over the past several years. I have confidence that he will succeed.

When I realized Jordan might have the opportunity to meet you in person, I penned this letter and gave it to him for safekeeping until he could deliver it personally. At the time of this writing, you will still be toddlers, so it will be several years yet before you actually see it. It is my sincere hope that he has carried out my wishes.

Well, my dear friends, I am tired and must rest. It is unfortunate that time travel cannot erase the ravages of age. My body is old but my spirit is still young. I have little time left in this world and look forward to the day that Maggie will join me and we will be together again for all eternity. I am not afraid to die. I know there is something more beyond this physical state. One day, Maggie will join me, as will both of you. I will miss my Maggie, but we have had fifty-eight wonderful years together thanks to you. There is nothing in this world that I could ever do to repay you. Know that I love you both, and I look forward to seeing you again one day. Give my best to Peter.

Take care of you...
Love, Jordan.

Andi clutched at her heart. "It hurts so much. I miss her."

Kale made no attempt to stem the flow of ears from his eyes as he brought the letter too his lips and kissed it tenderly.

"I love you, Jordan. I always have." He reached over to take Andi's hand in his own. "It warms my heart to know she was happy."

Andi smiled through her tears. "Me too."

Kale held the letter in front of both of them. "Jordan," he said out loud. "You said there was nothing in this world that you could do to repay us. Well, my friend, you were wrong. You are giving our child's life back to us. It doesn't get any better than that."

"Amen," Andi chimed in.

Kale leaned over and kissed Andi tenderly. "Have I told you today that I love you?"

Andi inhaled deeply. "I believe you have, but I never tire of hearing it. I love you too, Kale, across all space and time."

"Across all space and time."

Kale carefully folded Jordan's letter and placed it in his pocket, then rose to his feet and offered his hand to Andi. Soon, they were walking hand in hand back to the farm.

At that moment, if Kale and Andi had looked at Jordan's

headstone, they would have seen that it now mysteriously read;

Jordan Marie Lewis
Born September 20, 2073
Died July 4th, 2077
Free front the bonds of time, and held in the arms of love.
Thank you, Kale and Andi.

Author Karen D. Badger
Photo Credit: Brad Fowler, Song of Myself Photography

ABOUT THE AUTHOR

Karen D. Badger is the author of On A Wing And A Prayer, Yesterday Once More (a 2009 Golden Crown Literary Award winner for Speculative Fiction), In A Family Way, Unchained Memories, Happy Campers, Collective Identity Sweet Angel and Relative-ly Speaking (Books I, II, III, IV, V and VI of the Commitment Series), The Blue Feather, All My Tomorrows (sequel to the 2009 award winning Yesterday Once More) and her latest novel, 1140 Rue Royale…all released by Badger Bliss Books, which Karen co-owns with her wife Barbara Sawyer (aka, "Bliss').

Born and raised in Vermont, Karen is the second of five children raised by a fiercely independent mother, who remains one of her best friends to this day. Karen earned her B.A. in 1978 in Theater and in Elementary Education, and in 1994, earned a B.S. in mathematics. In addition to her novels, Karen is the author of many technical papers on photomask manufacturing, which she has presented at numerous semiconductor industry conferences, and is the holder if several technical patents. Karen is currently in her 38th year as an Principle Member of the Technical Staff with a prominent Semiconductor manufacturer in Vermont.

Karen and her wife, Barb (a retired Lt. Col., US Air Force) live in the beautiful state of Vermont—home of Ben and Jerry's. They spend their spare time with family as well as doing home improvement projects on both their homes in Vermont and New Mexico. They also enjoy camping, kayaking, motorcycling and singing Karaoke.

Please visit Karen's author website at www.karendbadger.com, or the Badger Bliss Books website at www.badgerblissbooks.com. Also like us on Facebook!

TITLES BY KAREN D. BADGER

www.badgerblissbooks.com

On A Wing and A Prayer
First edition published by Blue Feather Books, Sept, 2005
Second edition published by Badger Bliss Books – Sept, 2014
Third edition published by Badger Bliss Books – August, 2016
ISBN 13: 978-1-945761-01-0, ISBN 10: 1-945761-01-6

Yesterday Once More
First edition published by Blue Feather Books, July, 2008
Second edition published by Badger Bliss Books – Sept, 2014
Third edition published by Badger Bliss Books – August, 2016
ISBN 13: 978-1-945761-02-7, ISBN 10: 1-945761-02-4
2009 Golden Crown Literary Society Award - Speculative Fiction

In A Family Way – Book One of the Commitment Series
First edition published by Blue Feather Books, March, 2010
Second edition published by Badger Bliss Books – Sept, 2014 Third
edition published by Badger Bliss Books – August, 2016
ISBN 13: 978-1-945761-05-8, ISBN 10: 1-945761-05-9

Unchained Memories – Book Two of the Commitment Series
First edition published by Blue Feather Books, Oct, 2011
Second edition published by Badger Bliss Books – Sept, 2014 Third
edition published by Badger Bliss Books – August, 2016
ISBN 13: 978-1-945761-06-5, ISBN 10: 1-945761-06-7

Happy Campers - Book Three of the Commitment Series
First edition published by Blue Feather Books, Sept, 2013
Second edition published by Badger Bliss Books – Sept, 2014 Third
edition published by Badger Bliss Books – August, 2016
ISBN 13: 978-1-945761-07-2, ISBN 10: 1-945761-07-5

The Blue Feather
First edition published by Blue Feather Books, July, 2014
Second edition published by Badger Bliss Books – Sept, 2014 Third
edition published by Badger Bliss Books – August, 2016
ISBN 13: 978-1-945761-04-1, ISBN 10: 1-945761-04-0

Collective Identity – Book Four of the Commitment Series
First edition published by Badger Bliss Books – January, 2015
Second edition published by Badger Bliss Books – August, 2016
ISBN 13: 978-1-945761-08-9, ISBN 10: 1-945761-08-3

All My Tomorrows – Sequel to Yesterday Once More
First edition published by Badger Bliss Books – May, 2015 Second
edition published by Badger Bliss Books – August, 2016
ISBN 13: 978-1-945761-03-4, ISBN 10: 1-945761-03-2

Sweet Angel – Book Five of the Commitment Series
First edition published by Badger Bliss Books – June, 2015 Second
edition published by Badger Bliss Books – August, 2016
ISBN 13: 978-1-945761-09-6, ISBN 10: 1-945-761-09-1

Relative-ly Speaking – Book Six of the Commitment Series
First edition published by Badger Bliss Books – March, 2016
Second edition published by Badger Bliss Books – August, 2016
ISBN 13: 978-1-945761-10-2, ISBN 10: 1-945-761-10-5

1140 Rue Royale
First edition published by Badger Bliss Books – Sept, 2016
ISBN 13: 978-1-945761-00-3, ISBN 10: 1-945761-00-8

Sweet Angel

Book V of the Commitment Series

Coming soon from:

BADGER BLISS BOOKS

CHAPTER 1

It was an early Saturday afternoon. The sun was bright and high overhead. A slight breeze filled the air, but did little to dispel the heat. The sounds of suburbia were everywhere. Children playing…birds chirping…water splashing in a backyard pool…the sounds of a sprinkler gracing the neighbor's lawn with a much needed blanket of moisture…the steady hum of a lawn mower.

Billie pushed the mower back and forth across the front yard, leaving neat, overlapping stripes of mowed grass behind her. Beads of sweat lined her upper lip while streams of the salty sweat rolled down the side of her face from her hairline.

The sun beat down across tanned arms, shoulders, and long muscular legs, left bare by a scantily cut tank top and cut off denim shorts. On her head sat a baseball cap, lent to her by her son more than a year ago to cover up baldness from brain surgery. Dark hair, having long since grown out beyond her shoulders, was pulled back and neatly entwined in a French braid. White ankle socks and construction boots adorned her feet, while aviator sunglasses protected her piercing blue eyes from the sun's rays. The sun reflected off her bronzed skin that shimmered under a sheen of sweat. Motorists and passersby alike extended greetings as Billie pushed the mower across the yard.

Along the walkway leading from the front porch to the sidewalk, Cat busied herself planting fresh perennials. Kneeling in the grass along the walk, she dug straight, neat trenches with her garden spade, readying the soil to accept the colorful flowers. With a complexion too fair for prolonged exposure to the sun, Cat wore a wide-brimmed straw hat banded in white silk on her red-gold hair, which had also been entwined in a perfect French braid. A sleeveless button-down shirt with tails tied under her breasts exposed a firmly sculptured abdomen and tiny waist, while cut-off denim shorts adorned her slim hips and thighs. Leather sandals graced slender feet while John Lennon sunglasses perched on her finely chiseled nose. White garden gloves with red polka dots protected delicate hands from the grit and grime of gardening.

Cat sat back on her heels and wiped the sweat from her brow with the back of her gloved hand, spade still hanging loosely from it. She looked around and caught sight of Billie out of the corner of her eye and for the next few moments, watched her push the mower back and forth. She found herself admiring the way the muscles in Billie's legs contracted with each step, while deltoids bulged with the effort to push the mower along in a straight line.

Now that's what I call eye candy, she thought to herself, grinning smugly at the knowledge that the bronze goddess was all hers.

Cat couldn't believe she and Billie had been together for more than six years already. Seth was only six years old, and Tara was four when they met. She remembered how tenuous her relationship with Billie had been in the beginning. When they first met in an aerobics class, Cat didn't know Seth even existed. She only found out later that he had spent nearly six months in a coma after being hit by a drunk driver passing his school bus. That certainly explained why Billie was reluctant to spend time with her in the evenings. She discovered later that Billie spent each evening after teaching her aerobics class, sitting by the little boy's bedside in the hospital.

To be fair, Cat had to admit that she wasn't forthcoming about Tara's existence either at first. Billie only found out about her when she showed up at her apartment one day and the little girl answered the door because Cat was too ill with appendicitis to answer it herself. Cat credited Billie with saving her life that day. By that time, they had fallen in love and although their joint secrets added complication to their lives, they worked through it and committed themselves to each other and their children.

So much had happened to them since that first day at the gym. Not long after they blended their families and moved in together. Billie's ex-husband Brian broke into their home with intent to rob them in punishment of Billie for not giving him money for drugs. Unfortunately, Cat and the children were home, and in an attempt to protect the children from him, she succumbed to Brian's advances. The only good thing that came from that encounter was their baby girl, Skylar, who had just turned six years old.

Life changed significantly from that point on. As a lawyer, Billie successfully lobbied to change the marriage laws in their home state of New York, allowing them to legally marry, followed by the adoption of each other's children. Then the unthinkable happened—Brian once again invaded their lives and kidnapped Cat and the kids, shooting Billie in the head during an attempted rescue.

Cat felt tears fill her eyes as she recalled the painful memories. They almost lost Billie that day had it not been for the medical training Cat received years earlier while studying to become an anesthesiologist. She managed to tend to Billie's wounds while waiting for the ambulance and after a time, Billie made a full recovery…at least they thought she did.

Nearly a year after the shooting, Billie was unresponsive one morning and landed back in the hospital. It was discovered that scar tissue from the gunshot wound was blocking vital functions in her brain. Cat found herself in the unfortunate position of having to make a potentially catastrophic decision about Billie's treatment, one that may have put her in a wheelchair for the rest of her life. As it was, Billie recovered full mobility, but not her memory. Worst of all, Billie insisted she wasn't gay when she awoke from surgery.

Cat was devastated at the thought of losing the one person who made her complete. With the help of her family and their best friends, Jen and Fred Swenson, Billie's memory slowly returned. Cat truly didn't know how she would have coped without Jen's help. Jen kept her encouraged at times when Billie's lack of memory seemed hopeless, and she was always there for them when they needed someone to watch the kids at a moment's notice. She truly felt blessed to have such dedicated and loving friends in Jen and Fred.

Billie stopped and made eye contact with Cat. The lawn mower continued to purr beside her as she stood with one hand on her hip, the other holding the safety shutoff bar on the mower, her weight shifted to one hip, and her eyebrows perched high on her forehead. "You look like you're a thousand miles away, Cat. Is everything okay?" she asked.

Cat rose to her feet and approached Billie, stopping only when a hair's breadth separated their bodies. She looked into Billie's face and smiled seductively, then reached behind her neck to pull her down into a kiss.

The mower suddenly died as Billie released the emergency shutoff bar to wrap her arms around Cat. The kiss deepened until Cat's knees were too weak to support her. Little did they care that they were in full view of passersby and neighbors alike.

Moments later, they broke apart and looked once more into each other's eyes.

"Not that I'm complaining, mind you, but what was that for?" Billie asked.

"That was for being the most beautiful creature on Earth," Cat replied, grinning ear to ear.

"Not true," Billie replied. "And I know this because *I* am looking at the most beautiful creature on Earth right now," she added as she smiled and lowered her head for another kiss.

Suddenly, the sound of a man clearing his voice echoed in her ear. The ladies' heads turned quickly in the direction of the sound.

Cat smiled as she lowered her arms from around Billie's neck and turned around in her wife's embrace. Billie maintained her current position, with her arms circling Cat's waist from behind.

"Hi Bert!" Cat said cheerfully. "What have you got for us today?" she asked.

"Good afternoon, ladies," he said. "Well, let's see, a few bills, a sales flyer, and, oh yes, a letter, from...ah, let me see...yes, from Michigan," the elderly mailman said, shuffling through the envelopes before handing them to Cat.

Bert smiled at the ladies as he watched Cat flip through the envelopes. These two ladies held a special place in the old mailman's heart. Not only were they sociable, kind and very beautiful, but they treated him with respect, even going so far as to insist he come in from the cold and share hot chocolate with them one very frigid winter day as he delivered mail. And as far as their lifestyle was concerned, it didn't concern him one bit. He had seen some pretty unique people in his many years of delivering mail, but all that mattered to him was that they were good, decent people, and treated him considerately...just like these two ladies did. Bert wished all of his deliveries were this pleasant.

Cat handed the letter from Michigan over her shoulder to Billie. She thanked Bert as he walked away then said, "This one's addressed to you, love. It's from your Mom."

Billie released Cat from the circle of her arms as she took the letter. She looked at the handwriting, nervously recalling the first meeting she and Cat had with her mother just three months earlier.

The meeting had been uneasy and tense. Billie had learned that her mother, Laurel, sold her as a baby for drug money nearly thirty-four years earlier. She also learned that she had a half brother, Dylan, and a homophobic stepfather named Jim, whom she had yet to meet. That was one confrontation she was not looking forward to.

The search for her mother had started quite by accident. While attempting to construct genealogies for themselves, she and Cat discovered that the two people Billie had spent her entire life believing were her parents were in fact, not. They had purchased her on the black market and had raised her as their own. It wasn't until ten years after their deaths that she learned the truth.

While searching for their roots, Billie and Cat interviewed Cat's grandparents, Josephine Wycliffe and Alexandria Spirakis, a wealthy elderly couple from Charleston, South Carolina. The physical resemblance between Billie and Alexandria was stunning, so much so, that further investigation lead to the revelation that Alex had given birth to what she was told at the time, was a stillborn baby girl fifty-five years earlier. Even though Alex was told otherwise, she was convinced in her heart that the child was still alive. The connection she felt to Billie, combined with the physical resemblance between them, was too strong not to wonder if the child she had lost so many years earlier could be Billie's mother. So started the search that led to Laurel...Alex's daughter and Billie's biological mother.

Billie's first encounter with Laurel was unpleasant to say the least, mostly due the intense feelings of anger and betrayal she felt for the woman. She just could not understand how a mother could sell her child for drugs. Admitting that her life probably would not have turned out as wonderful as it had if

Laurel had kept her was not enough to erase the feelings of desertion and betrayal.

Several painful confrontations ensued before the women struggled to come to terms with each other in an attempt to build a mother-daughter relationship. Since that time, they exchanged letters, e-mails and phone calls, managing to build a friendly camaraderie, but lacking that deep emotional bond shared by a parent and child. Three months later, the relationship was still distant and admittedly, Billie was having a hard time completely letting go of the hurt.

"Billie?" Cat placed a hand on Billie's arm and drew her out of her trance as she stared at the envelope.

Billie snapped back to awareness at the sound of Cat's voice. She smiled nervously.

"Billie, are you all right?" Cat asked.

Billie just nodded and sat down on the porch steps. For several moments, she looked at the front of the envelope. The slope of the penmanship prompted a thought that her mother's handwriting was similar to her own. She slid her little finger under the flap and tore it along the top of the envelope. She retrieved the letter and placed the empty envelope on the step beside her and looked nervously at Cat.

"Do you want me to read it to you?" Cat asked.

Billie seriously considered Cat's offer for a few moments before she declined. "No, I'll do it, love."

Cat lowered herself to the step beside Billie and picked up the empty envelope. She inspected it absent-mindedly as Billie read the letter to herself. When Billie was finished, she took a deep breath and sighed.

"Is everything okay?" Cat asked.

Billie pulled Cat in for a hug. "Everything's fine, Cat. At least it is now," she replied.

"What do you mean?" Cat asked, concern edging her voice.

Billie held the letter in front of her. "Laurel says here that she and Jim went through some rough times after she returned from South Carolina. Apparently, Jim feels threatened by my presence...and Alex's," Billie explained.

"Threatened?" Cat asked. "How so?"

"She thinks he's afraid of losing her to us, I guess," Billie surmised.

"Billie, I hope he doesn't force her to choose between him and her child. If that happens, he will surely lose. Laurel made it very clear that she won't allow him to come between the two of you," Cat reminded her.

Billie nodded as she scanned the letter once more.

"Apparently, she let him have it with both barrels, accusing him of being insecure and close minded," Billie said, paraphrasing the letter.

"Wow!" Cat exclaimed. "But didn't you just say that everything's fine? I guess they worked it out."

"It appears so," Billie replied. "Maybe he realized that an open heart has limitless capacity?"

Cat smiled at her wife's eloquence. "I sincerely hope so, love. In any case, I'm glad they're okay now. I'd hate to see a good marriage ruined because of ignorance and bigotry."

"Amen to that."

"So what else does the letter say?" Cat asked.

"Well, it says here that she wants to come for a visit next month."

"That's great!" Cat exclaimed, sitting up straight, a smile beaming from her face. "I've been anxious for her to visit. I mean, she has yet to meet her grandchildren, and besides, the more time you spend with your mother, the stronger the bond will be between you. I think it's wonderful that she wants to visit."

"Yeah, wonderful," Billie said, almost sarcastically as she pulled Cat back into her embrace and rested her chin on top of Cat's head.

"Billie, I thought you agreed to work things out with her. Are you having second thoughts?"

Billie released Cat and stood up. She moved a short distance away and turned around to face her.

"Cat, while we were still in Michigan, I told you the anger is gone…and it is, but I am having a hard time letting go of the hurt. I'm having a hard time forgiving her. I really want to, but I don't know. It's just hard. I can't get over the fact that she sold me, Cat. She *sold* me! How could she do that? I would die before I did anything so heinous to any of our children."

Cat stood on the step and opened her arms, motioning Billie into them. From her vantage point on the steps, she was face to face, nose to nose with her.

"Well, we finally see eye to eye on something," Cat said, grinning. "Ouch!" she yelled as Billie slapped her behind. "I was only joking," she said rubbing her backside. "Look, honey, I totally understand how you feel. I could never do such a thing to a child, and to be honest, I'm pretty disappointed in Laurel myself, but she *is* your mother. Besides Alex and Seth, Laurel and Dylan are the only blood relatives you have," Cat explained. "Blood is thicker than water, you know."

Billie stubbornly held her gaze, not wanting to agree with Cat.

"Billie, you *know* I can see into your soul. You know I can see the struggle going on right now between your heart and your head. I can see it because your heart belongs to me. Sweetie, listen to your heart. It will never lead you astray as long as I possess it," Cat pleaded.

Billie leaned her head back and looked up at the sky as Cat's arms remained locked around her neck. She knew Cat was right, but her stubborn nature would not allow her to totally forgive and forget. Laurel had hurt her deeply, and it was a hurt that would take a long time to heal. She closed her eyes and released a long frustrated sigh.

"Billie, look at me," Cat urged as she placed one palm on the side of Billie's face and pulled her head back into an upright position. "Open your eyes, my love."

Billie never could resist Cat's requests. She opened her eyes and smiled at the mischievous grin on Cat's face.

"That's, better," Cat teased before continuing. "Honey, I think it's a good idea for Laurel to visit. After all, she hasn't met the kids yet, and I really think the two of you need time alone together...you know, to get acquainted," Cat explained.

"I'm not sure I *want* to get too acquainted with her, Cat."

"Billie, I know you are worried about being hurt again, but anything worth having is worth taking a risk for. I would love to see you have the kind of relationship with Laurel that you have with your own children...that I have with *my* own mother," Cat explained. "Now wouldn't that be rewarding?"

"Yeah, maybe you're right," Billie said as she lowered her head for a kiss, not quite reaching Cat's lips before a small body pressed itself between them.

Looking down, both ladies saw their youngest daughter wedged between them, her arms wrapped around Billie's thighs and her head resting on Billie's abdomen. Billie took a step back and picked the child up. Skylar immediately put her head on Billie's shoulder and closed her eyes. A frown creased Cat's forehead at her daughter's odd behavior.

"Where are brother and sister, love bug?" Billie asked.

"They're still at 'Rissa's and Stevie's," the little girl answered softly.

Cat brushed the red-gold hair off Skylar's forehead, noting the pale, ashen look to the child's skin. "Sky, honey, do you feel all right?" she asked. She placed her hand on the Skylar's forehead then looked at Billie. "She has a low-grade fever."

Skylar nodded her head 'yes', but continued to rest her head on Billie's shoulder.

Billie also reached up to feel the child's forehead. "Sky, are you sure you feel okay?" Billie asked. She glanced uneasily Cat.

Again, Skylar just nodded her head and snuggled deeper into Billie's neck.

"Billie, why don't you bring her inside and put her to bed? I'll get a couple of children's pain relievers from the medicine cabinet and bring them up to her, right after I call her pediatrician," Cat said.

Billie carried Skylar to her room and stripped the little girl of her shoes and jeans, leaving her socks and T-shirt on. She tucked her into bed and pulled the covers up under her arms. Billie kissed her on the forehead and once again, frowned at the heat radiating from her daughter's skin.

"Baby girl," Billie said, running the back of her hand across Skylar's forehead. "You feel hot, honey. Does it hurt anywhere?" she asked.

As before, Skylar just shook her head 'no', then yawned broadly while fighting to keep her eyes open.

Moments later, Cat entered the room with two chewable pain relievers and a glass of water. She approached the opposite side of the bed from Billie and sat down. "Here, sweetie," she said to the child, placing a hand on the child's back to help her sit, while her clinical mind, tempered by years of medical training, registered the intensity of heat she could feel through Skylar's T-shirt.

Skylar took the tablets from her mother's hand and chewed them, then drank the glass of water. Both mothers tucked her in and then sat with her while she drifted off to sleep.

Billie looked at Cat. "What did the doctor say?" she asked.

"He said just what I expected him to, that children will run fevers for no reason at all. If she's still sick tomorrow, we need to bring her in," Cat replied.

"You're a doctor, Cat. What do *you* think is wrong with her?" Billie asked worriedly while she stroked the hair from Skylar's forehead.

Cat hated to be put in this position. She completely understood why most doctors preferred not to treat family members. She was so afraid of making a bad diagnosis and having her loved one harmed or to suffer because of it.

"It's hard to tell, Billie. The doctor is right. It could be anything from an ear infection, to cutting her molars. If the fever is still there tomorrow, we'll have her looked at," Cat explained again.

"Okay," Billie replied.

"Come on, she's asleep," Cat said.

She kissed Skylar's cheek then rose from the bed and followed Billie out of the room.

www.ingramcontent.com/pod-product-compliance
Lightning Source LLC
Chambersburg PA
CBHW051242270626
47162CB00001BA/240